71/11

Wizard's Daughter

Titles by Catherine Coulter

FBI Suspense Thrillers

Wizard's Daughter

CATHERINE COULTER

**Doubleday Large Print
Home Library Edition**

JOVE BOOKS, NEW YORK

This Large Print Edition, prepared especially for Doubleday Large Print Home Library, contains the complete, unabridged text of the original Publisher's Edition.

THE BERKLEY PUBLISHING GROUP
Published by the Penguin Group
Penguin Group (USA) Inc.
375 Hudson Street, New York, New York 10014,
USA
Penguin Group (Canada), 90 Eglinton Avenue East, Suite 700, Toronto, Ontario M4P 2Y3, Canada
(a division of Pearson Penguin Canada Inc.)
Penguin Books Ltd., 80 Strand, London WC2R 0RL, England
Penguin Group Ireland, 25 St. Stephen's Green, Dublin 2, Ireland (a division of Penguin Books Ltd.)
Penguin Group (Australia), 250 Camberwell Road, Camberwell, Victoria 3124, Australia
(a division of Pearson Australia Group Pty. Ltd.)
Penguin Books India Pvt. Ltd., 11 Community Centre, Panchsheel Park, New Delhi—110 017, India
Penguin Group (NZ), 67 Apollo Drive, Rosedale, North Shore 0632, New Zealand
(a division of Pearson New Zealand Ltd.)
Penguin Books (South Africa) (Pty.) Ltd., 24 Sturdee Avenue, Rosebank, Johannesburg 2196, South Africa

Penguin Books Ltd., Registered Offices: 80 Strand, London WC2R 0RL, England

WIZARD'S DAUGHTER

A Jove Book / published by arrangement with the author

PRINTING HISTORY
Jove mass-market edition / January 2008

Group, a division of Penguin Group (USA) Inc.,
375 Hudson Street, New York, New York 10014.

ISBN: 978-0-7394-9072-3

JOVE®
Jove Books are published by The Berkley Publishing
Group, a division of Penguin Group (USA) Inc.,
375 Hudson Street, New York, New York 10014.
JOVE is a registered trademark of Penguin Group
(USA) Inc. The "J" design is a trademark belonging to
Penguin Group (USA) Inc.

PRINTED IN THE UNITED STATES OF AMERICA

**This Large Print Book carries the
Seal of Approval of N.A.V.H.**

To Penelope Williamson

You're a wonderful writer and rider,
and best of all,
you're a wonderful friend.

—CC

1

A long time ago

I knew something wasn't right. I was lying on my back and I couldn't move. A single light shined directly onto my face, but it wasn't strong enough to blind me. The light was strange, soft and vague, and seemed to throb ever so slightly.

"You are awake, I see."

A dark voice, a voice one would hear in the deepest part of the night; surely a man's voice, but unlike any I had ever heard before. Any normal man would be afraid of such a voice but, oddly, I found I was only mildly curious. I said, "Aye, I am awake. However, I cannot move."

"No, not yet. If you agree to do what I want, you will move again, as you did before I saved you and brought you to me."

"Who are you? Where are you?"

"I am behind the Cretan light. Lovely, is it not? Shimmery as a king's silks, warm and soft as a woman's fingers tracing over your face.

"I saved your life, Captain Jared Vail. In return I ask a favor. Will you agree?"

"How do you know my name?"

The Cretan light—whatever that was—seemed to brighten a moment, and harden into a column of trapped flame, then soften once more, the glow gentle, pulsing like a resting heart. Did it believe I had insulted the being behind it? Its master, perhaps? No, that was ridiculous; a light, no matter what it did, was without breath or feeling, without a soul—was it not?

"Why can't I move?"

Where was the bloody man? I wanted to see his face, wanted to see the human who spoke all those words.

"Because I do not wish you to as yet. Will you grant me a favor for saving your life?"

"A favor? Do you wish me to kill someone? I have not dispatched a pirate or a thieving dock rat for three years." Where had that pathetic attempt at humor come from? There was no laugh, more's the pity, for that would have made the voice human, and perhaps that was why I had tried to jest. Still, I was not afraid, even though I knew in some part of my brain that I should be scared out of my few wits. But I was not.

"Who are you?" I asked again.

"I am your savior. You owe me your life. Are you willing to repay your debt?"

"I have gone from granting a favor to paying a debt."

"What is your life worth, Captain Jared Vail?"

"My life is worth all that I am. Will you let me live if I do not agree?"

The Cretan light flashed bright blue for an instant, then flickered, as if brushed by a waving hand. Once again it settled. The shadows behind it remained impenetrable, like a black curtain covering an empty stage. My imagination was on fire. The voice brought me back. "Will I let you live? I do not know." A heavy pause. "I do not know."

"Then I have no choice, do I? I do not wish to die, although I would be well dead now had you not saved me. But I do not know how you managed it. The huge wave was on me, and the wound in my side—I would have died from that blow probably before the water crushed me."

I realized in that instant that I felt no pain from the gaping tear in my side that had hurled me into a madness of agony. I felt nothing at all except the strong, solid beating of my own heart, no stuttering with pain or fear, no gasping to find a breath.

"Ah, the pain. That is another debt you owe me, would you not agree?"

Why was I not afraid? The absence of fear made me feel cold to my soul. I was thinking it made me less a man, less—alive. Had he somehow removed my human fear? "How did you heal me?"

"I have many abilities," the black voice said, nothing more.

I retreated into my mind, trying to keep myself calm and focused, allowing no frightening stray thoughts to make me want to scream in terror, even though I knew any sane man would be babbling by now. He wanted me to pay him back for saving my life. I could certainly do that. But I asked, "I do not understand. You saved me in a way that no mortal could have saved me. If this is not an elaborate dream, if I am not dead, I would say you can do anything. What could I possibly do for you that you cannot do yourself?"

Cold silence stretched on and on. The Cretan light danced wildly, shooting off blue sparks that sprayed upward into the darkness, then suddenly there was calm. Was the light a mirror of my savior's feelings? The voice said, "I have sworn not to meddle. It is a curse that I must obey my own word."

"To whom have you sworn this?"

"You need not know that."

"Are you a man as I am a man?"

"Do I not speak incessantly as does a man, to hear the sound of his own voice? Did I not laugh like a man?"

Yes. No. "Will you tell me where I am?"

"It is not important, my friend."

His *friend*? If he was such a friend why could I not move? Suddenly I felt my fingers. I wiggled them a bit, but still I could not raise my arm and that was surely alarming. Yet I wasn't alarmed, truth be told, merely interested and intrigued, as a man of science would be at the discovery of something unexpected. Had he seen the thoughts in my brain? Now, that gave me pause.

I said slowly, "What could a ship captain possibly do for you? You have demonstrated powers I cannot begin to imagine. I was aboard my brigantine in the middle of the Mediterranean, five miles from Santorini, my last port, and a huge wave appeared out of nowhere. I heard the screams of my sailors, heard my first mate yell to God to save him as that nightmare swell crashed over us. Then a splintered board speared into my side, tearing me open, and then the crushing mountain of water, and yet—"

"And yet you are here, warm, whole."

"My men? My ship?"

"They are dead, your ship destroyed. But you are not."

I thought of Doxey, my first mate, loud and crude, loyal to me and no one else, and Elkins, the cook, always singing filthy ditties, always making lumpy porridge everyone hated. I said, "Perhaps I am dead, perhaps you are the Devil and you are toying with me, amusing yourself, making me believe I am still alive, when I am really as dead as—"

A laugh. Yes, it was a laugh, low and strangely hollow, and something else—the laugh wasn't quite a man's laugh—it seemed to me it was more the imitation of a laugh.

Was I in Hell? Would evil Uncle Ulson trip into my line of vision, ready to welcome me to his home? Why was I not afraid? Perhaps death removed a human's fear.

"I am not the Devil. He is a creature that is something else entirely. Will you pay your debt to me?"

"Yes, if I am actually alive."

I felt a bolt of pain so horrendous I would have welcomed death as a savior. My side gaped open; I could feel my flesh ripped away to my bones. I felt my guts oozing out of my belly. I screamed into the blackness. The Cretan light shot high, a wild mad blue. Then, as suddenly as it had started, the pain stopped. The Cretan light calmed.

"Did you feel your death blow from that falling beam?"

For a moment, I couldn't speak I was breathing so hard, bound in the memory of that ghastly agony. "Yes. I felt my own death but an instant away, so I must be dead, or—"

I heard amusement in that black voice, again somehow hollow, not quite right. "Or what?"

"If I am truly alive then you are a magician, a sorcerer, a wizard, though I am not at all certain there are grand differences amongst those titles. Or you are a being from above or below that a man of reason cannot accept. I know not and you will not tell me.

"You need me because you have promised not to meddle. *Meddle?* That is a curiously bloodless word, a word empty of threat or passion, like a promise a maiden aunt would make, is it not?"

"Will you pay your debt to me?"

I saw no hope for it. He was through with me. "Yes, I will pay my debt."

The Cretan light winked out. I was cast into darkness blacker than a sinner's heart. I was alone. But I had heard no retreating footfalls, no sound of any movement. There was no breathing in the still, black air but my own.

But what was my debt?

I fell asleep. I dreamed I sat at a grand table and ate a meal worthy of good Queen Bess herself, served by hands I could not see— roasted pheasant and other exotic meats, and dates and figs, and sweet flatbread I had never before eaten. Everything was delicious, and the tart ale from a golden flagon warmed my mouth and coursed through me like healing mother's milk. I was sated, I was content.

Suddenly the light in my dream shifted and a young girl appeared in front of me, hair red as the sunset off Gibraltar, loosely braided down her back. Her eyes were blue and freckles ran across her small nose. She seemed so real in that dazzling dream I felt I could reach out my hand and touch her. She threw her head back and she sang:

I dream of beauty and sightless night
I dream of strength and fevered might
I dream I'm not alone again
But I know of his death and her grievous sin.

A child's voice, sweet and true, it called forth feelings I had not known were in me, feelings to break my heart. But those strange words—what did they mean? Whose death? What grievous sin?

She sang the song again, more softly this time, and again her voice settled deep inside me as I listened to the strange minor key and the haunting sad notes that made me want to weep.

What did this small girl know of haunting or sin?

She went quiet. Slowly she took a step closer to me. Even though I knew this was a dream, I would swear I could hear her breath, hear her light footfalls. She smiled and spoke to me even as she seemed to fade into the soft air, and this time her words rang clear in my brain: *I am your debt.*

2

Present
April 22, 1835
London

Nicholas Vail stood at the edge of the large ballroom with its dozens of limp red and white silk banners hanging from the ceiling with military-precision distance between them—to give the feeling of a royal joust, don't you know, my lord, Lady Pinchon had said proudly, all puffed up with a purple turban on her head.

He agreed smoothly, mentioned it was a pity no knight and horse could fit into her magnificent ballroom, at which she looked very thoughtful.

He was sweating from the heat of all the too-close bodies and the countless numbers of dripping candles in every corner of the room. Of the long line of French doors that gave onto a large stone balcony, at least two were open to the still evening.

He pitied the women. They wore five petticoats—he'd counted them with the past several women he'd been with. He estimated there were two hundred women present, so that meant one thousand petticoats. It boggled the mind. And their gowns—the women looked like rich desserts in yards of heavy brocade or satin in every color invented by man, looped with braid and flounces that dusted the floor, wilted flowers and jewels in their hair—all of it had to weigh a good stone. He pictured the froth of petticoats in a mountainous pile in the middle of the ballroom, all those gowns dumped on top like frosting atop a cake, the lot sprinkled with the buckets of jewels that adorned their earlobes, necks, wrists. And that meant the women would be naked. Now, that was a fine picture to tease a man's brain. He saw one particularly heavy young matron, her chins quivering as she laughed, and quickly stifled that image.

As for the men, they looked dapper and prideful in their buttoned-up, nipped-in, long-tailed, proper black garb, starched and stiff, undoubtedly miserable in this heat. It made him shudder.

He knew exactly how they felt since he was dressed just as they were.

At least the women could bare half their chests, what with their gowns nearly falling off sloping white shoulders. He thought of walking around the ballroom, giving little tugs here and there to see what would happen. But those bare shoulders couldn't make up for those ridiculous long sleeves that stuck out so stiffly from their bodies. If he had to endure those sleeves, he would surely hunt down the insane misogynist who had foisted them on women. Were they supposed to make them more desirable? What they did was render each female a force to be reckoned with in sheer breadth.

It was time to get down to business. He raised his head, a wolf scenting prey. His hunt was over finally—she was here just as he'd known she would be—he felt her. The hair rose on his arms as the scent of her thickened in his nostrils. He turned quickly, nearly knocked the tray out of a footman's arms. He righted the footman, set his punch glass on the tray, and started toward her, pausing when he could finally see her face. She was young, obviously newly loosed on London, but he'd known she would be. She was laughing joyously, enjoying herself immensely. He could see her lovely white teeth flashing, her hair in thick braids stacked atop her head, making her look very tall indeed. As he drew nearer, he saw also that her pale blue satin gown didn't hang off sloping shoulders. Her shoulders didn't slope, but were strong, squared, her flesh as white as the beach sand on the leeward side of Coloane Island.

Her braids were dark red, a deep auburn it was written, perhaps Titian if one were a poet. It was she, no doubt in his mind at all. In odd moments over the years he'd wondered if he would die a doddering old man, not finding her, if it still wasn't the right time. But it was the right time and he was here and so was she. It was an unspeakable relief.

He walked toward her, aware that people were watching him; they usually did because he was an earl and no one knew a thing about him. London society loved a mystery, particularly if the mystery in question was an unattached presentable male with a title. There was his size too, one of his grandfather's gifts to him, and he knew he intimidated. With his black hair, pulled back and tied with a black velvet ribbon, he knew people looked at him and saw a man not quite civilized. They might have been right. He knew his eyes could turn cold as death, another gift from his grandfather—black eyes that made people think of wizards, perhaps, or executioners.

A couple danced into his path. He smoothly moved aside at the alarm on the man's face, but he scarcely noticed them, he was so focused on her.

Each of his senses recognized and accepted she was indeed the one he sought. She was waltzing now, her partner whirling her in wide circles, and her blue satin skirts swirled and ballooned around her. She was light on her feet, smoothly following her partner, an older man—old enough to be her father, only he wasn't paunchy and jowly like a father should be; he was tall and lean and graceful, his blue eyes bright as a summer sky, nearly the same light blue as hers, and that face of his was too handsome, his smile too charming. Her husband? Surely not, she was too young. He laughed at himself. Girls were married off at seventeen, some even sixteen, to men older than this one, who also looked fit and surely too spry for his age.

They danced by him. He saw her eyes were brighter than the gentleman's, she was that excited.

He stood quietly, watching. Around and around they whirled, the man keeping her to the perimeter so no one would dance into their path.

He could do nothing but wait, which he did, leaning negligently, arms crossed over his chest, against a wall beside a large palm tree that had a red bow fastened to one of its fronds. He didn't know her name, yet he already knew she wouldn't be a Mary or a Jane. No, her name would be exotic, but he couldn't ever think of a single English name exotic enough to fit his image of her.

He saw a pallid young gentleman and a lady who appeared to be his mother whispering as they looked toward him. He smiled at them, a black brow arching, not that he blamed them for their gossip. After all, he was the new Lord Mountjoy, and people were speculating on how he was adjusting to a title as empty as a gourd since the old earl had left all his wealth to Nicholas's three younger half brothers. All that was left to him

was the entailed moldering family estate in
Sussex, Wyverly Chase, built by the first Earl
of Mountjoy, who had fought the Spanish like
a Viking berserker and managed to charm
the eternal virgin Queen Elizabeth. She had
duly elevated Viscount Ashborough to his
earldom. Wyverly Chase was going on three
hundred years old, and showed every decade. As for the entailed three thousand
acres, his father had ensured it was as worthless as a lack of money and care could make
it by the time he'd died. His son was left with
nothing but fallow fields, desperate tenants,
and mountains of debt.

Was the young man's mama wondering
where he'd come from? He'd heard one man
whisper that the new earl was newly arrived
from China. That made him smile.

Nicholas saw a man looking toward him,
saw him say something to a portly man
beside him. Was he speculating on whether
Nicholas had yet met with his three half brothers, all young men now, two of them, he'd
heard, as wild as any Channel storm? Ah, but
most importantly, beggared as he was, had
he come to London to find an heiress?

The music stopped, the waltz finally
ended. Women smiled and laughed, waved

themselves vigorously with dainty fans, gentlemen tried not to let anyone see how winded they were.

Nicholas watched the older man lead her to a knot of people standing on the opposite side of the ballroom.

It was time to do what he was supposed to do, time to do what he was meant to do.

3

He walked directly to the older man who'd danced with her, and bowed. "Sir, I am Nicholas Vail and I would like to dance with—" Nicholas stalled. Could she be his wife? Surely not. His daughter? "Ah, this young lady, sir."

The man gave him a brief bow in return. "I know who you are. As for the young lady, she has already promised this waltz to my son."

Nicholas flashed a quick look at a young man around his own age, smiling at something the girl said to him. He looked up, cocked his head to one side, and nodded to

Nicholas. Then the girl turned to look at him, straight on, her eyes never leaving his face. So joyous she'd been, but now her expression was remote and unreadable. But he saw something in her eyes, something— knowledge, secrets, he didn't know. Ah, but he would, and soon. Then the young man spoke to her and she placed her hand on his forearm and let him lead her to the dance floor. She did not look back at him.

It seemed to Nicholas that she'd recognized him. Well, he knew her, so it made sense she would recognize him—but he just wasn't sure. She'd never met him, but her eyes—the light-filled blue, just as he'd known they would be—yes, he'd found her, even though he didn't yet know her name.

The older man cleared his throat and Nicholas realized he'd continued to stare after her. He said to Nicholas with amusement, "I am Ryder Sherbrooke. This is my wife, Sophia Sherbrooke."

Nicholas bowed to the woman, plump and pretty, her mouth full and soft, but she wasn't smiling, she was looking at him with a good deal of suspicion.

He felt huge relief. She wasn't *his* wife. He

bowed to Sophia Sherbrooke again. "Ma'am, a pleasure. I am Nicholas Vail, Lord Mountjoy. Your husband is an excellent dancer."

She squeezed her husband's arm, laughed, and said, "My husband tells me he was born with accomplished feet. When we were younger he would let me dance on his accomplished feet. I was known as the most graceful female of the season."

Nicholas was charmed.

Ryder said, "As I said, I have heard of you, Lord Mountjoy, and I am not at all certain I wish you to meet my ward, much less dance with her."

His ward? Nicholas admitted to surprise. He hadn't imagined anything like this.

"I have not been in England long enough to earn a reputation to alarm you, Mr. Sherbrooke. May I inquire why you feel concern about me?"

"Your father was a man I would have gladly challenged to a duel had he but once crossed the line rather than always toeing near it. I suppose I am foisting his deficiencies upon you, his son, grossly unfair of me, I know, but there it is."

"To be honest, sir," Nicholas said slowly, "I

escaped him as soon as I could. I rarely saw him after he wedded his second wife, which was during my fifth year."

An eyebrow went up. "I understand his three younger sons would gladly stick a knife in your throat." Ryder paused a moment, looked at the young man searchingly. "You are aware, I assume, that Richard, your eldest half brother, feels the title should be his?"

Nicholas shrugged. "Any or all of them are free to try for my gullet, sir, but I am a difficult man to dispatch. Others have tried."

Ryder believed him. He looked big and hard, a young man who'd had to make his own way, a man who knew who and what he was. He watched Nicholas Vail look yet again toward Rosalind, who was laughing, as she always did when she waltzed. Ryder said, "It grows late, sir. After this waltz, I am taking my family home."

"May I call upon you tomorrow morning?"

Ryder looked at him appraisingly. Nicholas felt the weight of that look, wondered if he would be found acceptable. Of course he'd heard of the Sherbrookes. But to find this couple acting as her guardians, he simply didn't understand, and he knew to his gut that complications would now billow up like a raging wind. How had it come about?

Ryder slowly nodded. "We are staying at the Sherbrooke town house, on Putnam Square."

"Thank you, sir. Ma'am, a pleasure. Until tomorrow, then." Nicholas strode from the ballroom, oblivious of the guests who moved out of his way.

Ryder Sherbrooke said to his wife, "I wonder what this young man is about."

"Rosalind is beautiful. It is probably the simple interest of a man in a woman."

"I doubt there is anything at all simple about Nicholas Vail. I wonder who and what he is."

"If he is a fortune hunter, he will learn soon enough that Rosalind isn't an heiress, and he will look elsewhere."

"Do you think he is in need of an heiress?"

Sophie said, "I've heard it said his father gave him naught but a title and a dilapidated property, and he did it apurpose. I wonder why. Is this young man in debt? I don't know. But I do know, Ryder, that pride and arrogance meld very nicely together in him, don't you think?"

Ryder laughed. "Yes, they do. I wonder if he realizes he is all the talk of London."

"Oh, yes, of course he does. I imagine it amuses him."

Neither of them noticed Rosalind staring after Nicholas Vail, who looked neither to the right nor to the left as he strode from the ballroom.

Nicholas was accepting his cane and hat from a liveried footman, palming him a shilling for his service, when a voice said, "Well, well, if it isn't the new Earl of Mountjoy, the sixth, I believe, in the flesh. Hello, brother."

Nicholas fancied he remembered that voice from his boyhood, but it took a moment for him to recognize that the young man facing him was his eldest half brother, Richard Vail. It occurred to him in that moment, staring at the young man, that he minded very much sharing his name. He looked into Richard's brilliant eyes, dark as his own, nearly black, and they glittered—with anger? No, it was more than simple anger, it was impotent rage. Richard Vail was not happy. Nicholas smiled at the young man. "It's a pity your memory has failed you, and here you are so very young—I am the seventh Earl of

Mountjoy, not the sixth, and the eighth Viscount Ashborough."

"Damn you, you shouldn't be either!"

"And you, Richard, should consider growing up."

The rage smoldered as Richard's hands clenched, unclenched. A knife to the gullet? Surely a possibility. Richard was a handsome young man, nearly Nicholas's size, big enough to look down on many of his peers. Richard said, "I am a man, more of a man than you will ever be. I am welcome in London. You are not. You do not belong here. Go back to your savage life. I heard you came from China. That is where you have lived, isn't it?"

Nicholas smiled and turned to look at another young man standing at Richard's elbow. "I recognize you. You are Lancelot, are you not?"

They could not have looked less like brothers. Unlike either Richard or Nicholas, this young man was slight, fair, and pale, the image of a delicate poet. Nicholas looked at his artist's hands, with their long fingers and beautiful shape. He wondered what his father had thought of this pretty son, who resembled his mother, Miranda, if Nicholas remembered aright.

Out of his pretty mouth came a petulant voice. "Everyone knows I am called Lance."

Nicholas drawled, "No knight then?"

"Make no jest with me, sir. It was paltry."

Nicholas raised a dark brow. "I? Certainly I wouldn't consider a jest with you. You are my family, after all."

"Only by bitter and unjust circumstance," Richard said. "We don't want you here. No one wants you here."

"How very strange," Nicholas said easily. "I am now the head of the Vail family, I am your eldest brother. You should welcome me, delight in my company, look to me for advice and counsel."

Lancelot made a rude noise.

"You are nothing more than a ne'er-do-well adventurer, sir, who should probably be in Newgate."

"An adventurer, hmmm. That has a nice ring to it, doesn't it?" Nicholas smiled at both young men impartially, strangers, both of them, and they hated him, doubtless made to hate him by his father and their mother. They'd been innocent children once; he remembered them from their last visit to Wyverly Chase, just before his grandfather had died. He'd been an ancient twelve. He said slowly, "I remember there are three of you. Where is—what is his name?"

"Aubrey," Richard said, tight-lipped. "He studies at Oxford."

Oxford, Nicholas thought; it sounded alien, it felt alien. "Do give Aubrey my best," he said, nodding to Richard and Lancelot.

"I heard you were staying at Grillon's," Richard called after him. "A pity Father didn't leave you the town house."

Lancelot snickered.

Nicholas turned back. "To be honest with you, Wyverly Chase is more than enough. I am relieved that decrepit Georgian pile on Epson Square wasn't entailed to me. The repairs alone must cost you at least three nights' winnings at the gaming table, if you ever win, that is."

Lancelot said, "Father wouldn't have left you Wyverly Chase either if it hadn't been entailed. A pity now that it will molder into the ground."

"It moldered long before my arrival," Nicholas said.

Lancelot said, "And you will not be able to

do anything about it. Everyone knows you're poor as a rooster catcher on the heath."

"I don't believe I am familiar with that term," Nicholas said.

"That's right, you are not a proper Englishman, are you?" Richard said, sneering. "It's a boy who handles the birds for cockfights, worthless little beggars with scarred hands from the birds biting them. We heard you sailed in from faraway China. We heard you even have several Chinaman servants."

Nicholas gave them both a schoolmaster's approving nod. "It is good that you listen. Myself, I recommend listening, I have always found it useful." As he turned to leave through the front door, held open by the same footman—all ears—he added, "Actually, I have always found listening more useful than talking. You might consider that."

Nicholas heard Lancelot huff out an angry breath. Richard's eyes were black with rage, his face flushed. Interesting how completely their father had bent their minds into hatred of him, Nicholas thought as he strode down the broad wide steps to the walkway. He remembered Richard had been a happy boy, and Lance a cherub, all pink and white and smiling, content to sit at his mother's feet whilst she played the harp. As for Aubrey, he'd been so small when Nicholas had last seen him—a little boy who loved nothing more than to hurl a ball and run up and down the long corridor, yelling at the top of his lungs. Nicholas remembered how he'd nearly gone tumbling down the front stairs. Nicholas had scooped him up just in time. He also remembered Miranda screaming at him, accusing him of trying to murder her son, and Aubrey between them, crying and afraid. His father, Nicholas recalled, had believed it, and taken a whip to him, cursed him, and called him a murdering little bastard. Nicholas's grandfather had been too ill to intervene, and he would have if he'd even been aware that his son and family had come to witness his death. Sweet hell, who knew why such memories burrowed into a man's brain?

There were at least two dozen carriages lining both sides of the street, both the drivers and the horses appearing to be asleep. It was a good long walk back to Grillon's Hotel. Not a single miscreant appeared in his path.

4

At the Sherbrooke breakfast table the following morning, a kipper poised on her fork, Rosalind asked Ryder, "Sir, who was that dark gentleman who wanted to dance with me last night? The young one with long hair black as All Hallows' Eve?"

Ryder was a fool to believe Nicholas Vail hadn't made an impression on her though she hadn't said a thing about him on their way home the previous evening. He said easily, "The young man is the Earl of Mountjoy, newly arrived on our shores, some say from faraway China."

"China," Rosalind said, stretching it out,

as if savoring the feel of it on her tongue. "How vastly romantic that sounds."

Grayson Sherbrooke grunted with disgust. "You girls—you'd say that riding in a tumbrel to the guillotine, shoulders squared, sounded romantic."

Rosalind gave Grayson a big grin and made a chopping motion with her hand. "You obviously have no soul, Grayson."

Grayson waved that away. "Everyone is speculating about him. I heard he's in town to find himself an heiress. At least that means you're safe, Rosalind."

"Of course I'm safe. I'm in the same hole with the church mouse."

"Regardless," Ryder said, "he asked me if he could pay us a visit this morning."

Rosalind sat forward in her chair, the nutty bun in her hand forgotten, eyes sparkling. "What? He wants to visit me?"

"Or Aunt Sophie," Ryder said. "Who knows? Perhaps he was taken with Grayson, and wants to hear a good ghost story." Ryder frowned. "Perhaps it was a mistake to tell him you were my ward."

"But why, sir? Oh, I see. As part of the Sherbrooke family, ward or not, he must assume I'm exceedingly plump in the pocket."

Rosalind wasn't about to tell Uncle Ryder or Grayson that she was more disappointed than warranted at this nasty bit of news.

"You're only discreetly plump," Ryder said.

Grayson said, "On the other hand, from what I have heard of the mysterious earl, he never acts until he knows exactly what he wants."

Rosalind said, "You mean he wants me even though I'm not an heiress? That's ridiculous, Grayson. Nobody would want me. Besides, he can't have me."

Grayson tapped his knife on the table-cloth. "I will be with you when he pays his visit this morning. We must know what he wants from you. If he's come to the mistaken conclusion you are an heiress, I will dispel that notion immediately."

Rosalind said, "He is very imposing."

"Yes," Ryder said, "he is. I sent a note to Horace Bingley—the Sherbrooke solicitor here in London—to tell us what he knows of the earl. We will see what he has to say about the young man's character."

Grayson said, "Excellent idea, Father, since no one really knows much about him. However, it does seem to be the consensus that he is a pauper and desperately needs to attach an heiress."

Ryder nodded. "I've also heard that the old earl left his heir nothing that wasn't nailed down in the entailment. He beggared his own son out of spite—the reason for this strange behavior no one seems to know. I will ask Horace to find out, if, that is, Nicholas Vail appeals to Rosalind."

He had indeed appealed to her, Rosalind thought, but didn't say that aloud. She didn't want to alarm Uncle Ryder before he'd ensured Nicholas Vail wasn't a bad man.

But she knew he wasn't; she knew it to her bones.

Grayson said, "We haven't given out any information about your early years, Rosalind."

"What is there to say? I am of no account, I am nothing at all."

Anger rippled through Ryder's voice. "You listen to me, Rosalind, you are not too old for me to wallop you."

"But it is only the truth, Uncle Ryder. I know you always prize the truth."

Ryder said to his wife as she came into the dining room, sniffing the air, "Rosalind has become impertinent, Sophie. What do you think we should do?"

"Wallop her, Father," Grayson said.

Sophie laughed. "Don't let her have one of Cook's nutty buns. That way I will have more and she will learn a valuable lesson."

"There are three left, Aunt Sophie," Rosalind said. "I swear I took only one; it's your son who is the glutton."

Grayson toasted her with his teacup.

Sophie said as she selected a nutty bun, "The Earl of Mountjoy presents the face of a man of mystery, a man with dark secrets. I have always found that a man of mystery piques a woman's curiosity, she cannot help herself. It is the nature of things."

Rosalind nodded. "He is mysterious, yes, but he also looked apart from everyone at the ball, as if he knew he had to be there but did he want to be?"

"That is called arrogance," Sophie said and took a blissful bite of one of the three remaining nutty buns. She chewed slowly, eyes closed. "Ah, Nirvana is close."

"I don't think women are allowed in Nirvana, Mother," Grayson said.

Sophie waved the last bit of nutty bun at him before she popped it into her mouth, and closed her eyes again. "Ah, you are wrong, my dearest. I have ascended."

Grayson said, "Nicholas Vail sounds like Uncle Douglas. He has a way of looking at a roomful of people as though their only purpose is to amuse him."

"He even has the look of Douglas when he was young," Ryder said thoughtfully.

Rosalind said, "He's coming to visit and I never even spoke to him. I could perhaps understand his wishing to visit me had he waltzed with me, since I am such a superb dancer, but he didn't. And he never enjoyed my wit, since I didn't have the opportunity to speak to him. Hmm, perhaps others spoke to him of my lovely way with words, my exquisite grace, do you think?" Even as she laughed at herself, she saw him very clearly in her mind. She could easily see him wearing a black cloak billowing in a night wind. He oozed mystery, dark boundless secrets, hidden and obscure.

Sophie said, "Regardless of his motive for wishing to see you, Rosalind, I would say he's a man who likes to be in control. One cannot be in control unless one knows about everything."

"Perhaps, my dear," Ryder said slowly, "just

perhaps you are right. The earl does look like he knows what he's about, and if that is indeed true, then he must know that you are not an heiress. So it's a mystery we have."

"It isn't always about a girl's dowry, is it, Uncle Ryder?"

"Yes," said Ryder.

"Ha," said Sophie. "You took me with naught but the chemise on my back."

Ryder Sherbrooke's blue eyes dilated, something neither his son nor his ward wanted to explore, something that made both of them vastly uncomfortable. Rosalind took another drink of her tea. Grayson played with his fork.

Sophie said, "He doesn't look like an easy man. All those secrets. He looks like he's seen many things, done many things, perhaps to survive." She sighed. "He is so very young."

"Not so young at all, Mother," Grayson said. "He is about my age. Perhaps I look mysterious as well?"

His mother, no fool, said immediately, "Of course you do, dearest. And your novels— goodness, there are so many terrifying happenings, so much mystery, my poor heart nearly leaps out of my chest, and one wonders where these black mysteries shrouded in dread and cunning come from. One must accept that they emerge from a mind that cannot be understood, only admired and marveled at."

Rosalind listened, feeling her own heart sound slow, hard strokes. She saw Nicholas Vail standing in front of Uncle Ryder, dark as a Barbary Coast pirate prince who would perhaps return to his opulent tent and lie at his ease on silk pillows, and watch veiled dancing girls. As for his size, well, he was larger than Uncle Douglas, she was certain of that. And he looked powerful, a hard disciplined man, both in mind and body. Nicholas Vail— she realized his name sounded through her mind with a strange sort of familiarity, and wasn't that odd? But she knew she'd never heard of the family. And he was an earl—Lord Mountjoy. She'd never heard the title before either. She wondered what he wanted with her. She was eighteen and not at all stupid. How she wished that Ryder Sherbrooke, the man whose blood she wished she carried, would let her meet with Nicholas Vail alone, completely alone. Unfortunately, she thought sadly, that wouldn't happen. It was not one of the benefits of being eighteen and unmarried.

5

At exactly eleven o'clock, Willicombe, his bald head shining brilliantly from the new recipe he'd used just that morning—aniseed, imagine that!—spoke in his lovely musical voice from the doorway of the first-floor drawing room, "The Earl of Mountjoy, madam."

Sophie said, "Do show the earl in, Willicombe."

Nicholas Vail paused a moment in the doorway. His eyes went to her immediately, as if no one else were in the room.

Ryder, who was standing by the fireplace, pushed off the mantel and walked to the young man, forcing his attention away from Rosalind. "My lord, do come in and meet my ward, and my son, Grayson."

Nicholas was a hunter, but he wasn't stupid. He bowed over Mrs. Sherbrooke's hand, then Rosalind's hand, but he didn't linger. He realized Grayson Sherbrooke was studying him intently, and said to him, "You write mysterious novels, Mr. Sherbrooke."

Grayson laughed. "Yes, I do, but there are primarily mysterious ghosts and otherworldly beings in my books, my lord, who enjoy meddling in the lives of men. And women."

Nicholas said, "I read *The Phantom of Drury Lane*. I enjoyed it immensely. It fair to curdled my innards."

Rosalind laughed, charmed to her toes, as, she knew, were Uncle Ryder and Aunt Sophie since they were Grayson's proud parents. Grayson beamed. "Yes, it curdled a lot of readers' innards, my lord, mine as well. I am pleased you liked it."

Sophie thought, what was a mother to do in the face of such a lovely compliment toward her beloved son? A mother would obviously unbend, and so Sophie unbent. "You are obviously a gentleman of excellent literary taste, my lord. You are possibly even worthy of one of Cook's excellent nutty buns. I begged her to bake more and she decided to please me. Willicombe, do bring in tea and any nutty buns that haven't already been filched off the plate."

Willicombe eyed the imposing young man who'd had the brain to compliment Master Grayson, and unbent himself. "Yes, madam," he said, and bowed low so the earl could enjoy the shine.

When Willicombe was gone, Nicholas said to Sophie, "His head—it near to blinded me."

Ryder said, "He was lucky to have that slash of sunlight hit it exactly right when he bowed. You see, my lord, Willicombe prides himself on a high shine. He is not bald, he shaves his head twice a week. He informed me this morning he applied a new recipe."

Nicholas laughed, still paying no particular attention to Rosalind. But he was aware of her, oh, yes, particularly of her rich deep red hair piled so artlessly atop her head this morning, lazy curls reaching down to brush her shoulders. Rosalind was an exotic name, he was pleased with it, but yet, somehow, her name didn't seem right. He would be patient; he would learn everything about her soon enough.

Because he was polite he took only one bite of a nutty bun. After he'd chewed that one bite he wished desperately he could stuff the entire bun into his mouth.

Ryder Sherbrooke said, "Where have you been for the past fourteen years, my lord?"

He said, without hesitation, "Many places, sir. For the past five years, though, I have lived in Macau."

Grayson sat forward on his chair. "The Chinese own it but the Portuguese administer it, do they not?"

Nicholas nodded. "The Portuguese landed in the early sixteenth century, claimed the peninsula even though it borders China. It was a major hub of Portuguese naval, commercial, and religious activities in East Asia for several hundred years." He shrugged. "But a country's fortunes change as alliances and trade markets shift. Macau is merely an outpost now, of little importance in the big scheme of things."

"What did you do there, my lord?"

At last, Nicholas thought, and turned to

face her. "I am in trade, Miss—" He stalled, on purpose, hoping she would give him her last name.

She did. "I am Rosalind de La Fontaine."

A dark brow shot straight up. "By any chance are you a fabulist?"

She beamed at him. "So you have read the fables by Jean de La Fontaine, sir?"

"My grandfather read many of them to me when I was a very young boy."

"Do you have a favorite?"

"Yes, 'The Hare and the Tortoise.'"

"Ah, a patient man."

He smiled at her. "And your favorite is?"

"'The Cicada and the Ant.'"

A black brow shot up. "Which one are you?"

"I am the ant, sir. Winter always comes. It's best to be prepared because one never knows when a storm might strike when least expected."

"That made no sense at all," Grayson said.

"I fear that it did," Ryder said, and Sophie nodded, and there were shadows in her eyes. "I had no idea, dearest, that you—"

They saw so much, Rosalind thought, too much, not, of course, that she hadn't just dished her biggest fear up to them on a platter. She laughed. "It's only a fable, Aunt Sophie. I truly would like to be more like the cicada, but there appears to be too much Puritan blood in my veins."

Nicholas said matter-of-factly, "Rosalind's virtue is prudence and mine is patience. What is yours, Grayson?"

"I hate flattery," Grayson said, "thus I suppose that I like 'The Crow and the Fox.'"

"Ah," Rosalind said, and poked Grayson's arm. "The fox flatters the crow, and the crow drops the food in his mouth to preen."

"Exactly."

Rosalind stuck out her small plate for a nutty bun.

Nicholas looked at that nutty bun, sighed, and slipped one of the remaining two off the plate onto hers.

"It is always so," Sophie said, grinning at him with only a dollop of sympathy, since she wanted the other bun. "Nutty buns are at a great premium in this household. The recipe comes from Cook at Northcliffe Hall. Because my husband prostrated himself at her feet, swore he would sing her arias beneath her window, she deigned to pass the recipe along to our cook."

"If you should show me to the kitchen, ma'am, I will prostrate myself as well. However, I don't know any arias."

"Neither does my husband. He is so charming, however, that it doesn't seem to matter."

Laughter. It felt good, Nicholas thought, surprised. He couldn't remember very much laughter in his life.

"It is a lovely morning," he said. "As I recall from my boyhood, this is a precious spectacle that shouldn't be squandered. May I ask Miss La Fontaine to walk with me in the park?"

"Which park?" Ryder asked.

"Hyde Park, sir. I have a carriage outside. I hired it, since the ones remaining at Wyverly Chase are from the previous century."

Grayson leaned forward. "Wyverly Chase? What a phenomenal name. I should like to hear the history behind it. It is your family seat?"

Nicholas nodded.

Rosalind knew Grayson's brain was already spinning a tale about Wyverly Chase, so she said, "I understand there is a small artists' fair this morning. Perhaps his lordship and I could see what is happening with that."

Grayson nodded and rose. "I shall accompany you."

Rosalind wanted to smack Grayson, but since he had to be a better choice for chaperone than either Aunt Sophie or Uncle Ryder, she nodded. She rose as well, and smiled. "I should enjoy that very much."

Ryder Sherbrooke, seeing no hope for it, slowly nodded.

It was the rare sort of English spring day—a blue sky so bright, a breeze so light and scented sweet with the blooming spring flowers, that it brought a tear to the jaded English eye. They discovered that the small artists' fair meant to take place in one corner of Hyde Park had turned into an event.

Hundreds of people milled through Hyde Park to stop at the food and drink vendors and the artists' stalls, or sit on the trampled grass to watch the jugglers and mimes come to share in the fun and profit. There was a good deal of laughter, some good-natured fisticuffs, perhaps a bit too much ale, and pickpockets who smiled happily as they adroitly worked through the crowds.

"There is more food here today than artists," Nicholas said. Both he and Grayson held Rosalind by an arm, not about to let her get pulled away in the boisterous crowd.

"And drink," Grayson said. Suddenly Grayson stopped still, stared off into the distance.

"Oh, I see," Rosalind said and poked him in the arm. "Bookstalls, a whole line of them."

Grayson was eyeing those bookstalls like a starved mongrel. Rosalind, seeing freedom within her grasp, stood on her tiptoes and kissed his cheek. "Off you go. I'll be perfectly safe with Lord Mountjoy. Go, Grayson. We will be just fine."

Nicholas's grin turned into his most responsible nod. "I swear to keep her safe." After but a moment of indecision, Grayson was off like a comet.

"He can move very quickly when properly motivated," Rosalind said.

Nicholas looked down at her upturned face. "What makes you think you'll be safe with me?"

She smiled up at his dark face, those black eyes of his. "Truth be told, I'd be perfectly safe by myself, as are you, I imagine." She eyed him up and down. "Were you to dare take liberties with my capable self, I should make you very sorry. I'm very strong, you know. And wily."

"And if you take liberties with me, then what am I to do?"

"Perhaps you could ask me to sing and that would distract me from those liberties."

He couldn't help it, he burst out laughing. Several people turned his way, smiling with him. One, Nicholas suspected, was a pick-pocket, one a housemaid with lovely thick black hair, and the third a matron with the look of a baker's wife, what with the streak of flour down the bodice of her gown, three children clinging to her skirts.

"It is his passion," Rosalind said, watching Grayson gracefully weave his way through a group of military men singing ditties at the top of their lungs, their voices well oiled with ale. "Grayson is immensely talented. He began telling ghost stories when he was a little boy. He never stopped."

Nicholas said. "Why did you kiss him?"

That brought her to a halt. She cocked her head to one side, looking up at him. "He is my cousin. He is like my brother. I love him. I have known him forever."

"You are no blood relation to him," Nicholas said, voice hard, dangerous.

An eyebrow shot up, but she said nothing, merely eyed him. Did she want to shoot him, or kiss him? She wasn't sure what to make of him. Was this an example of a man's possessiveness?

Rein in, rein in. Nicholas said, "I mean to say I heard Ryder Sherbrooke call you his ward."

"That too. It's all rather complicated and really none of your business, my lord."

"No, I suppose not. At least not yet."

Now, what do you mean by that? she wondered. *You thrive on mysteries and secrets, don't you?*

She ducked past a small boy running full speed toward a pasty vendor. "I am very glad my aunt and uncle didn't realize the beautiful weather would unleash the population of London into the park. This has turned into quite an affair. Oh, look, there are boys performing acrobatics. Let's go watch."

She grabbed his hand and pulled him to the edge of a circle to watch the three boys. "Oh, one of them is really a little girl. Would you look at how she leaps onto that boy's shoulders—so smooth and graceful, and she stands so tall on his shoulders—it looks easy, doesn't it?"

After he dutifully tossed several pennies into a large top hat, Nicholas bought her lemonade that tasted remarkably sour, and a hot beef pie. They walked away from the crowd to the far side of Hyde Park and sat on a small stone bench in front of a narrow, still pond.

"No ducks," Rosalind said.

"They're probably alarmed by all the bustle, hiding under those bushes over there."

"You're probably right. But I'll tell you, these ducks are great performers. They quack and leap about, knowing they'll get bread and biscuits. Hmm, I hope they're not in any of the vendors' pies."

"I wager they're also fast."

Rosalind bit into her beef pie, chewed, took another quick bite. "Here, have a bite. A small bite."

She fed him a bit of her pie. Nicholas looked at her while he chewed. Her hair was mussed, her color high; she was smiling and looked utterly pleased with herself and her world. Suddenly four young men, all dressed in red, came bursting through the trees to form a half circle around them. Nicholas was an instant away from having his derringer in his hand when they began to sing. *Sing!* And in lovely harmony. He settled back to listen. He realized soon enough they were singing to Rosalind. They knew her and she them. Now, this was interesting. He didn't like it, but— when they finished a lilting Scottish ballad about a bonny girl who loved a one-armed highwayman called Rabbie McPherson, Rosalind clapped and said, "That was lovely, gentlemen, do give Lord Mountjoy another."

Another song filled the sweet air, this one sounding like a tragic song from an Italian opera. So she knew them, did she? He didn't know if that was odd or not. It probably was.

When they had finished, each of them bowed low, and a short, plump young man with lovely blue eyes said, "Rosalind, we have sung for you. We have sung for your companion. It is your turn now. Come, we will blend our voices with yours."

Her turn?

She laughed, handed Nicholas the rest of her beef pie—telling him to hold it carefully and not eat it—then went to stand with them. She cleared her throat, looked straight at him, and began to sing. The men's voices came in under hers, harmonizing beautifully, never overpowering.

See the flight of the moon
Through the dark stretch of night
Bathing the earth in its radiant light.
All those in love who look to the sky
Fear not the death of the night's final
sigh.

When she sang the final haunting word, she dropped her head a moment, then raised her eyes to his face. It was the voice that made you weep deep inside where you didn't even know tears resided. It wasn't the child's voice, but it was still the same voice. The men applauded her even as he sat there stunned, mute, unable to move. Even though he'd known, still he trembled at the knowledge of what she was. And what he was to her.

She asked after a moment, "Ah, did you like it?"

He nodded, still without words.

He watched the young men move away and he still sat there on the bench, the rest of the beef pie clutched in his hand. He said slowly, looking up at her, "You spoke of Grayson's talent. Your voice, it is something one can scarce imagine. It sinks deep." He simply hadn't realized how deep.

6

"What a lovely thing to say." Rosalind laughed, suddenly uncertain. "But I am nothing compared to Grayson."

"You are different from Grayson, more powerful."

"Oh, well—" She laughed as she reached into her small reticule and scooped out some pennies. He watched her race after the young men. He heard laughter, then the first line of another familiar song, this one faintly Germanic.

When she came skipping back to him, he handed her the rest of her beef pie.

She ate it. "Gerard thanks you for the money."

"They were your pennies."

She shrugged. "Yes, but it is always the gentleman who must pay. It's some sort of ritual, so I suppose you must pay me back."

"You are temporarily short of funds?"

"Actually, those four pennies were the last of my fortune until my allowance next Wednesday. It is difficult, but I must give up a pound of my allowance for the collection plate." She sighed. "It is the right thing, of course, but when one is in London and visits the Pantheon—" She sighed, looking at him beneath her lashes.

He said nothing, his eyes still brooding, resting on the bushes behind her.

"What is wrong, my lord? You look fair to gut-shot. Are you temporarily penniless as well?"

That brought him back. This smiling girl was not a haunting vision of another time with a siren's voice to bring a man to his death—no, at least in this moment, she was a young lady who'd spent all her allowance. "Fair to gut-shot? I don't believe I have ever before heard a young lady say that."

"On the other hand you have been gone from England for many years. What do young ladies in Macau say?"

"The young ladies in Macau are mostly Portuguese, and there isn't an equivalent in Portuguese for 'gut-shot.' But in Patuá—that is a local language developed by the Portuguese settlers who came in the sixteenth century—" He paused, leaned down, picked up a skinny branch, and tossed it. Who cared about a language spoken by very few people in a settlement on the other side of the world?

"Patuá—what a lovely name. Do you speak the language?"

"One must."

"Say something in Patuá to me."

"Well, there is a Patuá poem a friend of mine turned into a song I've always believed very pretty—"

Nhonha na jinela
Co fula mogarim
Sua mae tancarera
Seu pai canarim.

He shook his head at her. "No, I will not attempt to sing it. You would run away, your hands clapped over your ears."

"Not I. I have great fortitude. Now, I don't have the least idea what you said, but the sounds are nice, like soft music."

"I'll translate it for you:

Young lady in the window
with a jasmine flower
Her mother is a Chinese fisherwoman
Her father is a Portuguese Indian.

"Imagine, you left England when you were only a boy and you went to this place where there are Chinese fisherwomen and Portugese Indians—a place so very different from England. Were you treated well there— a foreigner?"

No one had ever asked him that. Slowly, he nodded. "I was fortunate enough to do a good deed for a rich Portuguese merchant in Lisbon. He gave me a flattering introduction to the governor of Macau, who happened to be his brother-in-law. I was treated well because of him, even though I was English."

"What was your good deed?"

He laughed. "I saved his only daughter from a rather oily young man who was plying her with champagne on a balcony under a vastly romantic Lisbon moon. She was foolish, but her father didn't realize it then. She was very angry at me for that rescue, as I recall."

"How did you communicate with everyone in Macau?"

He shrugged. "I suppose you could say that I have a gift for languages. I already spoke Portuguese and I learned Mandarin Chinese and Patuá very quickly."

"I speak Italian," she announced, and puffed up.

He smiled at her. "You've got me there," he said, even though he was perfectly fluent in Italian.

"Have you missed England, my lord?"

"Perhaps. At odd times, like on a day like today, but, on the other hand, it's hard to remember days like today." He raised his head and sniffed the jasmine that grew not two feet away from them.

He said, "Tell me about your parents."

She jumped to her feet, dusted her hands on her skirts. "I believe I wish to see that one juggler we passed earlier."

Nicholas rose and offered her his arm. "As you like."

Grayson found the two of them clapping their hands along with the crowd of people standing in a circle around a giant of a man who was juggling five ale bottles. Every few minutes he snagged one of the bottles out of the circle and drank it down even as he continued to juggle. By the time every bottle was empty, he was staggering. Still, he never dropped a single bottle.

It was Grayson who had to pull out the rest of his coins to place in the giant's huge boot. Rosalind noticed Grayson's eyes were shining with excitement as he pulled them aside. "Just look what I found in a stall leaning against an old oak tree, set completely apart from the other bookstalls. I don't know why, but I went there like a homing pigeon." He held out an ancient and tattered bloodred leather-bound book set gently on his palm, but didn't let them touch it. "An old man was sitting on a rickety stool surrounded by piles of old books, whistling. But this one—the old man held it out to me and smiled." He added, his voice more reverent than a vicar's, "I couldn't believe it. It's an ancient copy of Sarimund's *Rules of the Pale*. I didn't believe any of them had survived."

"Who is Sarimund? What is a pale?" Rosalind stuck out her hand, but Grayson simply pulled the book to his chest, cradling it.

"No, it is too fragile. The Pale, Rosalind, is

a place that's beyond us, on the other side, mayhap in a different time. An otherworld, I suppose you could call it—it's where all sorts of strange beings exist and stranger things occur, frightening things, things we mortals cannot understand. At least that's what an ancient don at Oxford told me about it. Mr. Oakby didn't believe any more copies existed either, but here it is. I found it." Grayson was trembling with excitement. He said, "It's incredible, I cannot believe this old whistling man had a copy of it, that he actually handed it to me, as if he knew I would give most anything to have it. Do you know what? He refused to take any more than a single sovereign. My lord, you are looking strange. Do you happen to know of Sarimund? The *Rules of the Pale*?"

Nicholas nodded. "I know that the *Rules of the Pale* is about the exploits of a wizard who visited the Bulgar and somehow managed to penetrate into the Pale, and wrote down rules he discovered in order to survive there. He found his way back out and there the book stops. As for Magnus Sarimund, I understand his home was near York. He was a Viking descendant, claimed one of his ancestors had once ruled the Danelaw. A marvelous fiction."

"Fiction? Oh, no," Grayson said. "Surely not."

Nicholas said nothing.

"I did not know Sarimund's history," Grayson said. "A Viking descendant—you must tell me everything you know, my lord. I must write to Mr. Oakby at Oxford. He will be very excited. What luck for me. Imagine finding the *Rules of the Pale* here in a bookstall in Hyde Park."

Rosalind grabbed his arm. "Wait a moment, Grayson. I remember now. A pale isn't some sort of otherworldly place, it's nothing more than a commonplace stockade, a protective barrier of some sort. I remember reading of an English pale that encompassed some twenty miles around Dublin—a long time ago, built as a defense against marauding tribes. To be safe, you stayed within the pale, or the stockade. If you were outside the stockade, or beyond the pale, as the phrase goes, then it meant back then that you were in real danger."

Nicholas nodded, saying, "I recall there was also a pale built by Catherine the Great to keep the Jews safe. But this place by Sarimund, it is another kind of pale entirely."

Rosalind said, "Grayson, let's go to that bookstall. Would you take us there?"

"Well, all right, but it was the only copy, you know. There'll be no more there. I asked the old man. He shook his head at me, never stopped his whistling."

Nicholas nodded, then stuck out his hand. Rosalind didn't hesitate; she took his hand and stayed close to his side as they weaved through the crowds. When Grayson spotted the decrepit old stall leaning against an oak tree, set a goodly distance away from the other bookstalls, he broke into a trot, calling over his shoulder, "I don't remember that it looked quite this bad when I was here just minutes ago. Something must be wrong."

They stood in front of the dilapidated stall. There were no piles of old books on the rough plank counter, and no whistling old man. There was nothing at all except a collection of very old boards looking ready to collapse.

Grayson said, "Where could he have gone? And the books? There's not a single one. Do you think he sold all his books and simply left?"

Nicholas was silent.

Rosalind said, "Are you certain this is the right stall, Grayson?"

"Oh, yes," he said. "Let's ask the other vendors. I would like you to meet this old man."

Nicholas and Rosalind helped him make inquiries at all the nearest bookstalls. Two of the booksellers remembered, vaguely, see-ing an old man—*Yes, yes, he was whistling, wouldn't stop, the old bugger—And he set up away from the rest of us, and why did he do that? The next thing there was this rad-dled old stall with all these dusty old books piled around.* The other booksellers didn't remember the old man or his dilapidated bookstall set against the oak tree. At Nicholas's suggestion, they spoke once more to the first two booksellers, the two who had seen the old man—now all they remembered was seeing some ancient boards nailed together, but no books, noth-ing but those dilapidated boards.

Nicholas said, "I wager if we speak to them again in an hour, they will have no memory of anything."

"But—"

Nicholas merely shook his head at Grayson. "I don't understand it, but there you have it. You have the book, Grayson, and that is enough."

"But this makes no sense," Rosalind said. "Why did the booksellers remember him, then ten minutes later, forget him entirely?"

There was no reply from either Grayson or Nicholas.

"Why do you remember the old man and the stall if the others don't, Grayson?"

"I don't know, Rosalind, I don't know."

When they turned back to the decrepit old bookstall, it was to see several rough boards littering the ground.

Grayson felt a quiver of something scary deep inside. "This is passing strange." He gave them a false smile. "Nicholas is right. I have the *Rules of the Pale*. And that's what's important. Perhaps the book broke through the Pale to come to me through the old man. Maybe the old man was the ancient wizard. I remember Mr. Oakby said he'd heard from his own mentor many years before that Sarimund wrote of his talks with ghosts. Perhaps that is why the old man wanted me to have it. He knows of all the ghosts that litter my mental landscape." And he laughed, a laugh that hid questions and the fear of something not to be explained. He looked down at the book he held reverently in his hand. "I must think about all this. I will see you at home, Rosalind." He nodded to Nicholas and quickly left them.

Nicholas wanted that book, wanted it badly, but there was nothing he could do. As he escorted Rosalind back to his carriage, Rosalind said, "How do you know of Magnus Sarimund, my lord?"

"We have watched a drunken juggler, listened to a group of young men sing to you, and I have even eaten part of your lunch. You should call me Nicholas, if you please. How do I know of Sarimund? Well, my grandfather visited the Bulgar. He told me he supped with the Titled Wizard of the East, as he is called, an ancient relic whose beard tip actually brushed over his sandals. The Titled Wizard of the East told him that Sarimund lived five years in the caves of the Charon Labyrinth with other holy men and wizards, the caves more dangerous than any other caverns in the Bulgar, what with their sheer abysses and knife-sharp stalagmites to stab the unwary, more dangerous than even a mad sirocco, he said. The Titled Wizard of the East told him that during the five years of Sarimund's stay, travelers who happened to venture too close to the caves were met by strange frightening visions and plagued by demons in their dreams. My grandfather asked him if wizards still inhabited the caves and the wizard gave him a smile that bespoke many things he couldn't begin to understand, he or any other human being, for that matter. The wizard said only, 'Of course,' and nothing more."

"Did this Sarimund really speak to ghosts?"

"My grandfather believed he did." Nicholas assisted her up into the carriage. He nodded to the man sitting in the driver's seat, a leather hat pulled low over his forehead. "Back to Putnam Square, Lee."

"Certainly, my lord."

Rosalind said, "He sounds like a gentleman."

"He is," Nicholas said, and nothing more.

"Why is he wearing that lovely leather cap pulled nearly to his nose? Why is a gentleman your servant?"

He gave her a charming smile. "It is none of your affair, Rosalind."

When Nicholas had settled himself across from her, Rosalind cocked her head at him. "All right, it is none of my business. Now, you swear to me this Magnus Sarimund was a real man?"

"Oh, yes, Sarimund was quite real, according to my grandfather. He lived in the sixteenth century, mostly in York, but also spent a lot of his time in the Mediterranean. On the islands, I suppose, though no one knows where exactly. It is said he had a hidden sanctuary there where he conducted his magical experiments. Then he journeyed to the Bulgar. When he came out, he went to Constantinople, to be welcomed by Suleiman the Magnificent. He wrote the *Rules of the Pale* there. I believe he had twenty or so copies made of his manuscript. It is indeed something of magic in itself to find one of the copies here. And that Grayson found it."

"Evidently the old bookseller made certain Grayson had it. And now it would seem that the old bookseller simply disappeared— that was very strange, Nicholas."

He said nothing.

"How odd that both you and Grayson know about the *Rules of the Pale* and this Sarimund."

He merely nodded.

"Very well, keep your secrets. Did this Sarimund write other books?"

"Not that I know of, at least not that my grandfather said."

"And now the bookseller is gone," Rosalind shivered. "As if he never existed. You have read it, haven't you, Nicholas? You have actually seen another copy of the *Rules of the Pale.*"

"Yes, I have. My grandfather said he found a copy in a dusty old bookshop in York where Sarimund had lived."

"Did he read to you from the *Rules of the Pale*? Discuss it with you? Do you remember what it said?"

"No, he never exactly read to me from the book itself, simply told me stories about Sarimund before—well, never mind that."

"Was your grandfather a wizard, Nicholas? You said he visited the Bulgar, he met with this old man called the Titled Wizard of the East."

Nicholas said slowly as he stared out the carriage window, "I cannot really answer that. I remember he knew things that most men didn't, he could tell me things about people's thoughts and feelings, but did he simply make it all up? I don't know."

"Did you live with your grandfather?"

"After my mother died, yes, I did. My father remarried, you see, and his new wife didn't like me, particularly after she gave birth to a son of her own. I was five years old when my grandfather welcomed me to Wyverly Chase, the country seat of the Vails since the sixteenth century. He was the Earl of Mountjoy, you see, and there was nothing my father could do about it, not that he wanted me to remain."

"You were only five years old."

"Yes. In the following years, my father and his new family rarely visited Wyverly Chase. I remember my father was angry he had to wait to come into the title and my grandfather's wealth, though I knew he was very rich in his own right."

"But you were your father's heir. Surely that was more important than any dislike on the part of your stepmother. You were only a little boy, why—"

Nicholas merely shook his head at her and smiled. "Remember our giant drunk juggler? Before we left the park I saw him snoring beneath a bench by the Serpentine."

"Very well, Nicholas, keep your secrets. But I will clout you if you are not more forthcoming in the future. The near future."

He reached over and lightly clasped her

hand in his. He smiled at her, an intimate smile, one that made something very deep inside her stir to life.

How very odd, she thought later, that she knew to her bones that there would be a future. He was now in her life, and he would remain in her life.

7

An old man walked toward her, his long white robe brushing his sandals. A thick, twisted rope belted the robe, its frayed ends nearly reaching his knees. His beard was so long the tip nearly touched the hem of his robe. She saw large white toes. He smiled at her, his teeth shining as white as his toes. It was odd, but she wasn't the least bit afraid even though she was lying on her back on her bed and her bedchamber should be dark, but it wasn't. His skin looked soft and pale, as if he hadn't spent any time in the sun. He looked like a prophet, she thought, and he was here to see her. He bent down beside her bed, leaning close to her ear. She heard his voice, gentle as a soft whistle of a warm breeze. *I am Rennat, the Titled Wizard of the East. All know you will come into your own. You—* He turned to look toward her door, his head cocked to one side, as if listening to something she couldn't hear, something coming here, to her bedchamber. He turned back to her, his beard brushing her shoulder as he leaned close once again. She heard his whisper in her ear, *Obey the rules, obey the rules, obey—*

Rosalind jerked awake, heart pounding, her nightgown damp with sweat. She jerked up in bed, her palms against her chest, trying to grab a breath, trying to bring herself out of that dream. The strange old man standing over her—no, he wasn't here, standing by her bed, his beard brushing her shoulder, there was nothing here at all.

She looked over at the thick shadows on the other side of her bedchamber that could easily hide something frightening—she sucked in her breath—no, she was being absurd. It was a dream, only a dream about the *Rules of the Pale*, and that wizard Nicholas had told her about, and her mind had spun it into that strange dream. How odd that she'd seen the wizard in the greatest of detail. Rennat—that was his name, an odd name that tugged at something deep inside her. Had Nicholas said that name? Perhaps so, but she wasn't sure. It didn't matter; if he hadn't, that simply meant her mind had supplied it.

Obey the rules, obey the rules. Her heart thrummed, gooseflesh rippled her skin. She was not about to fall asleep again, not with those dreams waiting to leap out of the corner of her mind when she closed her eyes.

All know you will come into your own. That's what the old man had confided to her, so close he'd been she fancied she could still feel his warm breath on her ear, and his breath—she'd swear she could still smell that light scent of lemon. Come into her own *what*? Rosalind sat very still, calming herself, her breath slowing, her squirreling brain righting itself.

She wasn't afraid, not really, since she knew ghosts—at least, that's what she called the voices, for want of anything better. She'd lived with them for years. Sometimes she heard them murmuring from shadowed corners, but more often they came like thick mist in her dreams, whispering, always whispering, but unfortunately she could never understand them. And she wanted desperately to see them, but never could. Rosalind wished her ghosts would say actual words, as Rennat had.

Then she could ask them what her real name was.

Enough of mad hoary old men with skinny gray beards dangling to their big white toes, their breath smelling of lemons. She felt restless, twitchy, and strangely cold as well. Rosalind put on a robe and slippers, lit a lucifer and touched it to her bedside candle, and went down the great wide staircase, her hand cupping the candle flame. She was going to steal some of Uncle Ryder's brandy. Her hand was reaching toward the doorknob when she saw a flickering light coming from beneath the library door. What was this?

She raised her hand to knock, lowered it, and quietly opened the door. She saw Grayson sitting at the great mahogany desk in the far corner, a single candle at his elbow illuminating what she knew was the *Rules of the Pale*.

The candle was nearly gutted.

She hadn't seen him since he'd left her and Nicholas at Hyde Park. He hadn't appeared at dinner nor had he come to the drawing room for tea. Since his writing hours were erratic, no one else had thought anything of his absence—but she had. His hair was disordered, his shirt open at the neck.

She lightly touched her hand to his shoulder. "Grayson?"

He nearly jumped out of his chair. "Oh, Rosalind, you gave me a royal scare. It's the middle of the night. What are you doing out of bed at this hour?"

"I had a strange dream," she said. "You're still reading the *Rules of the Pale*?"

"I can't read it, at least not yet. It's in some sort of code I haven't been able to figure out. Sarimund starts off in an old formal sort of English I can read. Then he tells the reader he has written the *Rules* in his own personal code and he doubts the reader will be able to decipher it. You can almost see him preening over his own cleverness, the bastard. I'd shoot him if he weren't already dead."

The book lay open on the desktop. She waved to it. "Why didn't you tell your parents about it?"

"My parents are very comfortably set in the modern day, you know that, Rosalind."

"They accept the Virgin Bride. Even

though Uncle Ryder carps about it all being a bloody myth nurtured by the ladies of the family. You know as well as I do both of them believe in her."

Grayson shrugged. "Oh, aye, I believe in her too, this unfortunate young lady who's lived at Northcliffe Hall since Queen Bess was in full flower—but she's different. She's a ghost, long dead, yes, but she's not a chain-dragging ghoul out to terrify. She's part of the damned Sherbrooke family. Corrie tells me the Virgin Bride has visited the twins many times and they accept her just as they accept their nanny, Beth."

Of all the ghosts that hovered around Rosalind, the Virgin Bride wasn't among their number. On the other hand, she doubted the Sherbrooke ghost ever would visit her—she had no plans to marry a Sherbrooke and that seemed to be the prerequisite if you weren't of their blood.

Grayson threw down his pen. "When I read Sarimund's sniggering claim, I'll tell you I laughed. I truly thought I would be able to break his code. It's all written with what look like random letters, spaced apart like they're words, only they're not and I can't figure out how to make them into real words. I've spent the past"—he stared over at the ormolu clock on the mantelpiece—"well, since this afternoon trying to figure it out, but I haven't yet succeeded. My brain wants to explode."

Rosalind frowned. "That surprises me since you've always been good at solving puzzles and deciphering codes and such."

"Yes, until now. It's fair to driving me to the edge."

"Does Sarimund use any proper names, or are the names in code as well?"

"Well, he did write one name—Rennat."

Her heart started up a hard drumbeat again. "Rennat?"

He nodded. "Yes, strange name, isn't it?"

Rosalind thought she would expire. "Rennat," she repeated, her voice a skinny thread of sound.

"It could be a dog, really, but it makes sense to me that if Sarimund went to the trouble of not encoding the name, it must be a man, an important man."

"Grayson, my dream"—Rosalind swallowed—"that is the name of the old man who came to me in my dream. Rennat, the Titled Wizard of the East—that's who he said he was."

Grayson stared up at her, then threw his

nib pen at her. She snagged it right out of the air with her right hand. She always did. It had been a game between them for many years. No spattering ink since the nib was dry. Grayson said, "I can usually count on you for a better jest, Rosalind. Rennat came to you in a dream?—that isn't worthy of you. Come now, don't try to make me any more befuddled than I already am."

She opened her mouth to tell him it was no jest, but he'd already turned away, staring back down at the book.

"May I look at it?"

He shoved the book over to her. "I'm so bloody tired my mind's decided you're my mother."

"In that case, I could smack you and you'd have to take it."

Grayson rose and stretched, waved her to his chair. Rosalind sat down and slowly drew the book toward her. She looked down at the small, spidery handwriting, the faded black ink still quite legible. She lightly touched the pages. "Sarimund never had it printed. So twenty copies were hand-copied?"

"That's what Nicholas said. I don't know. Mr. Oakby at Oxford never said. I don't think he knew either."

Rosalind looked down at the page and her heart nearly stopped. Grayson was wrong. It wasn't a difficult code at all. She reached out and touched her hand to his arm. "Grayson, it's easy. I can read it."

8

Grayson was so startled he spurted out the tea he'd just gulped down, and coughed. "No," he said, staring at her, "that's not possible. Stop it, Rosalind."

"Listen to me, for whatever reason, I can indeed read it. And I did dream of this old man Rennat, it wasn't a jest. I can tell you what he looks like. He spoke to me. Maybe that's why I can read this. It's not in old stilted English, either—it's in modern English. I don't know, maybe he's allowing me to read it easily."

Grayson carefully set down his teacup. He looked bewildered. "No, that's not possible, Rosalind."

"It's easy, I tell you. All you have to do is switch the third letter of each word to the front, or, if the third letter happens to be a vowel, then it goes to the end or near the end of the word. All vowels represent the seventh, thirteenth, nineteenth, twentieth, or twenty-fifth letters of the alphabet, and those consonants represent the vowels. All the *u*'s are pointers to those words that are the subject—it's perfectly clear, Grayson, in lovely, clear English, not stilted and no strange words from the sixteenth century."

"Yes, yes, you move consonants about and the vowels fall into place and—" He stared at her, shook his head. "Damnation, what you said makes no sense at all, it's all nonsense. Besides, if it did make sense, if that was the key, it would take hours to rearrange all those bloody letters."

He took the book from her and saw his hands were shaking. Dear God, how he hated this. He looked down at the scrambled letters and heaved a huge sigh. What had she said about the consonants being vowels—and the *u*'s were what? Pointers? "No, you must be tired too, Rosalind. There's no sense to be made of this."

"Bloody hell, you stubborn jackass, it is

easy! Be quiet now and listen." She read slowly: *"A river slices like a sharp blade through the Vale of Augur, narrow and deep and treacherous—"*

Grayson jerked the book from her hands and scanned the page. "You made that up. I don't like you teasing me like this. This dream about Rennat, what you're pretending to read, no one could decipher that code so quickly. You should be writing the ghost novels, not I."

She laid her hand on his forearm. "Grayson, for whatever reason, the code translates itself to me instantly. I cannot explain it, but it's true."

He looked down at the book again. "There is no way you can make sense of that except—" He shook his head, thrust the book at her again. "All right, I'll transcribe what you say." And he began to write as she read.

"Smooth black stepping stones span the river like burned loaves of bread, but the stones reject a man's foot. That is because they are meant for the Tiber's hoof. A man may only dare to walk on the stones to cross the river when the three blood moons are full and have risen in concert over Mount Olyvan. Heed this rule or you will die."

She raised her head, and said, her voice thin as a thread, "Grayson, what is this place? Three full blood moons that rise together over this Mount Olyvan?" She shivered. "I'm afraid." And she was—very afraid. She said slowly, "Nicholas knows about this. He said his grandfather owned a copy."

Grayson lifted her from the chair and pulled her against him, lightly stroking her back, something he'd done to soothe her since she was a terrified child newly arrived at Brandon House. "I don't understand this either. But whatever it is, you're right— Nicholas Vail is a part of it. But what I don't understand is, why was I the one to find this particular book? Why did the old man at the bookstall call to me and not to you? After all, you're the one who can read it, not I. I'm willing to wager you my new saddle that Nicholas can read it too. And what happened to that whistling old man and his bookstall? It's as if he was waiting for me to come, then poof!—gone. All I see in my mind now are leaves blowing in the wind, a few rotted boards. Fact is, I'm afraid too." He eased her back against his arms. "There is something very odd going on here, but we will find out the truth of it, Rosalind. Now, I want you to read the book to me so that I may transcribe it while you read, all right?"

Suddenly she was excited, filled with energy, not fear. "Yes, of course I will. You know, Grayson, I'm thinking the old man showed the book to the right person." She turned to look a moment into the sluggish fire, nearly embers now. "Before I read more, let me tell you about my dream. I told you that Rennat the Titled Wizard of the East spoke to me."

"Yes, but—"

"Well, the thing is, I can't remember." And try as she might, she simply couldn't remember. "Grayson, I—" She stared up at him, helpless and mute. She was perfectly white now. "Why can't I remember? It's gone, the dream of Rennat, it's all gone now. And he was so clear to me, what he said, all of it—now it's just gone."

Grayson was suddenly scared to his feet. "What the devil is happening here?"

"I don't know." She pulled away and slammed her palms against her head. "I have a great memory. Why, I can remember that girl's name you took to the barn loft that July afternoon—Susie Abercrombie."

He stared at her with a fascinated eye. "You shouldn't know about that," he said slowly. "I was very careful, since my mother always knew all." They were both silent for a while. Grayson picked up the book. "Perhaps I should burn this damned thing."

She grabbed his hand. "No, oh, no, you can't. There is something here, Grayson, something that places you and me and Nicholas in the middle of something. We don't know what that something is right now, but we'll find out, you'll see. We must speak to Nicholas."

She didn't know where it came from, but she felt a smile on her face. Then the wild energy left her. She felt empty and so tired she could sleep on the carpet in front of the fireplace.

She heard Grayson say as if from a great distance, "You're right, we do need to speak to Nicholas Vail. I'm praying with all my might he'll have some ideas about how to proceed. We can send him a message first thing in the morning. You look very tired, Rosalind. Enough of this."

She said, "You don't want to wait, I can see it, you want to run all the way to Nicholas's house—no, he's staying at Grillon's Hotel. I'd like to run right along beside you, but I'm so tired, Grayson."

Grayson touched his fingers to her white cheek. "We will figure this out, trust me. Until tomorrow. Come, I'll walk you up."

Rosalind paused on the step, looking back down at him. He was cradling the book in his arms. She said, "Yesterday I was only concerned about the ball at Pinchon House, wearing the new gown Uncle Douglas ordered for me, dancing with at least three dukes, but now—everything is backwards and upside down now. I feel like we've strayed into the pages of one of your novels, Grayson."

Backwards and upside down, things you would say to children in the nursery, Grayson thought.

They parted at the top of the stairs, Grayson to his bedroom, the book now pressed tightly against his chest. Rosalind watched him until he paused at his bedroom door, looked back at her, and gave her a small salute.

Rosalind slipped into bed and fell immediately asleep. There were no more dreams. She slept soundly until Matilde, whose plentiful bosom was the envy of every female servant in Sherbrooke town house, shook her awake the following morning. "Miss Rosalind, come on now, it's time to wake up."

Rosalind's eyes flew open, suddenly aware that light flooded in on her from the window, and she shot up in bed. "Oh, goodness, what time is it, Matilde?"

"Going toward ten o'clock, Miss Rosalind. Mrs. Sophie told me to see if you were ill. I told her you were never ill, you did not even understand what it was like to suffer colds like I do, endlessly. I told her—"

Rosalind threw back the covers. "Yes, yes, Matilde. I understand. Have you seen Master Grayson?"

Matilde crossed her arms and tapped her foot. "He went out early, just as soon as he'd fed the last bit of bacon to that racing kitten of his, didn't tell anyone where he was going, at least that's what I heard Mr. Willicombe tell Mrs. Fernley."

Rosalind paused. "Did you notice if he was carrying anything, Matilde?"

Matilde, whose secret ambition was the stage, struck a pose, fingertips tapping her chin in rhythm with her tapping toe, eyes narrowed in deep thought. "Yes, there was a wrapped package beneath his right arm. Sly, Master Grayson was about it, and ever so protective."

She'd just bet he was furtive. Curse him, he hadn't waited for her, he'd gone by himself to see Nicholas. She would kill him.

Matilde said, "I heard Mrs. Fernley tell Mr. Willicombe that Master Grayson knocked at least three times on your door early this morning, but you were nestled in the wings of the angels."

Well, that was something, but not enough. She was still going to hurt him.

9

Rosalind was pacing the drawing room an hour later, alternately grinding her teeth and looking at the clock on the mantel. Where the devil was Grayson?

The *Rules of the Pale*—she wanted to read it before Nicholas did. Small of her, she knew, but somehow she simply knew deep down that she had to be the one to read it, and very soon now or—or what? She didn't know.

When Grayson came into the drawing room thirty minutes later, she grabbed his arms and shook him. "I know what you did, Grayson, you gave three paltry little knocks on my bedchamber door, probably just brushed your knuckles really, then off you went. You took the book to Nicholas, didn't you? You let him read it, didn't you? Oh, I'm going to bloody your nose and lay you flat. You treacherous blockhead, I'll just bet Nicholas—another treacherous blockhead—was ever so delighted to see you, wasn't he?" She shook him again, got right in his face, ready to lambaste him some more—blast him to the hereafter—when Grayson had the nerve to laugh at her.

She stuck her fist under his nose. "You dare to make light of this, Grayson Sherbrooke? You don't think I can kick you in the dirt?"

"Hello, Rosalind."

She whirled to see Nicholas Vail standing in the open drawing room doorway. He looked ever so fit, and dangerous, in truth, with his black hair wind-tossed, his boots so highly polished she knew she'd be able to see her face in the shine. A black brow was arched; he looked ready to laugh.

"You!"

"I believe so, yes. Do you really think Grayson and I are treacherous blockheads?"

"You are probably a good deal worse."

Grayson said, "I did knock on your door, Rosalind. Rather vigorously, but you were dreaming of dancing with your three dukes, deciding which one of the poor dolts you were going to nab. What was I to do? Of course I went to see Nicholas. Of course I showed him the book. You would have done the same thing in my shoes, you know it. Don't be a twit."

Nicholas never looked away from Rosalind as he walked into the drawing room. He took her hand and lifted it to his lips. A graceful, old-fashioned gesture, to be sure, but it fit him, and it fit the moment. His mouth was warm on her flesh, the look of amusement still making his dark eyes gleam, and at the touch of him . . . Rosalind grew very still. Something akin to shock crashed through her. It was only a man's mouth lightly touching her hand—the absolute frantic delight of what she felt astounded her. She opened her mouth, stared at him, mute, her confusion, her delight, clear on her face. She looked at his mouth—she thought it could be hard, perhaps cruel—but when his mouth had touched her hand, she'd wanted to plaster herself against him and kiss him until her lips fell off. As for Nicholas, that unconscious clod appeared unmoved, as if he hadn't a clue that her world had just shifted, as if he were thinking about a nice cup of tea. She wanted to kick him, yell at him to wake up, but Nicholas said, amusement rich in his voice, "Grayson came to me. He showed me the book, told me you could read the *Rules* as fluently as one of Mrs. North's gothic novels. I admit I disbelieved him because I couldn't read it, so how could you, a mere female? Now do you feel better?"

Are you lying, Nicholas?

Before she could pin him, Grayson said, "So it's only you, Rosalind, who has this ability, I suppose you could call it, this gift, this—"

"Yes, yes, I know, I'm different."

"So, Nicholas is of no use to us at all. Why do you look like you want to kick him? He didn't do anything at all. You're still the only star performer here, not either of us."

Nicholas said, "Fact is, even though my grandfather showed me the book, he never told me specifically what was written; he only told me about Sarimund. Had he broken the code as well? I remember him trying, endlessly, but I don't think he ever did."

She wondered again if he were lying and

wanted to connect her fist to his perfect nose. Unfortunately she had to keep her fists at her sides because Uncle Ryder and Aunt Sophie came into the drawing room at that moment. Their faces froze, all conversation died.

Ryder said smoothly to Nicholas, "Willicombe told us you'd arrived with Grayson."

"It is delightful to see you, sir, ma'am," Nicholas said, bowing to Sophie. "Your gown is quite charming."

Sophie grinned up at this dangerous young man. "No more charming than you, my lord."

Rosalind snorted.

Sophie asked, "From the looks on all your faces, you wish us to the Devil, but alas, we're staying right here. Now, what is all this about a book? This is the one you were reading yesterday, Grayson?"

Grayson nodded. "I, ah, had some questions about it, Mama. I wanted Nicholas to see it."

"But why didn't you show it to him yesterday? After all, the three of you were together at the park, weren't you?"

Grayson turned mute. Nicholas stared hard at a lovely shepherdess atop the mantel, and so Rosalind, giving them both a disgusted look, said, "You know how Grayson is, Aunt Sophie, he gets an idea and he goes off to hide. He left us in the park." *Unchaperoned.* "Er, that is, Grayson didn't really leave us, exactly, he suggested we come home immediately and so we did. Well, almost immediately."

Ryder Sherbrooke walked slowly to where his son stood. "You and Rosalind were always inept at dissimulation. I see that his lordship is no better. What is going on here?"

Nicholas said, "Grayson found a rare old book at the fair yesterday. It is in code. Are you good at deciphering code, sir?"

"Code? This old book is written in code? How very odd. Let me see it." Ryder held out his hand. Nothing else to do—Grayson handed his father the *Rules of the Pale*, though for an instant, he'd wanted to tuck it into his shirt and run.

Ryder, aware that his son was hovering, handled the book very gently. "It indeed appears to be very old. You found this in a bookstall at the artists' fair yesterday?"

Grayson said, "Yes, sir."

The three of them watched Ryder open the book at random, watched his forehead furrow as he studied the page, watched him frown. Finally, he raised his head. They held their collective breath. "It is a code I have never seen before. Douglas is very good at this sort of thing. We can show it to him." Grayson took the book from his father without a word.

"Douglas and Alexandra will be arriving on the morrow," Sophie said to Nicholas. "He is the Earl of Northcliffe, but you know that, don't you?"

"Someone mentioned it to me at the ball the other night. I look forward to making his lordship's acquaintance."

Sophie held out her hand to her son. "My turn."

To her disappointment, she couldn't make out the code either. "How very lowering. I thought my dear husband and I knew everything of importance. This depresses my spirits. As for Douglas, he is coming to lend more weight to Rosalind's coming out. There will be a ball here for her next Friday," Sophie said, her eyes never leaving Nicholas Vail's dark face.

Guileless as a nun, Rosalind said, "Lord Mountjoy came back with Grayson because I agreed to go riding in the park with him; he is

going to tell me all about Macau. I have a fascination for Portuguese colonies, you know."

Both Ryder and Sophie strongly doubted
Rosalind had even heard of Macau before
this. Still, Sophie found herself nodding. "I
suppose that will be all right. But don't forget,
dearest, you have a final fitting at Madame
Fouquet's this afternoon."

"Macau can wait," Grayson said. "The
book, Rosalind, we must work together on
the book. Nicholas as well."

It was odd, but Rosalind no longer felt any
urgency about the book. She felt urgency
about Nicholas. She said, "I will get more
information from Nicholas about it, Grayson.
It will assist us. When we return, we will all
work on it together."

"But why—"

"I have a headache. I need fresh air."

*   *   *

"That was very well done," Nicholas said as
he sat opposite Rosalind in his carriage.
"Your Uncle Ryder is wrong. You lie quite fluently." He thudded his cane against the roof.
"Tell Grace and Leopold to go leisurely to the
park, Lee."

"Yes, my lord." The carriage rolled forward.

"Grace and Leopold?"

"My grays. They're proud and know their own worth. If they feel someone has slighted them, they bite. Now, can you really read the *Rules of the Pale*?"

"You needn't play more games, my lord. You know I can read that wretched book. You knew all along. Or at least you very much hoped I could. My question to you is, why?"

There was a pause before he said, "Of course I am surprised. How could I possibly know? As for a plan, why, I have none except to provide whatever assistance I am able to you and Grayson when I return you home from the park. This ride I invited you for this morning, did I indicate any specific time?"

"A medium sort of time, if I remember aright. Don't change the subject. And you think I lie fluently. I am not near to your equal, my lord. I know you will hang over my shoulder to hear each word from the *Rules of the Pale*. I wish you would tell both Grayson and me what you know about it, Nicholas."

He gave her a lovely shrug with his powerful shoulders, but she had no intention of admiring him. "Certainly the book is of some interest to me, since even as a young boy, I knew it was a passion with my grandfather.

Perhaps I'll learn why it was his passion from the text itself."

Her gloved fingers drummed on her reticule. "You are quite adroit, aren't you, my lord?"

"My name is Nicholas. Adroit? I surely hope so or I doubt I would have survived to adult years."

When she looked at his mouth again, she forgot about his secrets, forgot about the *Rules of the Pale*, forgot that she didn't want to admire his shoulders. She didn't understand any of this, only knew she wanted him to touch her again, to feel him kiss her hand again, perhaps kiss the inside of her elbow, even her ear. She shuddered when she thought of his kissing her on the mouth, kissing her until she was stupid with it. That would be wicked, surely, but she imagined that a life without wickedness couldn't be much fun, could it?

She looked out the carriage window to see that they were passing by the entrance to the park. She didn't care a whit. It was overcast today, cooler, but she felt comfortably warm. There weren't that many people wandering about, not at this unfashionable hour, only a few children with their hoops, yelling to each other in sight of nannies and tutors. A flower girl and a pie vendor were walking about to find buyers. She said on a sigh, "So that I am not a complete liar, tell me about Macau."

"The air smells different there."

"Well, yes, of course it does. It is a foreign clime."

He laughed, shook his head. "And just what do you know of foreign climes?"

"Actually, London was a foreign clime to me until two weeks ago. I'll admit it, I'm a provincial. Do you despise me for it?"

"I don't think so. Should I?"

"Probably. When you are angry with me you will doubtless think of several reasons." Then she found herself once again staring at his mouth. She cleared her throat. What were they talking about? Oh, yes. "I'm sure the blue of the sky is different as well as the smell of the air in Macau. Tell me, how did you live?"

He stared at her, all of his dangerous suave self suddenly nonplussed. Until now, no one had shown the slightest interest in the life he had before London. "What do you mean?"

"Come now, Nicholas, I'm sure you were

very prosperous. All these nonsensical rumors about your not having a sou because your father purposefully beggared you, I don't believe it for an instant."

"But it is true," he said slowly. "My father's intention was to beggar me. He left me only the entailed family estate in Sussex with its three thousand acres of dying land."

"What he did doesn't matter to you. You have the funds to fix everything. Indeed, I imagine you have already begun setting things to right. I am willing to wager my next allowance that you have no need at all of an heiress."

"No, you're quite right. I have no need of an heiress."

"I knew it. I am equally sure you moved easily in Portuguese society in Macau. Tell me about your life there."

He gave her a brooding look. "Your eyes are the most incredible shade of blue. I was thinking of a soft blue blanket a Portuguese woman wove for me."

"A blanket? That sort of flattery could shatter a girl's heart. As for your eyes, Nicholas, they are black as any tar pit I have ever seen."

"Have you ever seen a tar pit?"

She shook her head, never looking away from his face. "Your eyes do not, thankfully, look like wet tar. They're simply black and deep and there are answers inside that you hide very well. You're a man brimming with secrets, Nicholas. I have secrets myself, only I don't know what they are."

A very strange thing to say, he thought, but said, "Shall I tell you about how beautiful I think your hair is? The shades of it—hair your color graces Titian's paintings."

He leaned toward her and lightly touched his fingertips to the curls over her ears. "I must adjust my opinion. The color of the stuff is richer than any red Titian ever produced. It is glorious hair you have, Rosalind."

"Why do you pay me such an extravagant compliment? Are you trying to atone for the blue blanket?"

"When I saw you at the ball Thursday night, I knew, I simply knew, that you were—"

"Were what?"

He frowned a moment out the window, and shrugged as he turned back to her. "You dance well," he said.

"Thank you. You're quite right about that. Uncle Ryder taught me himself. Stop avoiding the subject, Nicholas. I wish to hear about how you lived in Macau. I want to know how you dealt with daily life in a strange land."

"Ah," he said absently, "listen to all the noise outside the carriage window. And all the people moving about—black-frocked clerks, ladies with their maids, gentlemen of leisure strolling to their clubs, swinging their canes, solicitors muttering to themselves, vendors hawking pies, flower girls sur- rounded with splendid color. It was the same in Macau, only you wouldn't understand what anyone was saying."

"You are extraordinarily eloquent."

"Thank you. Now—"

"Now nothing. What did you do, Nicholas? Where did you live? How did you live?" *Did you love a woman? Many women?*

And out of his mouth came, "I will tell you when you agree to marry me."

She stared at him for an instant, then laughed so hard she hiccupped and fell sideways.

Then she straightened up, hiccupped again, and looked over at him—stiff, silent, wary. By everything that was glorious and splendid, he was serious. Her body hummed. She felt the leap of excitement, the feeling that very suddenly, so very unexpectedly, everything was right. It didn't matter that she'd seen him for the first time the night before last. She laughed again, joyously, and said, "Yes, I should like to marry you, Nicholas Vail."

He looked suddenly panicked. "But I—"

She leaned toward him and lightly laid her finger against his mouth. Then she kissed him.

10

☟

Rosalind read:

"**The Tiber is vicious. Only slight force is needed for its hooves to smash a man's face into pulp. The Tiber has one weakness. It craves the taste of the red Lasis. The black Lasis or the brown Lasis will not do, only the red Lasis. But the red Lasis, unlike the brown and black Lasis, is wily and reveals itself to the Tiber only when it can lead it to a covered pit. The red Lasis easily jumps the pit but the Tiber does not. It falls in and the Lasis sends fire spears into it until it is dead. A man must make friends with the red Lasis. Oth-**

erwise a man is destroyed by the Tiber. Sing to the red Lasis of your loyalty just as they sing to the Dragons of the Sallas Pond, and they will protect you."

Rosalind looked up. "It is like Sarimund is writing for a child—simple, basic, crude, if you will."

Nicholas sat on a sofa opposite her, holding a large silk pillow between his hands. He said as he tossed the pillow from one hand to the other, "Or he is writing an instruction manual and wants to make certain there is no misunderstanding. It is crude, you're right about that, Rosalind, and unfortunately it gives us no information at all that is helpful." And he wondered, as he had each time she read from Sarimund's book: *Why is this so clear to you and not to me?*

Grayson was rubbing his hand, cramped from writing so quickly to keep up with her. He said, "Or the Tiber and the red Lasis simply stand for something else—they're metaphors."

"Metaphors for what?" Nicholas said.

Grayson shrugged. "Perhaps concepts of the afterlife. The Tiber represents Hell, the Dragons of the Sallas Pond and the red Lasis—well, Heaven seems a bit of a stretch."

"Maybe the red Lasis are angels," Rosalind said, an eyebrow raised. "They protect men, help them to survive. I don't know, Grayson; even though Sarimund writes simply, I can see the red Lasis leaping over a pit meant for the Tiber. I can even picture a fire spear."

"But note there's no description of them, it only tells the reader that the Tiber has hooves," Grayson said. "It's interesting too, you have words like 'Tiber' and 'Lasis'—foreign, strange words—but then there are words we know, like 'moon' and 'spear.' Read, Rosalind. I have a feeling this will change. I know it will change."

He dipped his nib pen into the inkwell on the floor beside him and nodded to her.

She gave Nicholas a quick look and felt her insides glow even brighter. She fully intended to marry this man—it was astounding and absolutely mad. So few days earlier she hadn't even known he existed. He was a stranger, she knew nothing about him, yet she knew, simply knew to her soul, that this man was the one for her. She thought again of what she'd said to him as they'd walked into the house earlier.

She'd looked up at him sadly, shoulders

dropped, and sighed deeply as she'd whispered, "I hope no one believes me a failure."

That pulled him up short. "A failure?"

"Well, the fact is, my lord, you are not a duke."

His quick full laugh had made her want to jump on him.

Grayson snapped his fingers under her nose. "Come along, Rosalind, back from wherever you went. Why are you blushing? No, don't tell me. Read."

She studied the next sentence a moment, then raised her head. "This is strange. It's a new section, but there is no empty space between to mark the end of one and the beginning of the next. It also changes from narrative to first person." She read, *"I discovered the Dragons of the Sallas Pond only eat every three weeks, and only fire rocks, heated for those three weeks until they're soft and glowing. They have never eaten a man. When men venture to the Pale they cower inside caves and build fires, but learn quickly that the flying creatures swoop down upon them to kill the flame. It is a frightening sight, the dying flames, the creatures sucking at the embers, the men screaming, but withal, the flying creatures do not harm men.*

"The men who survive settle into the body of the Pale. Just as I did, they observe the Dragons of the Sallas Pond and see that their snouts are rich glittering gold and their eyes bright emeralds and their huge triangular scales, the sharp points glistening beneath the brilliant ice sun, are studded with diamonds.

"To the best of my knowledge, the Dragons of the Sallas Pond do not die. They exist for the now and the ever after. If a man holds himself perfectly silent, he will hear the Dragons singing to each other, perhaps telling about men, what very different creatures they are, foolish and lost and afraid. If a man has patience and can wait, the Dragons will determine if he is worthy, and if he is, as I was, the Dragons will teach him the rules of the Pale.

"For myself, their love songs moved me unutterably, for the mating of the Dragons of the Sallas Pond is for all eternity. They are your salvation. Never lie to a Dragon of the Sallas Pond. This is a rule of the Pale."

Rosalind stopped reading, frowning as she read again, silently, the last few lines. Grayson raised his hand and began rubbing it. Nicholas tossed the bright blue silk pillow to a brocade chair opposite him. He said, "Dragons of the Sallas Pond—it sounds like a tale spun out of an incredible imagination. What is the Sallas Pond, I wonder?"

Rosalind said thoughtfully, "A sacred place, perhaps like Delphi. And Mount Olyvan could be Mount Olympus, could it not? My throat is quite dry. Should you like some tea?"

"Nutty buns?" Nicholas asked, perking up.

"Stand up, Nicholas. Let me see your belly first." He obligingly rose and waited for her to come to him. At the last moment before she touched him, she saw Grayson was gaping at her, his mouth open.

Nicholas said mildly, catching her hand, "I am thin as a pole, Rosalind, no extra flesh on me. Any man who allows himself to gain flesh in his belly is doomed, and will be spat upon. This is a rule of the Nicholas."

His words, spoken with such seriousness, undid her. Laughter spurted out of her. Grayson didn't know whether to laugh or to hit this man who was on such friendly terms with Rosalind. She'd thought to touch her hand to his belly to see if it was flat—what the devil was going on here?

"Oh, goodness," she said, "does the rule of the Nicholas apply to the ladies as well?"

"Indeed it does. Heed me, for I speak true. Should I check your belly, Rosalind? I proclaim you exempt from this rule when you carry my—when you carry a child."

Grayson leapt to his feet and opened his mouth, only to close it when he saw Rosalind's face. Her eyes were wicked. He knew that look. She gave him a bow as she walked to the bell cord and gave it a tug. When Willicombe appeared in the library a scant three seconds later, Grayson said, "Willicombe, were you waiting outside? Did you somehow fathom that we were starving?"

"I am desolated to announce there are no more nutty buns, Master Grayson. I heard Cook say the last three were stolen right out of her kitchen, and it so upset her that she was unable to prepare more."

"Oh, dear, I swear I am not guilty," Rosalind said.

"I suspect my mother," said Grayson. "Nutty buns are her weakness. And she is sly."

Rosalind sighed. "Is it time for luncheon yet, Willicombe?"

"Actually, Miss Rosalind, I was on my way in to fetch the three of you. Cook has prepared

ham slices so thin you can see through them."
While Willicombe spoke, he looked at Sarimund's book. Rosalind could see his fingers
twitching. He bowed once again, holding it a
long moment so the full effect of his bald head
could be appreciated.

Rosalind watched Grayson carefully tuck
the *Rules of the Pale* into his jacket as they
followed in Willicombe's wake.

Nicholas said, leaning close to her ear, "I
could not examine the flatness of your belly.
Grayson would have surely run me through
with that ceremonial sword over the mantel."

"Perhaps if we slip around behind those
stairs, I can kiss you quickly even as I suck
in my stomach for your inspection," Rosalind
said and raced down the hallway.

He laughed. "Come back, Rosalind. I will
feed you a ham slice instead."

11

During luncheon, Grayson told his parents the plot of his new novel to distract them from the *Rules of the Pale*. His fond parents knew what he was doing, but they loved him, and told him they adored the idea of a young Oxford student dueling with a demon who held the heart of his beloved inside a magic gem, rumored to have been ripped out of Satan's crown. It wasn't bad, Rosalind thought, particularly since Grayson was making it up as he spoke.

The moment Aunt Sophie rose from the table, Rosalind pulled Nicholas into the small room that the Countess of Northcliffe had designed for ladies some two decades before.

"No," Nicholas said as he lightly touched his fingers to her cheek. "We mustn't say anything yet to anyone, particularly your aunt and uncle. We've known each other such a short time. Give them another day at least to witness how dazzled I am with you. So soft, you are, Rosalind."

"I don't wish to admit it, but you're right. Uncle Ryder would believe we'd both lost our wits. He might have you kidnapped and shipped back to Macau. You really think I'm soft?"

He touched the tip of his finger to her nose. "Your Uncle Ryder would not consider lost wits; he would believe lust rules us. Your Aunt Sophie would have stars in her eyes at the romance of it, but upon brief reflection she could agree with Uncle Ryder—nothing more than rampant lust, all on my part since you are such an innocent. I am a man of the world, they would say, and one must always beware a man of the world when it comes to a young girl who looks like you do. You're softer than a butterfly's wing."

"I will have you know I am not that innocent." She fidgeted a bit. "The fact is, Nicholas, I don't look like anything much."

"Perhaps you are right. Perhaps you aren't much at all."

She crossed her arms across her chest. Her foot tapped, tapped, tapped. He was enchanted. She said behind her teeth, "You needn't go that far. Now, this lust business—what a very strange word that is. I've never even thought about lust before. If it is lust that makes me want to leap on you and kiss you until you crumple to the carpet, then it is a powerful thing. I think I quite like it. Is that why you asked me to marry you so quickly, Nicholas? You've gone over the edge with lust for me?"

He hadn't wanted to consider lust with her, it wasn't what was important, but—he drew in a deep breath. Truth was truth, and it had to be faced. He said, "Lust is a fine thing, but I don't believe it is lust that rules us." Well, most of the truth was important.

She stared at him in amazement. "Never say so!"

He held back his laughter. She had to recognize it was more. "Well, it doesn't rule us entirely. I am not completely mad with lust for you. You realize that, don't you?"

She said slowly, her eyes going yet again to his mouth, "I honestly don't know what I realize, Nicholas. All I know is that it is right for me—you are right for me, no one else, just you. When you kissed my hand this morning, something deep inside me recognized that you were for me."

So quickly, and she knew? He knew he was the one too, of course he was the one, but he wouldn't tell her that until he had the vows from her, not until she was legally his. He said lightly, "Not even one of the three dukes?"

"Into the fire with the dukes."

He laughed again. He believed he'd laughed more in the past two days than in the past five years. "You have a wit that pleases me," he said.

And she said then, flooring him, "But there is more to this, Nicholas, and I suspect you are well aware of it. For me, it is these overwhelming feelings, this recognition of you, but I think—well, it sounds absurd, I know, but I feel you were perhaps looking for me, as I, perhaps, was looking for you."

"Looking for you? Actively searching for you? And you looking for me? You mean Fate guided our boats to the same shore?"

"I think our boats docked next to each other with our bows knocking together makes more sense than this place called the Pale with its Tibers and Dragons."

"Perhaps the Pale isn't real—perhaps it's a metaphor, as Grayson said."

"You believe it is real, Nicholas. I ask you, how is this book—the *Rules of the Pale*— possible? It was Grayson who found it, who was *led* to find it. Was this Fate or something stronger? And you say your grandfather had a copy of the book. This book boggles the mind. You know it is too much. And when I begin asking these sorts of questions, I become afraid."

The whole thing would frighten him too if he weren't so long used to it. He wanted to bring her against him, reassure her, but knew he'd be a fool to do it. He couldn't ruin things now. Even this conversation, con- ducted only a room away from her guardian, was madness.

Nicholas sighed. It had all happened too quickly. He said, "If you wish, we could attend the theater tonight. My solicitor told me, laughing, that my father neglected to stipulate that the theater box he bought some ten years ago be willed to my half brothers; thus it came to me by default. He told me my half brothers were rather distressed about it. My solicitor is a master of understatement. They would just as soon see me underground."

"Your half brothers? I don't know about them, Nicholas."

He stared at her, appalled at himself. He'd spoken so freely, without considering possible consequences, and it was very unlike him. Well, it was done. Unless she chanced to meet them, and believed whatever they may tell her in their spewing hatred of him, it wouldn't matter. She would be his wife. She would meet them, doubtless, and discover quickly enough that all three of them hated his guts. Yet though he'd known her only two days, he was sure she wouldn't hesitate to be utterly loyal to him, to attack anyone who was stupid enough to insult him. He smiled fatuously. No one had ever sought to protect him and yet he knew she would.

"But why do your half brothers hate you? You are the head of the Vail family. They owe you their respect just as you owe them your protection."

"They hate me because my father taught them to hate me, my father and their mother, Miranda. I saw the two oldest ones, for the first time since my return, on Thursday night, the night I first saw you. Will they be pests? I don't know, but it doesn't disturb me." His dark eyes glittered with banked violence. "And they would be fools to disturb you. Now, should you like to go with me this evening? With your aunt and uncle, of course."

"You've already asked Uncle Ryder, haven't you?"

"Yes. A man must know what is in the stew before he brings the spoon to his mouth."

She laughed. "That was a dreadful metaphor. What are we to see?"

"It is Charles Kean playing Hamlet. He is Edmund Kean's son, not as successful as his sire, but still, I understand after practicing his craft for several years in Scotland, he has returned to London and made this role his own. Do you like Shakespeare?"

"Oh, yes, very much. I have always believed, however, that a woman brought Shakespeare low, and that was the reason he brought Kate to such a wretched end. A revenge, of sorts. I mean, can you imagine a woman kneeling before her husband and promising to do whatever he wishes?"

His eyes nearly crossed. He swallowed. "Well, just perhaps—"

She lightly laid her fingers over his mouth. "No, I won't let you dig yourself into a big hole. You are a man. Aunt Sophie says if a woman is wily and imaginative, she can easily manage a man." She patted his arm. "No, don't groan. Now, when do you wish to tell everyone, Nicholas? Perhaps tomorrow? Sunday would be a splendid day to announce our betrothal to everyone. When do you wish to wed?"

"Let me think about that," he said, never looking away from her face.

"And what about the *Rules of the Pale*?"

He'd felt such urgency before, but oddly, it wasn't prodding him now. Now he had time, since he had the key—namely, her. "Tell Grayson we will continue with it tomorrow afternoon."

She nodded. "I will also tell Grayson to invite a young lady to the theater this evening. He is very popular, you know. The young ladies think he is vastly romantic."

12

Miss Lorelei Kilbourne, eldest of Viscount Ramey's five daughters, born and raised in Northumberland and in London for her first season, had, until this night, only worshipped Grayson Sherbrooke from afar. Rosalind had met her several times, and managed to listen, without snorting, to the young lady's outpourings about Grayson's magnificent physical self, his ever so lovely blue eyes, the ever so charming way he smiled, and his equally brilliant books. So when Grayson shrugged and said he could think of no particular young lady to ask to the theater on such short notice, she presented

Lorelei Kilbourne for his consideration. At his perfectly blank expression at the young lady's name, Rosalind punched him in the arm. "You are such an oblivious oaf. You've met her, Grayson. I believe you've even waltzed with her. Ask her, she adores you— admires you to the point of nausea. Even if she already has an engagement, I know she will break it for you."

"Hmmm," Grayson said. "Lorelei is a lovely name. Unusual. Strange that I don't remember it. I would like to ask her parents why they selected this particular name for her. Perhaps they thought of the sirens, perhaps—"

"Grayson, blessed hell, time grows short. Take yourself over to Kimberly Square and ask her. That's where she lives, at number twenty-three."

"She's the small girl? Shy, blushes a lot? Has glorious mink-colored hair?"

Mink? Trust a writer. "Yes, she's got the minkest-colored hair I've ever seen. Shy? Not with me, she wasn't shy. Not a single blush. Accept it, you're her hero. Go now."

Grayson laughed as he lightly touched a fingertip to her cheek. "Hmm, let me weigh this. Would I prefer to sit in a box next to a pretty girl who worships me . . . or to sit with loud, drunk, belching friends in the pit? This is very difficult. Ah, there are my parents sitting not two feet away from me, Rosalind. That doesn't make it so easy a question, now, does it?"

"You dolt, your parents will not be perched on your shoulder. They would not dream of disapproving of her, what with all the praise she will doubtless heap on your empty head. They'll probably join her, making you insufferable. Grayson, if you do not ask her, I will hurt you very badly. You know that I can."

Grayson remembered that long-ago day she'd lurked in the shadows on a second-floor balcony of Brandon House, waiting for him. When he'd walked below, whistling, minding his own business, she'd thrown a bucket of freezing soapy water on him, all because his ugly pug Jasper had chewed a pair of her slippers and he'd had the nerve to laugh. "All right, I will go around and speak to her. Does that make you happy?"

"You don't have to marry her, Grayson, so don't sound so put-upon. But you know, now that I think about it, you're nearly ripe enough—as Uncle Douglas says—to manage being a decent husband. Shall I ask him?"

Grayson looked ready to run. Then he began to look thoughtful. "Lorelei," he said, studying the Grecian urn on the mantel-piece, "it rather sings on the tongue, don't you think?" And he walked away, whistling.

She called after him, "All this worship for you, a moron of the first order, it fair to makes me gag."

He laughed, waggled his fingers at her, but didn't turn.

The Royal Theater, Drury Lane

Rosalind said behind her hand to Aunt Sophie, "Kean pauses so very long between his sentences, it's difficult to know if he has finished declaiming his monologue. Poor Ophelia thought he was through with that last one and began her lines—even from here I could see the nasty look he gave her, and then he mowed right over her."

"Ah," Aunt Sophie whispered close to her ear, "but the passion in him, my dear, it fairly radiates around him, and the dramatic poses, so moving, so evocative—and would you look at the lovely stage sets, Rosalind. It's said he strives with all his artistic might to make all the scenery and the settings accurate."

"Aunt Sophie, are you laughing at me?"

"A small chuckle, no more. I will say he is not his father, but he does the part well enough."

Nicholas sat quietly, his arms crossed over his chest. He looked on the point of nodding off.

Rosalind poked him in the ribs. "Don't you dare fall asleep, Nicholas. Your snoring would be the ruin of all of us."

He slowly turned to smile at her. It was only a smile, but it smote her. Rosalind actually felt her heart thump down heavily on the toes of her white satin slippers. *I saw him the first time only two nights ago,* she thought; *only this morning I felt his mouth kiss my hand, so meaningless in the course of things, but he made my world turn upside down. Or right side up. It doesn't matter. Whatever he did, he did me in.*

"No," he whispered, his breath warm on her cheek, "don't look at me like that. I'm a weak man, Rosalind, spare me."

"Weak, ha." She pressed her fist over her mouth to smother the giggle. She looked over at Grayson and Lorelei Kilbourne.

Grayson looked fascinated; she knew the signs. Unfortunately his fascination wasn't with his companion, it was with the drama unfolding on the stage. He was sitting slightly forward, his hands on his knees, absorbed. As for Lorelei, she wasn't looking at Kean; she was looking at Grayson, and the adoring look on her very pretty face made Rosalind want to kick her. She was a rug waiting for him to tread upon. But wait—did she, Rosalind de La Fontaine—look at Nicholas like that? Like a besotted half-wit? Oh, dear, could that be possible? She would get hold of herself. She would have dignity.

Nicholas whispered, "Lorelei is lovely and Grayson is basking."

"Not really," Rosalind said, eyes narrowed on Grayson's face. "The blind sod is more interested in what's happening on the stage."

"You're wrong. He is being smart; his seeming indifference to her is drawing her in and he well knows it."

"She's already drawn in. If he draws her in any more she'll be plastered to him. But if you're right, that must mean he likes her. And that means he'll probably make her the beleaguered heroine in his next book."

Kean yelled something toward the audience, clasped his hands to his breast, flailed about, and, head bowed, collapsed gracefully on a chaise, his posture artfully arranged. The green curtain swooped down. Applause rang out, loud and sustained.

When the applause, whistles, and stomping feet finally dwindled enough that they could hear the orange girls calling out, signaling the intermission, Rosalind said to Nicholas, "This is a lovely box. We can see everything and everyone. There are so many people. I'll wager nearly all three thousand seats are occupied tonight. How delightful your father forgot he owned it."

"Miranda is furious she couldn't get her hands on the box."

She saw he was staring toward a box to their left. She followed his line of vision and saw two young men staring back at her.

"Your half brothers, I presume?"

He nodded. "The eldest, the tall dark one who looks remarkably like me, is Richard Vail. The pallid young man beside him who looks like a tormented poet is Lancelot. Of the two of them, I would guess he's the more vicious, since he hates the way he looks, hates his name, wishes I were dead at his feet, and needs only a sharp stiletto. Or perhaps he would prefer a nice heavy rock."

"And the youngest brother?"

"Aubrey is his name. He is only eighteen, at Oxford for his first term. I have no idea of his character."

"Those two aren't smiling."

"No, they are not. They're probably wondering why I am with the Sherbrookes, a powerful family they dare not cross, and you, of course, who must be connected to the Sherbrookes. Perhaps they will come to visit during the intermission. Ah, I do believe they're leaving their friend's box." He waited, still as stone.

She whispered close to his ear, "Don't throw them over the side of the box, Nicholas, you might hurt some innocent below in the pit."

He gave her a swift smile.

Not four minutes later, the curtain at the back of the large box parted, and Richard Vail stepped inside. He immediately stepped toward Ryder and Sophie Sherbrooke and bowed. "Sir, madam. I am Richard Vail. This is my brother Lance. We did not know you were acquainted with our half brother, Nicholas."

Ryder nodded at the two young men, quite aware of the tension pouring off them. A gentleman to his toes, Ryder said pleasantly, "A pleasure. Allow me to introduce you to the rest of our party," which he did. "And of course you are well acquainted with your own brother."

"Half brother," Lancelot said.

There were curt nods from Lancelot and Richard, a bland smile from Nicholas. Because Rosalind was sitting close to Nicholas, she was closely scrutinized. She hated it because it was laced with malice.

Lancelot said to Grayson, "I have read your books, Mr. Sherbrooke. I have thought to write myself, perhaps a memoir since my life has been so very fascinating, but I am so very busy, you know."

Grayson nodded. "That is so often the case with people I have met. You must be very pleased to see your brother again after so long an absence."

"Half brother," Lancelot said.

An awkward silence filled the box. The air thrummed with animosity, but ingrained civility won out, that and the presence of Ryder and Sophie Sherbrooke. Richard nodded. "Oh, yes, to see Nicholas again must please us greatly, even though he is only our half brother, as Lance just said."

Grayson looked surprised at that. "What does it matter? A brother is a brother, don't you find that true?"

Finally, after a moment, Richard nodded. "As you say, Mr. Sherbrooke."

Ryder wasn't blind. It was clear that Rosalind had fallen hard for Nicholas Vail, and he knew next to nothing about him, and now here were two half brothers who would very much like to shoot the man dead. All the rumors Ryder had heard were obviously true.

And now his Rosalind was in love with this stranger, and he knew she'd made her decision. She'd only just met him. Ryder sighed. Well, how long did it take to fall in love? He would make inquiries immediately, starting with this hatred his half brothers had for Nicholas and focusing on any possible danger to Rosalind. He looked at Nicholas, who looked calm and somewhat ironic, his natural arrogance heightened, Ryder thought, because his two half brothers held him in such dislike.

Ryder wished he could leave London tonight and whisk Rosalind back to the

Cotswolds, where she'd be safe from this young man and his mysterious past, this man who kept secrets as well as Ryder's own father had.

There was also the case of Rosalind's background. Had she mentioned anything to Nicholas as of yet? What would happen when she did?

He heard Lorelei laugh. Should he have Sophie drop a hint in the girl's ear that it wasn't wise for her to worship Grayson so blatantly? On the other hand, Grayson looked like he was quite enjoying himself so maybe the young lady knew exactly what she was doing. So many swirling undercurrents. Thank God Douglas and Alex would arrive tomorrow. He needed reinforcements, badly.

He conversed easily with the half brothers, knowing they were staring at Rosalind, their anger simmering. Richard Vail finally asked Rosalind if she was enjoying London.

"Oh, yes, ever so much. Everyone is quite kind, you know. Do you enjoy London as well, Mr. Vail?"

He nodded. "You became quickly acquainted with our half brother."

"I surely hope so," she said with a sunny smile.

"And he only very recently arrived in London," Lancelot said. "One would think—" He paused, and because he was so pretty, it was a delicate pause.

Rosalind immediately filled the pause. "One would doubtless think I have immense good taste, is that what you wished to say, Mr. Vail?"

"Not really," Lancelot said. He shot a look at his brother, but Richard only shrugged, and worried his thumbnail.

"But of course you would know when Nicholas arrived in London, wouldn't you?" Rosalind patted her skirts. "After all, you are family."

There was an eternal moment of silence, then Richard and Lancelot Vail bowed to Ryder and Sophie and left the box.

"Wasn't that delightful," Rosalind said behind her hand. "I don't believe I am going to be tremendously fond of your brothers, Nicholas."

"Trust me, they won't be fond of you either," he said.

The theater darkened. Rosalind said low to Nicholas as the thick green curtain was hauled back up, "Don't worry, Nicholas, I won't let those wretched dolts hurt you, and they want to, particularly Lancelot, the pretty little sod." She raised her arm and made a muscle. "I could destroy him."

He laughed, simply couldn't help it. Then he cleared his throat. Laughter spurting out like that meant loss of control, no matter that it was for only a brief moment of time.

Ryder, who'd overheard this, sighed. Rosalind's heels were dug in so deep they were probably close to knocking down a Mandarin farmer in China.

Eventually, after Laertes artfully slew Hamlet with a poisoned sword and the stage was strewn with bodies, it required a good half hour to make their way through the crowds outside, then another twenty minutes for their carriage to be brought around. They drove to the Kilbourne town house first, all of them waiting in the carriage while Grayson escorted Lorelei up the wide stone steps to the front door. When the door opened, Grayson quickly realized that directly behind the butler stood Lorelei's father, looking closely at his little chick. What was he worried about? Grayson wondered. He gave Lord Ramey a bow, waved toward own his father and mother, who obligingly waved back, proving to Lord Ramey that their precious son hadn't debauched his precious daughter, and finally Grayson made his good-byes.

"Mr. Sherbrooke?"

Grayson turned. "Yes, Miss Kilbourne?"

"Would you care to come to a small recitation tomorrow afternoon? All young people, perhaps twenty in all. We are reading Mary Shelley's *Frankenstein*." She lowered her lids a trifle and stared up at him through lovely thick lashes. "I recommended it. I felt it would please you."

Well, it did. It was one of his favorite novels. However, Grayson wanted nothing more than to be left alone with Rosalind and have her translate the *Rules*. "Well, you see, Miss Kilbourne, I fear that—"

"Actually, after we've read a chapter from her book, we will read from your latest novel, sir, and would very much appreciate your lending your expertise to the discussion of vampires."

"Ah, well, in that case—perhaps a chapter or two would be stimulating," and it was done.

When Grayson climbed back into the carriage he looked so self-satisfied Rosalind wanted to clout him. After he'd told them what he would be doing on the following afternoon, Rosalind sneered at him. "You are so very weak. It is pitiful."

"You're just angry because I won't be home to do your bidding. Besides, this recitation meeting, it won't take very long. Unless, of course, they wish to read a goodly portion of my book, then—" He gave an obnoxious shrug. "If I'm not back in good time, Nicholas can take you for a ride in the park."

Rosalind snorted. "If all the young people present are like Lorelei, you won't escape for a week."

He gave her a very satisfied smile.

His father laughed. His mother patted his hand.

13

Ryder wasn't laughing the next afternoon when his brother Douglas Sherbrooke, the Earl of Northcliffe, said privately to him, "I am familiar with the Vail family, particularly this Nicholas's grandfather, Galardi Vail. I hate saying this because it sounds so absurd, but I was told he wasn't of this world."

"Wasn't of this world? What world, then? What the devil does that mean, Douglas?"

Douglas shrugged. "Fact is, the rumors were that Galardi Vail was some sort of magician, a wizard of sorts. As for his wife, I believe she died in childbirth."

"I wonder," Ryder said, "was he really a magician or a wizard, or did he simply believe he was?"

"I don't know. Rumors were rife about strange incantations chanted in a strange language, blue smoke rising above the forest, strange red lights glowing from behind draperies at the house, nonsense like that, and Galardi raised young Nicholas when his own father had removed him from his house at the time of his second marriage. He was around five years old, I believe. Nicholas was still a boy when his grandfather died. Well, I should say *supposedly* died. There was no physician in attendance and there were whispers there was no body." Douglas shrugged. "It sounds like one of Grayson's novels, but this is what I have heard. I remember it because it is so very out of the ordinary."

"From whom did you hear this?"

"My main source is Tysen's curate, Mr. Biggly, some two years ago when he first arrived at Glenclose-on-Rowan. Alex and I were visiting Tysen and Mary Rose and he spoke of his prior living at Gorton-Wimberley, a small village in Sussex, near where this strange old man lived. Mr. Biggly could weave an excellent tale, and that is what I thought it until I chanced to hear a friend of Nicholas Vail's father say much the same thing. He too claimed the old man was a wizard. What about young Nicholas? After Galardi's death, he said that young Nicholas simply disappeared. Now Nicholas Vail has resurfaced and assumed his title. May I ask what this is all about? How did you meet Nicholas Vail?"

"Did you also know that young Nicholas's father cut him off, leaving him only what was entailed?"

Douglas shook his head. "Is the young man a wastrel?"

"I don't think so, Douglas." Ryder sighed. "Before Sophie and Alex join us, let me tell you that Rosalind is in love with him. She met him Thursday night at the Pinchon ball. Four days. I hate to believe it, but you should see the way she looks at him. Our girl's in love, Douglas, tip over arse. And you know Rosalind. She never does anything by half measure. That's why I asked you what you knew about him."

Douglas Sherbrooke could but stare at his brother. "I'll admit I'm old, Ryder—but four days?"

"I know, it has fair to knocked me flat as well. Rosalind sees what she wants and she goes after it. The thing is, she also has excellent instincts. Remember that man who came to Brandon House to sell us wonderful bolts of material from France at a marvelous price?"

Douglas laughed. "Oh, yes. And Rosalind nailed him but good."

Ryder said, "She got all the children to unroll bolts of his expensive, supposedly fine brocade and, sure enough, there were moth holes throughout."

"He probably thought what with all the children, he would make a very pretty penny indeed and be well gone before he was discovered. So Rosalind approves this Nicholas Vail. But what about Nicholas Vail? Which way does the wind blow with him?"

"It blows in her direction."

"Have you told him why you are Rosalind's guardian? Has he inquired?"

Ryder shook his head. "I will let her tell him, when and if it comes to that. I don't think it's even occurred to her that there might be a serpent in the garden. Nicholas Vail is a peer of the realm. Blood and background are important."

"Perhaps she wants to wait until she is certain of him. Rosalind is very well grounded."

"In some ways, yes, but the other, Douglas—"

"Yes. What is Nicholas Vail all about? What do you want me to do, Ryder?"

"First I want you to meet the young man, take his measure. Then speak to your contacts in the foreign office. You've told me many times that what they don't know, they can easily find out—see what they know of him, of his family, of his half brothers, two of whom I met last night at Drury Lane. There's deep hatred there, Douglas.

"You also have several acquaintances with a reach into the underbelly of London. Ask them if they've heard anything about him. Nicholas Vail claims he lived in Macau for the past five years. I did find out from our solicitor that he is in shipping and that he's quite successful, and did not need any money from his father, even though the rumors would have you believe he is without a sou and looking for an heiress. As for the nine years before he settled in Macau, he was not specific. I've got to make sure Rosalind will be safe with him."

Douglas nodded. "Then he is twenty-six, near Grayson's age."

"But he is older than Grayson in experience, hard experience, the kind that brings you too close to death. I also believe he would be utterly ruthless, probably had to be to survive. He would be a dangerous man to cross."

"On his own since the age of twelve—that would either toughen a boy or he wouldn't survive."

Ryder nodded. "So he left after his grandfather's death, yet you tell me Tysen's curate spoke of there being no body to bury. Damnation, Douglas." Ryder slammed his fist into his palm, winced. "And there is this ancient book Grayson found in a bookstall in Hyde Park, written by a man whose idiot name is Sarimund. It's titled the *Rules of the Pale* and it's in code. Unbreakable code, I think you'll agree.

"And let me tell you what scares me to my toes: Rosalind can read it, quickly, no problem at all. Blessed hell, how the devil can one explain that? I most certainly can't. There's something going on here and the children know more about it all than I do. I hate that."

"Calm yourself, Ryder, we'll find out all we need to know, and quickly. I should like to see this book as well. Code, you say? Unbreakable? Except our Rosalind is able to decipher it?"

Ryder nodded. "This isn't good, Douglas. You know it isn't."

14

I've got to tell him, got to, got to, blessed hell, I've got no choice. Rosalind hated it, but it had to be done. Where was Nicholas? Why must he be late this afternoon of all afternoons? She couldn't lose her resolve. That would be completely dishonorable. But what if he looked at her like an unwanted snail in the garden, stomped her, and walked away?

No, surely he won't stomp me, but maybe he'll give me one of those dangerous cold looks and walk away. It doesn't matter. I've got to tell him, no choice.

Willicombe opened the door and said in his brilliant voice, "Lord Mountjoy, Miss Rosalind."

Nicholas cocked a dark eyebrow at the back of Willicombe's shiny bald head and smiled over at her. Rosalind jumped to her feet. She saw Willicombe wasn't happy about leaving them alone. She wished he knew, wished everyone knew that she and Nicholas were engaged. That would remove the bilious look from his face. Well, maybe not.

Willicombe eyed first one, then the other. He cleared his throat. "Miss Rosalind, shall I inquire if Mrs. Sherbrooke is available to, er, come and converse with the two of you? Perhaps guide your conversational gambits to a proper elevated plane?"

"Oh, no, Willicombe. We will be unchaperoned for a mere matter of two minutes, no more. His lordship is a gentleman of stern moral resolve. He was born on an elevated plane. I don't know if I was born elevated, but I was certainly raised that way. Don't worry yourself."

Willicombe still wasn't happy and so he gave them only a small bow, this time not bestowing upon them the full glory of his bald head.

As soon as the drawing room doors closed, Rosalind grabbed Nicholas's hand and pulled him toward the bow windows. "Nicholas, you are late."

"Not more than a minute or two. What is this? What is wrong, Rosalind?"

She dropped his hand and began to wring hers, and looked down at her feet.

He stared at those wringing hands, an eyebrow winging upward. "What is this? You are obviously upset. Tell me what is wrong, Rosalind."

"My name. It is my name that is wrong."

"Your name? Yes, well, La Fontaine is on the unusual side. But as you told me, your namesake was a name to be respected. Rosalind de La Fontaine. I like your name, Rosalind, it suits you. What of it?"

"You don't know who I am, Nicholas, you really don't. You don't know why Ryder Sherbrooke is my guardian. You don't know anything about me."

"Well, no, it hadn't really occurred to me. We've been rather occupied since we met. But you will feel free to tell me when it pleases you."

"You look very handsome today, Nicholas.

I like the buckskins and your riding jacket. Very smart."

"Thank you. I'm listening."

"Well, the thing is—" She stopped dead, then shook her head and paced to the far end of the drawing room, then back to him. "All right, I'll just spit it out. I hear ghosts," she said, coming to a stop right in front of him. "I know ghosts, I've lived with them for ten years. I've never seen them but I've heard them murmuring from shadowed corners or, most often, in my dreams."

"All right, for ten years you've heard ghosts. Tell me about this."

"I will spit it out, I will. I have heard ghosts since—well, since Uncle Ryder found me nearly beaten to death in an alley near the docks in Eastbourne."

He grew very still. How could this be? "I don't understand," he said slowly. "You were nearly beaten to death? You were only a young child. What is this, Rosalind?"

"They believed I was around eight years old. They even let me select a month and a day for my birthday and of course I picked the very next day after they told me. Uncle Ryder took me to Brandon House—it's where he brings children who have been abandoned or beaten or sold, children in awful situations—he raises them and loves them and educates them, and gives them hope. He told me the physicians weren't sure I would live, but I did. But, you see, when I finally regained my wits, I had no idea who I was. I still don't. My memory never came back. Just the ghosts lurking in the back of my mind, and they've never come forward, never told me who I am."

He studied her pale face. "You still don't know who you are?"

"No. The ghosts came and I've asked them over and over who I am, but I can never understand what they say, if indeed they themselves know."

"But your name—La Fontaine."

"I selected the name myself when I was ten years old because I liked Jean de La Fontaine's fables, as simple as that. I'm more of a fiction than his fables are—at least his fables have a moral. I don't have anything. I don't know who I am. At first Uncle Ryder and Uncle Douglas tried to find out about me, but they could discover nothing. Then they decided that whoever had tried to kill me could still be out there, and still want me dead. If someone hated me enough to try to kill me, then I must be worth very little. Or worth nothing at all."

Nicholas had never considered anything like this, never. It didn't matter. He hated that her eyes were sheened with tears, hated her pallor. He pulled her against him and kissed her, gently, as if she'd only just been beaten and he didn't want to hurt her more. "I'm so very sorry, Rosalind."

She pushed away from him. "No, no, you don't yet understand, Nicholas."

"I understand someone tried to murder a child but you survived thanks to Ryder Sherbrooke. I will be grateful to him for the remainder of my life."

"Yes, yes, of course, but that isn't it, Nicholas. Don't you see?" She drew in a deep breath. "You are the seventh Earl of Mountjoy—an *earl*, Nicholas, a peer of the realm. You have an impressive lineage, whereas, well, to say it plainly, I am nobody. I am very sorry I did not tell you immediately when you asked me to marry you, but the truth is, I simply didn't think about it. I wanted to kiss you too much and it all happened so very quickly and we've been tossed into the *Rules of the Pale*, trying to figure out what it all means, and I simply didn't think about it until I was lying in bed last night and it hit me in the nose. I cannot do this to you. I cannot marry you, Nicholas. Actually, it's you who cannot marry me."

Nicholas turned from her and walked to the bow windows. He pulled back the drapery and looked out onto the spring-ripening gardens across the street. There were daffodils swaying in a light breeze, their yellow vivid against the well-scythed green grass. He turned slowly to face her. "This is unacceptable, Rosalind."

She felt clouted to her soul. She wanted to burst into tears, but she didn't. When she'd realized at the advanced age of eight that her brain was perfectly blank, she'd wept until she was ill, and learned tears were good for exactly nothing. "I'm sorry," she said. "I'm very sorry I didn't tell you immediately. I allowed you to gain lust and fondness for me."

"Lust and fondness," he repeated, a dark brow arched. "You put that nicely. You misunderstand me. I find it unacceptable that someone tried to murder you—a child."

"That is because you are noble. But I survived. Listen, Nicholas, I could be a butcher's daughter, a pickpocket, a match girl. I could be a perfect nobody."

"No, you're not a nobody. Otherwise why would someone try to kill you, an eight-year-old child?"

"My Uncle Ryder and Uncle Douglas agree with you. They believe I must be the daughter of someone important, someone who made powerful enemies. It's true I was wearing very nice clothes when Uncle Ryder found me. Ripped and torn nearly off me, of course. And this." Rosalind unfastened a gold chain from around her neck. Hanging from the chain was a small heart locket. She handed it to him.

Nicholas held it in his palm. It was warm and smooth. He felt the small latch and opened the locket. Both sides were empty. He checked the thickness of the gold. No, there wasn't hidden space.

"It was empty when Ryder found you?"

She nodded. "Perhaps there were two pictures, one of my mother or father, and one of me. Perhaps, but I don't know. Were the pictures removed because someone might recognize them?" She shrugged. "But it doesn't matter, Nicholas. No one has any idea at all of who I am or who my parents are—or were—or if they're English or Italian. Uncle Ryder believes I'm possibly both, since when I began speaking, I spoke both Italian and English. Uncle Ryder also believes my parents must be dead or they would have searched the earth for me. Of course that is what he would do if Grayson disappeared. It's a damnable thing, Nicholas, but I am a blank page."

"No, you're not at all blank. You have an ability that none of us have—you can easily read the *Rules of the Pale*. This is a gift, so perhaps you come from parents with a similar gift. You've accepted this gift of yours without question. I would say this gift is only one of many."

One of many? Hmm. "So much has happened so quickly. I haven't even wondered why I can read that blasted book." She gave him a pathetic attempt at a smile. "I will ask the ghosts when I next hear them. They come to me less often now. It's odd, but I miss them. It's like they're my only link to my lost past. And now they're giving up on me."

"Ghosts," he repeated. "Ghosts around you."

"You don't think me mad, do you?"

He looked distracted. He drummed his fingertips on the mantelpiece. "Mad? Oh, no. My grandfather, I believe he was intimately acquainted with ghosts, and he wasn't mad, believe me." He shrugged. "To be honest, I suppose I assumed you were of my class. Say we discover you aren't, Rosalind. What does that mean in the long course of events? Not much of anything. My own father was a weak man, manipulated by my stepmother, but vicious as only a weak man can be. Whoever you are doesn't matter to me. You're Rosalind de La Fontaine. You will shortly be mine, Rosalind Vail, the Countess of Mountjoy."

"You cannot be so noble, Nicholas, so elevated in your spirit, you cannot—"

"Hush. That's quite enough. Let's be sensible here. You would like to know who you really are. I am acquainted with many different sorts of people from all over the world. I will have your portrait painted, perhaps a dozen miniatures, and I will have them sent out. We will discover who your parents were, Rosalind. Or, perhaps, one morning you will wake up next to me, and smile, and you will remember. I quite understand why your Uncle Ryder and Uncle Douglas stopped the search. But you will not worry about anyone ever hurting you again. I will protect you with my life."

Rosalind turned and ran out of the drawing room.

15

"Rosalind!"

"My lord, Miss Rosalind scampered out of the house. Are you responsible for this, my lord? Did you insult that sweet young pullet?" Willicombe, all puffed up, actually barred Nicholas's way.

"The pullet has nothing but air between her pretty ears. She ran out for no reason at all." Nicholas lifted Willicombe beneath his armpits, set him down to one side, and ran after her through the open front door. He paused when he saw a flash of her blue skirt swing around the corner.

He heard a yell and a shout. He came

around the corner at a dead run to see her on her backside on the sidewalk, skirts billowed about her. Beside her sat a heavy matron, flushed to her eyebrows, hat askew, a lovely ruffled petticoat fluffed up about her knees, parcels scattered around her, her mouth open to yell again.

Nicholas quickly helped the woman to her feet, not an easy task, and gathered her parcels for her.

Chins wobbled as she shook her fist at Rosalind. "I am Mrs. Pratt, sir, and I am the wife of Deacon Pratt of Pear Tree Lane. This young lady, sir, came flying out at me, fair to sending me to my maker, and it's Deacon Pratt who wants that pleasure. Lucky it was that my precious pork knivers didn't scatter themselves on the dirty ground. If she's your wife, sir, you need to clout her good."

"Yes, she is my wife, but she doesn't deserve a clout in this instance, ma'am, since it is my fault she was running and had the dreadful misfortune to hit you."

Mrs. Pratt crossed ample arms over her equally ample bosom and tapped her puce-colored boots. "Is that so? And what did you do, sir, to make this sweet young lady flee from you?"

"Well, I must be honest here, Mrs. Pratt. You deserve honesty. The fact is she isn't yet my wife. The second fact is that I asked her to marry me but she doesn't feel she's good enough for me, which is absurd. All right, I admit that if you look at her now, ma'am, sitting there rubbing her rear parts, looking as though she wants to burst into tears and scream at me at the same time, perhaps you'd agree with her. But standing upright or waltzing, an enchanting smile on her face, she's very fine indeed and will do me proud. And when she marries me, I will surely keep her from running over respectable ladies out doing their shopping."

"I've never eaten a pork kniver," Rosalind said.

The woman eyed Rosalind with disfavor. "You likely don't deserve one. Marry him or I will introduce him to my sweet nieces, who would never consider taking a single step away from him. Just look at him—he has all his teeth and nice and white they are, and there is no fat hanging off his middle, unlike Deacon Pratt, who wears a very wide belt to hold himself into his shirts. I have told him repeatedly not to be a glutton, but he looks at me and says a man must take his pleasure where he can. The gall, I tell him. Marry him, missy, marry him."

Rosalind stared up at Nicholas, wringing her hands again. "But, Nicholas—"

"You're not getting any younger," the woman said. "If I show him my nieces, he might turn his back on you fast enough. My little Lucretia is only seventeen."

Since Rosalind ignored Nicholas's outstretched hand, he turned to say to Mrs. Pratt, "Pray accept my apologies, ma'am, but she will wed me and thus I will not be available to make the acquaintance of Lucretia." Nicholas gave her a marvelous bow and a fat smile that made her chins wobble anew. Mrs. Pratt gave him a look that Rosalind now recognized as fast-crumbling female principles, and said, just this side of a simper, "Perhaps my lovely Lucretia is on the young side for you, sir, perhaps it is an older, more experienced lady who would suit you"—she patted the fat sausage curls over her ears then stared down at Rosalind with a good deal of antipathy—"not this harebrained knot-head who ran away from you."

"But you caught the knot-head for me, ma'am, and I thank you."

"Only in a very remote manner of speaking, sir. Well, now, I suppose there was no harm done." And Mrs. Pratt, all her parcels tucked beneath her arms, was gone with one long wistful backwards look at Nicholas and a sneer at Rosalind.

He stood over her, hands on hips. "Do you really want to sacrifice me to Mrs. Pratt's niece Lucretia?"

"She's only seventeen. You could mold her."

"You're only eighteen and I would rather mold you. Are you all right?"

"It is about time you inquired. No, I'm humiliated, and you had to rub my nose in it with your fine conversation with Mrs. Pratt."

"One must consider all offers. I'm sorry to say this, but you deserved to be humiliated. Would you care to tell me why you bolted, or was I right on the mark?"

She looked away from him. "I simply couldn't bear it."

"Bear what, for heaven's sake?"

"Your—your nobility."

He could but stare at her. "If only you knew," he said finally. He reached down a hand and jerked her up and into him, hard.

She said, her breath warm on his chin, "It's depressing, my lord. I cannot even execute a dramatic exit with any style at all. Blessed hell, I wish I'd scattered that dreadful woman's wretched pork knivers in the street. What *is* a pork kniver?"

"A cutlet that's baked with peonies and thyme until it resembles the leather on the bottom of your slippers. It is a challenge to all teeth. Quite tasty really."

He held her close, ignored the nanny and two children who passed close by. "So I am noble?"

"Yes, but what's important here is that I'm trying to be noble as well." She looked at his mouth, leaned forward, and kissed his neck. She actually felt the surge of energy pound through him. "It's difficult to be noble when you're holding me like this. Nicholas, are you perhaps feeling lust for me from that wee little kiss on your neck?"

"No, damn you, what I am feeling is abused. Now we have a good half dozen people staring at us, Rosalind. I am an important personage. Come along back to the house."

She took a step away from him. "All right, I have some distance from you and thus some perspective. Here it is, Nicholas. You are noble, I am noble. I will not, cannot, marry you. Take it to heart, for I mean it well."

"That sounds like you're quoting from Shakespeare."

"Well, naturally, since he provided me my name."

Nicholas said to the heavens, "I wonder if it would help me understand if I pounded my head against that stone wall over there." He looked at her, reached out, and managed to grab her hand. He pulled her after him back to the Sherbrooke town house. She didn't yell, for which he was profoundly grateful.

* * *

Douglas Sherbrooke, imposing in his black evening clothes and his head of thick white hair, eyed the newly arrived Nicholas Vail, Earl of Mountjoy, and felt a bolt of fear for Rosalind. This young man was indeed honed hard to the bone, just as Ryder had said, and ruthless, he'd wager.

He watched the young man's eyes search the room until they found Rosalind, who was seated quietly in a wing chair by the fireplace. She looked pale to Douglas, not at all her usual laughing self, and the pale yellowish-green gown she wore didn't help. He frowned. Who had selected that gown for her? He would make sure she never wore it again.

He pulled his attention from Rosalind and her unfortunate gown as Ryder introduced him to Nicholas Vail.

The young man bowed, looked him straight in the eye. Bedamned, Nicholas Vail was as dark as he was, his eyes as black, and his swarthy skin wasn't entirely due to his months at sea.

Nicholas Vail could be my son, Douglas thought, *and isn't that a kick to the head?*

"My lord," Nicholas said. "It is my pleasure and honor to meet you."

Before Douglas could bear him off to seclusion in the estate room to pry every past sin out of him, Willicombe glided into the drawing room and announced dinner, addressing both the Countess of Northcliffe, all beautiful in dark green, her magnificent red hair twisted up about her finely shaped head (Willicombe occasionally entertained a vision of the countess's head as nicely shaved as his own) and Mrs. Sophie (such a gentle iron fist she had, and a lovely manner). "Cook requested that I inform you that she has prepared a very fine half calf's head, tongue, and brains, quite in the French way, although 'execrable' springs to mind when one speaks of the Frogs cooking anything."

The Countess of Northcliffe asked, "Is there perhaps something not quite so unambiguous she is also serving?"

"Fortunately yes, my lady. Not to be overlooked is her famous boiled bacon-cheek, garnished with spoonfuls of spinach followed by a compote of gooseberries, and cauliflower with cream sauce, all blessedly prepared in the English way."

"My dreams have come true," Sophie said.

"I do not see Master Grayson," Willicombe said.

"He is dining at his club," Ryder said.

Willicombe bowed and walked from the drawing room, head tilted back, assuming, rightfully, that his betters would quickly follow, which they did.

"He is amazing," Nicholas said.

"That is what *he* told me when he became our London butler," Douglas said.

Alexandra had placed Nicholas and Rosalind across the table from each other, as Rosalind had asked her to. One of Nicholas's black eyebrows shot up, but he said nothing. Douglas spoke about his twin sons' own sets of twins, how they were the pictures of their respective fathers, which meant they were so fine looking it curdled his innards. As conversation and laughter flowed, Rosalind served herself some stewed Spanish onions, and screwed up her courage. She waited until everyone was served and there was a lull in the conversation. She cleared her throat and announced to the table at large, "Nicholas Vail, Lord Mountjoy, has asked me to marry him. It struck me between the eyes, and only after I accepted, that he did not know who I was, or who I wasn't, and I knew it would be a gross misalliance.

"I wish to announce that I will not marry Nicholas Vail, even though he is insisting upon it because he is very fond of my person and my singing voice and yes, it must be said, he enjoys kissing me. He also speaks of Fate bringing us together, as if it were a meant thing, which sounds romantic, and somewhat mystical, but not at all to the point. He is noble. I am proving that I am noble as well." She stopped and spooned up some stewed Spanish onions, sweet with a punch of black pepper.

There was perhaps three seconds of stunned silence. As for Nicholas, he slowly put down his fork and smiled over at her. He said to Ryder and Sophie, "You are doubtless surprised that I have proposed marriage to her so quickly, perhaps more surprised that I did not speak with you first, sir. I apologize for that, but when a man is faced with his mate, the passage of time seems irrelevant. I wished to wait to speak to you, sir, to allow you more time to get to know me, to perhaps judge me as acceptable, but Rosalind has changed the game.

"I fear I must say it—she isn't being noble, she is being a knot-head, as a recent acquaintance of mine remarked. There is no one at this table who believes she is not worthy of me, that is, not worthy to be a peer's wife. Otherwise, I daresay Mr. Ryder Sherbrooke would not have made her his legal ward and brought her to London for her season. Am I correct, sir?"

Ryder was betwixt and between. He had to hand it to Nicholas Vail, he'd pinned him very nicely. He nodded, nothing else to do, his eyes never leaving Rosalind's face, now flushed because—why? Because Nicholas hadn't folded his tent, but rather addressed the matter head on and with a great deal of skill? Ryder said slowly, unconsciously mangling a dinner roll in his hand, "Yes, we firmly believe she is wellborn. Actually, we have had no doubts from the time she finally opened her mouth and spoke, six months after I found her. However, Nicholas, we have been unable to locate her parents, or any relatives, for that matter. And we gave up because, honestly, someone had indeed tried to murder a child, and we feared if we found her parents, she would still be in danger.

"Even today, ten years later, who is to say the motives for this deed aren't still valid in this person's mind? No, we have kept quiet and we will continue to keep all our inquiries to ourselves. She will continue to be Rosalind de La Fontaine until she regains her memory, something our physician doubts will happen, given that she's remembered nothing at all over the years."

Douglas focused his dark eyes on Nicholas Vail's face. "Understand, my lord, we are her family now and we will keep her safe."

"As will I," Nicholas said. "I swear it to all of you. No one will harm her in my care."

Rosalind leaned toward Nicholas. "Listen to me, Nicholas Vail. I am no more real than Shakespeare's Rosalind. I found my name

in *As You Like It*, but I had preferred
Ganymede—you remember, Rosalind dis-
guised herself as a shepherd and called herself Ganymede—since I was living a sort of
disguise myself, but Uncle Ryder and Aunt
Sophie felt the name was perhaps a bit too
unconventional. You must realize I could be
the descendant of Attila the Hun or Ivan the
Terrible, an alarming thought, don't you
agree?"

Sophie ignored her. "When you began
speaking, Rosalind, your English was clearly
that of a well-bred young English girl and we
knew that you were wellborn. Your Italian
was equally good, perhaps the result of an
Italian nanny or an Italian parent.

"It was obvious there were evil persons in
your background, evil persons who saw you
as some sort of threat and acted on it. That
is all we know for sure. Please don't embroi-
der yourself into the Devil's spawn, else I
must consider boxing your ears."

Ryder said, "My love, remember some of
the pranks Rosalind pulled the children into
in her younger years?"

Sophie nodded. "Yes, you're right. Upon
reflection, perhaps the Devil's spawn might
apply."

There was a spot of laughter, but not much. Ryder continued, "And your singing voice, my dear girl—the voice teacher we brought in to instruct you said you had received excellent instruction for at least the previous two years. To be honest here, I do not wish to know who you really are because I would fear for you. I want you safe. Naturally we discussed fully the chance we were taking with your safety bringing you to London for a season. Who's to say someone wouldn't recognize you? I will admit that sometimes I feel a certain foreboding about it, but no matter. Now, unless you remember someday, you will remain Rosalind. We are your family and we love you."

16

After dinner, Nicholas steered Rosalind to the music room, hoping for a bit of privacy. She eyed him a moment before saying, "I used to spin stories about who my parents were—the Czar and Czarina of Russia or dashing pirates in the Caribbean. In each scenario there was a wicked witch who was afraid of my precocious self and yet jealous of my immense fairness of form and face."

"Excuse me a moment, Rosalind. You say your mother was also a pirate?"

"Oh, yes, and she would wield her cutlass and wear a white shirt with flowing sleeves. Boots to her knees, of course. She and my father were the terror of the Caribbean. Yes, yes, I realize the odds of my speaking won- derful English are slim given that particular set of parents."

"No Italian counts in your scenarios?"

She frowned. "No, I've always shied away from anything Italian. Now that I think of it, that's odd, isn't it?"

Nicholas opened his mouth to reply, but closed it when he heard the countess's voice coming toward them. The private conversa- tion he'd hoped for was not to be.

"Ah, dearest," Alexandra said, beaming a bright smile on the two of them, "how perfect to find you here in the music room. We have all decided to beg you to sing for us." The rest of the party followed her in.

Rosalind wanted to grab Nicholas and haul him away to some nice private nook or cranny in this immense house. At the same time she also wanted to kick him out the front door. She wanted to smack him for handling her family with such finesse and kiss him stupid that he'd so neatly cornered her.

"That would be quite nice," Nicholas said. "Do sit down at the pianoforte and sing me a love song. Perhaps one of the love songs sung by the Dragons of the Sallas Pond."

"Dragons of what?" Sophie asked.

Nicholas said calmly, "It's the name of beings in the *Rules of the Pale*, the book Grayson bought at the fair in Hyde Park."

Rosalind saw questions were ready to burst out of Aunt Sophie's mouth, questions she didn't want to address, so she quickly ran her fingers over the keys. She had intended to sing something Scottish and amusing, for her Scottish accent was quite decent, but what came out of her mouth was the song that had lived deep within her for as long as she could remember, never distant from her thoughts, a song she didn't understand, a song that made her feel both tranquil and unsettled at the same time. Of course she didn't remember how she had come to learn this particular song, but she knew it was from before. It was odd, but it felt as if it were drawn out of her, no choice for her at all. She sang:

I dream of beauty and sightless night
I dream of strength and fevered might
I dream I'm not alone again

But I know of his death and her grievous sin.

Sophie said quietly, "Every time I hear you sing that song, Rosalind, it makes me want to weep. Nicholas, if you did not know, those were the first words Rosalind spoke when she finally opened her mouth six months after Ryder found her."

"She didn't exactly say them," Ryder said, "she rather hummed them, not quite a song, but almost."

Nicholas said, "You have no memories from before you were eight years old, but this song was inside you. The words are curious. *His* death—whose death? And *her*—who is she? And what was her grievous sin? It seems to me the four lines are filled with clues about who and what you were, Rosalind."

Douglas nodded to the young man. "Yes, that is what we have all thought, but Rosalind has no memory at all of what the words could mean."

Rosalind shied away from thinking about the strange words. She began playing a Scottish reel, a clever tale about a bonnie lass who loved to dance for the prince of the faeries. Everyone tapped their toes on the pale blue and cream Aubusson carpet.

When Rosalind walked Nicholas to the front door after a lovely tea an hour later, Willicombe clearing his throat discreetly not six feet behind them, she said, "You know Uncle Ryder is standing not twelve feet away, back by the drawing room door, ever vigilant. I believe Willicombe is his forward guard."

He looked down into those blue, blue eyes of hers. "I don't doubt I'll be doing the same thing when our daughter is your age."

Her jaw dropped and she pressed her palms to her cheeks. "Oh, dear, that brings such a clear picture to my brain. It is appalling, Nicholas. I am only eighteen."

"I know," he said and smiled down at her. He lightly cupped her cheek with his own palm. "Only consider all the time you and I will spend bringing this about. Will you marry me, Rosalind? Will you let me be your Orlando?"

"A man who knows Shakespeare. It is a powerful temptation, Nicholas, but—"

"Perhaps it is I who am not worthy of you. Look at me, a merchant of Macau, an earl through an accident of birth, detested by his father. Not at all worthy of you."

She chewed on her bottom lip. Finally, she raised her face to his. "Perhaps I would not lose *all* my nobility if I married you."

"You would not lose a whit. Indeed, you would gain in worthiness."

"Very well, then it is time you spoke to Uncle Ryder."

Nicholas raised his head and nodded first to Willicombe, then toward Ryder Sherbrooke, still standing against the door of the drawing room, his arms still crossed over his chest. "Excuse me, Rosalind."

She watched Nicholas walk back to her uncle and speak to him low, then he came back to her, lightly patted her cheek, and left.

Ryder merely nodded to her and went back into the drawing room, where she knew Uncle Douglas waited.

17

The following afternoon Nicholas emerged from the Sherbrooke estate room looking thoughtful. When he walked into the study, Grayson said, "It's about time you came. Rosalind wouldn't translate the *Rules of the Pale* until you got here."

Nicholas nodded toward Rosalind, smiling automatically when he saw her. Good, she thought, it was done. She was going to marry Nicholas Vail, a man she didn't know at all. She hoped she would have fifty years to learn all his bad habits. Her Aunt Sophie had once told her that Uncle Ryder still came up with a new crop of bad habits every single spring and it required great ingenuity to stamp them all out. Rosalind was smiling as she lowered her eyes to the ancient book and read:

The most amazing thing has happened. The Dragons of the Sallas Pond have sung to me that they believe me ready to join the wizards. Because the Dragons can read a man's thoughts, they sang to me that the wizards were men like myself who maintained the balance of the different worlds tied to the Pale. These men, the Dragons of the Sallas Pond sang, were only wizards, not gods. One Dragon told me his name was Taranis. I remembered quickly enough that Taranis was the Celtic god of thunder. The thunder god of the Celts and a Dragon of the Sallas Pond, also a god, both carried the same name?

Taranis told me to sit between his mighty scales and hold on. For the first time I saw the Pale from above, where clouds the color of eggplant rolled like mighty waves through the sky. On and on Taranis flew, his powerful wings nearly soundless in the still air. I looked down to see many rivers and lakes, all as thin as thread, but never ending, and so blue

they looked like raised veins on a man's hands and arms, but it was the fortress of black stone I saw atop a huge mountain that froze my blood.

Taranis sang to me that this was the pride of the wizards, that the fear it engendered helped them to maintain their veil of power. The wizards' fortress, brooding like a black vulture atop Mount Olyvan, was called Blood Rock. I saw the reason for the name. Streaks of blood snaked down the black rock, like the rivers on the land below. The streaks were as red as blood just shed.

We were welcomed by a young man who greeted Taranis with great deference, almost reverence, I thought, and bowed low to me. He told me his name was Belenus—I remembered that Belenus was the Celtic god of agriculture who also was the giver of the life force and brought the healing power of the sun to earth and to man. The Romans called him Apollo Belenus and named the great May first festival after him, Beltane. Another Celtic god? When Taranis left, Belenus invited me into a small room hung with rich crimson draperies and gave me a bronze cup of witmas tea. It tasted of strawberries stirred with garlic.

Belenus had a great red beard that covered his face, leaving only bright blue eyes showing beneath his shag of more fierce red hair. He had big square teeth and he seemed to grow younger even as I spoke to him and drank the witmas tea. I drank a great deal of witmas tea during our time together and the taste changed with every sip, from strawberries and garlic to harsh green tea to a sort of beef broth. I was a wizard, I thought, and so I tried to change the witmas tea, but it ended up filthy black mud. It was very humiliating, but Belenus only laughed.

I met another that day as well, Epona, and she wasn't a wizard, she was a witch, known to the Celts as the horse goddess because her father hated women and thus mated with a horse; she was the result. She represented, I knew, beauty, speed, bravery, and sexual vigor. It was a good thing that her father gave her his face, I thought, since her mother's would not have gained the same result at all. The Romans, naturally, adopted her and held a festival in her honor each year in

December. Odd that she was fully human and yet her mother was a horse. As to her sexual vigor, never would I have guessed at that moment what would come to pass with the witch Epona.

Belenus told me the other wizards wished me to join them. I knew deep down that if I did not remain with them, perhaps my blood would join the wet streaks on the fortress's walls. And so I remained for close to a year. But one morning I thought hard that I wished to leave Blood Rock, where I seemed to forget as much as I was told, surely because of a spell they'd cast upon me. Soon, as I stood on the ramparts, hungrily searching the horizon through the eggplant clouds, I saw Taranis flying to Blood Rock to fetch me.

"That is why you remember so little," Taranis sang to me. "They knew you would not choose to remain with them. I had hoped you would, for all the Dragons worry about the future with that vicious crop of wizards up there."

On odd days I remembered the wizards had given me the name Lugh, pronounced "Loo," the Celtic "shining god" who was a fierce warrior, magician, and craftsman. It

was a very important name—the Romans had Latinized it into Londinium, which later became London.

Rosalind paused and drank some water. She said, "The Celts. This is very odd. Why are there Celtic gods in the Pale?"

"Why not?" Grayson said. "If there are Tibers, surely we can accept Celtic gods." He shrugged. "We still didn't learn anything at all useful, but I will say that this is a powerful story. I can see the fortress of Blood Rock clearly in my mind."

Nicholas said, "You think it is a fiction, spun out of Sarimund's brain?"

Grayson shrugged. "Were there not so many odd things about how I came upon the book, I should say yes immediately. But there were odd things, more than odd, really. Magical things. I find myself enjoying it as I would any good tale."

Nicholas rose and prowled around the room, pausing here and there to pick up a cushion or a teacup or a book off a table. He said, "I don't like any of this. It is as if Sarimund is playing with us, perhaps mocking us, and perhaps this Blood Rock is something he created to ease the boredom of his time in the Bulgar."

Rosalind said, "There are only a few pages left. Shall I finish them today?"

Grayson consulted his watch and rose. "Let us finish it tomorrow. I must be off. I have an engagement."

"Aha," Rosalind said, grinning shamelessly at him. "An engagement with the lovely Lorelei? Will her father be hanging over your shoulder the whole time? Perhaps her four sisters will giggle in a circle around you?"

"I am not the one scandalizing my parents," he said. "Look at the two of you—engaged! I tell you, Rosalind, it fair to curdles my belly to think of you married, and you wore pigtails only weeks ago, I would swear it. Nicholas, I will tell you about her misspent childhood, how she was as bad as any demon I ever created, led all the children into mischief, always with a wicked smile, drove my parents and Jane—Jane is the directress of Brandon House—quite mad. Yes, Mother is right, you were a Devil's spawn, Rosalind."

Nicholas sat down on an embroidered green wing chair, stretched out his long legs in front of him, and crossed his hands over his belly. "Tell me one evil deed this Devil child executed, Grayson—only one, because I don't wish to become disillusioned."

Grayson struck a thoughtful pose and grinned at Rosalind as he said, "When she was fourteen, she decided to visit the band of gypsies camping on the eastern corner of my father's fields. I refused to go with her, and since she was afraid to go alone, one evening she took a dozen of the children to the gypsy camp, all of them wearing kerchiefs on their heads and banging cymbals and bells and hitting sticks on bottles, and whistling. The gypsies were surprised and amused and, luckily, welcomed them.

"My father was even more surprised when at the stroke of midnight several of the gypsies appeared at our door leading the children, who'd all drunk some gypsy punch Rosalind had given them. The children were vilely ill for the remainder of the night. As I recall, my father spanked you good and proper, the one and only time, as I remember."

"Yes, he did, but it wasn't fair. There were so many other times when it would have been fair, but not that one. I intended us to have a marvelous lesson, perhaps sing songs with the gypsies, learn how to dance as they did, you know, twirling about the huge campfire, skirts swinging. Then I saw a little gypsy girl drinking punch out of a big barrel. When I told her we were thirsty, she gave us all some. How was I to know that it would make everyone so sick?"

"You were sick as well, Rosalind?"

Grayson said, "No, she was the only one who wasn't ill. I was certain you didn't drink any of the punch. You didn't, did you, Rosalind?"

"Yes. I drank at least three cups and it tasted so good. I don't know why I didn't get sick." She was aware Nicholas was giving her a brooding look. There was calculation in that look, she was sure of it, and what did that signify?

18

Tuesday afternoon, Nicholas, Rosalind, and Grayson were seated in Nicholas's small drawing room at Grillon's Hotel, cups of tea on a silver tray next to Rosalind's elbow, brought to them by Lee Po, Nicholas's man of all affairs. The two men had spoken quietly in what Nicholas told them was Mandarin Chinese. When Lee Po had bowed himself out, Grayson said to Nicholas he'd never before heard sounds like that coming from a human throat.

Nicholas laughed. "Lee Po says the same thing about English, though he speaks the King's English like a little Etonian." He shrugged. "Since I lived and traded in Macau, it was necessary that I learn Mandarin. Lee Po corrects me regularly. However, I'm not able to correct his English."

Rosalind laughed. "Why didn't he speak English to us?"

"He tells me no civilized tongue should sound like a knife chipping ice."

"Where did he learn English?" Grayson asked.

"He was married to an Englishwoman, ten years, he told me, before she died in child-birth with their only child. She'd been a missionary and a teacher."

"How very sad," Rosalind said. "Why is he so completely loyal to you?"

Nicholas looked off into the distance, seeing something neither Grayson nor Rosalind could see. "I saved his life when a Portuguese governor wanted to hang him."

Rosalind gave him a shrewd look. "What did you do to the Portuguese governor?"

He smiled at her. "I merely told him what would happen if he attempted anything like that again."

Rosalind said thoughtfully, "Lee Po was looking at me rather pointedly. Does that mean he knows we will marry?"

Nicholas nodded.

"It's time to see if my tongue can form these strange sounds. How do I say thank you to him?"

"*Shesh shesh* is how you would pronounce it."

Rosalind said it over a couple of times, then called out, "*Shesh shesh*, Lee Po!"

She heard him mumble something and grinned at Nicholas. "What did he say?"

"He said you are welcome, redheaded soon-to-be ladyship of his vaunted lordship."

"You made that up!"

He gave her a crooked grin that made her knees lock. It was powerful, that grin of his.

Grayson asked, "Does Lee Po know about the book?"

Nicholas nodded. "I believe Lee Po knows about everything that is important to me."

"Speaking of the book," Rosalind said as she opened the *Rules of the Pale*, "we haven't much time. I must be fitted for my wedding gown in two hours. I believe we have time to finish."

Grayson said, "Lorelei told me she is to accompany you. She told me she helped select the pattern."

Rosalind rolled her eyes at Grayson. "She

simply agreed—with great enthusiasm—
with everything my Uncle Douglas said. I
had some ideas, but do you think anyone listened to me, the future bride? No, not even
the assistant with the tape measure."

Nicholas laughed. "Your Uncle Douglas
told me you have unfortunate taste in
gowns, Rosalind, and that is why he has
selected nearly all your clothes for your season. He then questioned me about my own
taste. I told him I had never had the opportunity to select a woman's gown and thus I
didn't know if I was gifted with this special
talent. However, I told him that Lee Po
assured me I have very fine taste indeed, so
we would see. I do have a bit of news for
you, Rosalind."

She was grumbling under her breath, but
not under enough. "Here I am a grown
woman with taste, good taste, I tell you, and
yet it's a gentleman who has the final word in
what I wear. It's not fair. And now here you
are claiming Lee Po worships your bloody
taste."

"I understand. Now, I said I had some
news for you, along the lines of taste as a
matter of fact." At her raised eyebrow, he
said, "I'm to accompany you to Madame

Fouquet's shop. Your Uncle Douglas wishes to test me."

Grayson burst into laughter. "Test you? Ah, and will you let Nicholas measure you, Rosalind?"

But Rosalind was studying him, her fingertips tapping her chin. "I fear we will see, Grayson, that his lordship is a toady."

Grayson laughed, shook his head. "Uncle Douglas doesn't like toadying. Only agree with him two out of three times, Nicholas, no more than that or he will blight you. Now, we need to finish up the *Rules*. Hopefully Sarimund will spin us more than just a fine ending to this tale." They heard the front door to the suite close.

"Where is Lee Po going?"

"He is visiting an apothecary shop in Spitalfields, at my request."

"And what request was that?" Rosalind asked. "You are not ill, are you?"

"Never you mind. Read, Rosalind."

Rosalind frowned at him as she carefully opened the book, cleared her throat, and read:

I realized I hadn't been much of a wizard here in the Pale and so I cast a spell upon a red Lasis. To my surprise, it turned

great eyes to me, came up and butted my shoulder, and sang to me, soft and sweet, its voice rather high. The red Lasis said his name was Bifrost, and he was the oldest red Lasis in the Pale. He had waited for a very long time for me to speak to him, since, of course, a red Lasis never spoke first. It was considered rude. He told me I was a mighty wizard, despite the fact that I'd let those boneheaded wizards and witches in Blood Rock roll my brain around like an empty gourd. He sang to me that it was time for me to leave, that I had left my seed in Epona, which was why they had wanted me to come in the first place. A good thing, he sang to me.

Left my seed? He saw that I was both appalled and disbelieving, though faint memories stirred, memories I'd forgotten, truth be told. He told me the tea they served me had left me senseless save the most important part of me. It was foretold, the red Lasis sang in his lovely airy voice, that Epona would birth a wizard who would be the greatest ever known and he would rule in the Pale until Mount Olyvan sank into dust.

I would have a son—only I would never

see him. I knew it would hurt me deeply, but not until later when the reality of it sank into me. I told Bifrost that I was ready to leave but I didn't know how I'd arrived in the first place, only that I'd awakened and I was here, but I had no idea of where the door—or whatever it was that got me here—was located so I could get back. He sang a laugh, which was very pleasing to the ear. He then sang that the Dragons of the Sallas Pond had brought me to the Pale, that this was how they judged possible new brethren for that vipers' nest of wizards and witches upon Mount Olyvan. He sang they didn't want me, however, that I was too set in my ways, but my son would do, a son I would never know. Bifrost sang to me that he would ensure my son knew about me. Then Bifrost sang that he would show me how to leave. But he did nothing at all. I saw him trap a Tiber in a pit and kill it with a fire spear through its big neck, and set to his meal ferociously. Then he left me. I felt abandoned. I did not understand Bifrost or anything else in this outlandish place. And I was leaving my son here.

When I finally fell asleep beneath a

sharp-toothed angle tree I dreamed I was in a mighty desert storm, sand whipping around me, choking me, blinding me. There was no escape and I knew I would die. Then the storm stopped and I saw I was back in the Bulgar. I felt wonderful. I had no idea what Bifrost had done, but I knew it was magic, ancient magic from a strange otherworld. And Rennat, the Titled Wizard of the East, was there standing over me, and he kindly asked me if I had slept well the previous night, and I nodded. The previous night? He said even a single night spent away from all the other graybeard wizards was good for the spirit. Only a single night?

Is the Pale naught but a dream? Did this mean I also had no son? That none of it really happened, that my stay in the Pale was spun from my fevered brain? I told no one about this. What would I say?

It was on the following day when I was bathing that I saw the healed scars from a Tiber's claws on my leg and knew the Pale was real and yet, and yet—how could I believe in a place that seemed to be someplace else, perhaps sometime else as well?

Rosalind turned the page. She suddenly stopped talking. She stared at the book, turned another page, studied it closely, then turned another and yet another. She finally closed the book and held it close to her chest for a moment. She felt her heart thudding against the book, fast strokes because she was afraid.

Nicholas said, "Rosalind, what is wrong?"

"There is more," she said, drawing a steadying breath. "About six more pages. However, I am unable to read any of them."

Nicholas stared at her. "No, that is not possible, you must be able to."

"I am sorry, my lord, but it makes no sense to me either. It appears to be in the very same code, but the meaning of it is gone to me."

Grayson struck his fist on his thigh. "What is the game Sarimund is playing?" He took the book from Rosalind and opened it to the final six pages. Then he turned back to the beginning and compared the pages. He raised his head, frowning deeply. "She is right, they look exactly alike, but—you really can't make any sense of them, Rosalind?"

She shook her head. "It's rather scary," she said finally. "It's scary being able to read most of it so easily, but then to have it stop—that scares me more, I think. It's as if there had been magic at work in me but now it's gone. Nicholas, why don't you look at the final pages, see if you can read them."

He took the book and gently turned each of the final pages and studied them a long time. His lips moved but he didn't say anything. Finally, he looked up. "Sorry, it's like the beginning, nothing but a series of jumbled letters to me."

Grayson had to study the book again himself, comparing the final pages to all the others. "Nothing," he said at last. He cursed, which surprised Rosalind, for, as with his father, it was a rare thing, except for "blessed hell," of course, the Sherbrooke curse of many generations. "Forgive me," he said, "but I cannot bear it to end like this."

Rosalind said, "But would it not be something to travel to the Bulgar and see if the Dragons of the Sallas Pond would whisk us away to this magical place? I wonder who named this place the Pale and why? A pale is only a blockade, after all, to protect those within it. So why that name?" She sighed. "I surely would like to meet Sarimund's son in Blood Rock."

"I wonder if the son is still alive," Grayson said. "After all, Sarimund wrote this in the sixteenth century."

Nicholas said slowly, "Epona, his mother, if she is indeed the Celtic goddess, then she is very old indeed. Immortal, I should say."

They all looked at each other.

"I wouldn't want to tangle with the Tiber," Rosalind said. "You do realize that there aren't all that many rules, yet that is the wretched title. So what is the purpose of leading you to buy this thin little book, Grayson? And who did the leading?"

"It wasn't meant for me, but you, Rosalind," Grayson said. "After all, you're the only one who can read it, and read it easily, I might add. Except for the final pages. Ah, that teases the brain."

"Then why wasn't I directed to the bookseller's stall rather than you, Grayson?"

Grayson looked over at Nicholas, who was writing something in a small dark blue notebook Rosalind hadn't seen before. "Perhaps Grayson is the catalyst," Nicholas said.

There was a perplexed moment of silence.

"What is that book, Nicholas?" she asked. He smiled over at her, closed it, and slipped it back into his pocket, the small pencil with it. "Merely a list of appointments I was in danger of forgetting."

"What do you mean I am the catalyst?" Grayson asked.

Nicholas shrugged. "You must be the spark to set this all off. Ah, who knows? At least Rosalind could read most of it. Like you, though, I do wonder why she can't read the final pages. Perhaps you are right, Grayson, perhaps this is meant only as a fine tale to amuse and tease. But enough for today. Rosalind, are you ready to go to Madame Fouquet's to meet your Uncle Douglas?"

"For your bloody test in good taste?"

He grinned at her.

"Will you toady up to him, Nicholas?"

"We will have to see, won't we?"

"I," Grayson said as he rose, "have decided that you have no need of Lorelei at your fitting. I am taking her for a walk in the park."

19

After Grayson left, Nicholas slowly rose and walked to her, gave her his hand, and pulled her to her feet. He realized in that moment he wanted to kiss every inch of her. He said, "Perhaps you will find me quite useful in the future, if, that is, I pass his lordship's test."

The future, she thought as she walked beside him out of Grillon's Hotel. She looked up at his profile. He looked stern and preoccupied. She hated it. She thought, *He is my future. I will not let him go away from me once he is mine.*

Once she was seated in the carriage, her full green skirts spread around her, she thought again: *He is my future.* But what was the future going to be about? To be honest with herself, Rosalind hadn't given a thought to the future, save that it would be perfect, a fairy-tale ending. What a dolt she was. Nothing was ever perfect. So many bad things could happen, did happen, all too often. Look at what had happened to her. What had her parents thought? Had they loved her? She had disappeared—simply there, then gone. Had they searched for her? Had they grieved?

She sighed. She'd asked herself these questions dozens of times, perhaps even more times than she could count. She wished she had more of a past than a measly ten years. Only the ghosts knew about her first eight years. Ghosts, she thought, those vague memories that crowded around her in quiet moments, memories and faces she could never grasp.

And now a future spread out before her with this man beside her, a future all blank, ready to be filled in. She felt a ripple of uncertainty. No, that was absurd, she was being absurd. For heaven's sake, he was about to be tested to see if he had good taste. No strangeness or evil could be attached to such a man. But then there were the missing years in Nicholas's life—not to him, of course—but she knew nothing about what that boy of twelve had done to survive. Then there was Macau—what sort of person lived in a place few people had even heard of? What Englishman spoke Mandarin Chinese? Did men have harems in Macau? No, the Portuguese were there, all Catholics, surely, not Muslims.

She became aware suddenly that he was studying her, just as she'd studied him. She turned to him and asked, "Nicholas, are you Church of England?"

"I suppose that's as good as any," he said, and studied his knuckles.

"Come, answer me. Are you a religious man?"

"Yes, I suppose I am. My boyhood years with my grandfather meant Sundays in the village church, but after I left England—well, to be honest, survival was more important than attending church, at least until I managed to make my way in Portugal. I believe I tend more toward Catholicism—the repetition of the ritual, the sound of Latin on my tongue—but it isn't deep inside me. And you, Rosalind, what religion are you?"

"I have been one of the local vicar's favorite parishioners for several years, since I began organizing fairs and gathering clothes for the poorer families. Before I came to Brandon House?" She shrugged. "I have no idea. But sometimes there are feelings that come, feelings for God, but a God not quite like the Church of England's God. Does that make sense?"

"It probably means you were raised in another religion before someone tried to kill you. If you're Italian, it would mean you're probably Catholic."

He'd said it so calmly, so—so emotionlessly. Someone had tried to kill her and she'd been only a child. Odd, she felt rather emotionless about it as well, since it had never been part of what she was, what she had become. Could she be Italian? Catholic?

She said, "A monster, I always believed it was a monster. When Uncle Ryder first brought me to Brandon House, I knew the monster was close by, especially at night, and I knew he would kill me and eat me whole. I remember Jane had me sleep with little Amy, to protect her, Jane said, from her bad dreams. Amy was an adorable little girl who wanted to design and make bonnets when she grew up. I remember one Sunday, Aunt Sophie wore one of Amy's first efforts to church. A bunch of grapes were hanging down over her forehead, but she never took it off."

"And she protected you?"

"Jane was very smart. I soon forgot about the monster, since I was so worried about Amy's nightmares. She never had a single nightmare, as I recall. Now that I'm grown, the monster is flesh and blood, and whoever he is, wherever he is, he brims with malevolence. Whenever I remember waking up to see Ryder Sherbrooke holding me, whenever I remember the black nights, I can still feel the fright of the child, but it's vague now. Now it doesn't raise any horror or terror in me."

He took her hand, looked her directly in her eyes. "No one will ever hurt you again, Rosalind. I swear it to you. Do you believe me?"

"Yes, I believe you. But what if someday I remember and I know who tried to kill me?"

"If that day comes, we will deal with it. I promise you that as well."

The carriage hit a brick in the roadway and she was nearly thrown into his lap. A nice thing, she thought as she regretfully settled herself back against her seat. "Where will we go on our honeymoon?"

He hadn't given it a thought, and she saw it on his face.

She punched her fist into his arm. "What is wrong with you, Nicholas? Surely you must have given at least a small passing thought to our honeymoon, since it will be the official place where you may indulge yourself with my fair person."

Just saying those words made her cheeks flush, and he saw she was both excited and embarrassed. He smiled at her, which was difficult, since he wanted to indulge himself now. But of course he didn't. "It's not that I haven't thought about it, precisely." He gave her a look that made her feel absolutely naked. She didn't know what to do, what to say. He continued easily, "However, I sincerely doubt we will reach a destination before I indulge both of us."

He nearly leapt upon her when she looked about the carriage, obviously eyeing the cushions with lovemaking in mind, something, he imagined, she knew very little about. But she loved the forbidden wickedness of it. He wondered what she'd think when he had her naked, what she'd do when he kissed her white belly, pulled her equally white legs over his shoulders.

"I heard Aunt Sophie say to Aunt Alexandra that she feared all of society will believe I'm increasing since we are marrying so quickly. Although now that I think of it, we are wedding too quickly for me to even realize I'm pregnant, if, naturally, we'd been wicked immediately upon our acquaintance, say within a half hour of meeting."

In that moment, Nicholas actually saw himself coming into her. He cleared his throat. "I imagine you will be soon enough."

Rosalind fell back as if he'd shot her. Gone was the look of wickedness. He saw she was shocked and appalled.

Rosalind thought, *Soon enough? SOON ENOUGH?* It boggled her mind. It was the same when he'd spoken about their daughter. No, this "soon enough" business wasn't going to happen. She wasn't ready to stop running across the fields, leaping ditches, tying her skirts around her waist so she could shimmy up the apple trees in Uncle Ryder's fruit orchard. She saw herself fat, waddling about, her belly huge, and made a grab for the carriage door handle.

He grabbed her hand, brought it to his mouth, and kissed her palm. "Don't worry, Rosalind. I will take very good care of you."

"I know, of course," she said slowly, voice as thin as Cook's ham slices, "that lust leads one to make love, which then leads to babies."

"That is the normal way of things, yes. What's wrong, Rosalind?" He kissed her palm again. "Why is the light of exploration gone from your eyes?"

"I don't think I wish to have any more lust for a while, Nicholas. I am eighteen. I am too young. So please do not kiss my palm again, it makes me want to hurl myself into all sorts of wicked experiments that might lead to my own undoing." She pulled her hand away from his, clenched it into a fist, and began to hit it against her leg.

He stared at her fist. "You're trying to erase the wicked feelings?"

"Yes, and they are very nearly gone now."

"Rosalind, if you do not wish to have a child immediately I will take steps to prevent conception."

"You can do that? It is possible?"

He nodded. "It is not always successful, but I will try."

"Well, that is good. Yes, that is very good. I'm pleased you're a reasonable man. It greatly relieves my mind. I like to race, you know, both on my own feet and atop a horse's back. I want to continue racing for perhaps another five or so years."

Was he a reasonable man? "Fine," he said, knowing he had to calm her, reassure her, give her no reason to doubt him, "we will speak of my heir again when I am thirty."

"Now that we have solved that small problem"—she beamed at him—"let me tell you again that it is your duty to select our honeymoon, Nicholas. Apply yourself to the task."

He grinned easily at her, a grin he'd known for many years usually gained him his way with women. He saw her ease. She smiled back at him, a blinding smile that made him stare at her. Potent, that smile of hers. He wondered if she knew how effective her smile was.

When they arrived at Madame Fouquet's, the Earl of Northcliffe showed Nicholas a dozen drawings of desperately elongated females who looked to weigh no more than the feathers that adorned their gowns, and more bolts of different-colored materials than

Nicholas would have dreamed existed, and asked at least two dozen questions. Everyone else stood about, paying close attention. Finally, Nicholas was pronounced to have satisfactory taste. "Rosalind," the earl said to her, lightly patting her cheek, "you are blessed. Nicholas has sufficient taste at the present time. I am certain it will improve even more as the years pass. I don't mind telling you I was worried. I find it odd that so many ladies in my life select colors that make their complexions look like oatmeal.

"But no matter, you needn't worry about looking like your breakfast since Nicholas has presented himself. All will be well." The earl pointed down to a drawing of a willowy lady who seemed to be floating at least three inches off the floor. "You won't embarrass yourself wearing that hideous shade of green with those ridiculous rows of flounces at the hem. Would you look at this? It fair to shrivels my liver."

But it didn't shrivel Rosalind's liver. In fact, she particularly liked those flounces. Those lovely flounces would make her look as if she were floating too. Because she wasn't a dolt, she kept quiet. She saw Nicholas and Uncle Douglas exchange a look.

As for Madame Fouquet, she looked at Uncle Douglas with too fond an eye, Rosalind observed, and agreed with everything he said. Uncle Douglas didn't appear to mind the toadying from her.

When at last her wedding gown was pronounced acceptable by Uncle Douglas, she and Nicholas were dismissed. Nicholas winked at her and took her hand. When they arrived back at the Sherbrooke town house, Willicombe, his bald head sweating, came flying out of the front door, his face pale, and told them Miss Lorelei Kilbourne had been kidnapped, and everyone was tip over arse, and they must do something.

20

It seemed Grayson and Lorelei were strolling in Hyde Park, hand in hand, when suddenly two ruffians, handkerchiefs over their faces, jumped from the bushes and coshed Grayson over the head. When he awoke, Lorelei was gone.

But then, not more than two hours later, she was dumped unceremoniously on the Sherbrooke front door, bruised, her clothing dirty and ripped, and a bit dazed, but not hurt. All the Kilbournes—father, mother, four other daughters—were clustered in the drawing room, Alexandra and Sophie trying to keep them calm.

The gentlemen had just returned from examining the abduction spot in Hyde Park and suddenly, there she was in the open doorway, supported by Willicombe. Her mother screamed, pressed her palms over her bosom, and ran to enfold her precious chick. "God returned my oldest treasure to me," Lorelei's mother said over and over, clasping her child to her soft bosom. The four other treasures cried, and Lord Ramey looked like he needed brandy badly.

It was Grayson who placed a snifter of his uncle's finest French brandy into Lord Ramey's hand. Since Grayson had been the one to lose his daughter, he hoped this would begin his redemption in her father's eyes. It was particularly fine brandy, and Uncle Douglas's favorite.

At Uncle Douglas's request, Sir Robert Peel appeared some thirty minutes after the reunion to question Miss Kilbourne, who was reclining gracefully on a pale blue brocade chaise, a lovely shawl spread over her legs, a dainty cup of hot tea in her hand, Grayson standing behind her, his hand on her shoulder. Since Grayson had wisely told her he was impressed by her wonderful bravery, despite her mother's and sisters' tears Lorelei didn't hesitate when she spoke. "I feared Mr. Sherbrooke was dead since one of those brutal men struck him so very hard on the head. I fought them, Sir Robert, but they were stronger and one of them picked me up and threw me over his shoulder. He carried me to a carriage hidden in a nasty alley and threw me inside onto the floor. One man climbed in and gagged me and tied my hands behind my back. He didn't say anything to me, just sort of grunted, as if satisfied he'd done a good job. The door slammed and the other man whipped up the horses.

"Perhaps fifteen minutes later the carriage stopped and one of the men opened the carriage door"—here she looked up at Grayson, who nodded encouragement at her—"but before I could do anything, he pulled the gag out of my mouth and pressed a handkerchief over my face. I breathed in a sickly sweet odor. I suppose I must have become unconscious, for I do not remember anything more.

"When I woke up I was lying on the carriage seat. My head ached, and I felt all logy, as if my legs were too heavy to move. Then the carriage stopped and one of the men opened the door and dragged me out. He tossed me on the doorstep. I looked up to see them driving away very fast. I kicked the door so someone would come. Willicombe untied my hands and helped me up."

Sir Robert Peel, blessed with a judge's unbending shoulders and beautifully dressed all in gray, nodded slowly at the pretty young girl and looked wise, which he was. "That was very well stated, Miss Kilbourne. Did you notice anything distinctive about the men who took you, or the carriage?"

Lorelei thought about this. "The men were toughs, the sort you see lurking around the tavern in our village at home, dirty clothes and mean eyes, as though they'd rip out your gullet and not regret it for a moment."

"They didn't call each other by name or say anything at all?"

"I heard one of them say he hoped the young lad hadn't croaked it since the other man had struck him so hard, and they hadn't been paid to croak anyone." She paused. "The carriage had some sort of crest on the door, Sir Robert. It was as if the men had tried to cover it with a cloth, but it had gone askew and I saw—" She put her hands to her head and pressed.

Her mother, with a moan, rose to go to

her, but Sir Robert forestalled her, and she sat again. He said, "You are doing fine, Miss Kilbourne. Think about it for a moment." And he gave Lady Ramey a charming smile and a small shake of the head. He said to Lord Ramey, "You must be very proud of your daughter, my lord. She is no fainting miss."

The other four daughters eyed each other, then their sister, then straightened their shoulders and tried to look competent. Since the youngest daughter, Alice, was no more than thirteen, Rosalind was impressed.

If Lorelei had considered fainting, she didn't consider it now. Grayson had taken her hand and was lightly rubbing his thumb over her knuckles. "The crest," Grayson said. "Were there colors, shapes, you can remember?"

"I saw the door for only a very brief moment," she said, "but yes, I could make out the legs of a lion, I think, standing upright, and there was the lower part of a red circle and a band of gold around it. It was as if the lion were holding up the world. I'm sorry, that's all I can remember."

"They bound and gagged you but they didn't hurt you? Didn't threaten you? Gave you no idea that they were kidnapping you for ransom?"

"No. They cursed a lot, particularly when I bit one man's hand, but he didn't hit me or speak, just cursed. And after they put that handkerchief against my nose, I have no memory of anything."

Sir Robert took his leave, well aware that more was going on in the Sherbrooke drawing room than anyone would ever tell him. It was another fifteen minutes before the Kilbourne women took their leave, Lady Ramey's daughters now supporting her since Lorelei seemed just fine.

Lord Ramey, after drinking three snifters of the earl's magnificent brandy, was still giving Grayson accusing looks for losing his daughter. However, a date was made for the following day, should Grayson feel up to it. No doubt about that, Rosalind thought, given his fatuous smile at Lorelei.

The drawing room was silent when the front door closed behind Lord Ramey.

It was Grayson who finally said aloud what everyone was thinking. "The men made a mistake. There is no doubt in my mind those men believed Lorelei was Rosalind."

Ryder said, "They drove for fifteen minutes, so Miss Kilbourne believed, drugged her with the chloroform-soaked handkerchief, and obviously took her into a house where those who wanted Rosalind were waiting. They saw it wasn't Rosalind and didn't kill Lorelei. Whoever it was balked at the murder of an innocent. That is something at least. They sent her back."

Rosalind was sitting next to Grayson, speaking low, when she heard Uncle Douglas say, "Where is Nicholas?"

But Nicholas wasn't there. He was gone.

* * *

Lee Po pulled up Grace and Leopold in front of a well-tended redbrick Georgian town house at 14 Epson Square.

As he walked up the steps to the front door, Nicholas said over his shoulder, "No, don't argue with me, Lee. I want you to tool the grays around the square. Don't worry about me, I know what I'm about. I shouldn't be long."

Lee Po didn't like it, but there was nothing he could do. He knew who lived in this house.

Nicholas hadn't been inside the town house since he was a small boy—namely, at his father's wedding to Miranda Carstairs, youngest child of Baron Carstairs, barely five months after Nicholas's mother had died.

His knock was answered by a pallid, furtive-looking young man, his hair so blond it appeared white in the dim light of the entrance hall.

"Yes?" A very suspicious voice, Nicholas thought, and handed him his card, then watched him look at it and give a nervous start. *That's right, you little bugger,* he thought, *I'm here.*

He said in a quiet voice, "I wish to see my half brothers, one or all of them. Now."

"Ah, my lord, allow me to see if Master Richard is available." The butler led Nicholas into a drawing room he remembered reeking of attar of roses, his father's new wife's scent. He hated the smell to this day.

The walls were oak paneled, the cornices classical, the fireplace ornate, and the furniture light and airy, making the drawing room feel more spacious than it actually was. Like the outside of the house, it was well tended. It required quite a lot of money to maintain this property, Nicholas knew; he wondered how deep his brothers' pockets were. He looked for any sign that Lorelei had been in this room, but he saw nothing out of the ordinary.

He turned when the door opened and his half brother Richard strolled in, looking quite

elegant in dark brown trousers and a waist-
coat of brown and cream stripes. His coat
was dark brown velvet. He looked quite fine
and indolent, a young gentleman with nothing more on his mind than his evening's
entertainment. Ah, but in his dark eyes: wari-
ness. No, even more, Nicholas could see he
was alarmed.

In his cultivated bored voice, Richard
said, "Well, well, if it isn't a Vail I never
expected to see here. What do you want?"

Nicholas walked to his stepbrother, drew
back his fist, and slammed it in his jaw.
Richard fell back, hit the arm of a chair, and
went down. He was stunned for a moment.
Nicholas moved to stand over him, hands on
his hips.

"I didn't hit you that hard, you little puke,
get yourself together."

Richard Vail shook his head and rubbed
his jaw. He looked up at Nicholas and slowly
got to his feet.

Then, without warning, he leapt upon
Nicholas.

He was strong and fast. Both of them
went down. Richard sent his fist into
Nicholas's belly. It hurt, but not all that much.
Nicholas smiled as he struck Richard's

throat with the heel of his hand, sending him scrambling backwards, gagging, to fetch up against the wall, all the while his hands wildly rubbing his neck. Nicholas grabbed him by the collar and hauled him upright. He didn't hit him, but took two steps back and sent his foot into his belly. Richard grunted and stumbled back against the fireplace, now clutching his stomach.

Nicholas said, "I could hit you lower, would you like that?"

"No!" Richard yelled, trying to get his breath, turning quickly to the side to protect himself.

Nicholas stood quietly, waiting.

"You bastard! You kicked my belly into my backbone. I've never seen anything like that. Is that from your heathen Chinese friends?"

"I will tell you this one time, Richard, then if you act again, I will kill you. Today you kidnapped the wrong girl. If you ever attempt to take Rosalind again, you are a dead man. Do you understand me?"

Richard Vail didn't attempt to deny his complicity. He looked upon his half brother with hatred and a good deal of fear. His stomach burned ferociously.

Nicholas said, his voice even lower, quieter, "Do you understand?"

Finally, Richard nodded.

"Good," Nicholas said, dusted his britches, and turned to leave. He paused at the doorway. "You hired two incompetent toughs, that's how Lorelei Kilbourne described your men. You have all your father's money. Surely you could have purchased better talent. Do you know the fools let the cloth fall away a bit from our father's family crest on the carriage and Lorelei saw it? I would have known it was you without that information but it makes me feel better to have it verified."

Richard Vail leaned against the mantelpiece, his swarthy face pale, impotent fury in his eyes. "I only wanted to talk to this girl you're going to marry, this girl who is of no importance at all, who has no money save what the Sherbrookes will give you as a dowry. I wanted to tell her what you were really like, warn her she was making a big mistake."

"If you wished to speak to the lady, why didn't you simply pay her a visit? Didn't your dear mother teach you any manners at all?"

Richard said nothing.

"Ah, of course you wanted to add on the threats, didn't you? Do you know, I venture to say that if someone were stupid enough to threaten Rosalind, he would sorely regret it. She is"—Nicholas found himself looking at a statuette of a limp shepherdess sitting beside Richard's ear atop the mantelpiece—"she is quite fierce." And he realized, as he turned on his heel to leave, that he was smiling. But then he stopped in his tracks and whirled around. "If, by any mad chance, you weren't considering threats, if you planned to weigh her down and throw her into the Thames to be rid of her once and for all—" Nicholas realized he was shaking. He said very quietly, "If you were considering making my betrothed simply disappear, don't, Richard. If anything happens to Rosalind, Lancelot will be next in line for my title. You will be dead."

"Damn you to hell! I hope she plays you false!"

Nicholas laughed at that.

The pale young man who'd greeted him at the front door stood not a foot outside the drawing room, wringing his hands. He was darting frantic looks behind Nicholas's left shoulder.

"What are you doing here?"

Nicholas turned to see Lancelot Vail trip quickly down the front staircase, dressed elegantly, like his older brother, his face flushed at the sight of Nicholas.

"I was on the point of leaving, Lancelot," Nicholas said. "Why don't you go pour your brother a nice snifter of brandy?"

21

Rosalind was staring out the bow window at the daffodils waving in the Wednesday afternoon breeze, waiting for Nicholas, when the door opened. But it was Willicombe who came into the drawing room. She was impatient and worried, but still she smiled at him because Grayson had recently confided in her that he was making Willicombe a magician in his next novel, with a head full of red hair, and it was to be a surprise. Rosalind cocked an eyebrow at him.

"Lady Mountjoy is here to see you, Miss Rosalind."

Wrong Mountjoy.

Lady Mountjoy didn't simply walk into the drawing room, she sailed in, a figurehead swathed in lavender from her boots to her big bonnet decorated with big clusters of purple grapes. She was short and on the plump side, but still, she looked ready to take on the Roman legions, something both to alarm and impress. Beneath the awesome bonnet, her hair was quite blond, the few gray strands difficult to see. Her eyes were very light, perhaps blue or gray. Lancelot was the picture of his mama. So this was Nicholas's stepmother, Miranda, the woman who had spawned three sons and taught them to hate Nicholas.

Lady Mountjoy didn't look happy, but she did look determined, and to Rosalind's eyes, she looked fretful, lines of discontent bracketing her mouth. She looked on the edge, as if afraid that something was happening she couldn't control. *Ah, perhaps she's upset that her sons failed to get rid of me to prevent Nicholas from having a boy child off me, and she's come to convince me to break off my betrothal to Nicholas herself.* Rosalind hoped the woman didn't have a stiletto in her lovely beaded reticule.

She eyed her future stepmama-in-law and

hoped this was her mission; she could get her teeth into that. Maybe she was here to try to buy her off. Rosalind remained silent as Lady Mountjoy stopped a foot short of her nose—very rude, to be sure—but Rosalind found she wanted to laugh at this plump little peahen of a woman trying to intimidate her. Lady Mountjoy looked her up and down, and snorted. She took one step back, as if realizing she was at a disadvantage since Rosalind topped her by a good six inches, and announced, "You are young and don't look as if you have much sense. I am surprised Nicholas would choose you, but then again, perhaps he is desperate. Tell me, missy, how much of a dowry are the Sherbrookes putting in his pockets?"

Missy?

A straight shot over the bow, no namby-pamby attack for this one. "Ah, I presume you are Nicholas's stepmother?"

"Unfortunately that is true."

"I understand you haven't seen your stepson since he left after his grandfather's death. What was he, twelve years old? And how many times did you and his father visit him while he was living with the former earl's father? Once, twice? It appears to me, madam, that you do not even know him; Nicholas is a stranger to you. You could pass him on the street and not know him. Why then are you surprised at whom he would choose?"

Lady Mountjoy waved her hand around. "One hears things from one's relatives and one's friends. All agree he is not stupid and therefore choosing you has left them bewildered, perhaps believing you seduced him."

"Hmmm. I only met him a week ago. A very fast seduction, don't you think?"

"Don't you make sport with me, missy!"

Rosalind gave her a sunny smile and a wave of the hand. "How do you do, Lady Mountjoy? To what do I owe the honor of your presence?"

"You ask me how I am? Very well, I will tell you how I am. My spirits are upended; I am perturbed. I didn't wish to ever meet you, missy, yet here I am forced to come. I wish you no honor with my presence."

"Should you care to leave? I will not force you to remain."

Rosalind got a fat diamond-adorned nanny finger shaken in her face. "You will be quiet. You are really quite common, although it does not surprise me."

"Perhaps I could sing for you. I'm told I have a lovely voice, that when one listens to me sing, one easily forgets my youth and my commonness. I do not even need a pianoforte to accompany me. What you think?" Rosalind didn't smile, she simply stood there, waiting to see what Lady Mountjoy would do.

"I do not wish to hear you sing. That is ridiculous. Now, I am looking for Nicholas, though I imagine he will be rude and not show himself."

"Did not your relatives and your friends tell you his residence is currently at Grillon's Hotel? He has a lovely suite of rooms there and all the staff are quite deferential to him. Should you like the direction to Grillon's?"

"I know where Grillon's Hotel is located, you impertinent little no-account. I have also heard he has a heathen servant who is very likely more dangerous than he is. No, I shall not go there."

"Lee Po, dangerous?" Rosalind nodded thoughtfully. "Possibly so. As for Nicholas being dangerous, I cannot be certain about that. However, in all honesty, he can be rather curt, but it is because he feels things so very deeply, you know."

Lady Mountjoy snarled. "He is a man, you ninny. Men rarely feel much of anything that is worth remarking upon. It is true they feel lust in their younger years, but in their older years one must pry the brandy bottle from their hands."

Perhaps that was part of the reason for Lady Mountjoy's discontent—no lovemaking and no brandy. Rosalind said, "It is a great pity you don't know your stepson at all, ma'am, for I believe him to be truly remarkable.

"I fear Nicholas isn't here at the moment. I believe he went off with my uncles to shoot at Manton's. I wanted to go, but they do not yet allow ladies. Would you care for a cup of tea?"

Lady Mountjoy grabbed Rosalind's hand and held on tight, making the grapes on her bonnet dance. "I don't want tea, you stupid girl, I want to tell you to call off this absurd wedding with Nicholas. I'm trying to save you even though you are as common as a weed and don't deserve to be saved." She lowered her voice to a hiss. "Your life is in danger. Nicholas Vail is a scoundrel. When his father kicked him out, he didn't have a single sou—"

Ah, so she was finally getting to it. Rosalind said easily, "Well, how could he have a single sou when his father kicked him out? Wasn't he a little boy?"

"It is one and the same thing. My dear husband told me the old earl gave Nicholas quite a lot of money before he died, but I ask you, what happened to it? We heard Nicholas simply disappeared—I know he gambled the money away. He was sly and mean, a good-for-nothing from the age of five. He had nothing when he left England."

"Do you know, I don't believe Nicholas gambles at all, but I shall ask him. I wonder too what happened to the money if his grandfather did indeed give him some. Was he robbed? Perhaps left for dead?"

"Control your melodrama. Nicholas was a wastrel when he was a boy, and I'm sure he's remained one. Whatever happened, Nicholas lost the money his grandfather gave to him. All know he is still poor. He has a title and no money and thus he needs an heiress. So I am here to tell you the truth. He is only after the money the Sherbrookes will give you. He will get a boy child off you, then murder you in your bed. If you trust him you are more a fool than I believe you are."

"As in the fruit never falls far from the paternal or maternal tree?"

Rosalind believed for an instant that Lady Mountjoy would strike her. Her bosom heaved, she turned alarmingly red in the face, and her breath was as loud as a bellows. But she held herself still. Rosalind realized in that instant if the woman had hit her, she would have retaliated, knocked her flat, with great enjoyment. Chin up, shoulders squared, Lady Mountjoy said, "My sons are gentlemen, nurtured by the parental and maternal tree. They know what is what, they know how to behave. If possible, my husband would have declared Nicholas a bastard, but the boy had the gall to look the picture of him, curse the fates."

Rosalind managed to pull her hand free of Lady Mountjoy's surprisingly strong grip. She turned away from the woman to sit down on the sofa. She watched Lady Mountjoy pace in front of her. Her imposing bosom looked ready to topple her, but didn't, possibly because she was so tightly corseted. She had once been very pretty, Rosalind thought.

Rosalind said finally, "I met your sons Richard and Lancelot, at Drury Lane, to see *Hamlet*. I, myself, didn't care for Kean's performance all that much. Have you seen him as Hamlet?"

"You are trying to distract me and it won't work. Be quiet." She paused, eyed Rosalind up and down. "Besides, I know you are a fraud yourself."

"Ah, so I am no longer the victim. Like Nicholas, am I now a scoundrel too? If that is what you believe, then why are you concerned? We are both poor and we are both scoundrels. Like to like. Don't you think it fitting?"

Rosalind thought the woman would explode. That made her feel quite good. She was learning an excellent lesson: *Hold on to your temper with both hands, and breathe.* As for Lady Mountjoy, she hadn't learned this lesson. Her face was alarmingly flushed. "You mock me, you worthless excuse for a proper lady. The only reason society is forced to pay any attention to you at all is because of the Sherbrookes."

"Well, of course that's quite right. What is your point, ma'am? That I am not good enough to marry the Earl of Mountjoy, even though you believe he is poor and a scoundrel?"

A spasm of rage seamed Lady Mountjoy's mouth. She realized she was getting far afield and couldn't find the road. "You are certainly not good enough to marry the real Earl of Mountjoy! Nicholas, the earl? Bah, I say. Neither of you should carry that proud name! And your name—La Fontaine—the man wrote nothing but silly fables about rabbits and turtles racing, of all things— ridiculous!—morality tales that have no bearing whatsoever on life."

"Well, to be honest yet again, I fear you are right. But don't you see, I somehow misplaced my own name and had to cast about for a new one. Since I love sly foxes and vain crows, you can imagine my delight when I learned that Jean de La Fontaine wrote such charming tales. La Fontaine—it floats rather nicely on the tongue, don't you think?"

Lady Mountjoy looked both amazed and furious. In fact, she looked as though if she'd had a gun, Rosalind would be lying dead at her feet. She shook a plump white fist, three large rings on her fingers, in Rosalind's face. "None of this is to the point, my girl. You will be quiet."

"Then why, ma'am, did you bring it up?"

Lady Mountjoy heaved and huffed and Rosalind feared for her stays. "The fact remains, you are not a real La Fontaine."

Rosalind said, "Well, naturally not. I

already explained that to you. I must say, ma'am, you don't seem to have found out very much about me. Perhaps you don't have a very competent solicitor."

"Glendenning is an idiot. He even allowed Nicholas to claim my son's title. It is my very special friend, Alfred Lemming, who is competent. Unfortunately he is in Cornwall at the moment, visiting his moldering estate in Penzance."

Lady Mountjoy had a lover? Rosalind said, "You mustn't blame poor Glendenning about losing the title. I believe the law of primogeniture prevents any other course of action. Nicholas was the firstborn, after all, and despite his father's machinations, he is the rightful Earl of Mountjoy."

"Primogeniture, what a ridiculous word, what an outmoded, outrageously unfair bit of law. It is ancient, not at all to the point in the modern world.

"Nicholas should never have come into the title and that's the truth of it. My precious Richard should be the earl.

"I have friends, missy, friends who know the Sherbrookes, friends who have told me about Ryder Sherbrooke and his collection of little beggars, one of which you have been for over ten years. Ah, I can see the shame in your eyes. What do you have to say to that?"

"I say thank you to God, every single night, that Ryder Sherbrooke found me and saved me life. Do you think I should do more? Oh, dear, all my money comes from him as well. I did knit him some socks one year for Christmas, and he did wear them, bless him."

Rosalind sincerely prayed Lady Mountjoy wouldn't fall over with apoplexy. Her powerful lungs looked ready to burst through her lavender bodice, her fists knotted at her sides. Perhaps Rosalind should stop laying it on with a trowel.

Miranda, Lady Mountjoy, was frustrated and baffled by this far too smart young lady with her glorious red hair, which even Richard had remarked favorably upon, unwillingly, of course. She wished the girl's hair were coarse and vulgar, what with all the thick riotous curls, but it wasn't. And those blue eyes—her own boys' father had had such blue eyes, beautiful eyes—but he was dead, that inconsiderate lout who'd really been too old for her at the time she married him, but she'd insisted—and then he'd had the gall to croak after barely twenty years. She yelled at Rosalind, "You are not paying proper attention to me, missy!"

"Ah, it just occurred to me that once I am wed to Nicholas, I shall take precedence over you. You will call me Lady Mountjoy and curtsy. You will be the Dowager Lady Mountjoy."

Lady Mountjoy picked up what was close at hand—a lovely green brocade pillow—and hurled it at her. Rosalind plucked it out of the air, laughing. She was very relieved that Lady Mountjoy did not have a cane in her hand.

"Pray, ma'am, if you would care to be seated and converse like a reasonable person, I would be delighted to respond in kind. Do you wish to leave or do you wish to sit down and calm yourself?"

Even as Lady Mountjoy's vision blurred in her rage, she sat herself down across from Rosalind in a high-backed brocade chair that matched the pillow. The lines on either side of her mouth appeared even deeper, a pity. She sat perfectly straight as if a board were down her back, imperious as a judge, Rosalind thought. But there was an air of uncertainty about her now. Could it be that she'd fired all her cannon? She could think of no more insults, no more attacks?

Rosalind rose and walked to the fireplace and pulled on the bell cord beside it. When Willicombe appeared barely ten seconds later, Rosalind asked him for tea and cakes.

"Shall I inquire if Mistress Sophia is available, Miss Rosalind?"

"Oh, no, Lady Mountjoy and I are having a charming time. She is to be my future stepmother-in-law, you know."

Willicombe did know and it took all his training not to tell the old besom to climb back on her broom and ride out of there.

The two ladies sat across from each other, Lady Mountjoy tapping her fingertips on the arm of the chair, frustration pouring off her. Rosalind swung her foot and whistled a lilting tune until Willicombe made his stately way back into the drawing room, bearing a silver tray with tea and cakes. When all was in order, Rosalind found she nearly had to shove Willicombe out. She closed and locked the door.

She smiled pleasantly at Lady Mountjoy. "My Uncle Ryder always says if there is bile to be spilled, it is wise to lock the door. He also says there is nothing quite like a good cup of hot tea to set things aright."

"A man would say something stupid like that, curse all of them to the Devil."

22

"So, ma'am, would you care for tea?"

Lady Mountjoy told her she wasn't thirsty, requested two sugars and a drop of milk, and proceeded to pour it down her gullet.

"My Uncle Ryder is quite right about the bile spilling, don't you think?"

"He is not your uncle!"

Rosalind said quietly, "I know. I often wonder if I have an uncle by blood out there somewhere. Perhaps he is still looking for me. More likely, he believes I died many years ago."

Lady Mountjoy appeared momentarily disconcerted. She managed a substantial snort and then snarled; "I certainly would not look for you."

That was an impressive blow. Rosalind sat back, her cup of tea in her hand. "You never told me why Nicholas's father sent his five-year-old firstborn son away. I imagine it was after you wedded his father, is that right?"

"When Richard was born, my dear husband knew he was the rightful son, the one who deserved to follow in his footsteps, not Nicholas."

"What was Nicholas like, ma'am?"

"He was an impossible child, sly, always hiding and spying on me. He hated me, hated his father, claimed his father had murdered his mother and that I had helped him. I knew he would try his best to murder poor little Richard once he was born, and so my husband sent him to live with his grandfather, that mad old man. But he came back. Damn him, he had the gall to come back!"

"I believe his mother had only been dead five months when you and his father wed?"

"What does that matter? We were in love, we'd waited long enough. His mother was a pious creature, one to rival the vicar in black looks and condemnation. When she died of a lung infection, it was a great relief to everyone, particularly her husband. Even though she fancied herself a saint, she still complained endlessly that it wasn't fair the old earl was still alive—I must admit she was quite right about that. The old man had enjoyed quite enough years on this earth." She sipped at her tea. "Mary Smithson— yes, that was the name everyone had to call her. As for the old earl, he simply became more and more eccentric—thought himself some sort of magician, if you can believe that. He was mad, I always thought. He raised Nicholas to hate us all the more—"

"But why?"

Lady Mountjoy eyed her with loathing. "That is none of your business. Let me tell you, missy, you are not clever. You string words together that sound clever, but they are not. The old man taught Nicholas strange things, otherworldly cants and mysterious rituals, mad ceremonies with ghosts and spirits invited, the brewing of deadly potions. There was wicked magic going on at Wyverly Chase, all knew it."

The words clogged in Rosalind's throat,

then broke loose. "Do you really think Nicholas's grandfather was mad? Or deep down do you believe he was a wizard?"

"Don't be a blockhead. There is no such thing. I told you—the old man was mad, nothing more, and he taught Nicholas bad things. I believe it quite possible that Nicholas could inherit this madness from his grandfather, that he could become crazed, and thus any boy child you presented to him could carry the seeds of madness."

"If that is your belief, it is very sad, ma'am, for that means you are discouraging your own three sons from wedding and providing you with grandchildren because of the taint of madness."

"You have the brain of a scallop. It is well known that madness passes only to the eldest, never to the other children."

"I have never heard that."

"That is because you are ignorant. Since the old man had Nicholas to mold, he paid no attention to my three sons, didn't even acknowledge their birthdays. Even without any of the old man's wealth, they grew up straight and tall and worthy to be what they are, the sons of an earl."

"I understand your husband wasn't

supposed to be the earl, that he had an older brother."

"I never met him but I know that Edward was a small-minded varmint of a man, always dreamy-eyed, and could never answer a question sensibly. My husband told me he spoke to rosebushes while he stroked their petals. Then Edward died and the title came to the rightful son, Gervais, and he became Viscount Ashborough."

Rosalind was no longer listening to the vitriol pouring from Lady Mountjoy's mouth, she was thinking of Nicholas's grandfather. Why had she asked if he was a wizard? Because something deep inside her believed it was true, that was why, and it was all wrapped up with Sarimund and the *Rules of the Pale*. She remembered Nicholas had told her his grandfather also had a copy of the book and had told him all about Sarimund. But he hadn't told him what was in the book, because obviously he couldn't read it.

Rosalind said, "What was the old earl's name?"

"Galardi. Stupid foreign-sounding name."

"How old was your husband when his older brother, Edward, died, ma'am?"

"He was newly down from Oxford, only

twenty. Wait, are you accusing my husband of murder? You believe he murdered his older brother and his own wife, Mary Smithson? You are a vile-minded no-account, stupid as a mole."

"Ah, so thinking about that worries you as well, does it?" Rosalind held up her hand. "If Nicholas doesn't marry me, he will marry someone else, someone probably not nearly as nice as I am, someone who would refuse to listen to your rantings, someone who would instruct her butler to close the door in your face.

"I would say you're blessed, ma'am, in having me for your future stepdaughter-in-law. Are we not drinking tea together? Did I not give you two sugars? I am so courteous I am not even berating you for your sons' misdeeds."

"There is nothing to berate!"

Rosalind tapped her fingertips against her chin. "Only imagine if Richard and Lancelot had managed to get their hands on me rather than poor Lorelei Kilbourne. And just imagine they wanted to do more than warn me away from marrying Nicholas. Just imagine they had murdered me, all to keep me from becoming their stepsister-in-law, all to prevent me from having a boy child. Imagine all that, Lady Mountjoy. I fancy it must bring you a certain amount of melancholy."

"Nicholas hoved in poor Richard's ribs!"

"I'm sorry, what?"

"I don't wish Nicholas to attack my poor Richard again; he fights like an alley tough. My poor Richard said Nicholas is vicious, no better than an apish dockworker. Yes, Nicholas forced his way into the house and attacked my son viciously, with no provocation at all. Richard is delicate. His health is precarious. He could be badly damaged—"

Rosalind was relieved that she had swallowed her tea; otherwise it would have spewed out of her mouth. "Excuse me. I thought we were speaking of Richard Vail, that very tall and fit young man who looks very much like Nicholas? You're saying that Nicholas attacked him? There was no provocation? I wonder what Lord Ramey would say to that. He is Lorelei's father, you know. I will check Nicholas's knuckles, see if they are skinned. Drat him, he knew Richard was behind Lorelei's kidnapping, and he didn't tell me. Did he hurt Richard badly? Did he really hit him that hard? Ah, his poor fists."

"No, you pork-brained ninny, he didn't hit

him with his fists all that much, he used his foot—*his foot!*—he kicked poor Richard in the stomach, knocked him backwards. It makes me ill that this barbarian is now the Earl of Mountjoy."

"Hmm. I wonder if he could teach me to do that."

"Be quiet! I don't want him to murder my son, do you hear me?" Lady Mountjoy jumped to her feet and waved her fist at Rosalind.

"He won't, ma'am, if your sons don't try to hurt me. Do tell them that."

Lady Mountjoy went silent.

Rosalind hoped she had expended her venom. If so, it had certainly taken long enough.

There was a knock on the door.

Rosalind jumped to her feet to race over and unlock the door. She was profoundly relieved to see Grayson stroll in. The last person she wanted in her drawing room at this moment was Nicholas. Nicholas and his stepmama in the same room would not be a pretty sight.

Grayson nodded to Lady Mountjoy. "You are the parent of the two young men who should have had their arses kicked many times before the age of fourteen. Richard is a bully, but I'm betting soft-looking Lancelot is the more vicious of the two. But to give them credit, they did have the brains to return the young lady their men had mistakenly abducted. They scared her to death, but they didn't hurt her. By the way, ma'am, I am Grayson Sherbrooke."

"I am Lady Mountjoy, not this one here."

Grayson sketched her a brief bow. He was very relieved neither of his parents was here. From what he'd heard in the corridor, both his mother and his father would have rushed in and pounded this dreadful woman into the wainscoting.

"That is all a lie! My poor sweet Lancelot, vicious? Nonsense! Nor is he soft looking. His is a gentle soul, he harbors a poet's heart. Know this, Mr. Sherbrooke, my sons would never kidnap a young lady, even the wrong one."

Rosalind said, "Despite your belief in their innocence, ma'am, I would suggest you impress upon your sons that if anything happens to me, they will be dead."

Lady Mountjoy leapt to her feet, sending her empty teacup tumbling to the carpet. She waved her fist in Rosalind's face. "You are a liar and a hussy. My fine sons wouldn't touch you, they would scarce look at you unless they were forced to. You are a nasty bit of goods." After malevolent looks at both Rosalind and Grayson, Lady Mountjoy swept out of the drawing room. They heard Willicombe moving quickly to open the front door for the lady.

Grayson's eyebrow shot up a good inch. "She called you a liar. Now, that's all right because you are indeed an excellent liar. But a nasty bit of goods isn't at all accurate."

"I suppose she couldn't think of anything else to call me, poor woman, and so it popped out. Actually, she fired off insults at everyone. I also got the impression she wasn't too fond of her husband. And she also has a special friend, an Alfred Lemming.

"She knows all about my background, Grayson. I made it seem that everyone knew and who cared?"

"Poor woman, she picked the wrong target. Hmm, now that I think about it, you always have a light hand when there is unpleasantness to deter."

"Well, yes, I try. I suppose it's because when I first arrived at Brandon House I was terrified that if I yelled back at anyone, your father would kick me out. No, no, I know I was wrong, but still, I was very young and afraid. Imagine not knowing who you are, Grayson, no memories of anything at all." She shrugged. "I suppose a way of behaving begun at an early age sticks well."

"I didn't know that," Grayson said slowly. "I remember when Father first brought you home, he trembled with rage at what had been done to you, a child. And the pain in him that you would die. I remember Dr. Pomphrey and my parents spent hours at your bedside when your injuries brought on that horrible fever. I remember clearly how my father shouted to the rafters when he came running down the stairs to say you would live. Your father and mother weren't there loving you, Rosalind, but mine were. Never doubt that. Never forget that."

She felt tears sting her eyes and swallowed. "No, I won't. Thank you for telling me, Grayson. In any case, none of it matters now. A light hand was the best way to make her spit out nuggets as well as bile. I learned a lot from her."

"Everyone views you as a mystery, and it is ever so romantic how you came to be with us, even though it was actually quite awful since you could have so easily died. You're not a no-account, Rosalind. I daresay if someone happens to remark that you are, all you would have to do is sing for them and they would admire you endlessly."

"I did offer to sing for her, but she refused."

He laughed. "I wasn't joking. Your voice is magic."

"You used to think so when we were young," she said and he grinned at her, showing those beautiful white Sherbrooke teeth of his. "How is Lorelei today?"

To her astonishment, he merely shrugged, then pulled his watch out of his vest pocket and consulted it. "I suppose she is fine now. I'm off to my literary meeting. I'll see you later at the Branson ball." And he was gone before she could say a thing, such as, *In matters of the heart, Grayson, you are a blockhead.* What had poor Lorelei done?

23

That evening at the Branson ball, Nicholas gave Rosalind a brooding look after a particularly exciting waltz that left her dizzy with pleasure. She studied his face a moment, accepted a glass of champagne punch from a passing waiter, drank down a good half glass, and realized the problem. "Ah, I see, you somehow found out about your stepmama's visit to me this afternoon. I dealt with her, Nicholas, you needn't worry. Did you really kick Richard in the ribs with your foot? You really got your leg that high? Please, Nicholas, please teach me how to do that."

"Unfortunately you cannot do it because of all your petticoats."

"I can wear pants. Teach me, Nicholas, perhaps on our honeymoon. What do you think?"

He pictured her wearing a pair of his trousers and grinned. "We'll see." He stared down at her. "You should have told me she'd had the gall to insult you."

Rosalind only shrugged. "She didn't overly concern me. I must tell you, though, I had to open all the drawing room windows to air out the vitriol."

"She tried to warn you away from me, didn't she?"

"She certainly tried."

He laughed, marveling at her good humor. It pleased him, most of the time. He wondered if she would laugh when he took her to bed. He wouldn't mind her starting out with a laugh, but—since he'd never made love to a woman who was laughing at the same time—he didn't know. He took her glass and drank the rest of the punch. He shook his head. "Two glasses of this stuff and you would leap upon one of the tables and do a dance that would make my eyes cross."

She leaned up and whispered against his neck, "Would I dance slowly and take off each item of clothing?"

He pictured her quite clearly on a lovely table in the corner. "I'm thinking of all the ridiculous petticoats you wear, the silk stockings, and don't forget the corset and chemise. There is simply no way you could do it by yourself."

He gently placed his fingertips over her mouth. "I want you to be serious now. Listen to me; my dear stepmama is a bitch. She sows discontent and sees herself as sorely abused. I don't wish you to see her again."

Rosalind frowned at him. "How do you know this about her? You haven't seen her in twenty-odd years."

"She hated me when I was five years old, wanted me dead, but since that didn't happen, she wanted me gone. Why would she change? You have only to look at her sons." He couldn't believe he'd said that. "I have an excellent solicitor. I asked him to give me complete reports on all my relatives. He is right, isn't he?"

She snagged another glass of champagne off a waiter's tray, saying, "Do you know, I think she was there to convince me her beloved sons had nothing to do with Lorelei's kidnapping, meaning they were no threat to me. I think she is afraid you will kill Richard and Lancelot. She was trying to protect them. She simply doesn't have the talent to go about it smoothly, not like you would have done. Yes, you would be smooth, and you would be deadly."

"The only reason I didn't kill Richard this time was because he bungled the job so badly. However, if Richard and Lancelot ever attempt to touch you again, I will kill them."

"You told them that?"

"Oh, yes, one must be perfectly clear when dealing with villains, particularly young ones, because they lack sense, and experience in the pain of consequences." He eyed the glass that was tilted to her mouth.

"Am I wedding a tippler, Rosalind?"

She grinned at him. "Perhaps once you rid me of my ignorance of wickedness, I will forgo this tasty stuff that makes my head all light, and makes unexpected words pop out of my mouth. Perhaps, my lord, you will ensure that I have no need of it."

He took the glass from her and set it on a table. He didn't want to dance with her, he wanted to fling her over his shoulder and run down the stone steps that led into the deep-shadowed gardens. He said, "Waltz with me."

She grinned up at him as he led her to the dance floor. "I read I was to marry you in the *Gazette* this morning."

"Yes, you are well and fairly caught." He sounded inordinately pleased with himself. Since she was very pleased with him too, she didn't remark upon it.

When later she danced with Uncle Ryder, he said, "Dearest, Willicombe told me about Lady Mountjoy's visit to you this afternoon. He also told me you handled the old bat very well."

"I thought he was eavesdropping."

"We have a long line of successful eaves-droppers in the Sherbrooke family. Willi-combe is one of the leading lights. Just as Sinjun passed it down to Meggie, I believe Hollis passed it to Willicombe. Hmm, do you eavesdrop well, Rosalind?"

"Oh, yes, very well. Don't you remember, Uncle Ryder? If there was anything you ever wished to know about what was going on at Brandon House, what Jane was feeling at any particular moment, you asked me. If I didn't know it, I knew which door to listen at to find out what you wanted to know."

Ryder laughed and swung her around the floor. Nicholas looked up from his conversation with Grayson, just arrived at the ball, at the sound of her bright laughter.

Grayson said, "Her laugh is nearly as magic as her voice. I imagine my father is questioning her about your stepmother's visit."

"And she will tell him everything?"

"Oh, no. She will pick and choose. She's quite good at it. Since she loves my father, she has no wish to overly distress him. Don't get me wrong, if a problem grabs her by the heels, she'll always go to my father or mother for advice. Come to think of it, I suppose I tend to trust both of them myself."

Nicholas said without thinking, "I've wondered what that would be like, having a father and mother one loved and admired and trusted."

"Oh, yes, and it is a pity you did not, but you had your grandfather."

"Yes—I did have my grandfather, didn't I? Ah, I see Miss Kilbourne on the other side of the room and she is waving at you. You never told me how your reading went at her literary salon."

"My head was nearly so big by the time I left, it was a good thing I was riding King because I couldn't have stuffed my head through a carriage door."

"Worshipped to the point of nausea?"

Grayson nodded. He was studiously avoiding looking at Lorelei. As a young lady, she could not detach herself from her mother and come to him. He said, "I read your announcement in the newspaper this morning. Well done. Now, I believe I shall ask Alice Grand to waltz," and he strolled off.

Nicholas was pleased with the wedding announcement he'd written; it had been effective. He'd been congratulated a good three dozen times since he'd arrived at the Branson town house. Soon she would be his wife and—and then what?

Nicholas normally did not meddle, but when he chanced to look at Lorelei Kilbourne again, he saw she was staring piteously at Grayson waltzing with Alice Grand, a buxom young lady with a ready laugh and a heavy wit that could fell an ox. He found himself walking to Lady Ramey, and asking her if he could have the pleasure.

Some five minutes later, after laborious conversation with Lady Ramey, the orchestra started up another waltz and he led Lorelei to the dance floor.

She was a good dancer, fitting to his style with ease and grace. He looked down at her, saw the misery in her eyes, knew to his boots that he should keep his mouth shut, and said, "What happened?"

She said without hesitation, "I don't know. Do you know?"

"Only that something is amiss, at least from Grayson's point of view."

"Would you find out what, my lord? I haven't much experience with gentlemen and find I'm at a loss to explain what is wrong with him."

Such an innocent, Nicholas thought, charming and quite pretty, really. He saw tears pooling in her eyes. What was a poor man to do? He cursed to himself and gave up. "I will try to find out, Miss Kilbourne."

Her soft mouth firmed. "Since I was kidnapped in the place of your damned betrothed, you could call me Lorelei, you know."

A touch of vinegar, he thought, and was pleased. He nodded. "Lorelei."

* * *

Nicholas knew he shouldn't interfere, only a fool interfered between a man and a woman, but yet, here he was wending his way through the gloomy exhibit halls of the British Museum in search of Grayson. He finally found him bending over a glass case, a look of near reverence on his face.

"What is it?"

Grayson jerked up, blinked in surprise, and motioned him over. "Look at this, Nicholas. The card claims it is the scepter used by a long-ago king of Persia."

Nicholas studied the ancient gold scepter, noted the empty holes on its hilt where precious gems had once been embedded. "It says it is from the time of King Darius. Do you think it was his?"

"No. It belonged to someone of greater magnitude—I think it belonged to a wizard. Cannot you feel the power of it, the magic—sort of like a vibration deep in your gut?"

Nicholas automatically shook his head. There was no way he would admit to such things as vibrations, but the damned thing seemed to glow and pulse in its ill-polished glass case. He could very nearly feel it, warm in his hand. "How long has it been here?"

"I don't know. I discovered it last week and find that I keep coming back to it. Even the director doesn't know exactly when it arrived here and who brought it. He checked and told me there weren't any records. Now, isn't that strange? It's as if it suddenly appeared. What are you doing here, Nicholas?"

"You are ignoring Lorelei because you're afraid she could be hurt again."

Grayson Sherbrooke stared at the big man who was two inches taller than he, built like his uncle Douglas and his cousins, James and Jason. And he had the look of Uncle Douglas, dark and swarthy and dangerous, at least until he smiled. It didn't occur to Grayson to tell him to mind his own business. He said simply, "I promised her father I would not see her again. He told me he would be very happy if I weren't to tell Lorelei why, and I haven't, but there you have it. You guessed it immediately."

"I am many things, but not blind. To be honest, I am very surprised Lorelei hasn't figured it out as well."

"She is innocent. However, I agree with Lord Ramey because I don't want to have to worry about her. Once all this is resolved, then we will see."

"You know, from Lorelei's description of the crest she saw on the carriage door, I knew it belonged to my father, and now to my half brothers, so I had my proof. I spoke to Richard."

"I heard you smashed your foot into his middle, chopped his neck, fighting moves he'd never seen before. Well done. Too bad you didn't kill the blighter."

"If he or Lancelot ever tries anything else, they know I will kill them. I don't believe they're that stupid. They won't do anything more. Should you like me to speak to Lord Ramey? Assure him there is no more danger to his daughter?"

Grayson looked away from him, down at the scepter again. "You are remarkably naive, Nicholas, given your experiences of the last dozen or so years. I met Richard and Lancelot Vail, remember? At Drury Lane. The danger is not over. They will not stop. It simply isn't in their nature. Richard was raised to believe himself the rightful Earl of Mountjoy. I heard one of my friends say Richard even used the title Viscount Ashborough once your father became the earl. He did not, however, ever call himself the Earl of Mountjoy upon your father's death. He couldn't go that far. Probably because he knew he'd be laughed at.

"As for Lancelot, I believe his innate

viciousness provides sufficient motive to kill you. He's more dangerous than his brother."

"Perhaps," Nicholas said after a moment, "if this scepter did belong to a powerful wizard, he visited the Pale."

"It is certainly possible," Grayson said. "I've thought it odd how the Pale appears like another world, or in another dimension, and we are the ones beyond the pale."

"Beyond the pale," Nicholas repeated slowly, "beyond the fortress, the designated safe place, the sanctuary where all is civilized, and to be outside of it means danger, savagery, and death."

Grayson nodded. "But Sarimund's Pale isn't a civilized place at all. Tibers try to kill the red Lasis, and the Dragons kill whatever animal displeases them. As for the wizards on Mount Olyvan, they reside within the Pale, keep a balance of sorts, and yet there is no safety there. It is a place of violence and magic. It is all very strange."

Nicholas said. "Perhaps you are right, Grayson, perhaps the Pale is a metaphor, for the earth perhaps, where chaos reigns given the least opportunity and where men kill each other with keen abandon." They were silent a moment. Nicholas laid his hand on

Grayson's arm. "Believe this, Grayson, if Richard and Lancelot try to do anything more, I will kill them. They know this and they believe me."

"Not if I kill them first," Grayson said, his voice utterly emotionless.

Nicholas nodded and left Grayson to stare once again at the scepter in the glass case.

As for Nicholas, he was shaking his head at Grayson's words. He was naive? Grayson was wrong in this. He'd dealt with countless villains. He suddenly saw Richard Vail's face in his mind's eye, a face filled with black malice, unspoken rage, the satisfying physical pain that Nicholas had inflicted on him, and something more—it was determination; a promise of violence? Revenge? Retribution? As for Lancelot, Nicholas believed that since he'd met the pretty butler at the Vail town house he now understood Lancelot very well.

He cursed, then turned to call to the young boy holding Clyde's reins. Clyde nickered when he saw him, then butted the boy's arm. The boy's face split into a big grin, showing a space between his two front teeth. "Oh, my, guv, wot splendid words I 'eard ye string together. This 'ere big boy sure likes the sugar cubes ye left for 'im. I gives 'im jest one at a time, so's not to overload 'is belly. Aye, me and the big bad boy understands each other."

Nicholas was thoughtful as he rode through Russell Square and slowly made his way through heavy traffic toward Fleet Street, where his solicitor kept his sparse offices. When he pulled Clyde sharply to the side to avoid a dray filled with beer kegs, and felt the stinging slap of hot air against his cheek as the bullet flew by, he thought, *Hell, Grayson was right.*

24

"I tell you I'm not a murderer! I did not try to shoot you nor did I hire anyone." Suddenly Richard's angry flush died. He gave Nicholas a superior sneer as he flicked a piece of lint off his coat sleeve. "Believe me, if I'd wanted you dead, dear brother, I would do it myself."

Nicholas couldn't say why, but he simply knew in his gut that Richard was telling the truth. This time. It both galled him and worried him. There were so many unknowns plaguing him right now, he hated adding another. "Where is Lancelot?"

"What? Now you believe my younger brother tried to kill you? Well, he didn't. He's visiting a friend near Folkestone, left early this morning."

Now that could be a meaty lie. "Give me Lancelot's destination and his friend's name."

Richard Vail gave it, his sneer intensifying. "It seems to me you have more enemies than a man should have. You've only been in England, what, two months?"

"About that, yes," Nicholas said as he jotted the information into the small book he carried in his vest pocket. He looked at his half brother. "I didn't see your pretty young butler at the front door."

Richard shrugged. "He is also Lance's valet. I believe he accompanied him to Folkestone."

There was a rush of silks at the drawing room door and a strident voice boomed out. "What are you doing here? You leave him alone, you no-account barbarian!"

Nicholas turned to see a plump little woman, beautifully gowned in violet, every uncovered inch of her sporting jewels, actually run into the drawing room, her fist waving at him. He recognized her voice and her eyes, eyes both uncompromising and hard, eyes that had scared him to death when he'd been five years old. However, he wasn't a small boy anymore.

On her heels was a fat gentleman, barely two inches taller than she was. Nicholas had seen him gambling at White's a couple of times. Was this his dear stepmama's lover, Alfred Lemming, whom Rosalind had mentioned to him?

He waited until she was very close before he arched a black brow and said mildly, "I believed only my betrothed was a no-account."

"She is, more no-account than you are, sir. At least your antecedents are known, more's the pity. What are you doing here? Don't you dare try to murder my son again!"

"Someone tried to kill him," Richard said to his mother. "A gun shot right past his ear. A pity whoever it was did not succeed. I told him I had nothing at all to do with it. I was at my club, my friends will vouch for that. So now he is questioning me about Lance."

"You were nearly shot?" said Lady Mountjoy, blatant disappointment in those hard eyes of hers. She looked him up and down.

"So you are Nicholas Vail. You look even more like the old earl than you do your father, and those two were nearly twins."

"I suppose you must also say that about Richard," Nicholas said.

"Perhaps. I told that impertinent girl you wish to wed that you would likely pass on your grandfather's insanity, but it was for naught. The chit exhibited no understanding of the human brain." Miranda, Lady Mountjoy, looked from him to Richard and back again, and frowned. They were even dressed similarly this morning, and everyone in the drawing room knew they looked clearly like brothers, unlike her precious Lancelot.

"Tell me, ma'am, where is my third half brother, Aubrey?"

"Ah, so now you think he's a murderer? Well, Aubrey isn't in London," Lady Mountjoy said, and sighed. "He is at Oxford. Aubrey is a scholar, if you must know, studious from his earliest years, always surrounded by his books."

Richard said, "Aubrey wouldn't know which end of a gun to use, so forget about him."

Miranda thought about the thick violent

red hair that covered his scholar's head—Aubrey's hair was almost the exact color of that little hussy who would take precedence over her if she indeed married Nicholas, and that was surely a revolting prospect.

Miranda pictured Aubrey in her mind. How she hated that his shoulders were stooped, that he had to wear glasses because he'd surely read every book at Oxford. Ah, how she'd begged him to let Richard take him to his private boxing salon, straighten his back, get his chin to go up, to show pride in his heritage, perhaps give him a dollop of aggression. How could a man stand up for himself if his shoulders were round as a bowl? His father hadn't been any help, he'd simply clouted the boy whenever he chanced to say something clever or quote from an ancient Greek philosopher. Ah, but she wasn't about to tell this interloper any of that.

As for Lancelot—at least he shot well, enjoyed hunting and riding. Even though he comported himself like a romantic poet, his shoulders were straight. Even though there wasn't much hair on his face for that valet of his to shave, he could still sneer as well as Richard.

And now here was Nicholas standing in the drawing room, her drawing room, big and fit and hard, just like her precious Richard, but there was something more in his dark eyes, something that bespoke experiences and fantastic adventures and something else—and what was that? Pain, black and deep?—no, she wouldn't think about his life after his grandfather died. After hearing nothing from him for years, they'd believed him dead, and in her heart, she'd rejoiced at the justice of it and swelled with pride when she looked at Richard.

Only Nicholas wasn't dead. He was alive and looming, ready to kill her boys. "You could have died when you were a boy," she said, "so why didn't you?" Miranda was aware that Richard was staring at her and she shut her mouth.

"I am like a tough strip of leather, ma'am, although"—he looked her up and down—"perhaps I am not as tough a piece of leather as you are."

"See here," Richard said, taking a step forward.

"No, dear," said Miranda, halting him. "So someone tried to put a period to you—well, you can forget about any of my sons."

"No," Nicholas said, "I don't think it was Richard. We'll have to see about Lancelot, won't we?"

"See here, my name is Lance, damn you!"

"Lancelot—" Nicholas rolled the name around on his tongue as he turned to see his half brother, the sunken-chested, pallid butler standing just behind him.

"Lance! My precious boy, what are you doing back in London? Richard told us you were visiting a friend in Folkestone."

Lancelot shrugged. "We had a wheel break on the carriage. No choice but to come back. So what? What is he doing here?"

"So you might easily have been the one to try to put a bullet through my brain this morning," Nicholas said, a blast of cold in his voice, wondering how long it would take him to strangle this supercilious little sot, and enjoy every second of it.

"Nonsense," Lancelot said, and frowned at a tiny speck of dirt on his burgundy velvet jacket. "I am an excellent shot. If I had been in London, if I had shot at you, you'd be lying dead on your damned back."

"You're not as good a shot as I am," the butler suddenly said. "Don't you remember our competition? And Master Richard is the best of all of us."

The butler was very free in his speech with his employers, Nicholas thought, and watched his stepmother gape at him. Nicholas asked, "What is your name?"

"I? I am called David Smythe-Jones."

Nicholas couldn't help himself, he laughed. "Davy Jones? Your parents are seafaring people then, with strong ties to irony?"

"No, they believe in treasure, trapped in long-ago sunken Spanish galleons, lying deep in the sea. However, since they live in Liverpool and haven't a groat to go searching for their prize, it isn't likely they will ever find it. Still my mother spends her life searching out old treasure maps and making plans."

Nicholas studied the young man, his petulant mouth, his nervous hands always moving. Then he looked at his two half brothers. So very different they were. And here, of all things, the third half brother, Aubrey, was a scholar. He wondered what his sire had thought about what his seed had produced. He raised his hand to get their attention. "No more bickering, no more insults, no more protestations of innocence. Including you, sir," he added to Alfred Lemming, who was standing on his tiptoes, ready to leap. "All of you will listen to me now. I am Lord Mountjoy, the Earl of Mountjoy. None of you will ever take that title. My son will follow me and his son will follow him down through future generations. If your mother taught you this was really your birthright, and not mine, if she taught you that you were the rightful heirs, then she did you a grave disservice.

"I will say this only once. If anything happens to me, I have several close friends who will avenge me." He turned to face Richard. "If I die, you will die, and Lancelot will die. Given my friends' rage were I to be murdered, I doubt Aubrey would survive either. Then there will be no Vails, the line will be dead as all of us. Do all of you understand me?"

Lady Mountjoy yelled, shaking her fist at him, "You're utterly mad! You are so mad you threaten my sweet boys who have never harmed you."

"Attend her, my lord, for that is the truth!"

Alfred Lemming bellowed, his face now alarmingly red.

Nicholas sketched his stepmother a brief bow. "I will see that you are not killed, ma'am. I would want you and your fat lover to continue on; perhaps eventually you would feel despair that you taught them to hate me, taught them I was an enemy to be destroyed, rather than their brother whose responsibility it would be to protect them, to be at their backs, perhaps even to assist them. In the end, madam, you would realize you were surrounded by nothing at all."

There was stone silence for a moment before Alfred Lemming stepped forward on small well-shod feet and said, barely above a whisper, "I say, my lord, you should not make such a blanket statement as that." His very white brow was damp with perspiration, but he persevered. "Despite the venom and threats floating around the drawing room, it is no excuse for bad manners. I am Lord Heissen and I will personally vouch for the young gentlemen. That is the point, my lord. They are gentlemen, not hooligans. You have come from heathen places, doubtless tracked by heathen enemies with no sense of what is suitable in a civilized world. No English gentleman would fire a gun in the midst of traffic—to possibly be seen and identified. It is absurd that you would be suspicious of these fine upstanding boys."

Nicholas eyed the very dapper Alfred Lemming, Lord Heissen, whose white hands were as plump and beringed as his stepmother's. "I am pleased to hear your opinion, my lord. Since you appear to be slithering about in this pit of vipers, I have decided to add you to the list. If I die, this entire drawing room will be cleaned out, save for my venomous stepmother. I bid you good-bye. Oh, yes, madam, stay away from my betrothed."

"Betrothed! It is not to be borne. Why, I—"

Nicholas took a step toward her at the same time one of Alfred Lemming's white hands gently pressed down over her mouth. Nicholas nodded at him, noted that despite its apparent softness, that hand of his looked, surprisingly, very strong. Nicholas said, "Keep it there, my lord, for her own safety."

When he passed by David Smythe-Jones, he said, "You really should consider a new name."

"What? It is a noble name, it is a name

that carries countless unspoken tales of bravery and adventure."

"How long have you been employed here as the butler?"

The soft, white chin went straight up. "I took care of Master Lance at Oxford. I was ready to assume greater duties in London. I am now in charge of this magnificent house. All look to me to resolve difficulties, to train the tweeny, to ensure Master Lance's cravats are white as a virgin's spit, and well folded. I am perfection and that is what I demand from all the servants."

Nicholas had a sudden memory of actually smelling the rot eating away at the books in the library just down the corridor. It was odd for a five-year-old boy to remember that. He looked over the young man's head at Lancelot. "See that you keep your butler in line," he said, and he paused in the doorway, looked at each of them, his expression pensive. Then he left the town house, seeing their stony faces in his mind's eye. As he took the front steps, he heard his stepmother yell, "Why did you even let him in, Smythe-Jones? That is not perfection, that is serious bungling. What sort of butler are you?"

"But I wasn't even here! Master Lance

and I were still at least a mile away when he shoved his way in. Had I been here, he would have walked on my face. I didn't have my gun so I couldn't have shot him. He is dangerous, that big fellow."

Big fellow? Clyde nickered. Nicholas smiled.

25

An hour later, Nicholas was closeted with Ryder Sherbrooke. Thankfully the Earl of Northcliffe had escorted the wives and Rosalind to Madame Fouquet's. It was a vast relief because Nicholas knew Rosalind would realize something was wrong, and then the three of them would hold him down and question him until he spurted out everything he knew or imagined he knew. And then they would all throw their opinions into the ring and it would be chaos. Rosalind, he thought, something of a fatuous smile on his mouth, would have gotten a gun and gone off to murder the lot of the half brothers. And his stepmother as well, he imagined.

He said now to Ryder, "One of them is behind the attempt on my life, I simply cannot prove which one it was and so I threatened all of them. Funny thing is, I do have friends who would gladly avenge me. If I leave word, as I most assuredly will, all that pernicious family would be wiped out were I to die.

"However, since I do not believe them stupid, perhaps that is the end to it." He paused a moment, looking toward the empty fireplace grate. "Still, I cannot be certain. Fact is, I don't know what to do, sir."

Ryder paced the beautiful Aubusson carpet in the library, a splendid room filled with five thousand books covering three walls, floor to ceiling. Ryder remembered his father gently cutting each of the pages, handling all the books with incredible gentleness, placing them carefully on the shelves. "The world is in this room, Ryder," he'd told him.

After the silence stretched long, Nicholas said, defeat leaching out all emotion in his voice, "I will leave right this moment and never return if you believe it the thing to do."

Ryder looked down at a massive globe, spun it slowly, watched England appear, then quickly disappear. So small, he thought, England was so very small, insignificant really, in terms of the size of the earth, but still— He said finally, looking over at the young man, "I want to agree with you, Nicholas, I really do, but I cannot. Actually, you will add me to the list of your avengers.

"But I do not believe murder will be done. We will take steps to ensure it does not. Now, I know Rosalind wants you for her husband. I know that Rosalind being what she is, being made how she is, being as loyal as she is, she would doubtless follow you back to Macau if you tried to leave her. Thus, I don't believe I have any choice in how to proceed."

Ryder rubbed his forehead, cursed low and fluent. "You and Rosalind must wed immediately and leave London. What do you think of Wyverly Chase? I know you spent time there before you came to London."

"Yes, nearly a month there, putting repairs into motion, so many needed since my father left that beautiful old estate to rot. As for all the tenant farmers, they were in dreadful straits, but that is being corrected as well. I have an excellent estate manager there to oversee repairs."

"I trust you have sufficient funds to see to all of it?"

"Yes, of course. The penniless boy who left England at the age of twelve made good, sir, as the vernacular goes. You wonder if Wyverly Chase is a good sanctuary. That is what you mean, isn't it, sir? You want Rosalind safe while I sort all this out."

"Yes. Do you think you and Rosalind will be safe there or should you simply leave the country for a time?"

Nicholas marveled at the decency of this man, his logical brain, and the fact that, when it came down to the meat of the matter, he was doing what Nicholas wished him to do. Nicholas wondered if Rosalind would really follow him to Macau. He said slowly, "Wyverly Chase is set atop a lovely hill with open views all around. There is a thick pine and maple forest that ends a good one hundred yards from the house.

"As I said, I have an excellent estate manager, Peter Pritchard, the son of my grandfather's man. I have already hired servants, all local, which bodes well for loyalty to me. The tenant farmers are very pleased with me, as

is the town of Wyverly-on-Arden since I've
ordered most all our supplies from the local
merchants. I honestly believe both of us will
be safe there until I am able to find out who
is behind this."

"You don't wish to take Rosalind on a honeymoon?"

"Not yet, sir. There would be too many
risks to her safety. Let her settle into Wyverly
first, see what she thinks of the place."

Ryder eyed him a moment. "I hate to tell
you this, but it wouldn't matter if Wyverly
were a grand palace, she would still redeco-
rate it. She will doubtless redesign and
replant the gardens, she will add peacocks,
and heaven knows the racket they make."

Nicholas's left eyebrow shot up.

"It's in her blood, she says, whatever
blood that is. She was always trying to
change Brandon House, and when Jane
refused, Rosalind brought herself to our
house and made immediate plans to change
the draperies in my estate room as well as
rearrange all my furniture." He grinned. "She
has no taste in clothes, but show her a room
and she will make it glorious very quickly
indeed. But first—I strongly suggest that this
wedding take place as quickly as possible.

Hmm, it's Thursday. How about Saturday? Do you think it sufficient time?"

Nicholas nodded. "I shall visit Bishop Dundridge to procure a special license. I know Rosalind is having her final fitting today with the earl and his wife and yours."

Ryder nodded. "I will meet with Willicombe and Cook to see that all is in order for Saturday morning." He paused a moment, then nodded to himself. "We shall invite all your relatives, Nicholas." He quickly raised his hand. "No, this is important. Trust me on this."

"They won't come."

"You are the head of the family. Society would not look kindly upon them if they refused to attend your wedding. And trust me, society will know if they come since I will ensure that all know."

"But—"

"No, it must be done. Your half brothers and your stepmother must see that it is done, it is over. Douglas and I will be there. It will be all right."

Nicholas left the Sherbrooke town house feeling a bit light-headed. He paid a visit to Sir Robert Peel on Bow Street, then returned to Grillon's Hotel to inform Lee Po of the new plans.

Lee Po raised a thin black brow that was already arched high, sending it nearly into his hair, and said in perfect English, "And I had thought to be bored in this frigid rain-soaked country. But instead, you and your betrothed are both in mortal danger, not to mention the magic and mystery of this Pale place—what an excellent diversion, my lord. You can be sure I shall be on my guard. None of the three half-wit brothers will harm you when I am about."

Nicholas laughed. "Thank you. Now, there is much to be done." Then he told Lee Po about the two men Sir Robert Peel was sending to him.

*　*　*

Rosalind found out quite by accident about the attempt on Nicholas's life. She had raised her hand to knock on the estate room door, when she heard Uncle Ryder's low voice and pressed her ear to the door. Uncle Ryder was telling Uncle Douglas about someone firing a gun at Nicholas.

"You fleabrain," she whispered to the absent Nicholas. "You will learn to confide in me if I have to box your ears." But since the debacle was the catalyst for their quick marriage, and that was surely very fine, she kept her peace. She had years in front of her to bring Nicholas around to trusting her absolutely. Given his unfortunate childhood, not to mention the villains he'd surely had to deal with since he was twelve, she knew it would be small of her not to accept his silence, but still, it hurt. What hurt too, but angered her more, was the attempt on his life. She wished she had Richard Vail's neck between her hands.

It was Grayson, told by his father that Rosalind had very likely eavesdropped when he told Uncle Douglas about the murder attempt, who warned Nicholas to stay away. Grayson told him, "Otherwise, she might call it all off and shoot you herself. She's a fine shot, my word on that, so don't take any chances. My father fed her some drivel about a problem at Wyverly Chase and that was why you needed to have the wedding moved to Saturday. Rosalind pretended to believe him, though I know very well she didn't. Truth be told, I don't know what she's thinking right now, she's been very quiet, perhaps too quiet."

Nicholas said, "I would wager every groat in my pocket she's planning something."

Grayson agreed, told him to keep his distance, and wished him the best of luck.

Nicholas called after him, "Please invite Lorelei Kilbourne, Grayson. Both Rosalind and I are very fond of her. Since she suffered for Rosalind, it's only right she be invited."

Grayson said stiffly, "I will consult her father."

"Ask her parents to come as well," Nicholas said.

"And her four sisters?"

"Naturally."

Nicholas laughed when Grayson muttered, "The giggling gaggle."

26

At ten o'clock Saturday morning, Rosalind was modestly accepting all the fulsome compliments, knowing she looked very fine indeed in Madame Fouquet's pale yellow silk gown, but she wasn't thinking about this, her wedding day, she was thinking about Nicholas's half brothers, how they should be dispatched to Hell.

And they were coming to her wedding.

Perhaps she should carry a small knife. And what about their mother, Lady Mountjoy, probably escorted by Alfred Lemming? Perhaps Rosalind should carry a knife up her other sleeve as well. She wondered idly how long Alfred Lemming had been Lady Mount-joy's lover. Before her husband had died? She wondered about the third son, Aubrey. For all she knew, he could be devout as a vicar, or as rotten as his brothers.

"Just look at this lovely nightgown and peignoir Alex has given you, dearest," Aunt Sophie was saying. "Ah, I venture to say your groom's eyes will roll back in his head when he sees you in it."

"Peach silk," Alex said, "it makes a man's heels drum. The silk is as sheer as your veil, Rosalind."

Rosalind saw herself standing in front of Nicholas wearing this delicious, sinful confection, and Nicholas, eyes blazing hot, striding to her, those big hands of his outstretched to touch her. She saw his big hands molding over the silk and—

Sophie said, "Ah, dearest, I only wish you could have been married at Brandon House. How the children would have loved that. They always accepted you, Rosalind, just as they always knew you were different."

She hugged Aunt Sophie close. "Let us have another wedding for them, all right?

Perhaps in a few months. I have already bought them all presents here in London—I will save them until Nicholas and I come to Brandon House. Ah, how I wish Nicholas were not constrained to return to his home so very quickly. I cannot imagine what has happened to necessitate this terrific rush. Do you know?"

Alex and Sophie had no clue Rosalind was lying through her teeth, since she had perfected the necessary lie very early on. "No," Alex said, demure as a nun, "we have no idea what happened." She gave Rosalind a fat smile and hoped Nicholas came up with some plausible catastrophe before they arrived at his family home. "Nicholas told me Wyverly Chase was named after an heiress in the sixteenth century who filled the family coffers and paid for the house—Catherine Wyverly, a duke's daughter. Nicholas told us her ghost roams about the vast corridors of the east wing, though he admitted he'd never seen her."

"Now, dearest"—Sophie patted the sheer material that sheathed Rosalind's arms—"forget about the ghost, I understand Douglas has declared your groom sufficiently blessed with good taste to clothe you properly. Ah, how very wonderful it all is. I am so excited." And Sophie wiped away a tear she'd managed to manufacture to distract Rosalind.

Alex said, "How quickly the past ten years have flown by. I remember so clearly the day you first sang for us, Rosalind, that strange song in its sad minor key, so hauntingly lovely it was.

"Now, don't forget, dearest, to savor the present since the future is always lurking right around the corner to grab you by the throat."

"I won't forget, Aunt Alex." She loved them both, knew they were trying to protect her, and evidently that meant to everyone in this blasted house to keep her in ignorance. She wanted to tell them she didn't need protecting, what she needed was to know everything so she could devise strategies to keep both her and Nicholas safe. Perhaps she could even figure out herself who was responsible for this misery. Truth be told, she believed Nicholas needed more protecting than she did. Well, she would see to it.

Sophie consulted the ormolu clock on the mantel. "It's time to go downstairs, dearest. It is but four minutes until ten o'clock, and you know how Bishop Dundridge believes in the power of time. He is probably already tapping his foot, frowning at his watch hands, worried that you or Nicholas will bolt."

Rosalind tried her best to float down the wide staircase since Nicholas was standing at the bottom, dressed in black, his linen white as his teeth, so very strong and fit, that jaw of his hard and stubborn, looking up at her, no smile whatsoever on his face. He looked stern, like a Puritan minister ready to blast his sinful flock. In that instant, she didn't want to do this. She didn't know this dangerous man, she— He watched her very slowly raise her gloved hand to lay it on his forearm. He said nothing, nor did she. He led her into the drawing room filled with white roses and the scent of vanilla.

Bishop Dundridge placed his watch with its shiny silver chain back into his pocket, and hummed. Then he smiled at the pair, looked back briefly at the assorted people in the drawing room, all of whom he knew. They clustered in two separate groups, neither group speaking to the other save in the stiffest of voices. He looked at the Countess of Northcliffe, acknowledging to himself, but only to himself, that he'd admired her immensely for a good twenty years now. He wanted to sigh as he stared at her, but he wasn't that stupid. He watched Mrs. Ryder Sherbrooke, who, along with the countess, had followed the bride and groom into the drawing room. She walked to stand by her husband, a lovely smile on her face. He looked toward the four younger girls who crowded together around a very lovely young lady who was in turn staring at Grayson Sherbrooke, who stood alone by the fireplace, arms crossed over his chest, looking remote. Now what was all this about? A very protective father hovered over the flock of ladies, eyeing the earl's three half brothers in the other group with ill-disguised loathing. The two looked as if they would rather shoot arrows into the groom, like the sainted and martyred Saint Sebastian, than celebrate his nuptials. And the mother, Lady Mountjoy—he found himself staring at the two bright circles of rouge painted on her cheeks.

Bishop Dundridge suddenly realized the bride looked ready to run. As for the groom, he looked as determined as Wellington at Waterloo. Well, no matter what the undercurrents swirling about the drawing room, it was time to marry these two beautiful young people who would doubtless produce beautiful children.

Bishop Dundridge married them in four and a half minutes.

"My lord," he announced in his deep plummy voice, "you may now kiss your bride," and he beamed at them. Both had said their vows in clear voices. He heard some muttering from one of the half brothers, but ignored it.

They were married, Nicholas thought, a bit stunned, and he very slowly raised Rosalind's veil. Her face was pale, her eyes slightly dilated. "It will be all right now," he said low, for both of them. "Let me kiss you." And he did, only a light touch of his mouth against hers. She made no move whatsoever, kept her eyes open and staring up at him. He would swear he heard her gulp.

When he raised his head, he lightly touched his knuckles to her cheek. "I like the smell of vanilla."

As if the spell were broken, she grinned up at him. "It was my idea."

"I knew you would be a very smart wife.

Now, let's see if that unpleasant group of carrion over there will deign to congratulate us."

Nicholas hated to admit it, but Ryder Sherbrooke was right. It was good his family was here. They now knew it was done. Perhaps they could get past their murderous hatred of him. Perhaps his half brothers would realize now that the money they'd inherited from their father was quite sufficient for any sane man. Richard managed to spit out a meager congratulations. Lancelot looked straight ahead. A male throat cleared. Richard frowned, but was forced to introduce Rosalind to the third brother, Aubrey Vail. Nicholas was struck at how similar his youngest half brother looked to his wife—like brother and sister, what with the nearly identical shade of red hair, Aubrey's nearly as thick and curly as Rosalind's. His eyes were blue, nearly as rich a blue as hers. It was as if the lid had come off the boiling pot—Aubrey began talking. He never stopped, a good thing since he drowned out the rest of his family's deadening silence.

"I am writing a book," he announced as he sat himself at Rosalind's right at the breakfast table, paying not a bit of attention to where his hostess wished him to be seated. "Ah, what a splendid feast this is. At Oxford, we are fed well, but nothing like this," and he picked up his newly poured glass of champagne and drank it down. "Should I have waited for a toast? Ah, well, no problem." And he motioned for a footman to refill his glass.

Rosalind, buffeted by his endless and entertaining monologue, said, "You don't hate your half brother? You don't wish to murder him?"

Aubrey drank down the second glass, gently belched, and carefully placed his champagne flute at an exact thirty-degree angle to his plate. "Murder Nicholas? Why, I don't even know Nicholas. He looks like Richard, doesn't he? Really, a remarkable resemblance. Let me tell you about the book I am writing."

"In a moment, Aubrey," Nicholas said easily. "I believe Rosalind's uncle wishes to make a toast."

"He is not her bloody uncle," Lancelot said in a low voice, but not low enough.

"Ah, I have need of more champagne," Aubrey said, covering his brother's words, and he held up his flute. He beamed at Rosalind. "You are quite beautiful, Rosalind. If I were not too young to wed, I would have thrown my hat at your feet. However, as a girl, you are the perfect age, the accepted age. Odd, isn't it? I have always believed our English mores more baffling than not."

Uncle Douglas said, smiling, "I rather think it is the fact that boys mature more slowly than girls, thus they must have more time to season."

Aubrey said with a considering frown, "I believe I'm already well seasoned. Lance, now, he must needs have another decade so he may attempt to grow some hair on his chin." Aubrey toasted his brother and laughed, ignoring the black look he got.

Ryder Sherbrooke tapped his champagne flute with his knife. He rose to his feet, raised his glass, and smiled toward Rosalind. "Rosalind is the daughter of my heart. When she and Nicholas have children, I hope they will call me grandfather. I foresee that they will never bore each other. They each make the other laugh, you see, and that is a very fine thing." And he saluted them.

"Hear, hear," Douglas called out.

"A grandmother," Sophie said, "I should like being a grandmother."

Finally, because Bishop Dundridge was seated next to Lady Mountjoy, and she saw she had little choice, she said behind her teeth, "Hear, hear." Richard and Lancelot, Nicholas's eyes on them, echoed their mother.

"Just think," Aubrey announced to the table at large, "when you have children, I shall become an uncle." He beamed a big smile to show a mouthful of very white teeth. "Here's to me, the future uncle."

There was laughter this time, not from the Vails, to be sure, but Sophie Sherbrooke, in particular, was looking at this redheaded young gentleman with approval. She said, "I heard you telling Rosalind that you are writing a book, Mr. Vail. What is it about?"

Over the magnificent breakfast feast featuring Cook's famous crimped cod and oyster sauce—delicious with the kippers and the mountain of scrambled eggs as yellow as the dining room walls—Aubrey said, "The book I am writing deals with the ancient Druids." And he said no more, simply began forking up eggs as if he hadn't eaten in a week.

Grayson called out, "Is it a story or a history?"

"I have not made up my mind as of yet," Aubrey said, "but I will tell you that the Druids' use of mistletoe to heal was an excellent thing, and yet our Christian church ignored mistletoe's natural curative powers and turned it into a kissing ball—bah!—and all to collect a few more pagan souls into the Christian basket." His mouth was full now of a scone, some crumbs falling off his chin. He dabbed them up with the tip of his finger wet in his own mouth, and grinned around the table. "I forget to eat at Oxford." Nothing more, and there was more laughter, and again, none of it from the Vails.

The Earl of Northcliffe had gladly relinquished his place to Nicholas since he wished to keep a close eye on the Vails. Who knew if Miranda, now the Dowager Countess of Mountjoy, carried a vial of poison in her reticule? He took his wife's soft hand and kissed it. "All is going very well. What do you think of the third Vail brother?"

"His hair is as red as Rosalind's and as—"

"No, not yours, dearest. Your hair is unique—Titian would have killed to paint your hair since it is better than the insipid red he produced."

Rosalind heard their soft words as she eyed her new husband. He was toying with his cod, not eating much, she saw, but again, neither was she.

After three more toasts, the level of laughter had tripled, her own included. Aubrey Vail, in particular, appeared to be enjoying himself immensely if six glasses of champagne were any measure. Richard Vail looked dark and still, Lancelot looked soft and furious. Lady Mountjoy's mouth looked pinched, as did her lover's, Alfred Lemming.

When Nicholas leaned close and said against Rosalind's ear, "It is noon and time for us to leave," wickedness and excitement roared through her. She took a sip of champagne, lightly touched her tongue to her bottom lip. "As in, you and I will be alone in your carriage?"

"That's it," he said, and gave her a shameless grin. He gave one last look at his half brothers and his stepmother, and slowly nodded. "They've all drunk too much champagne to stick a knife in my ribs on our way out."

Aubrey was sitting back, his hands clasped over his stomach, smiling widely, eyes glazed, telling how the Druids loved cats, the priests walked about with cats on their shoulders, all proud and arrogant.

At one o'clock in the afternoon, Rosalind and Nicholas were off for Wyverly Chase, in the middle of Sussex, merely a six-hour drive from London.

27

Rosalind's first sight of Wyverly Chase was at the exact moment Nicholas's tongue eased into her mouth. She squeaked, jerked back from him, and stared at the incredible house up on top of a smooth hillock. He kissed her again. She flattened her palms against his chest, and lightly butted her forehead to his—she'd learned that move from a little boy who'd been a wharf rat before Ryder Sherbrooke had brought him to Brandon House. A head butt always got the other person's attention.

He couldn't believe she'd done that. He gave his head a shake, rubbed his forehead, and stared at her, bemused. "Why did you do that? What's wrong?"

She touched the tip of her tongue with her finger, and he stared at her tongue, ready to throw all finesse to the wind and leap on her, but he managed to hold himself in check because she looked so damned silly gaping at him. She said, "Nicholas, oh, dear, how difficult this is to say, but the fact is you stuck your tongue in my mouth. You actually touched my tongue with yours. I'm trying not to think about that but I can't seem to help it. I suppose it's something men feel they must do so that—no, no, let's speak of that house—is that Wyverly Chase?"

He'd kept his distance during their six-hour trip, truly he had, at least for the most part, until just three seconds ago when he simply couldn't bear it anymore. Her mouth—staring at her mouth while she spoke of the red Lasis and its fire spears— but not really hearing much of what she said, her words lovely background noise while he thought of cupping her breasts in his hands and kissing them, pressing his face against her warm flesh, then her mouth, her tongue—it had done him in. He'd wanted to wait for the simple reason that taking a virgin on the seat of a moving carriage lacked a certain finesse. Yes, he'd planned to wait until he had her in the huge master suite at Wyverly with its immense mahogany bed and thick soft feather ticking. He'd planned to have her in that bed not more than six minutes after he carried her over the threshold—the greeting of Peter Pritchard and Block his butler, and all the servants—very well, he could have her in the middle of that bed in eight minutes. But then she'd wet her lips with her tongue as she'd wondered aloud if the red Lasis ever attacked that disagreeable lot of wizards and witches with their Celtic god and goddess names who resided atop Mount Olyvan. Done in, he thought, dazed, as he'd slipped his tongue into her mouth. But he didn't get the result he'd expected—actually, he nearly shocked her out of her slippers. Of course she'd never been kissed like that before. He grinned fatuously.

What had she said? Oh, yes, she'd asked about Wyverly Chase. He focused his eyes on his home and managed to clear his throat. "Yes, that's Wyverly Chase, our country home, built in the sixteenth century by the Wyverly heiress who saved the first Vail's bacon with her immense number of groats. Ah, what do you think of your new home?" He realized in that moment that his house wasn't perhaps what a new bride would expect. It wasn't in the Palladian style, nor was there a single Elizabeth diamond pane to be seen. No moat, so a castle was out as well. It was, quite frankly, outlandish, not to him, certainly, but— What was she seeing, thinking? He found he was holding his breath.

She straightened, righting her charming little green hat with its cream-colored feathers that curved around her cheek. She remained silent, her eyes widening as the carriage bowled up the long winding drive, the graveled road surrounded by thick maple and pine trees, up, up, to the top of a bare gentle slope, thinking it rather looked like a full-bearded man with a bald head. He waited, praying she wouldn't laugh.

"It's magic," she whispered, wonder and excitement in her voice. "Magic. The Wyverly heiress, she built it? She was magic, Nicholas. You know that, don't you?"

He looked at the nearly white stone that rose up and up, almost touching the clouds, and the late afternoon sun beamed a silver spear through the clouds to strike a certain point on the back eastern turret and make the stone sparkle like raindrops. There were four rounded stone towers that rose high above the house itself. No, not really a house—it was simply Wyverly, his home. Was it magic? No, surely that was absurd, and yet—yet he knew deep in his gut that what was happening right this instant was very, very important.

He said slowly, feeling his way, "Magic? No, not the Wyverly heiress. The newly created earl built it. Before Queen Bess tapped him on the shoulder with the ceremonial sword, he was the captain of the *Bellissima*, Sir Walter Raleigh's forward ship in the battle with the Spanish in 1578. He saved Raleigh's ship *Falcon* from a broadside. Since Raleigh won the battle and was in good stead with the queen, she thanked him with gold in his coffers, and at Raleigh's request, she bestowed land and an earldom upon my ancestor, making him the first Earl of Mountjoy."

"Where does the title Mountjoy come from?"

"It had become extinct but the year before, displeasing the queen, even though she herself had beheaded the final earl in the line. But the first earl didn't settle down. You see, he was a very successful trader before he threw in his lot with Raleigh, and so he went out again. Not three months later, his ship sank in the Mediterranean. He was the only survivor. He never wrote about it, only that he'd been both cursed and blessed, whatever that means.

"My grandfather told me the first earl kept a journal. He'd written that he'd pictured this house or castle or manor house, whatever you wish to call it, in his mind, all full-blown down to the last white round tower stone, and his new heiress wife had enthusiastically poured all her money into the venture, and Wyverly Chase was the result."

"I trust the Wyverly heiress gained an excellent husband for her money."

"Well, they both lived a long time, if that is any measure. His name was Jared Vail. From his portrait—it's in the long picture gallery in the east wing—he was a strapping gentleman, the flashing dark eyes of a pirate, face ruddy from the wind and sea, and a wicked smile. Fortunately, the Vail men have been fairly astute in dealing with finances over the years and have flourished." Nicholas grinned. "Do you know Captain Jared also wrote of that dreadful day in 1618 when Raleigh was beheaded with an axe? He claimed Raleigh boomed out before the axe fell, 'This is a sharp Medicine, but it is a Physician for all Diseases.'"

She studied his face. "I agree, the Wyverly heiress wasn't the magic one, it was this ship captain, Jared Vail, he was magic and you know it, else he couldn't have built this magnificent house that must whisper of secrets and ancient magic rattling about behind its walls. You also know it because you carry your grandfather's blood and his teachings, and he carried his father's blood all the way back to Jared Vail. I want to see your grandfather's library, Nicholas. I want to see his copy of the *Rules of the Pale.*"

"You will," he said, looked at her mouth again, and lifted her onto his lap. "Let me kiss you, and don't try to leap away from me in shock."

For the moment, the magnificent magic house receded to the back of her mind. Rosalind gave him a slow smile. "I've never had a man's tongue in my mouth, Nicholas. I've been kissed before you, naturally, but not this way. Grayson was the first."

"Grayson?" His temperature of his voice plummeted. "Grayson?"

Rosalind poked him in the arm. "Yes, but truth be told, I goaded him into doing it. I told him Raymond Sikes was the best kisser in all of Lower Slaughter and I was willing to wager a shilling that Grayson couldn't come close to him." She laughed. "Poor Grayson, he didn't know what to do. I was fourteen and he was quite the young man, newly up from Oxford, ready to sample all London's wickedness. I remember I puckered up when he forced himself to lean down and peck my mouth." She paused a moment, remembering the appalled look on his face, then giggled, a delightful sound Nicholas had never heard out of her before. Who knew Rosalind could giggle like any other young girl? Then she laughed. "Poor Grayson looked so revolted, so guilty, really, and so I told him I'd kissed a frog not more than five minutes before he'd kissed me—he fled to London. I didn't see him for six months. Do you know that I was convinced to kiss three more frogs?"

"None of them turned into princes, I gather."

"Not even a duke. I worried for months I would get warts, but I didn't."

"What about Raymond Sikes?"

"Oh, I made him up. Poor Grayson never knew I'd plucked the name out of nothing at all. I suppose now that I am married, I should tell him. He can't smack a wife, can he?"

"It would be very bad form," Nicholas said, then shook his head. "So Grayson gave you your first and only kiss before me?"

"Well, to be perfectly honest about it, yes."

He kissed her again, this time running his tongue over her bottom lip, and whispered, his breath hot and exciting, "Open your mouth, Rosalind. Open now."

She did. All of his focus was on her mouth. He wanted the warmth and wet of her and so he eased his tongue—

The new footman he'd hired himself a month before yelled right outside the window, "My lord! We've arrived! Shall I open the door for you and her ladyship or would you prefer that Mr. Lee Po and I carry in all the luggage and leave you alone here with your new bride, perhaps until it is dark?"

Nicholas hadn't even realized the carriage had stopped in the wide circular drive in front of Wyverly. Given the dazed expression in Rosalind's eyes, neither had she. He wanted to kill. He wanted to cry. Instead, he rolled his eyes and removed his tongue from his wife's mouth. His wife, what a thought that was. He'd known her for nine days, and she was now his wife.

He pulled himself together and stuck his head out of the carriage window. "Thank you for felling me with your wit, John. Ah, I see Block is opening the front doors. Tell him we need several more footmen. Introduce him to Lee Po. Go."

John didn't want to go. He wanted a nice long look into the carriage even though a blind man would know exactly what was going on. He was being small and nosy, and enjoying it immensely. He sighed.

"Go!"

Nicholas straightened Rosalind's gown, her bonnet, lightly touched his fingertip to her mouth, still open in surprise, and wondered if he could have her in his bed in under five minutes.

"Goodness," she said and lightly touched her fingertips to her mouth.

"I plan to treat you to the unexpected for the next thirty years. What do you think?"

She looked up at him through her lashes. "Perhaps I'll have some unexpected surprises for you too, Nicholas."

His eyes nearly crossed. He lifted her down from the carriage and walked beside her up the foot-worn stone steps. "You're ignorant," he said, not looking at her. "You don't know a blessed thing, much less anything about surprises."

"Aunt Sophie gave me a book. With pictures. She said they're not as explicit as the naked statues at Northcliffe Hall, which I was never allowed to see, by the way, but informative enough."

"You will show me this book."

She gave him a wicked smile.

Block said to him without preamble, "It is not all a disaster, my lord. There are a few of us who have stuck and will continue to stick. As will Mr. Pritchard, who is sleeping in the entrance hall to guard us."

28

She blinked at the instant change in her new husband. He now looked suddenly hard, ready to fight. He looked dangerous. She'd swear his eyes had darkened to black, but his voice was calm, low. "Peter is guarding you? What the devil is going on here, Block?"

"I did not mean to overly alarm you, my lord."

"Ah, so I take it that rats are racing through the kitchen? Perhaps smoke is billowing out of the bedchamber fireplace? Oh, yes, Block, this is my new wife, Lady Mountjoy. Rosalind, this is Block. He was with my grandfather for twenty years. To the best of my knowledge, Block has never encountered a problem he couldn't resolve."

Rosalind smiled at the old man, who looked ancient as the single pine tree whose gnarly branches waved against the second story of the house. He walked right up to her, eyed her briefly, then said close to Nicholas's ear, "It is not rats or smoke, my lord, it is the return of the old earl. No, no, don't think for a moment he is displeased. He appears quite happy that you are wed and that you and your new wife are here at Wyverly. Since he has never presented himself before, I must assume it is because you have wed and returned home.

"We have heard him singing at the top of his lungs, and laughing, and banging into things, as if he were blind and couldn't see that the old Indian chest was right in front of him. He told me I had at least seven more years before I departed to the hereafter. I told him it wasn't enough years but he told me to get hold of myself, that I would be older than he was when I finally croaked it. Unfortunately, he wasn't specific about my final destination. He sang it all in rhymes that were not at all felicitous."

"I see," Nicholas said slowly, eyeing Block, whose expression never changed, remaining aloof, only a slight tic at the corner of his left eye. "Well, then, since my grandfather is singing because her ladyship is here now, he is bound to sing even louder when he meets her."

"I would, were I he," Block said, and gave her a formal bow and a smile that showed a near full mouth of beautiful teeth. "It is a pleasure, my lady. Welcome to Wyverly Chase. If it would please you, my lady, I will also sing to you. I would accompany myself on the pianoforte. Do you like rousing Scottish tunes? Do you know, his old lordship doesn't ever sing Scottish ditties."

Rosalind was charmed even though she didn't have the slightest idea what was going on. There was a ghost singing in the house? Nicholas's grandfather?

She smiled at Block. "I should love to hear you sing, Block." She noticed the old man's linen was as white as the cumulus clouds overhead, his black suit such a shiny black she could see herself. She said, "Willicombe, our butler in London, has always wished for his trousers and coat to be shiny like yours, Block, but has never managed results such as yours. Perhaps you could write to him and tell him how it is done?"

"I have done nothing, my lady," Block said. "These clothes are as ancient as the Moorish tiles in the bathing closet. What you see is the high shine of honest age. How I enjoy viewing my noble countenance when I chance to gaze down at my sleeve, and thus have refused new clothes. Our laundress knows how to brush them just so, so they remain shiny. Do not be alarmed. I assure you that no moths hunker down in my seams, my lady."

"Thank you, Block. I will communicate with Willicombe and tell him to simply refuse all new clothes. So our laundress hasn't left?"

"She and her assistant are too far away from the library to hear the old earl sing and bang into furniture. Cook tells me that as long as she feeds Mrs. Bates and Chloe her excellent stuffed chicken necks, they will be content to remain and wash and iron."

Nicholas heard Peter Pritchard's deep melodic voice. "The old earl was singing a moment ago in the library, my lord. Earlier in the day I believe he was reading. If you would care to assure him that you and your new wife are home to remain, perhaps he will depart the premises and continue on to the heavenly climes."

Block said, "Perhaps it is the possibility of traveling in the other direction that keeps him earthbound."

Rosalind looked from one face to the next. She stared at Peter Pritchard. "What does he sing, Mr. Pritchard?"

"Ditties, my lady. At least they sound like something a man might sing while striding a ship deck."

To the best of Nicholas's knowledge, his grandfather had never set foot on a ship deck in his life.

Rosalind asked, "What does he read?"

Peter gave her a lovely bow. "Forgive me, my lady, I am Peter Pritchard, the earl's estate manager. I fear I have been a bit distracted."

You have a ghost in the house. No wonder.

Peter said, "Yes, things have been rather at sixes and sevens here for the past several days, actually, since the day his lordship sent a messenger informing us of his plans to return home with a wife. Forgive me, my lady. You asked me what the old earl reads. There are piles of books on the floor beside his favorite chair. The one on top is a treatise on hermit wizards who dwell in caves in the Bulgar and eschew all human contact."

Rosalind said, "If they eschew all human contact, I wonder how anyone could write a treatise about them."

Nicholas laughed.

Rosalind slipped her hand into his. "I should like to accompany his lordship to the library and make the acquaintance of my grandfather-in-law's ghost."

Block heaved a sigh. "How fortuitous that you do not appear to be of a highly sensitive nature, my lady. Indeed, an overabundance of nerves could possibly prove fatal to your marital bliss, given our current visitation."

"Not I, Block. I am as stout of heart as Lee Po."

"Ah, his lordship's man of affairs. Lee Po tells the grandest stories. Come now, Cook has chilled one of the old earl's bottles of French champagne and made her exquisite gooseberry tarts. If you would like to enter, my lady, I will introduce you to the maid, Marigold, who appears to be about the same age as that young maid of yours, who looks really rather alarmed and a bit white about the mouth."

Rosalind turned to Matilde and smiled. "Come along, Matilde, everything is all right."

Matilde nodded even though she didn't think anything was all right, and dutifully trailed after Rosalind into the massive ugly house, which gave her the shudders. At least Mr. Lee Po was here. No one and nothing would try to harm her whilst he was about.

Only one young girl, dressed in a dark muslin gown, a white cap perched on the side of her head, stood at attention in the center of the massive black-and-white-tiled entrance hall. She saw Nicholas and Rosalind and quickly dropped a curtsy. "Oh, dear, here ye are, standing right here in front of me eyes." She bobbed another curtsy. "Me name's Marigold. Me mum loves yellow, she does, that's why she named me Marigold." And she curtsied again.

Block said, "Marigold laughs when the old earl sings. Or sings along with him, depending on her mood."

"He doesn't carry enough of a beat for me to dance," Marigold said. "But we do make lovely harmony."

Rosalind smiled at her and said, "This is Matilde. If you would show her to her room,

Marigold, and introduce her to Cook, Mrs. Bates, Chloe, and the tweeny."

"The tweeny would be Mrs. Sweet, my lady. She's fair to doddering, but still can polish an armoire to a high shine. Not as high a shine as Mr. Block's suits, but high enough to remark upon."

Rosalind hadn't met many tweenies, but she'd never heard of one older than sixteen. "How old is Mrs. Sweet, Marigold?"

"Older than me mum, my lady, got three teeth left in 'er mouth, all in the front, a good thing, me mum says, else she'd have to gnaw 'er food with 'er gums."

"I see. I would also like you to give Matilde a tour of the house. Matilde, when you are finished, come to my room. Go along now. Thank you, Marigold."

"Yes, my lady." And yet another curtsy, this one deeper, nearly toppling her onto her face. "Matilde, now that's a purty name too, I'll ask me mum what she thinks of it." And off they went.

Nicholas was looking toward the library, listening.

Block said, "I suppose even a ghost must occasionally take a respite."

At that moment, they heard a strong loud bass voice sing out,

I went to sea as a wee young goat.
I crossed the waves in a very small boat.
I learned to swim—I can tell you that!
And never once did I wear a hat.
Hey ho. Hiddy ho.
The sun burned and blistered but there I sat
And not once did I wear a hat.

There were three more eminently forgettable verses, then silence, dead and utter silence.

Peter gave them a crooked smile. "The hair on my arms no longer rises. To become used to the presence of the ghost of my old master, now, doesn't that bespeak a tortured brain? But the fact is he is indeed here and so what is one to do?"

Nicholas saw a pallet lying in the corner. Peter's bed, he supposed. "Rosalind, why don't you accompany Block upstairs and I will go bid Grandfather hello."

Like that would ever happen, she thought. "Oh, no, I'm coming with you. Do you know, perhaps the two of us can sing a duet."

Peter Pritchard gave her an amazed look, then laughed and coughed behind his hand.

Nicholas gave one final fond thought to his huge bed upstairs with Rosalind naked on her back in the middle of it, perhaps beckoning to him, smiling, then took a resolute step toward the closed library door at the end of the long corridor.

"I leave the door open," Peter said, "but it always closes. Always. At first I was disconcerted, frightened to my booted heels, to be honest about it, but now—" He shrugged and gave Rosalind another smile. "You do not appear to be afraid, my lady."

"Oh, no, I adore singing," Rosalind said and gave the young man with the clever eyes and tousled bronze hair a sunny smile.

29

Silence, dead silence. Appropriate, Nicholas thought, given his grandfather was dead and really shouldn't have anything to say about it.

He and Rosalind stepped into the huge library, so shadowed and so long you couldn't see either end of it. It was rather narrow and there were more books than Rosalind had ever seen in a single library in her entire life, and that was saying something, given Uncle Douglas's immense library at Northcliffe Hall, not to mention Uncle Tysen's vast collection at the parsonage.

"Are there windows anywhere in this room?" she asked.

"Yes," Nicholas said and strode to the front end and flung back the thick dark gold velvet draperies. He looped the thick braided cords over golden hooks. Then he flung open the windows. Light and fresh spring air flooded into the room. He sucked in the blessed fresh air, then turned to say—

There was a moan.

Both Nicholas and Rosalind froze where they stood.

"I'm sorry, I forgot to tell you," Peter said, now coming into the library, "but I suppose he doesn't like the light. Perhaps if you've been dead a long time, you're quite used to the dark. If you wait a bit, those draperies will close themselves again."

Nicholas didn't look away from his grandfather's old wing chair that sat at an angle to the fireplace, perfectly empty. He said, without looking away from that chair, "Have you actually seen him, Peter?"

"No, I haven't."

Nicholas nodded. "Thank you, Peter. Leave us now."

"Er, you are certain, my lord? I worry that her ladyship—"

"Her ladyship could face down a band of Portuguese bandits," Nicholas said, smiling.

"She will be fine. Leave us, everything is all right. My grandfather returned because she was coming, that is what Block said, so let him meet her."

When Peter walked out of the library, he left the door open, a demonstration, Rosalind supposed. As they watched, the door very slowly closed itself.

"Well, Grandfather," Nicholas said to the empty chair, "it seems you're causing quite a commotion. I would just as soon not hear another moan, to be honest here. Come, speak to me and Rosalind. That's why you're here, isn't it? To meet her?"

Nothing but silence, then, a very soft old voice chanted in a singsong voice,

At last the girl comes home
A girl who never belonged
To her is owed the debt
Well met, my lad, well met.

Nicholas would have fallen over if he hadn't been leaning against the mantelpiece. *The debt*, he thought, *the bloody debt*. He still didn't understand this debt business but it was deep inside him, spun out in the dream that had filled his youth, and with it the need to pay this debt. He looked at Rosalind. She was no longer the little girl in his dream, but she was his debt, this woman, now his wife.

The old voice sang again, from everywhere and nowhere, surrounding them, yet sounding hollow, puffed out of an old reed, ancient as yellowed parchment.

> **The little girl nearly died**
> **The monster nearly won**
> **The debt was paid by another**
> **But the race must still be run.**

The wispy voice faded into the soft air and they were alone, quite suddenly they were utterly alone, and both of them knew it. The draperies remained open.

Rosalind sang softly into the still air, toward the empty wing chair,

> **I dream of beauty and sightless night**
> **I dream of strength and fevered might**
> **I dream I'm not alone again**
> **But I know of his death and her grievous**
> **sin.**

The ancient chair toppled onto its side. The draperies flew closed.

"Well, that certainly got a rise out of the old boy," Nicholas said. He pulled Rosalind close. "What do you think of my home now?"

"I think," she said, looking up at him, "that we have something very important to accomplish."

"Yes," he said. "Yes, we do. Do you know, I've never before heard my grandfather sing. I remember once he told me his voice scared small children and dogs."

Rosalind said nothing, but she still stared at the empty wing chair lying on its side on the carpet.

30

Nicholas took a bite of his roast pork, and chewed quickly. Dinner had been the last thing on his mind when Block had waylaid them coming out of the library. "Now that you are in the country, my lord, it is country hours you must observe." He bowed. "It is now well after six o'clock, nearly seven as a matter of fact and Cook is anxious to present you with her *pee-ss de resistence*."

What was a poor beleaguered very newly married man to do? *Strangle Block, that's a good start.*

After Rosalind met the cook, Mrs. Clopper, tall and bony, dressed all in white, not a single food stain to be seen, and a mustache that looked like a thin swatch of black satin, Block steered them into the massive dining room.

Nicholas had no fond memories of this airless, gloomy room, but the table was set for the two of them and candles were lit. "After this, Block," he said, "we will have our meals in the breakfast room. This room is so dark a half dozen thieves could be hiding in the shadows. I don't wish to come armed to my dinner."

Block bowed. "As you wish, my lord. Ah, I will now fetch Cook's white soup. It is renowned. She never serves her soup first, as perhaps you may remember, my lord, but tonight, she believed . . ."

Rosalind wasn't listening, she was breathing in murky air and studying dark corners. A single twelve-branch of candles stood in the middle of the table and cast strange shadows on a large bowl of muddy-looking grapes. She said, "If Grayson saw this table, he would say it was at least three coffins long."

"At least," he said and gave her hand a squeeze, all of her he could reach. He heard Block clear his throat yet again, and whispered, "Eat as much as you want, Rosalind, for I plan enough activity to skinny you to the bone."

She smiled at him, though he saw that her eyes were a bit dilated, perhaps her face a bit pale.

The two of them, if asked, would have said the dinner was quite delicious, but in truth, neither particularly noticed the succession of dishes brought out by Block.

"I am quite fond of fig pudding," Rosalind said finally, and forked up a small bite.

"I believe that is an apple tart."

"Oh, dear."

"Figs, apples, it doesn't matter, keep eating. You will need your strength."

She took another bite. "I believe you are right, it is apple. Do you know, Nicholas, I wonder if your grandfather will visit us in your bedchamber."

"*Our* bedchamber. If Grandfather comes to sing us a lullaby, we will listen, I suppose, then applaud and politely ask him to leave, else he will find himself shocked to his ghostly toes."

"If I know the lullaby, I could sing it with him." She gave him a look from beneath her lashes.

She felt the urgency in him, heard it in his voice even though he sounded light and amused. Despite her excitement, she knew this was uncharted territory. She had to admit to a bit of apprehension, a bloodless word, really, when she felt her innards jumping with excitement mixed with terror.

"Nicholas? About this lovemaking business."

He came to full attention, his focus on her. "Yes?"

She waved her hand around her. "This is all very civilized, I mean, we're eating our apple tarts, but now I'm thinking about what you're going to do to me as soon as you get me into the bedchamber."

He did indeed have plans, wonderful, detailed plans. "Did you look at all the pictures in the book Aunt Sophie gave you?"

"I tried to thumb through it quickly, but neither aunt would give me a moment's peace. I think they were embarrassed and regretted immediately giving it to me, but I held on, let me tell you."

"If you wish, when we are in our bedchamber, we can look at the pictures together. Should you like that?"

"Yes. Well, no. I don't think I could do that

with you peering over my shoulder, your eyes on the same things mine are on. The couples don't have any clothes on, Nicholas. There is not a single petticoat to froth up and hide things."

"And the gentlemen in the pictures? Are they unclothed as well?"

"I looked at as many as I could while Aunt Sophie was trying to gently tug it out of my arms. I think I managed to get a brief glimpse of a good half dozen before—to be on the safe side—I folded it beneath my chemises in my valise hoping they wouldn't filch it. The gentlemen"—she cleared her throat— "well, they looked very strange, not at all like the little boys at Brandon House."

"Strange how?"

"The front of them, low on the front of them—they looked deformed, big and puffed out and, well, one could not help but think there was a tree trunk sticking out of their stomachs."

Nicholas laughed. "Sounds to me like the artist was a man with a grand view of himself, a man who wanted to impress, and that led to a good deal of exaggeration to carry home the point."

She sat forward, her fingers locked

together. "What point? I didn't see a point. Now, I don't wish to speak of that book anymore. I don't wish to dive beneath this table to hide my mortified self. I don't like to think what could be under this bloody table when it is dark, and no feet are there in a row to keep strange creatures away."

He merely smiled at her. "Finish your fig pudding. Let's go to the library and request that Grandfather not pay us any bridal visits. Then, we will enjoy ourselves, Rosalind. I promise you everything will be fine. I am your husband and you will trust me."

She chewed on that a moment, then said to his surprise, "Nicholas, do you know why your grandfather's chair fell over when I sang my song?"

Oh, he'd thought about that all right. "We will discuss it, tomorrow at noon, at the earliest."

Block came into the dining room, carrying another branch of lit candles. The light haloed his face, making him look like a ruddy-cheeked devil. "I fancied you might wish to have your port now, my lord."

Was that irony in Block's voice? Nicholas folded his napkin and laid it beside his plate.

"No, thank you, Block. We are going upstairs now. Is the house quiet and secure?"

"Yes, my lord. May I say I thought it particularly sensitive of Mr. Pritchard not to dine with you this evening, what with this being your very first evening together at Wyverly Chase, er, and your very first evening together as a married couple?"

"No, Block, you may not say it."

Rosalind choked back a laugh. "Please thank Cook for the delicious meal, Block. My lord?"

Nicholas pulled back her chair and took her arm. "Good night, Block. Ah, tell Mr. Pritchard to hire some additional staff. I can't imagine Cook was pleased to clean all the pots and pans by herself. I will personally speak to each of them, allay their ghostly concerns."

"Very well, my lord, but I don't hold much hope of gaining an additional servant. There's talk in the village, you see, and people are remembering your grandfather and the fact that *there was no body*."

"I assure you, Block, when Grandfather died, he left his earthly remains behind. After all, what use would he have for his corporeal self in the hereafter?"

"As to that, my lord, you were only a lad, and didn't know anything at all. I remember well what was said by He Who Should Know."

"Who would that be?"

"The physician. You remember Dr. Blankenship, my lord, a fussy little man with wheat-colored hair and eyes so pale he could stare at you and you wouldn't know it? He evidently whispered to his sister that when he made his final visit, the old earl wasn't snug in his coffin, as he should have been. You, my lord, were, of course, already gone."

"I remember Blankenship. What happened to him?"

"I believe he went to France, my lord."

"Well, now, there you have it," Rosalind said. "Very fitting. Anyone who would claim such a thing deserves to wind up in France."

Block nodded. "I must admit that Dr. Blankenship was a strange little man. However, as you may imagine, having the old earl's body missing was a titillating tale. However, we will try, nonetheless, despite knowing we will fail, to bring more servants here."

"What happened to Dr. Blankenship's sister, the one he whispered this to?"

"Why, she still lives in her brother's house

in the village, still dines out on her brother's whisper. It appears that our fellow man never tires of hearing about otherworldly phenomena. Unfortunately she is now also drooling in her soup. Ancient she is."

Block trailed them into the library, watched by the door as they spoke briefly to the empty chair in front of the fireplace.

When they came out, Block cleared his throat and stood his ground. "My lord, it is Lee Po."

"What about Lee Po?"

"It is Cook, my lord. At dinner she asked him to prepare a Chinese dish for her."

"I see."

"He told her he was a master at noodle preparation, but little else, to which Cook said she'd heard that heathens ate raw octopus and live squid still trying to crawl off your plate. Lee Po laughed, my lord. He informed her that he'd always allowed octopi and squid to escape although many times they tangled themselves up in his noodles. Cook was charmed. She batted her eyelashes at him. Such a thing hasn't happened since she was eighteen and fancied herself in love with Willie, the old butcher's son." Block sighed. "I don't know what she will do now. If that weren't enough, Marigold wanted to touch him. He allowed her to lightly lay her palm on his cheek to see if yellow came off on her hand. It didn't. She remarked in a throaty voice that his skin was very nice, soft as—then she began reciting colors. I fear there might be a rivalry brewing between Cook and Marigold, for Lee Po's favor."

"He is quite used to females admiring him, Block. Don't worry about it," Nicholas said. "I remember he even once impressed the empress with his superior tailoring of a sable robe." Nicholas frowned a bit. Lee Po also had a way of making events unfold just as he wished them to. He'd told Nicholas once that they fit together very nicely, both of them with abilities that flew above the heads of normal men. Nicholas didn't like to think about what Lee Po had meant by that.

When he and Rosalind had the master bedchamber within sight four and a half minutes later, Nicholas was breathing hard and fast, his eyes a bit on the glazed side. Rosalind was matching him, step for step. He saw her so clearly—lying naked beneath him and she— He ran the last dozen steps, pulling her with him now. He closed the door, thought about it a moment, then locked it. He left the key in the lock. "Not that a locked door would stop him if Grandfather decides to stir from the library."

"I don't think he was in the library."

Nicholas said, "Perhaps he was sleeping."

Rosalind didn't say anything. She was staring over at the massive bed.

31

Nicholas laughed as she walked over to the fireplace and began to desperately warm her hands.

At least there were a good three dozen candles lit against the darkness, but still it wasn't enough. "Is this a lovely room, Nicholas, when the sun is shining strong through the windows? There are windows, aren't there?"

"A good score of them. Big windows, I promise. Think of it as being nice and cozy in here right now, all right? Now, come to me, Rosalind, and I will play your maid."

"But—"

"No, don't worry about Matilde. I told Block to inform her that she was free to get to know Marigold and Mrs. Sweet and Cook and Lee Po this evening."

"I see my nightgown is lying on the bed. Perhaps your grandfather is snuggled beneath it."

"Forget Grandfather." Nicholas fetched her nightgown and laid it on the back of a lovely brocade wing chair facing the fireplace. He said, "This was my grandfather's favorite chair when I lived here, this one and the one in the library. When I was a boy I spent many hours sitting on that worn hassock listening to him tell me stories about the great wizard, Sarimund. He told me Sarimund was married, but no one ever saw his wife. It was said by some, he told me, that she was a figment of his tortured brain, not a real woman, but then one day he was strutting about demanding everyone congratulate him on the birth of his little daughter, and surely she would be an explosion of light in the dark English skies. This announcement was met with skepticism. As far as Grandfather knew, no one ever saw the daughter either."

She grinned up at him. "Is there any written record of her?"

Nicholas shrugged, cupped her chin in his palm, raised her face, and ran his thumbs over her jaw. "I don't know, Lady Mountjoy. Ah, such a lovely name." He leaned down and kissed her. It wasn't the sort of kiss meant to stir her blood and make her heart pound like a battle drum, but rather a light touch of his lips against hers, and his tongue, always his tongue, now tracing the outline of her bottom lip. Such an odd feeling it was. He continued to kiss her until she lay her palms flat against his chest. She felt his heart thudding loud and fast beneath her palms.

To Nicholas's delight and relief, she snuggled up against him, wrapped her arms around his back.

He knew he needed patience, a difficult thing for a man on his wedding night after weeks of abstinence. He knew she could feel him against her belly, she was so close now, and he wondered if she believed a tree trunk was pressing against her. He kissed her mouth a dozen more times, licked and nibbled on her earlobe. Her hands moved to his shoulders, squeezing him, hard. Ah, good, she wanted more, he couldn't be wrong about that, and so he said against her warm mouth, "Open, Rosalind, let's try this tongue business again."

"Your tongue has been all over me, licking me between nibbles. Even my chin is wet."

A lot more of you is going to be wet, he thought, but managed to hold his tongue.

She opened her mouth wide, and he laughed. "No, not quite that wide, just a little bit. Tease me."

Her eyes flew open and she stared at him. "You're sure about this, Nicholas?"

"Oh, yes." And he slipped his tongue into her mouth after again nibbling her bottom lip. "Yes, that's right. Give me your tongue, Rosalind. I'm suffering here."

To his besotted relief, she did, and with a good deal of enthusiasm. His hands cupped her even though she was separated from his hands by at least five layers of clothes. He'd swear he could feel her. He wanted to take her to the floor this very minute. He felt her start in surprise, and that firmed his brain a bit.

Rosalind heard a moan, stiffened, but it wasn't from his grandfather, thank the good Lord, nor was it from Nicholas. Oh, dear, it appeared to be from her, from deep in her throat, from a place she didn't even know was there, then there was something else—

A low cackle came from behind them. Nicholas whirled around, ready to kill.

No one was there.

There was another cackle.

Nicholas turned back to her and touched his forehead to hers. He drew in a deep breath and raised his head. "Grandfather, go away."

There came yet another cackle.

Nicholas cursed with great and long fluency, involving goats and chickens and the sharp quills of feathers.

"You are very good at that."

"Thank you." He picked her up in his arms, grabbed a small branch of lit candles, and walked to the door. He managed to turn the key in the lock, no small feat, and not scorch either of them with the candle flame. He said over his shoulder, "Old man, I am taking my wife to another bedchamber. You will take yourself off, back to the library, or I swear we will leave to return to London in the morning. All the servants will leave then and you will have no one to appreciate your wretched songs."

And he slammed the master bedchamber door.

When he opened a door near to the opposite end of the endless stretch of hallway, he carried her into a room small enough so the branch of candles lit every corner. There was a narrow bed in the center, an armoire and a desk against the far wall. In front of the small fireplace was a dark blue rug with a wide green border, well worn, a very old chair sitting on it, high-backed, its seat sunk in. A lot of bottoms had settled in that chair over the years. Rosalind said, "I like this bedchamber." Then she shut up fast when he laid her on her back in the center of the bed.

He was breathing hard, unable to focus on her words, on anything. "Now, Rosalind. Now."

"Wait, Nicholas!"

"What? What is it?"

"This room, ah, I think it suits you more than that massive earl's chamber—particularly with your grandfather in it."

She was afraid, dammit. He had to slow himself down even though he knew it would kill him. He owed his grandfather a fist to the nose, if a ghost had a nose. He set the branch of candles on the small table beside the bed, managed to say in a credibly calm voice, "It was my bedchamber as a boy. I spent many happy hours here. I plan to spend many more this night."

And the dam broke. His hands were all over the buttons on her gown. His fingers were nimble, a vast relief, and when he pulled the gown off her shoulders and down her arms, imprisoning her, she lay on her back, looking up at him. "Nicholas?"

"Hmm."

"That cackle we heard in your bed-chamber—maybe that was a chicken we heard and not your grandfather."

Laughter spurted out of his mouth, and he turned away, holding his stomach he laughed so hard. He finally caught his breath, leaned down, and pulled her up against him. He whispered against her cheek, "How is a man supposed to perform his marital duties if he's howling with laughter?"

"I'd rather it was a chicken."

He kissed her, then laid her onto her back again. "Perhaps," Nicholas said, laughter bubbling up again, "if it was Grandfather, he will sing advice to me tomorrow."

"Oh, dear, do you need it?"

That got his attention. He prepared to lunge.

"Nicholas, no, wait. You've got me half-undressed and here you are still in your bloody coat."

In record time, his record at least, he was naked, his boots tossed at right angles next to his boy's chair, his clothes scattered on the floor at his big bare feet.

She made a funny noise in her throat.

"Rosalind?"

He saw himself then through her eyes and cursed, this time detailing a goat who mistook a boot for a female goat. He was naked. Could he be any more of a clod? What to do? He couldn't very well grab a blanket and wrap it around himself, that would lack finesse, it would be, quite frankly, unworthy of a man who knew what was what. So he faced her, arms to his sides, and didn't move. "I'm a man, Rosalind, just a man. I am sorry if you are disappointed there is no tree trunk sticking out from my belly."

What if she were repulsed? What if she thought him the ugliest creature on God's earth?

She was breathing hard; he heard it and wondered what she was thinking, feeling. He continued to stand there, looking down at his big toe, stubbed in his haste to get her away from his grandfather's bedchamber. It pulsed with pain. It steadied him. What was she thinking? What—

She came up on her elbows, never looking away from him. "You are beautiful, Nicholas. I never imagined a man could look like you do, all hard and smooth. I mean—" She actually broke off, swallowed, and her eyes went right to his sex.

He was aroused, nothing he could do about it. He was beautiful? He cleared his throat. "You think all of me is beautiful? Or just parts? Or maybe just my feet? I was told once that I had David's feet, you know, Michelangelo's sculpture? What do you think?"

Whatever she thought remained unspoken. She looked utterly absorbed, staring, staring, and her eyes were looking nowhere near his face. Because he was a man, because a woman's attention was focused on him, he predictably got bigger.

She sat up suddenly, swung her legs over the bed, and reached out her hand toward him. Then her face flamed red and she dropped her hand back to her lap. A pity that, he thought. She whispered, "Oh, dear, as fascinating as you look, I don't think this will work. I'm very sorry, Nicholas."

"It will work, I promise you." He walked to the narrow bed. She squeaked, rolled, and nearly fell off the other side.

"Didn't you see it work quite well in your book? And all those gentlemen were far more well-endowed than I am."

She clutched a pillow to her chest. "Well, yes, I suppose so. But you're not a drawing, Nicholas, you're a man, all real flesh and blood and you're standing right by my bed."

"We will go slowly," he said, and prayed he could manage that tall order. It would be a close thing, but he was determined not to muck it up. "Come back to me, sweetheart, and let me see you. You want to be fair about this, don't you?"

"No."

"Here I am, naked to my feet, and you're still dressed ready for a ball."

She gave him a long, considering look. "All right," she said and scooted back to him. She lay on her back, her arms at her sides, and closed her eyes.

Again, he couldn't help himself, he laughed. "If you would clasp your hands together over your breasts, I could slip a lily between your fingers. Oh, Lord, Rosalind, you look like a half-dressed sacrifice."

Her eyes remained tightly shut. "I am."

He was still laughing when he tossed her gown to the foot of the bed. He studied the acres of virginal white petticoats, her slippered toes sticking out. He must be careful not to rip the lovely lace-edged white chemise. He got her slippers off, pulled her stockings down, smiled at the hand-stitched pale blue garters she wore. He looked at those long narrow feet of hers, the nice arches. He wanted to lick her toes.

Her eyes popped open when he lifted her bare foot to his mouth. "What are you doing?"

He licked and caressed his way up to her knees. "You are really going to like this." He raised her leg, her petticoats frothing around them, and began kissing and licking the back of her knee.

Bless her heart, she didn't move, but since his ears were attuned to any sort of sound she might make, he heard her breathing jerk a bit. Suddenly, she shot upright and leapt on him, taking him backwards. They rolled off the bed and landed on the floor, Nicholas thankfully on bottom. A rug was beneath his butt but his back was on the bare oak planks, scratchy and cold.

Who cared?

She kissed his nose, his chin, his ears, licked his jaw, and he thought he'd die when she slipped her tongue inside his mouth.

He went to work on the billowing petticoats—five of them—and soon they looked like small snow mounds scattered across the small bedchamber. When she was wearing naught but her lovely chemise, she was lying on top of him, her hands all over his face, tugging at his hair, kissing his nose, his eyebrows, his mouth. He eased his hands beneath the chemise and nearly expired at the feel of her.

"Now there is nothing between thee and me," he said.

32

She reared up, stared down at him as he kneaded her flesh. She moaned, looked horrified, then she whispered, "Nicholas," and kissed him again.

His fingers stroked her inner thighs, moving upward until he found her. He stopped breathing. He eased a finger inside her, and to his utter joy, that blessed finger set off a cataclysm. She began to move frantically against him, making small mewling sounds that drove him mad. His finger deepened and butted against her maidenhead. Nothing could have brought him to attention as that did.

Her maidenhead. He knew she'd have one, virgins did, though he'd never before been this close to one. But feeling it, actually touching her maidenhead nearly made him howl. He grabbed her up and tossed her onto the bed, came down over her, and shoved her legs wide.

He breathed hard and fast into her mouth. "Rosalind, tell me you want me this very instant."

"I want you. But I'm still wearing my chemise."

He cursed, reared back, and tore the chemise off her.

"Oh, dear, Nicholas, we mustn't tell Aunt Sophie what happened to the chemise she made. Perhaps—"

He knelt between those lovely white legs, pushed them wide, lifted her hips, and gave her his mouth.

She yelled so loud surely Cook could hear her, and jerked away, pressing hard against the headboard of the bed, her knees drawn up to her chin, and jerked the covers over her.

Nicholas stared at her. His mouth was wet with her, her scent in his nostrils, her taste in his mouth, and his brain empty. He was panting hard. He wanted to cry. What to say? She didn't look frightened, she looked appalled. He must be a man of the world here, fluent and self-assured. Was he capable? He cleared his throat. "Listen to me, Rosalind, this is very important to me. Kissing you with my mouth is vital to me, it is what a man must have in order to gain pleasure from coupling. Surely you know that, don't you?"

"No, I've never heard of such a thing. That can't be right, Nicholas, it is a mistake, your aim was wrong. You wanted the back of my knee again, or perhaps you wished to lick the bottom of my foot, not—oh, dear."

"You would deny me pleasure on our wedding night? You do not care for me at all?"

She saw him between her legs, his mouth, his tongue, touching her, kissing her, and she nearly folded up into nothing at all at the mortification of it.

He gave a very deep sigh. "I see you do not trust me to do what is right and proper." He sighed again, not looking at her, but at his toe, which was throbbing again.

"Oh, no, Nicholas, it isn't that, it's—"

A man made a decision and acted, he thought. He grabbed her, flattened her onto her back again, pulled her legs apart, and sat on his heels between them. "Now," he said, "you will enjoy this." Again he gave her his mouth and this time, to be on the safe side, he held her down with the flat of his hand on her belly. When, thank the blessed Lord, her shock became astonished pleasure, she moaned, twisted the sheets in her fists, and moaned again. If he could have thought of any words, he would have sung to the heavens. When her hands were wild on his naked back, on his hips, her nails scoring his flesh, he was quite willing and ready to conquer the world.

Her fists struck his shoulders, her fingers shoveled in his hair, yanking hard, but it was nothing. Suddenly, quite suddenly, she heaved up, arched her back, and screamed as her orgasm tore through her. It was wonderful, beyond wonderful, and he reveled in it, holding her firmly in those precious moments, pushing her, giving her all he could. He welcomed the strength of it, the intensity of it, and it burrowed deeply inside him. He began to love her more gently now as he felt her ease. Finally, when she was as limp as the sheets, he raised his head to see her staring up at him, her eyes a deeper blue, if that were possible, dreamy and bewildered. Her red hair was tangled around her head and face and all her beautiful white flesh, her legs sprawled—he reared up and came inside her, hard and fast and deep. When she screamed again, as he knew she must, his palm was over her mouth. He felt her pain, but he didn't stop, not until he pressed against her womb. His heart pounded, he trembled like a palsied man, but discipline was the important thing here.

He pressed his forehead against hers. "Your maidenhead," he managed to whisper against her hot skin, "I had to get through your maidenhead. I swear it will never hurt again. Lie still, get used to me. Let your muscles relax. No, don't curse me, you'll just make me laugh. Breathe deeply. Feel me in you, Rosalind. All right?"

Relax? With that man part deep inside her? How could that be possible? Curses bubbled up, but she held them in. She leaned up and bit his earlobe. Not at all lov-

ing or gentle, but that was all right, it steadied him. He whispered against her temple, "I
won't move, I promise. Please, try to relax."

She bit him again.

Not such a violent bite this time. He kissed
her cheek, the tip of her nose. He was a man
in pain, a man whose muscles would lock for
all eternity if he didn't move, and quickly.
"Surely this is the hardest thing I have ever
attempted to do. Surely this makes me a
very fine man indeed. Lie still, that's right,
just lie still."

How could his voice sound so soothing,
so gentle, when he'd skewered her? Men
came into women, she wasn't stupid, but
still, she'd simply never imagined how it
would actually work. She could feel him, and
wasn't that the oddest thing, hard and
smooth and he was pulsing. How could that
be?

He was heavy on top of her, and hot and
sweaty. He didn't move. Nor did she.

She began to ease, began to let herself
feel the length of him, the heat of him, and
how very alive he felt. It was the small
clenching of muscles deep inside her that
sent him over the edge.

"Rosalind." His brain blurred, every feeling centered on her, driving into her—and her womb, oh, merciful heavens, her womb—he yelled his release.

He collapsed on top of her, feeling the slick of her sweat. Blessed be, he was still alive and of this earth, and she was holding him, her arms tight around his back.

Rosalind said against his shoulder, "I can feel you inside me. It is a very strange thing, Nicholas."

He'd never understood how women could find the breath and brain to speak after having sex. No, this wasn't simple sex, this was the hurtling of self into chaos, and exploding, so many vivid colors filling his brain. This was the most wonderful thing that had ever happened to him.

He nuzzled her neck. "I can feel you too. You're soft now, Rosalind, and wet from my seed and wet from you. Did I yell louder than you did?"

She leaned her head up and bit his shoulder, then licked where she'd bitten. Now that was a lovely bite and so he pushed a little, felt her tighten, and stopped. She said, her eyes as bemused as her voice, "I did yell, didn't I? I couldn't help it, it just came bursting out of my mouth. It was probably close either way. I love the taste of you, Nicholas." And she bit and licked him yet again. "And the way you made me feel—your mouth on me—it is something I could not have imagined."

Her words settled deep inside him where he usually didn't spend much time, deep burrowing feelings, powerful feelings that pooled into soul-deep pleasure, filling all the empty corners of him. He managed to bring himself up on his elbows. He wanted to say something clever, something with a touch of world-wit to it, but instead, he stared down at her face, her cheeks flushed in the candlelight, her hair stark red against the white pillow, and those eyes of hers, the blue so deep, so fathomless. No, no, he was fast becoming a moron. A woman's eyes weren't fathomless. He swallowed. He realized in that instant that this woman was his. She was his wife until he died. If her eyes were fathomless, so be it. He felt her muscles squeezing him, then easing. A man could happily expire.

She smiled up at him. "You're sweating, Nicholas."

"So are you."

She looked thoughtful. "Do you know I've never liked sweating before, but now?" She gave him a dazzling smile. "Now, who cares? That was wonderful, really, until you had to shove yourself inside me."

"My coming inside you, that was your reward, your bonus for being a very good wife and letting me love you with my mouth."

"Oh, dear." She pressed her face into his shoulder.

"Rosalind, I am inside of you, my naked self is pressed against your naked self. There is no reason for you to be embarrassed, ever again."

She looked at him. "Some reward. It hurt."

"I know, but do you hurt now?"

"Well, no, not really. But you are very big, Nicholas, and I'm not. Surely the men in all those pictures, as bountifully as they were portrayed, they still aren't built like you are."

I'm deformed?

"Still, to be fair, despite your size, it wasn't really so very bad after a while." She leaned up and kissed him, a shy kiss, on his mouth. And fatigue suddenly fled. He wanted to make love to her all over again, right this instant, but he didn't move. It was difficult being sensitive to the fact that she must be sore. He nibbled on her chin, whispered in her mouth, "Thank you for explaining everything so clearly to me."

"I hope your grandfather isn't standing in the corner watching us."

He only smiled and kissed her again, on her mouth, a bit swollen, he could feel it, and so he licked her bottom lip. "You're my wife now, legally now."

"And you're now my husband, legally now."

"Ah, I'm much more than that, Rosalind." The words spilled out of him. "I'm the man who sought you out in London, the man who knew who you were the moment he saw you, even before he saw you, the man who must figure out what—" He broke off, cursed himself along with the goat's boot, then realized it didn't matter. Rosalind was asleep. He eased away from her to lie on his side beside her. He stroked her hair, easing out the tangles, picturing her head thrashing on the pillow when she'd fallen headfirst into her first orgasm, not a timid little orgasm, but a loud, ankle-thrumming, bone-melting orgasm. He gently pressed the wild curls behind her ear. "Yes," he whispered against her temple, "you're now legally my wife."

He spooned her, his hand on her belly, and kissed the nape of her neck. She tasted like salty jasmine.

He'd listened to men over the years talk about their mistresses and their wives. The biggest difference, they'd say and laugh, was that a wife followed you to your grave, or placed you in it, whereas a mistress perforce caressed whatever it was you instructed her to caress, and hopefully she would mourn your death perhaps a week before finding a new protector.

Wives, the talk usually continued, were to be taken quickly, without fuss and candlelight, in hushed darkness, a husband fast, done, and gone, all modesty preserved. Whereas a mistress, she was fashioned to enjoy a man, to enjoy his slavering all over her.

He'd always believed the men idiots.

Tonight, he'd proven it. He imagined that Ryder Sherbrooke would agree with him wholeheartedly.

He wondered what it would be like to have Rosalind take him into her mouth. He nearly shuddered himself off the bed.

He fell asleep with her scent in his nostrils, the taste of her on his mouth.

He didn't love her, couldn't love her, for a man couldn't love a debt. Could he?

33

Nicholas handed her the ancient leather book. "Here is my grandfather's copy of the *Rules of the Pale*. As you can see from the meager number of pages, it appears only to be an extract."

"Perhaps this is something of an introduction that will have explanations." But her voice didn't hold out much hope.

Rosalind sat in his grandfather's chair by the fireplace. The seat was warm even through her petticoats and her gown, and that made her wonder, but since there came no moans or groans when she'd sat down, she would deal with the possibility of sitting

on a spirit. Hopefully the old earl was prowl-
ing elsewhere this morning, perhaps still
hovering about in his former gloomy bedchamber, or standing on the other side of
the room, watching her in his chair.

She let the skinny volume fall open at random. It was in the same code, she recognized it, and she could read it as easily as
the other. She read:

**The wizards and witches who reside
on Mount Olyvan are an unscrupulous
lot, endlessly contentious and vain. They
hurl spells and curses at each other, so
vicious the heavens hiss.**

**I realized at last that they could not
leave Mount Olyvan, perhaps they could
not even step off of Blood Rock, this cold
and grim fortress that seems older than
the Pale itself. Not one of the residents
seemed to know where the fortress name
came from, or the fortress itself, for that
matter. I asked Belenus and he said
vaguely, "Ah, we are from before time
decided to travel forward." What a typical
wizard answer, I thought, and wanted to
kick him.**

**Another time I asked Belenus how old
he was and he ran large fingers through**

his thick red beard, showed me his white teeth, and said finally, "Years are a meaningless measure created by men who have to count them to ensure they get their fair share, which men never do because to kill each other fulfills them more than continued life." On this, I fancied he had a point.

I asked Latobius, the Celtic god of mountains and sky, if he was really a god, if he was immortal, and he raised his hand and a flame speared out from the tip of his finger and exploded an exquisite glass sculpture across the vast chamber. From King Agamemnon's palace in Mycenae, someone had told me. I remember the shards flew outward, cascades of vibrant color.

And I thought, You are a wizard, not a god, and I pointed my finger and hurled a spear of flame at a sconce on the stone wall. To tell the truth, it relieved me to see it burst apart. We both stood there watching the heavy shards hit the marble floor and scatter. He said nothing. It was difficult, but I didn't either.

And Epona? My son's mother? I never saw her again after the sixth night I spent in her white bed.

What are these beings?

I knew there were servants, but they were only flashes of shadow and light, as if they moved about in a slightly different time and place, out of phase, like a moon hovering just outside your vision. They certainly kept the fortress clean, its inhabitants well garbed, but they were separate from the witches and wizards, separate from me as well. Did they take their direction from something outside the fortress? Perhaps they were guards, or bodyguards. There were cooks too because the meals were splendid.

"Where are the servants?" I once asked Epona. She wore only white, her gowns always spotless. Her bedchamber was also completely white, it seemed to me the air was white around her. "We call them only when we need them," she told me, but that didn't sound right at all. "So they are not really here then? Where do they go? Where do they come from?" But she only shook her head, smoothing one white hand through my hair, and began kissing down my belly. And I wondered, before my brain became nothing more than empty space between my ears, Do you have any idea who or what these creatures are who serve you?

Rosalind raised her face. "Nicholas, this book isn't an extract from the other, it's completely different."

His heart was beating hard, strong strokes. "Yes, so it seems. Keep reading, Rosalind, there aren't many more pages."

There came a night when Blood Rock heaved and groaned and spewed rock and dirt high into the sky. Flames speared into the moonless black sky, the three bloodred moons inexplicably gone from the heavens. I heard screaming and shrieks, like demons from the deepest pits of Hell. The wizards and witches? Or the other creatures I didn't know about? Rocks tumbled down the steep sides of Mount Olyvan. I could not hear them crash at the bottom, and I feared for a moment that there was no longer a bottom, no longer a valley below. I ran to the ramparts and prepared to face my death. But I didn't die, Blood Rock did not tumble down Mount Olyvan. As suddenly as the cataclysm had begun, it ended. It was still, utterly still, as if the air itself were afraid to stir.

I didn't want to remain here and so I sent a silent plea to Taranis, the Dragon of the Sallas Pond who'd carried me to Blood Rock, and soon he came, swooping down gracefully onto the ramparts. No wizards or witches came to bid me farewell, indeed I hadn't seen a single one after the upheaval that had shaken the bowels of the fortress. My bowels as well. Had they all died?

Taranis lifted his mighty body gracefully from the ground and winged away from Mount Olyvan. When I looked back, everything seemed as it had been. I wondered yet again at all their Celtic god and goddess names, for none of them ever seemed to worship anything at all—and at Taranis the Dragon of the Sallas Pond, who was named after the Celtic god of thunder, the god who demanded human sacrifices. Had Taranis caused the mayhem on Mount Olyvan? He was immortal, he'd told me, unlike those bedeviling wizards and malignant witches in Blood Rock. I asked him if the wizards and witches had survived. Taranis told me the creatures of Blood Rock were cowering within their individual enchantments, a

**cowardly lot. I wanted to ask him about
my son, if he had indeed been born of
Epona's body, if indeed he had ever
existed, but Taranis chose that moment to
dive straight toward the earth and I lost
what few wits were in my head, and my
bowels were again in question.**

She looked up again. "Sarimund is occasionally amusing in this account. It's completely different from the other. I wonder
what really happened? Or if any of it happened at all."

"Perhaps the Blood Rock wizards and
witches unleashed all their powers."

"Unleashed their powers on what? The
fortress? The mountain itself? On each
other?"

"I don't know."

"I wonder if Sarimund ever found out what
happened. Perhaps there is a third thin volume somewhere. Oh, dear, do you think his
son survived? Epona's son? Was he even
born yet? This is very frustrating, Nicholas."

"Read the final pages, Rosalind."

She tried to turn the page, but it was
stuck. It wouldn't part. She looked at her
husband, saw he was frowning at that page.
"Drat, Nicholas, I cannot turn the page. It

seems stuck together with the last page. Remember with the other *Rules of the Pale*, I simply couldn't read the code on the final pages. With this little one, the bloody pages refuse to come free. I really would like to hurl this across the library."

Was that a rustling sound she suddenly heard?

There was a knock on the library door.

Nicholas looked ready to curse. Rosalind quickly got to her feet. "Let's see what's happening now."

It was Peter Pritchard, his young face haggard, his pale eyes ringed with shadows, his dark hair standing on end. His clothes, however, looked freshly pressed and his boots were polished. Behind him stood six women and four men in the vast entrance hall, all waiting, Peter told them, to be convinced by Nicholas to come to work at Wyverly, which was surely an opportunity only a dolt would deny—just imagine, a lifetime of tales to whisper about in front of winter fires.

"Give us a moment, Peter," Nicholas told him and shut the library door in his face. He'd forgotten. He didn't want to deal with convincing a bunch of villagers to work at Wyverly, and Rosalind saw it. She also saw his mouth, ah, his mouth, when he'd kissed her, when he'd caressed her with his mouth. She shivered, remembering how when she'd awakened, he was gone, and she wanted to howl. As she stretched sore muscles she hadn't been aware of even having, she thought about burrowing against him in her sleep, and waking to kiss him, letting him—well, she'd kissed him at the breakfast table, in a small, really quite lovely room with huge windows that gave onto the front drive, kissed him until Marigold had staggered into the room balancing heavy silver-domed trays on her arms. She'd stopped in her tracks and stared and stared, then grinned from ear to ear.

And after breakfast, when Rosalind had thought perhaps Nicholas would carry her up to his boyhood bedchamber, he hadn't. He'd brought her to the library and handed her the thin leather book. She knew this was vital, she knew it, but still—

She smiled at him now, tossed him the thin volume. "Why don't you slip out into the gardens, Nicholas, and think about this. See if you can free those final pages. Did you notice there are no more rules? Yes, you go to the gardens. Since I am the Wyverly mistress, it is only right that I deal with hiring our staff." She patted his arm. "I am very good at convincing people to do what I want."

He looked down at the book, opened his mouth, but she lightly placed her fingertips against his lips.

"The book has been here for a very long time. It isn't going to fly out the window. Try to get the last page unstuck, though I don't hold much hope. Now, let me see what I can do. We need to get Wyverly back to its former glory. Ah, there was former glory, wasn't there?"

"There was until my father became ill, actually faced his own mortality and realized the house and lands would come to me. He moved his family to London and left everything here to rot. Not all that long ago, thank God. I was very lucky Peter Pritchard was available."

"I'm sorry, Nicholas. What a wretched old wart your father was. I wish he were here so I could punch him in the nose."

He laughed, bent down and gave her a hard, violent kiss, and took himself out of the glass doors into a small overgrown garden. He heard animals scurrying about in the underbrush. He called out over his shoulder, "We need gardeners."

She opened the library door and ushered Peter in. "Peter," she said, turning to face him, "I think I should like to speak to all of them at once. I trust you have ensured that none are ripe to steal the silver?"

"The old earl told my father, who told me, that Nicholas once stole three silver spoons forged during the time of Queen Bess so he could sell them in Grantham and buy himself a pony. The old earl, my father told me, thought it was very well done of him. The pony was treated like a prince here at Wyverly Chase. Indeed, he still resides in the stables, content to be brushed and fed carrots." Peter paused, slapped himself, and said, "I'm sorry but that has nothing to do with the matter at hand. As best I can ascertain, we have no thieves in this bunch."

"All right, Peter, bring in our people."

"They're not ours yet, my lady, and I doubt—"

She merely shook her head at him. When they were all lined up in front of her, many looking frankly alarmed to be in the old earl's library, the rumored seat of all ghostly occurrences, several of the men trying to sneer away their fear, Rosalind smiled at each of them in turn, and said, "I am Lady Mountjoy.

My husband and I are newly arrived at Wyverly Chase." She leaned closer. "Let me tell you all truthfully—I played chess with the old earl's ghost last evening, and do you know what? I beat him every time. He grumbled and threw several chess pieces across the library, but all in all, he took it well."

There were several gasps, a couple of indrawn male breaths.

"The old earl is in transit, I suppose you could say. He is neither here nor there, but currently more here than there, if you know what I mean. He is not dangerous, not at all alarming, indeed, I find that he is a good listener and I enjoy singing duets with him.

"Do any of you sing?"

34

Dead silence. An older woman's hand slowly crept up. "I do, my lady. The vicar told me I have the sweetest voice in his whole flock."

"Then doubtless you will have to carry the duet with the old earl, as his voice isn't all that true. Do you think you would enjoy that, Mrs.—"

"Mrs. McGiver, my lady. Mr. Pritchard spoke to me about the housekeeper position."

"The old earl knows some clever songs, Mrs. McGiver."

"'E's not the old earl, 'e's a ghost," one of the men said, "a bloody ghost wot doesn't belong aboveground! Singing duets, it isn't right. All this talk about playing chess with a ghost—there's evil and bad business, that's what everyone says. No good will come to anyone who stays 'ere."

Rosalind nodded at the older gentleman with a rooster tail of white hair. "I understand your concerns, Mr.—"

"Macklin, my lady, Horace Macklin. I was the 'ead gardener 'ere before the old earl came back to 'aunt."

"The gardens are in dire need of your help, Mr. Macklin. Now, listen to me. I have discussed this with the old earl and he assures me he is not evil, he is, indeed, of a happy frame of mind. The reason he is happy is that he is very glad his grandson is here and wed.

"He told me about many of you, how kind you were, how pleasant and witty, how very good you all were. He also said he hoped you would come back and scrub things up so Wyverly Chase can be brought back to its former glory."

Still uncertain looks, at least two appalled faces.

Rosalind leaned a bit closer to the group and lowered her voice. "I can tell you this: He will add interest to your lives, he will make you smile after you become used to hearing his booming voice. When he breaks into song, I daresay you will soon find yourselves singing along with him. Who among you can be so timid, so fearful, as to turn down this very rare opportunity? Isn't this an adventure, something to tell your grandchildren? Your friends? I daresay they will all be hanging off your words, buying you glasses of ale to hear you talk."

Ah, most of the faces weren't quite so stony now.

She continued, "All great houses have their ghosts. Without ghosts, great houses simply don't come up to the mark. Now, the old earl's ghost isn't ancient and thus he hasn't yet decided whether or not he wishes to settle here. As I said, he is still afloat, but eager to greet all of you. Will he remain? I don't know. We will see."

She stepped back and let them huddle. Voices were muted but they were talking, and that was good. Eyes darted around the library, but the old earl remained quiet, if he was even here.

Finally, the woman with the sweet voice, Mrs. McGiver, took a step forward and said,

"All but Robert will come, my lady. Robert is afraid, a sorry thing for a man to be—"

"'Ere now! I ain't afeared!"

Mrs. McGiver sneered at him. "Then sign on, my lad. You won't even have a chance to hear the old earl sing, or sing with him for that matter, since you'll be yanking up weeds in the gardens. You too afraid to do that?"

More grumbling, then Robert nodded. "All right, I'll stay on the grounds, but niver will I come into this den of iniquity. A ghost in the library—it fair to beetles the brow."

Thankfully, the old earl's den of iniquity remained quiet, the air unruffled and warm.

Rosalind heard Peter Pritchard tell the group as he ushered them out of the library, "If you would all begin today, his lordship and ladyship would be very pleased. Do you know that I myself have sung a duet with the old earl? His is not a very good voice, I must say, but he does try. I'm thinking there must be heavenly points for singing rather than simply speaking. What do you think, Mrs. McGiver?"

"He never had a good voice, at least I wouldn't imagine he did. I never heard him sing, truth be told."

Robert said, "Well, now, the old earl's dead, ain't 'e? Who could sing good with grave dirt in 'is mouth?"

Mumbled agreement. Thank the good Lord no one mentioned there hadn't been a body in the old earl's casket.

Rosalind was grinning when she joined Nicholas in the small overgrown garden with hummingbirds dipping into the rich tangled rose blooms. The air was soft, the sun shining down hot from a clear sky.

"I like my new home, Nicholas. We now have ten additional servants. All will be well. Our new housekeeper is Mrs. McGiver, and I have to hand the prize to her. She's got a backbone, in addition to a lovely voice."

"However you and Mrs. McGiver managed it, I am impressed." He kissed her. The hummingbirds were blurs in the air, swooping closer when he took her to the ground behind a thick-pedestaled sundial. She asked him between kisses if the earl ever visited this small garden.

Nicholas, no fool, said, "No, never. He hated flowers, hated the bright sun. Do you know, I hated leaving you this morning, I ground my teeth, kicked the chair on my way out the door. Do you know you clutched me to you when I tried to leave? Ah, be quiet now."

"Then why did you leave?"

"You had to be sore," he said between kisses. "I didn't want to hurt you. You're better now, aren't you, Rosalind?"

"Oh, yes," she said into his mouth even as she pulled his ears, "I am perfect."

He laughed.

Because Peter Pritchard wasn't a fool either, when he heard voices in the garden he immediately turned himself about and went back into the old earl's library. He thought about the widow Damson, her lovely smile, her pillowy breasts, and decided it was time to pay a visit.

Twenty minutes later, Nicholas helped Rosalind to her feet and straightened her gown. She fussed with her hair. "Oh, dear, how do I look?"

He was so sated, so contented, not a care in his brain, his eyes heavily hooded, that he wanted to fall in a heap and grin like an idiot. His fingers touched her cheek. "You look like a queen." Since this was perhaps not all that accurate, Rosalind punched his arm. He grinned down at her, kissed her mouth again because he couldn't help himself, and said,

"You look happy and satisfied with yourself. You look silly and adorable as well. There were three twigs sticking out of your head like horns. This look of yours befits a new bride. Don't concern yourself—no one will know what you've done beneath the sundial. Trust me, you also look like the stern mistress of Wyverly just so long, well, so long as one doesn't look at your eyes."

"What's wrong with my eyes?"

He kissed her again. "Not a thing. However, the terms 'vague' and 'dreamy' come to mind." Like his own eyes, he guessed. "That sundial is very old, you know, at least two hundred years. I'm pleased it didn't fall on us when you kicked out with your foot." He lightly touched his fingertips to her cheek. "I am very pleased with you, Rosalind. Very pleased."

Rosalind didn't look up at him. "I am pleased with you as well, Nicholas. I know I should be shocked at what I most willingly wanted you to do to me—again—things that you did to my great satisfaction—again—but I'm not." That tongue of hers licked over her bottom lip. He went *en pointe*. She stood on her tiptoes and whispered against his ear,

"There are things I wish to try, only you didn't give me a chance."

He could practically feel her long white legs, sleek with muscle, squeezing his flanks, and consulted his watch. It was ten o'clock in the morning. Perhaps after luncheon he could take her riding to the small copse where a stream ran through it surrounded by soft grass, and larks sang their sweet songs overhead on the maple tree branches. He beamed down at her. "I will give you a chance. We will ask Cook to make us a picnic."

"Oh, yes. Would you look at all the hummingbirds. Do you know how long they live?"

"Only about three years, I believe."

"They move about awfully fast, don't they? Always moving. Do you think with all our activity we will shorten our lives?"

He stared down at her, kissed her because he simply couldn't stop himself, and said, "I wouldn't mind." He felt the book in his pocket. He cleared his throat. "I couldn't free the last pages. The answers are there, I'm thinking, only something or someone is preventing us from finding them." And he kissed her again.

When she would have taken him behind the sundial again, he raised his head and smoothed his thumb over her lower lip. "What do you think?"

"I think it's time to use your brain rather than other parts, my lord," she said and laughed as she tugged him back into the library. They both stopped cold on the threshold when a scratchy old voice boomed out,

Sins of the flesh
Sins of the flesh
A bloodless bore the world would be
Without sins of the flesh.

Rosalind shook her fist toward the empty chair. "We committed no sin. We are married. You are surely a lecherous old ghost. Be quiet."

"The thing is," Nicholas said slowly, after hearing nothing else from the old earl for several moments, "my grandfather never sang a note in his life. Why should he begin singing in his death?"

"What?"

He drew in his breath. "I can never remember him singing when I was a boy. I've been wondering how a dead man would begin to sing when the living man never had."

"But that's all he does, only sings out one ridiculous ditty after another, no rhyme nor reason."

"Well, this last one was pointed and fairly accurate, I'd say. I've given this a lot of thought. Fact is, I don't think it's my grandfather."

"Then who?"

"I think we need to go back to Sarimund's century, to someone he knew firsthand. We need to go back to the time of the first Earl of Mountjoy. Fact is, Rosalind, I think our ghost is our long-ago captain, Jared Vail."

"But why is he here? Why did he welcome me?"

Two excellent questions, Nicholas thought, and asked the empty chair, "Are you indeed Captain Jared Vail?"

There was a faint cackle, from behind the wainscoting, Rosalind thought, or maybe it came from that empty spot above a painting of a seventeenth-century Vail with a very elaborate curled black wig, holding a ripe peach in his hand, some sort of ancient ruin behind him.

"So, if you are Captain Jared Vail, why are you glad to see me?" she asked, looking in that direction.

Nothing at all, just calm peaceful air, no lurking ghost to stir it up.

Then the painting cocked itself crooked.

35

Two hours later, Rosalind went in search of Nicholas. She paused when she heard Mrs. McGiver's rich contralto coming from the library. She was singing a clever song about a young girl in Leeds who fell in love with a cooper's son and how things went awry over a beer barrel.

Rosalind moved closer to the library door, listening, then, finally, a scratchy old voice sang out,

Three girls are better than two
Two girls are better than one
Nail one and it's fun

Nail two and swoon
Nail three or more
And the lion roars.

Praise be, Praise be.
I always nailed three
Until I had to wed
And take the fat cow to bed.
Alas, my cock fell dead, so dead.

She heard Mrs. McGiver's sharp voice, "What a nasty thing to sing, my lord! It was somewhat funny, I'll grant you that—but I must say your words aren't what the vicar would consider respectful. And what is this about a cow for a wife? Your wife was never fat. She was a thin little mite as I recall. For shame." And in the next moment, Mrs. McGiver, plump cheeks flushed, came striding out of the library. She shut the door sharply behind her. She pulled up short when she saw Rosalind.

"Oh, my lady, did you hear that nasty old—" She waved a work-roughened hand toward the library.

Rosalind said, "I heard you sing very prettily, Mrs. McGiver, and yes, I heard the old earl's reply." There was no need to tell Mrs. McGiver which old earl—a two-hundred-year-old ghost might not go over as easily as one who'd just gained his ghostly wings only ten years before. Still, Mrs. McGiver was clearly outraged, not because she'd heard a ghost sing, but because of the words of his bawdy song. Rosalind couldn't help herself, she burst into laughter. She cleared her throat, and quickly said, "Do forgive me, but don't you see? Our ghost listened to you. He was probably enchanted by your lovely voice and trying to think of a song to flatter you, to amuse you, but unfortunately those appalling rude verses were all he could think of. Don't forget, Mrs. McGiver, he was still a man, and you know what men are." Rosalind herself didn't know much about what men were and weren't, but she was married, after all, and so she gave it her best.

To her surprise and relief, Mrs. McGiver's outrage disappeared. "Hmm. My lady, do you think he really liked my song? But, *take the fat cow to bed*—I mean, how spiteful—well, perhaps you have the right of it, perhaps our old earl couldn't think of a more uplifting tune. The odd thing is, though, I can't ever remember the old earl harking so often to the pleasures of the flesh. You don't think that ghosts—?"

"No, no, surely not. The thing about our ghost . . . He realizes that he upset you, Mrs. McGiver. Perhaps next time, he will moderate his content."

To Rosalind's astonishment, Mrs. McGiver giggled. Then she harrumphed and cleared her throat. "Well, as to that, I must say now that I think about it, it was fairly amusing. Now, I left him, my lady, all upset, perhaps his ghostly innards twisted with shame and embarrassment, and I realize I must go back in the library and dust. Mrs. Sweet told me it fair to shriveled her liver to work in the library, particularly after the old earl's chair tilted from one leg to the other to work itself closer to the fireplace, right in front of her."

"I know. Mrs. Sweet has a fine set of lungs. You're an example to all the staff, Mrs. McGiver."

"Well, that's as may be. I told Mrs. Sweet that since he was a ghost, there was little if anything at all left to him now, so didn't it make sense that he had to have more warmth?"

"But the fireplace isn't lit."

"Aye, that's true enough, and I'll admit I did hold my breath, but luckily Mrs. Sweet accepted the explanation. Aye, in addition to singing like an angel, I'm a very brave woman, and that's what my father told me when I married Mr. McGiver. Of course it didn't take much bravery to crack Mr. McGiver's head with a cooking pot when he sent his fist to my jaw, now did it?"

"You were fast?"

"Oh, yes, it only required a couple of smacks right in his face—a man with a black eye doesn't like to be questioned about it by other men—and Mr. McGiver turned into a model husband. As you said, my lady, the old earl was still a man, whatever else he is now."

"Hmmm."

Mrs. McGiver whirled around at the sound of the deep male voice, a deep male voice that warmed Rosalind to her toes, and she would swear that deep male voice made those toes flush. She'd been working with Peter Pritchard, and hadn't seen Nicholas for two hours—too long a time without him. Mrs. McGiver quickly bobbed the new earl a curtsy. "Oh, my lord. So you're here and not somewhere else. Well, these sorts of things must occasionally happen, I suppose. It is still a pity you were close by, if, that is, you chanced to hear anything you should not have heard." And Mrs. McGiver bobbed him another curtsy and took herself off.

"I'm a critter?"

"Doubtless a model critter, my lord."

She saw that he was carrying several old books, and raised a brow.

"I found these in an ancient trunk on the third floor." He stepped closer. "They're Captain Jared Vail's journals, Rosalind."

"Oh, my." The books he held were ancient cracked black leather, laden with dust, and looked ready to crumble. She eyed those books. "They are very old indeed. You told me your grandfather said Captain Jared kept a journal, but how did you know where to find it?"

"Come into the library. I don't want any of the servants to hear this. They'd think I am quite mad and send for the magistrate. Wait, I am the magistrate. Unfortunately, I still might just declare myself ready for Bedlam." He gave her a crooked grin and led her back into the library. He closed and locked the door. "I don't know how good Captain Jared's ghost is with locked doors. Perhaps we'll find out." He looked down at the books lying in the palm of his hand. "Or maybe he's seated right there. If so, perhaps he'll want to sing about the journals."

She didn't tell him that the ghost had just

sung a bawdy ditty to Mrs. McGiver. "But how did you find them, Nicholas?"

"Fact is, I think when the old fellow saw I'd figured out who he really was, he knew it was time to direct me to his journals."

He touched her cheek with a dirty finger. "Sorry." And he pulled a handkerchief out of his pocket and wiped her cheek. "Perhaps you will believe me when I say I knew, I simply knew. From one moment to the next, I knew there would be something in a corner room on the third floor in the east wing, and so I went up there. Sure enough there was this ancient trunk tucked snug under a window beneath a pile of equally ancient draperies, so moth-eaten they fell to pieces when I lifted them off the trunk. Nothing else in the room, just that old trunk. Inside the trunk was a mound of clothes, and at the bottom of the trunk, wrapped in a tattered yellowed petticoat, were these three volumes." He grinned. "What's wonderful is they aren't in code. I can actually read them."

Rosalind was frowning at him. "I don't understand, Nicholas. As a boy, you must have explored every inch of Wyverly. Why didn't you find the trunk?"

He frowned, stared toward the library

door he'd firmly closed and locked when they'd come in here. Now it was the tiniest bit open. He hadn't heard a key turning in the lock, he hadn't heard a thing. How had Captain Jared managed to unlock it? He walked over and closed it again, and once again turned the huge old key in the lock, saying over his shoulder to her, "Yes, I did explore every inch of this place during the seven years I lived here. So did my grandfather— he would brag that he knew where every splinter was, where every creaky stair step was. But even though he knew about Captain Jared's journals, he didn't know where they were." He stared down at the key a moment, then pulled it from the lock. He looked around the room as he waved the key about. "Come and get it, you old sea dog," he said, and slipped it into his jacket pocket.

"So the trunk with the journals just somehow appears? This is getting rather alarming, Nicholas."

He shrugged. "Who knows? I think I shall wrap the journals in cheesecloth and take them on our picnic. We can study them in private, with no ghost or servants to peer over our shoulders."

36

An hour later, Nicholas helped her down from Old Velvet's back in a maple copse set at the back of the Wyverly property. Rosalind was carrying the cheesecloth-wrapped journals as tenderly as she would a baby.

Old Velvet, he'd told her when he'd introduced her to the bay mare with lovely white socks, had been intended to mate with Beltane. Unfortunately, Beltane wasn't interested, a blow to Nicholas and to Velvet, who proceeded to eat every oat she could find and became quite fat. "They still ignore each other," he said, and patted the old mare's nose.

After they tethered the horses, Nicholas carried the picnic basket and a large tartan blanket, the plaid of Scottish Highland cousins many times removed, and led her deeper into the maple copse.

The air was as soft as Old Velvet's nose, soft like silk lightly touching her cheek. The scent of wild roses and star jasmine filled the air. Was that lilac she smelled? There were animals rustling about in the woods around them. A lone nightingale sang from the top branch of a maple tree.

Rosalind looked around her, touched the leaves of a wild rosebush. "What a wonderful place. It is perfect."

He nodded. He was standing very still, his eyes closed. "When I was a boy I always thought something good and fine lived here a very long time ago. Whatever it was, or whoever it was, it left an echo of sweetness behind. And joy," he added, then flushed.

This hard tough man, she thought, who'd carved himself an empire with his brain and his back, and he thought of an echo of sweetness. And joy. And he was flushing because surely a man shouldn't speak so poetically.

He'd seen her and wanted her. Only her.

He hadn't cared that she could very well be less than a nobody.

She watched him fall to his knees and spread out the tartan, and arrange the food atop it. She stood there, the journals still clasped protectively to her chest, and marveled at him. At Fate. At a two-hundred-year-old ghost and the journals he'd led Nicholas to find.

He smiled up at her, patted the plaid. "Come, sit down."

"I must be very careful not to hurt the journals."

He said with absolute conviction, "They're not about to disintegrate on us now, since I—we—were meant to find them. Hand them to me, Rosalind."

He laid them on the tartan. "Let's eat first, I'm starving to death, unless—"

"Unless what?"

He shrugged, all indifferent, picked up a leg of baked chicken, and bit into it.

She said, "Unless perhaps you would care to kiss me first?"

He chewed on the chicken and looked at that mouth of hers, and slowly smiled. "A very nice idea."

She laughed aloud and leapt on him. He

fell onto his back, tossed the chicken leg
over his head, heard a small animal scurry
to pinch it, and brought her over him.

He would never tire of kissing her, he
thought, never, and when his hands touched
her bare flesh, he trembled. She didn't know
what to do—until she felt the earth suddenly
tilt and all her embarrassment fell out of her
head. She grabbed his hair to yank him
down to her.

When she lay quietly, her head on his
shoulder, her breathing finally smoothing out
again, he sighed. "I am a selfless man, a
man so noble he ignores his own needs,
content to bask in the pleasure he gives his
wife. Ah, if I feed you, Rosalind, will you have
the energy to perform your marital duties?"

"But, you—" She reared up and grinned
down at him. She struck a pose. "Ah, I
understand. You want more than one marital
duty from me. Do you know, I have some
ideas about that." She remembered one
drawing in the book her aunts had reluc-
tantly given her that showed a woman on
her knees in front of a standing man and he
had his hands clenched in her hair while she
was pressing her face against his belly. At
least at the time she'd thought it was his

belly, and hadn't understood why that was of enough interest to merit a page in the book, but now she knew the truth. She gave him a look to cramp his guts.

They didn't touch the journals until an hour later. Even then, Nicholas really didn't give a good damn. He was stretched out on his back, naked, his shirt, pants, and boots tossed to the ground beyond his right arm, a silly grin on his face, his eyes closed against the spear of sunlight coming through the maple leaves, basking in utter contentment, remembering when she'd dropped to her knees in front of him. "Tell me what to do," she'd said, her warm breath on his flesh, but he'd said nothing at all.

"Nicholas?"

A soft voice, a sweet voice, coming from above him, insistent, that voice. She kissed him. Slowly he opened his eyes and looked up at her. What to say when the earth had opened beneath his feet, and he'd dived right in? "That was very fine, Rosalind."

She preened, she actually preened. If he'd had the energy, he would have laughed.

She nearly sang it out. "You were as wild as I was, Nicholas."

His eyes crossed. He blinked. "Perhaps,"

he said. "Perhaps. I suppose you wish me to get myself together, don't you?"

"Yes. I just looked over at the journals, and I swear to you, they've moved closer to us."

Nicholas sincerely hoped that Captain Jared's ghost hadn't nudged them closer since that would mean the old boy had gotten himself a ghostly eyeful. He raised his hand and lightly touched his fingertips to her lips. "I love your mouth."

She ran her tongue over her bottom lip and he swelled, ready to take her down again. He swelled even more when she looked down at him.

No, he had to get a grip on himself. At least she was wearing her chemise—how did that happen? But a chemise didn't matter since he was a young man and he was newly married and—he took her down, both of them laughing wildly, then there were only whispers and deep sighs. This time, he managed to work her chemise up to her neck.

When he buried his face against her breasts, and moaned deeply, all those dark places inside himself that had been empty far too long, bubbled and filled, perhaps even overflowed. It was astounding.

When he handed her his handkerchief,

she walked into the trees, giving him a quick smile over her shoulder. Her wild curling red hair tangled about her shoulders. He lay back and closed his eyes, grinning like a fool, he couldn't help it. When she came back, her chemise was in place again.

He dressed himself, then assisted her with the buttons on her wrinkled gown, even rubbed at the grass stains, and knew the laundress would know well what had happened to the mistress's gown.

"It is two hours after noon, Nicholas, only the second day of our union, and you have already loved me three times." She gave him a huge grin. "And I loved you."

"I have always liked the number four. Would you—"

She raised her face to the cloud-tumbled sky. "I am stalwart, I am focused, I will not let you distract yet again. Ah, but you are beautiful, Nicholas."

He had to clear his throat three times before his brain was focused enough to read from the first ancient journal. The handwriting was spidery and barely legible, the years had so scarred and faded the ink.

"This entry is dated the same year as his marriage to the Wyverly heiress," he said.

"Goodness, you remember that?"

"No," he said absently, "Captain Vail wrote it here."

"Have you already read the journals, Nicholas?'

"Just a few pages here and there. In this first one, he chats about what was happening at the time—how his decision to wed the heiress was a good one because his pockets were so empty they were dragging the ground. His creditors were six feet behind him, and closing fast. You will like this: *She is eager, a fine thing for a virgin of seventeen, and even though she has an arse the size of a cow's—*"

"What a nasty thing to write, particularly when she saved him."

"Yes, very true," Nicholas said. "He goes on to detail the actual building of Wyverly— at great boring length, I might add—and the workmen he'd like to kick in the arse. Ah, he appears to have an obsession with this rear part. All right, here we go. Now he writes about what happened to him the previous year when he lost everything in the Mediterranean, his ship, his cargo, his crew, yet he was saved. He writes, *I knew something wasn't right. I was lying on my back and I couldn't move. A single light shone directly onto my face, but it wasn't a strong light so it didn't blind me. The light was strange, all soft and vague, and it seemed to pulse like a beating heart.*

. . . I don't know who or what this being is, but I indeed promised to pay my debt so that I would continue living.

. . . A young girl appeared in front of me, her hair streaked with sunlight, loosely braided down her back, eyes blue as an Irish stream, freckles across her small nose, a sturdy little girl with narrow hands and feet. She threw her head back and she sang.

"What did she sing, Nicholas?"

He saw that she knew well what the little girl sang.

He read:

I dream of beauty and sightless night
I dream of strength and fevered might
I dream I'm not alone again
But I know of his death and her grievous
**   sin.**

He looked up at her. Neither said a word. He knew she also realized she was the little girl. Rosalind whispered, "Then what does he write?"

A child's voice, sweet and true, it called forth feelings I hadn't known were in me, feelings to break my heart. But those strange words—what did they mean? What male died? What female's grievous sin?

. . . She spoke again; this time her words rang clear in my brain: I am your debt.

She said slowly, "I don't suppose we can escape it now. I was the little girl and who-ever, whatever it was who demanded Captain Jared pay this debt—whatever this debt is—I'm it."

37

They gathered up the remains of their picnic and rode silently back to Wyverly. Nicholas felt the fear in her, just as he felt it in his own gut. He didn't like it and sought to distract her. He spoke of their tenant farmers and the repairs he was making on their cottages, the new equipment he'd provided for their fields. He was nearly hoarse from talking so much when at last they were sitting again in the library, both of them looking over at the earl's chair. It remained perfectly still, and hopefully vacant.

Rosalind said, "I wonder where our ghost goes when he's not in this room."

"Don't be afraid," he said abruptly.

"That isn't possible," Rosalind said. "I've never felt such fear, not since I was eight years old, woke up to hear I'd nearly died, and couldn't remember who I was. Worse yet, I still don't know who I am. I only know I am a debt." She slammed her fist on the chair arm. "What bloody debt?"

Suddenly, one of Captain Jared's songs was clear in her mind. She recited the verses slowly aloud.

> **At last the girl comes home**
> **A girl who never belonged**
> **To her is owed the debt**
> **Well met, my lad, well met.**
>
> **The little girl nearly died**
> **The monster nearly won**
> **The debt was paid by another**
> **But the race must still be run.**

How could she remember the words so clearly, so easily? She looked up to see Nicholas studying her, his fingers steepled.

"Yes," he said, "I remember them as well. It all began when a being whose identity we don't know, whose identity Captain Jared never learned either, a being who saved his life, took him to this unidentified place, told him he had to pay this debt because, as this being told him, *I have sworn not to meddle. It is a curse that I must obey my own word."*

"What being would promise not to meddle, Nicholas? That is what a magic being does—it meddles, it plays, or it devastates. And I am the debt, yes, I will accept that though I was also seemingly the debt over two hundred years ago, the debt Captain Jared was to have paid, and how can that be? Who was he to pay a magic debt?

"I don't know anything of a debt, I don't even know who I am. All I know is that wretched song. It's always been inside me, you know it was the first thing out of my mouth when I finally began to speak after Uncle Ryder brought me home.

"I don't know who the monster is in the song. Obviously it was Uncle Ryder who saved me. *The race must still be run.* So it's still there, the monster, the mystery, the need to pay the debt, whatever it is.

"And then after you came, we found Sarimund's book, the *Rules of the Pale*. Or rather Grayson did. What does that wretched book have to do with anything? Why can I read it and not you or Grayson? Who cares about this red Lasis who kills the Tibers in fire pits? None of this makes any bloody sense and I'll tell you, Nicholas, I'm very sick of all of it."

She jumped to her feet, grabbed a pillow, and threw it at the old earl's chair. The very heavy chair tilted a bit, then settled again.

"Oh, go away, you miserable old fright! I didn't strike the chair hard enough to make it move. I am a normal female person now, not some sort of planted dream from hundreds of years ago. Am I a wizard's debt, for God's sake? A wizard who's sworn not to meddle?"

The chair tilted again, then settled.

They both stared at it. Rosalind growled deep in her throat and threw the other pillow at Nicholas. He snatched it out of the air six inches from his face. "Sit down, sweetheart. It's time—" His brain closed down a moment. No, he had to say this, he had to tell her the truth now. No choice.

"Time for what?"

"It's time I was completely honest with you. It's time I told you who I am and what I know of this."

Something was very wrong here, and she knew she really didn't want to know. But there was no hope for it. Her heart jumped, then begin to thud, slow hard strokes. She sat beside him and clutched his arm. She said, her mouth so dry she could barely form the words, "What do you mean, *who I am*? You actually know something? Tell me who you really are. Tell me what is going on, Nicholas."

He took her hand in his, began stroking her long fingers. He stared into the empty fireplace as he said, "I was eleven years old when I first dreamed of you. You were a little girl, skinny, your glorious red hair in braids, the line of freckles scattered across your nose. You had the sweetest face. Then you sang your song to me. After you'd sung, you fell silent and looked at me, sad and empty, and you said, *I am your debt.*

"I finally told my grandfather about the dream after I'd dreamed it a half dozen times. Always the same, always your face, your voice, that haunting sad song.

"To my astonishment, Grandfather told me he'd had the same dream as a boy but it had simply stopped when he'd been about sixteen, but he'd never forgotten it or you or the sense of failure. He said his father had told him the same thing, but he'd never understood the debt either, and his dream had stopped also when he'd been a young man. It was as if, my grandfather said, whoever or whatever had brought on the dreams had given up. My grandfather supposed it went all the way back, although exactly how far he didn't know, and it always came to the eldest son and he always dreamed that dream, but then, as he gained years, it simply stopped. But not the feelings of loss, the feelings of something vital left undone.

"I asked him about my father. Had he dreamed the dream? My grandfather told me my father was the second son and he denied any such dream, as did his older brother, the first-born son.

"And so it came to me. Then he recited the words of the song, looked at me sadly. 'I never did a thing, Nicholas, never did a thing because I didn't know what to do, like all the men in our line, I suppose. But now it is your turn. It is up to you to pay the debt, if the debt finally appears.' He told me he believed the little girl had somehow been out of time, and surely that was beyond a man's comprehension, but he knew she would appear when it was right for her to appear, and not before.

"Perhaps, he told me, now it was time and

she would be there for me, but in truth, he didn't know, though he was hopeful."

Nicholas fell silent.

"Did the dream fade away when you were a young man?"

He shook his head. "No, and that is how I knew I was the Vail to pay the debt. I dreamed the identical dream perhaps twice a month. After I met you I dreamed it every night, until we wed. But not last night."

Rosalind said slowly, "Perhaps this all ties together with the *Rules of the Pale*. It was your grandfather who told you about Sarimund the wizard and Rennat the Titled Wizard of the East. I dreamed of Rennat, and he told me I would come into my own and to obey the *Rules of the Pale*, and he kept repeating it."

He stared at her. "Rennat actually appeared to you? He told you you would come into your own? Those were his words?"

She nodded, searching his face. "So the *Rules of the Pale* must fit in all this mess somehow. What is this all about, Nicholas? Who am I?—*What am I?*"

Nicholas smoothed his thumb over her palm. "I kept dreaming about you, the little girl with the rich red hair and eyes as blue as the summer sky, and the beautiful haunting voice. I knew someday, Rosalind, knew all the way to my soul that I would find you and I would save you since you were now my debt. It was time, you see, it was the right time, and something deep inside me knew it was the right time. And so I came for you."

"To pay Captain Jared's debt?"

"Yes."

"You came to London, you saw me, recognized me, married me. A debt is one thing, but—why did you marry me, Nicholas?"

Not a single word came to his brain.

"You didn't succumb to the *coup de foudre*, as the French say, did you? You did see me across the ballroom, but your heart didn't fall to your feet, did it? You said you recognized me, Nicholas. And you came to me. Why didn't you simply tell me who you were, what this was all about?"

"I couldn't very well tell you when I had no idea what I was to do. What would I have said to you? Besides, whatever I could have said, you would have believed me mad. Your Uncle Ryder certainly would have put his boot to my back and kicked me out."

"So you believed so strongly in this debt business that you married a girl you didn't even know?"

38

"There was more to it than that, Rosalind."

"Yes, there was the *Rules of the Pale*. And Sarimund and your grandfather—who just happened to have another sort of *Rules of the Pale* written by this Sarimund character. Now that's a universe of madness in itself, isn't it? You must have been so excited when it turned out I could read the bloody thing—but the *Rules of the Pale* didn't tell us anything, nor did the scribblings of Sarimund that your grandfather had in his possession. He couldn't read it either. That's what you told me."

"No, he couldn't. And it drove him to near madness. The hours he spent trying to decipher it. I can remember him sitting up until late into the night studying the code, trying to figure it out."

"But he couldn't, because it isn't really a code. It's magic, some sort of enchantment."

"Yes, perhaps so. Who knows?"

"So since I'm the only one who can read the bloody thing, I must be magic as well. Do you agree?" She laughed over his silence, an ugly sound because it was filled with fear and something else he couldn't identify. "Oh, yes, I'm so magic I was nearly beaten to death. I'm so magic I can't even remember who I am or how I could possibly be any-one's debt." She jumped to her feet and paced the length of the library. "That visit of Rennat the Titled Wizard of the East in my dream—and what does that ridiculous title mean anyway?—*I'm to come into my own.* How would he know that? Why did he come to me? What does he want me to do?"

"Perhaps Rennat was the wizard or being who saved Captain Jared's life. After all, he isn't a simple plain wizard, he's the Titled Wizard of the East. Perhaps he also caused the storm, the being who brought the huge wave that destroyed Captain Jared's ship and killed all his men. He set it all up so Captain Jared would believe he did owe him a great debt."

"You believe Rennat brought the storm? That bespeaks a power neither of us can comprehend, Nicholas. Could a wizard do that, even a wizard with a bloody title?"

"I don't want to believe it but there doesn't seem to be a choice for me. It also means that this is a very powerful being, if this being did indeed bring Captain Jared Vail under his thumb. It can only mean that Jared Vail was the only man to pay this debt. If it wasn't Rennat, was it Belenus, the wizard Sarimund wrote about at Blood Rock? Or Taranis, the Dragon of the Sallas Pond? He was the god, after all, supposedly immortal and all-powerful. Is that why we were led to the *Rules of the Pale*? But again, why Grayson and not one of us?"

She walked over to the big mahogany desk, pausing a moment by the ghost's chair. She leaned down to say into an invisible ear, "You might try to be of some assistance here. A song perhaps that isn't lewd, a song that really means something."

There was nothing from the chair.

Rosalind sat behind the desk in the over-large leather chair. "Let me get a piece of foolscap and a pencil. I want to list out all the questions. Then we will try to go about answering them one at a time." She sat down and began writing. He watched her silently until at last she looked up at him. She said very precisely, "The question at the very top of my list, Nicholas, is why did you marry me? You are the only one who knows the answer to that question. Tell me now."

His brain, working at a furious speed until this moment, shut down. Nothing at all came out of his mouth.

She said, her voice utterly expression-less, "Very well, I don't really blame you for keeping quiet. Your answer wouldn't be excessively gratifying to a new bride, would it? So allow me to answer it for you. You married me because you knew if you were ever to figure out this debt business, figure out what exactly was owed to me, figure out exactly what you had to do in order to rid yourself of the wretched dream, and this immense sense of obligation you feel, that the men of your family have felt for many generations, then I had to be close to you, I would have to be tied to you. Yes, I can understand that you would be terrified I would get away from you.

"So as I see it, you married me because you felt you had to." And she wrote it down.

He lunged to his feet. "Bloody hell, no!"

She looked him dead in the eye. He was pale, his eyes blacker than midnight. Slowly, at last, he nodded, and his black eyes were now desolate, his face leached of color. "Yes, that is what happened."

Rosalind slowly rose, the pencil still in her hand. "So much has happened since I met you, so many inexplicable things. I'll wager it's because the two main players are finally together. Do you remember I asked you once if your grandfather was a wizard and you told me you didn't know? But then you told me he knew things, guessed things that no one else would know?"

"I remember," he said. "There was something in him, something magic. I can say that now without feeling contempt for myself."

"I accept that your grandfather was magic. This magic goes all the way back to Captain Jared Vail, it simply has to, and it puts magic in you as well. No, don't argue.

"Now, do you believe this being who saved Captain Jared is some ancestor of mine?"

He didn't want to answer, she saw it clearly, but finally he said, "It is possible."

"All right, if Captain Jared was a wizard, and Rennat the Titled Wizard of the East saved him in order to wring agreement from him, then it also makes sense that he knew I was in trouble—or would be in trouble—and in need of saving whenever the time was right. You know, when something bad would happen to me."

Slowly he nodded.

"Do you believe I'm a witch, Nicholas? Do you believe that someone tried to kill me because they recognized me for what I was, recognized I was from this long line of wizards, and was afraid I could harm them in some way? And so this someone tried to destroy the witch, or tried to destroy the spawn of this long-ago wizard?"

"I don't know."

He walked to where she now stood, and placed his hands on her shoulders. "I simply don't know, Rosalind, but I do know that everything is becoming clearer."

"Nothing is clear at all, Nicholas, save that like the Wyverly heiress, you married me because you felt you had to."

"Marrying you was the most important thing I have ever done in my life."

"It didn't matter to you what I wanted."

"You wanted me. That's what you told me. This marriage has been a two-way road, Rosalind. I didn't force you to do anything you didn't want to do."

"But our reasons for marrying each other were quite different."

When he said nothing, she continued. "That's beside the point in any case. It didn't matter to you who I was, where I'd come from, what I believed."

"Don't be an idiot. Of course it mattered."

"How were you so certain I was that little girl when you saw me at the ball that night, Nicholas? Surely I bear only the slightest resemblance to the little girl?"

He shrugged but didn't release his hold on her. Was he afraid she'd bolt? *Probably.* "I knew. I simply knew, there's nothing more I can tell you."

"All right, so you'd found the little girl you'd dreamed about, you were led right to her, is that correct?"

He nodded.

"She was now a woman and that added layers of problems. And your solution was to marry her—me."

"Yes. But there is so much more, Ros-

alind. From the beginning you were important to me."

"Well, naturally I'm important to you. If I
hadn't wanted you desperately, why then,
you would be cursed to dream that dreadful
dream for the rest of your days."

"Yes," he said, "that is the truth."

"What if I am indeed a witch, Nicholas?
Remember Rennat told me I would come
into my own, whatever that means."

He drew in a deep breath and his hands
tightened on her shoulders. "Then you are a
witch and my wife, and we will deal with it."

"When I come into my own—my own—
what will you do, Nicholas?"

"Do you mean you will smite the land and
bring famine to the world?"

She didn't laugh. "What will you do,
Nicholas?"

"I don't know. How can I know something
before it happens? *If* it happens? Or what
the result will be?"

She looked up at him, studied the face
that had become so beloved to her in such a
short time. She felt deadening pain. It was
difficult to force the words out of her tight
throat. "The most important fact of all of this
is you don't love me, Nicholas."

"Rosalind—"

She held out her hand. "You're an honorable man, Nicholas. Give me the key."

"But we need to study Captain Jared's journals, see if he's hidden some information to help us, to—"

"Give me the key, Nicholas."

He released her and gave her the key.

She walked quickly away from him, turned, and said, "I know you want me, Nicholas, I know well you enjoy making love to me. However, from what I've heard, it seems a man is content with any woman who wanders into his vicinity. She simply has to be available."

"No. Well, yes, perhaps there's some truth to that. But you, Rosalind, you are very special to me, you—"

She raised her hand. "You don't love me, Nicholas. That's the truth of it. How could a man love a debt?"

And she unlocked the library door and left.

Nicholas stood frozen in the middle of the room. He heard a deep sigh from behind him.

"Go to the Devil," he said and went out into the gardens.

39

Two hours later, he went looking for her. He finally found her in the long portrait gallery in the east wing, staring up at Captain Jared Vail, the first Earl of Mountjoy. She was looking up at a man in his prime, a big man, his legs in the tight leggings of the Elizabethan times. Broad shoulders, a chin possibly more stubborn than Nicholas's. She started when she studied his eyes. His eyes—they looked familiar. She'd seen those eyes, hadn't she? No, that didn't seem possible. His eyes were a glorious blue, bright, filled with wickedness and endless dreams and wonders, and mayhem.

She knew the moment Nicholas entered the gallery. He walked with lazy grace, but she saw the tension in him. They stood only three feet apart, but in truth, there was a chasm between them.

"He was quite a man, was Captain Jared," he said, looking up at the portrait.

She eyed him a moment, then said, "You said you simply knew who I was, simply knew I was the child you'd lived with nearly all your life in your dream. Come, Nicholas, how did you recognize me? I was a woman, not the child you dreamed about."

"I told you the truth. I simply knew. I realize it must sound impossible to you, but I knew you would be at that ball, knew it all the way to the deepest part of me, and I knew you the moment I saw you. Does that mean nothing to you, Rosalind? Can't you see? We were meant to know each other, meant to be together."

She crossed her arms over her chest, tapped her toes. "Listen to me, Nicholas. Despite all that's happening here, despite all the questions, the mystery, it is still my life. Mine. And you married me under false pretenses."

Yes, true enough, damn me for an idiot.

He reached out his hand to her, dropped it when she didn't respond. "Rosalind, I did what I had to do. Whatever this debt is, I know to my bones that both of us, together, must figure it out. We must figure it out because I know I am meant to save you."

"Ah, so now you believe the debt is to save my life? Uncle Ryder saved me first and now it is your turn?"

"No, I'm not certain that is the debt, but it seems certain to be a part of it."

She said nothing for a very long time, merely stared at him, through him really, and he had no idea what she was seeing, thinking. She said at last, "That first night I sneaked a look over my shoulder at you even while Grayson was leading me to the dance floor. I will be honest here, Nicholas. You fascinated me from the first moment I saw you. You looked so mysterious, so dangerous." She stared back up at Captain Jared. "You made me feel things I didn't know existed. You made my insides want to shout with joy. I felt drawn to you. In some deep part of me, I knew you were meant for me. I was very glad when Uncle Ryder told me you were coming to visit that next morning. And you came and I knew I wanted you, desperately." She paused a moment, thoughtful. "And now you will say that I too recognized you, recognized you as what— my knight? My husband? What?"

He said, without looking at his wife, "I've been wondering why you can't read the final pages of the *Rules of the Pale*."

"All right, so you are not ready to deal with my questions. Aunt Sophie says that a man, if he is smart, can distract with great skill, he can avoid facing something that makes him uncomfortable. Perhaps you would like to deal with this question: If Grayson hadn't been led to the *Rules of the Pale*, by whomever or whatever, if we didn't know about Sarimund and his damnable rules at all, there would have been nothing to focus on, nothing to draw us into this mystery. What would you have done? Would you simply have hung around me, hoping something evil would try to do away with me and you would slay it?"

"I don't know. I didn't think of it, truth be told. Everything has happened so very quickly. I only knew that finally, in this span of almost three hundred years, it was I, Nicholas Vail, not Captain Jared or any of the other following firstborn Vail sons, who was finally in the right place at the right time. And there you were, in the middle of it. Waiting for me."

"I wasn't waiting for anyone or anything except my memory to return. I didn't know there was anyone for me or anything to wait for. No, that's not true—the song was always there, waiting to be understood, I suppose you could say."

"Yes, it is. Even without the *Rules of the Pale*, the song is a focus. And where would you say it comes from, Rosalind?"

"I suppose I would say it's always been printed in my mind and on my soul. Even losing my memory made no difference to the song."

"Just as my knowing you, recognizing you, was deep inside my mind, always there."

"But Nicholas, you must see that I don't know anything else. I sing the song, but I don't know what it means, didn't really care, not after so many years. Without your coming, there would never have been a mystery, no debt I knew of, that my adopted family knew of. In the long view of things, what does a simple song have to do with anything at all?"

"Richard tried to take you."

"Yes, he did, and that is quite interesting. I wonder why he did. To keep us from getting married? So that I wouldn't bear you an heir? So that he could kill you at his leisure and then take the title and estate? We'd only just met, Nicholas. Why would Richard act so speedily on something that probably wouldn't even come to pass?"

"I don't know Richard, I don't understand him. Was that his motive? It sounds logical, given that he's a very angry man, mayhap a very bad man, albeit too young a man to be so accomplished at sin already."

"You indeed look like brothers, nearly twins, save you do look a bit older. He is only twenty-one, so very young to be thinking of murdering his brother, or murdering me."

"You've seen what a rotter Lancelot is. Can you imagine what he will be like when he is thirty? If he lives that long. As for Aubrey, who can say? At our wedding breakfast, he was certainly interesting and clever for one so young."

Rosalind said, "I agree you are not blessed in your remaining relatives. Do you think perhaps Richard wanted me for himself—for some reason we don't yet know? Or perhaps he saw me and he is the one who fell head over heels in love? The infamous *coup de foudre*? He had to have me or die trying?"

"Now that's a mawkish thought." Nicholas took a step toward her. Rosalind looked him squarely in the eye, then down at his out-stretched hand.

"Don't," she said.

He drew a deep breath, but didn't back away. He dropped his hand to his side. She saw a flash of anger in his eyes, but he said only, "The fact is, you are very important to someone. The people who tried to murder the child, are they still about? Would they recognize you like I did? And Rennat the Titled Wizard of the East—who is he to you? What is he? A long-ago ancestor? Or per-haps simply a beneficent being assigned to look after you? If so, he didn't do a very good job of it when you were eight years old. Who are your parents? Are they still alive? Where are they?"

"You know I have no answers to these questions. You also know when I finally spoke, I spoke fluent English and Italian. Which am I?"

"I told you I would send off inquiries and so I shall."

"Just what would you inquire about?"

"That's easy enough—any renowned wealthy family who mysteriously lost a child ten years ago. No, don't doubt that. How else could you speak two languages fluently? Your English is obviously a lady's English; your Italian, I am certain, is the same. Well, let's see." He spoke Italian to her, not an educated, aristocratic Italian, since he'd learned it from an Italian mistress from Naples, but he did indeed know educated Italian when he heard it. In the next moment, she answered his question about her favorite hobbies in smooth upper-class Italian.

Nicholas nodded. "Ryder told me your clothes were well-made, though ripped to rags. And there is your gold locket. Someone will recognize it." He said it with absolute conviction. "Now, after you left me alone with the old earl's ghost, I finished reading Captain Jared's journals. I told him his assistance was worth spit, that he hadn't written a single helpful thing. He didn't even tilt the chair."

"Perhaps he is embarrassed."

"I'm thinking he simply doesn't know himself since he never found the little girl to whom he owed his debt."

She said, "For me, it always comes back to why would anyone wish to murder a child?"

"Don't forget that whoever it was, he didn't get the job done. He failed. Now that is something to consider, isn't it?"

Now that she thought of it, she realized he was right. "Surely it wouldn't be all that difficult to kill a child. It's not as if the child could defend herself."

"And why on the docks in Eastbourne? Say you are Italian, then why were you here in England? Were you with your parents? Were you kidnapped from them here? No, that can't be right. Your parents would have raised a mighty hue and cry and Ryder Sherbrooke would have heard about it. No, you were likely taken from Italy. By whom? And why would he or she or whoever want to murder you here? In Eastbourne?"

"For that matter, why not simply toss me over the side of the ship in the English Channel?"

He sent his fist into the wall right beside Captain Jared's portrait, making its heavy gilt frame tilt. When he faced her, he looked dangerous, his eyes dark, opaque, vicious, she thought, his mouth cruel. "Bloody hell, don't be angry at me, Rosalind. I did what I had to do."

She sighed. "I know."

He felt a surge of relief, felt the rage fade a bit. "You do?"

"Of course. Tell me, Nicholas, when all this is resolved, will you journey back to Macau? Are the laws different enough there to enable you to have a wife in England and one in this Portuguese colony?"

He froze. He looked primed for violence, his face now even harder, colder. He said very precisely, "You are my bloody wife. You will remain my bloody wife until the day we die."

"No," she said, her face still, "I am your debt."

She heard him cursing as she walked away from him down the long gallery, vicious curses. She didn't recognize many of the animal parts he used so fluently. She did understand the occasional reference to a woman whose ears he wanted to box.

* * *

When Nicholas walked into the master bed-chamber late that night, Rosalind wasn't where he'd believed she would be—namely, in bed. He didn't expect her to want to make love to him, but he'd believed she'd be there, possibly pretending sleep, he didn't know, but she'd be there. Perhaps because she feared a ghost's machinations, and his company was better than none at all.

At dinner, she'd spoken calmly, detailing plans she'd made with Peter and Mrs. McGiver for improvements within the house and work on the grounds. She'd played the piano, and he leaned his head back, closing his eyes to listen. And when she'd added her voice to the songs, he'd sighed with pleasure. When she crashed down on the final chords of a Beethoven sonata, they both looked up to hear applause coming from the corridor outside the drawing room. Peter Pritchard stuck his head in, smiling, pointing to the audience of servants.

She'd played a song for Mrs. McGiver to sing, and that had been very fine indeed. Then all the servants had been encouraged to sing, and they'd had an impromptu musicale. It had been, he thought, quite nice.

Where the devil are you, Rosalind?

Yes, she'd been calm whenever she'd

spoken to him or looked at him. Nicholas realized finally, after following her up to bed, that he'd thought of more questions, and decided that once they made their way to the cursed center of this maze, he never again wanted to hear another question in his natural life. Ah, but if there was magic in him, maybe nothing in his life would be natural. If he'd had magic in him from as far back as Captain Jared, then why had he been forced to eat roots in Portugal when he'd been a starving twelve-year-old?

As he paced the large bedchamber, he remembered that storm in the Pacific, near the Sea of Japan, when one of his sailors had nearly been swept overboard and Nicholas, through sheer luck—or something else—had managed to loop a rope around the man's flailing hand, surely an unlikely feat, and haul him upright. The first thing the sailor had done was cross himself a good six times, others of his men as well, and none of them had ever looked at him again in quite the same way. On a very deep level, they'd feared him.

The candlelight flickered.

"Go away," he said.

The light calmed. That ancient old sea dog was ready and willing to keep him company, but not his wife.

He went to the adjoining room door and turned the knob. It was locked. She'd locked a door against him.

He knocked on the door. "Rosalind, let me in. I wish to speak to you."

Nothing.

"Dammit, I'm your husband. You will obey me. You will open this damned door now."

"I know well who you are, my lord. I, however, have nothing more to say to you. Go away. Good night."

His booted foot itched to break down the door. Instead, he walked quickly to the main door off the hallway. It was locked too. He felt like a fool. He stood against the opposite wall, his arms crossed over his chest, staring at the locked door, and finally managed to calm himself. Let her stew. Let her get cold during the night without him to warm her. Let her be frightened of all the unknowns all by herself. Curse her.

When he finally fell asleep, alone and naked in that big bed, a heavy dose of fatalism settling into him, he realized what he wanted was to make her angry enough to try to murder him. He yearned for violence, violence he could handle, anything but her polite disinterest.

He thought he heard an ancient old voice humming and resolutely ignored it.

40

At exactly three in the morning, Nicholas sat straight up in bed at a deafening roar. Windows shuddered, the room rocked. Thunder, he thought, heart racing, it was only thunder. It was odd, though, because it hadn't looked to storm when he'd finally fallen into his bed. Another clap of thunder shook his bed. Suddenly, a jagged sword of lightning struck directly into his bedchamber and he was bathed in light. Only thing was, the light didn't fade. It was as if a dazzling sun was trapped in his bedchamber.

This isn't right, isn't right at all.

He looked toward the windows as he

jumped out of bed. And waited, standing by his bed, but there were no more slashes of lightning, no more thunder to rattle the windows and shake the room, but still, the huge bedchamber remained pure white. And he thought, *No, this is whiter than sunlight. This is something else entirely,* only he didn't have a clue what was happening. *The Pale,* he thought, *this is a message from Rennat.*

He remained standing beside his bed, breathing hard, wondering what the devil was going on, trying not to let his imagination run wild and his heart slam out of his chest. Or perhaps—he said, "Are you here, Captain Jared? If this is one of your bizarre performances, stop it at once, do you hear me?"

No sound, nothing at all, just the empty stark white. Dead white, he thought, as dead white as the face of a bandit he'd killed outside of Macau the previous year.

He heard Rosalind scream.

He ran to the adjoining door, kicked his foot into the wood close to the lock, but the door didn't give. He cursed, then rubbed his injured foot. Not broken, thank God. He pounded the door. "Rosalind! Open the damned door!"

Suddenly, the door swung wide open and he was nearly blinded. The countess's bedchamber looked even whiter than his own vast room, the white light nearly blinding. He could see every corner of the room, every detail of the furnishings and draperies. Even the light layer of dust on the vanity table glittered the same dead white, as if encased in ice.

Rosalind stood beside her bed, a white nightgown covering her from neck to toe, her vivid red hair now as white as the room, tangling over her shoulders and down her back. Her face looked dead. He knew his face must look the same, and wasn't that an image to turn his innards to water?

"Rosalind? Are you all right?"

She didn't move, said nothing. She seemed unaware of him, seemed not to even hear him, much less see him.

He stopped cold when he neared her and saw she held a knife. It was dripping blood. Only, the blood drops were white.

She's been hurt, she's been—

He looked closely at her white face, at her hair still white as an old woman's. Why didn't the white fade away? Unless it wasn't natural. His wife holding a dripping knife in her hand was far from natural as well.

He looked down at the knife, saw the steady drip, drip, drip of white blood onto the carpet beneath her bare feet. Where was all the blood coming from?

He watched a white blood droplet splash on her left foot. White on white. It was obscene.

He didn't touch her, merely held out his hand. "It's all right, sweetheart, I'm here. It will be all right. Give me the knife."

She didn't look at him, didn't respond at all. Finally, she stretched out her hand to him. He gently uncurled her fingers from around the knife handle.

He realized soon enough that he'd seen the knife in the library beneath glass in a small case on one of the bookshelves, locked to the young boy who'd once tried to open it. Had it belonged to his grandfather, or had it gone all the way back to Captain Jared Vail? He didn't know. The knife looked vaguely Moorish, the blade curved like a scimitar, gems embedded in the ivory handle. He didn't remember what sorts of gems they were and couldn't tell now because they were utterly without color.

He raised his voice. "If it isn't you, Captain Jared, is it Rennat? I don't care who is causing this—stop it now. I am tired of this trick, do you hear me? Stop it now!"

To his relief, and, he admitted, to his surprise, the room went slowly dark, fading finally into the simple dark of night. He turned toward the window to see rain streaking down the windowpane. He realized there'd been no more thunder, if indeed thunder it had been. As for the strange lightning, no, lightning wasn't the word for it either.

He carefully laid the knife on the night table beside the bed. It no longer dripped white blood, no surprise, since whoever, whatever, had stopped the magic.

He clasped Rosalind's shoulders in his big hands and lightly shook her. "Rosalind, come back. Everything's over now."

Slowly, she raised her head to look up at him.

Her eyes, once dilated, were normal now, and blue once again, her hair vivid red, her face no longer the dead white, but still too pale. "Sweetheart," he whispered against her temple, "it will be all right. I'm here with you now. I can protect you, well, perhaps not completely. I nearly broke my foot trying to break down your door." He pulled her tightly against him, pressed his palm against her head until she rested on his shoulder.

Her breathing was slow. She said facing his neck, "I'm sorry about your foot."

He rocked her where they stood, kissed her hair, began to smooth out the tangles. "Can you tell me what happened?"

She pressed closer. He held her tight, felt her nails digging into his back. "It's all right," he said, and repeated it once more, twice.

She said finally, her voice thread thin, "I was dreaming I saw a man I'd never seen before. He was very handsome, Nicholas, like a golden angel, with the most beautiful pale blue eyes, but I knew there was darkness behind those pale eyes of his, and that sounds strange, but it's true. Too much darkness, and such intensity. I felt his intensity to my soul. Even though he looked at me he didn't seem to see me, didn't seem to know I was there, although I was standing right in front of him, on the other side of a huge fire. He was brewing something in a large pot and I thought he must be careful else the flames would burn him, for they were leaping upward, spewing, then funneling, forming peculiar shapes. I'd never seen a fire like that before in my life. I told him to be careful of those mad flames, but he didn't hear me. For him, I suppose I wasn't there. It was as if there was a wall between us and it was clear only from my side.

"He continued to stir the pot with some sort of long-handled metal spoon. I watched the pot bubble and hiss and the flames roar, as if an unseen bellows blew on it. I realized he was chanting something and I thought, *Why can't he hear me if I can hear him?*"

She fell silent, her hands in fists now against his shoulders. He continued to hold her tightly, running his hands up and down her back.

"*There is a clear wall between us,* I thought as I watched him, but it made no sense to me and so I stuck out my hand to touch it. There was nothing there. I stepped to the side of the fire, and stuck my hand out again." She shuddered against him. "I touched his shoulder. He jumped in surprise. Believe me, so did I. He stopped stirring, stopped his chanting, and looked straight at me, and I knew he could see me now. Nicholas, he smiled at me."

"He *what*?"

"He smiled at me, and said in this deep voice, '*You are mine. Isn't it odd how the light always brings clarity?'* Then he looked back over his shoulder as if hearing something or someone coming that alarmed him. Then he turned back to me and he put his fingertips to his lips. He stared at me. I saw something strange and scared in his eyes, but it was gone quickly. His eyes were so intense, Nicholas, so powerful, I felt he was looking into my soul. He whispered, *'Be careful, look to the book, and you will be here, soon now, soon now—'"*

She looked up at him now, and he saw her eyes were clearing, becoming more focused.

"What happened then?"

"Suddenly it was as if I was hurtled into a huge well of white, like a blizzard, but there was no wind, no movement of any kind, no cold, nothing save blinding white. Then you were holding me and talking to me and I slowly came back into myself. Was it the white that frightened him? Or was he the one who stopped it when you commanded it? Nicholas, what was in the pot? What did he mean that I had to be careful?"

"For once a being in a dream says something that makes sense. This being believes you're in danger, he's warning you."

"But who was he?"

"We will find out, don't worry."

"And the book, I'm to look to the book. That has got to mean Sarimund's the *Rules of the Pale* or Sarimund's short book that belonged to your grandfather. All right, I can do that. I can read both books again, we can study them more closely."

"Yes, we will even look at the book seams, see if there is anything hidden within the covers. Another helpful clue. We're getting there, Rosalind."

"And what did he mean when he said I would be there soon? In the Pale?"

He didn't like it, but he said, "Yes, very likely. As to the light bringing clarity, that requires more thought. We will figure it all out." He pointed to the knife. "When I came in, you were holding this knife. Blood was dripping off the tip, only the drops were white like everything else. Do you know where it came from?"

She looked horrified. "No, no, I've never seen it before. It wasn't in my dream. I was holding it and it was dripping white drops of blood?" She sounded terrified now and he couldn't blame her. "But wait, Nicholas, you were wrong, there's no blood on it, white or red."

He picked up the knife, looked down, and felt his heart stop. She was right—there was no blood, no sign there had ever been any blood. The blade was glittering silver. He immediately released her and fell to his knees to study the carpet. No blood.

Nicholas slowly rose, felt his heart tripping. He hated that there was something going on here he couldn't begin to understand, hated not understanding, not knowing what it was. He felt helpless, impotent. What if she'd been with him? Would she have dreamed the same dream? Would there have been the same thunder, the terrifying white that filled everything? Would he have seen the knife appear in her hand? He said, "Wait, I saw blood drip on your bare foot." She raised her foot. There was nothing at all. She raised her other foot. Nothing.

"Well," he said, trying to center himself, trying to think clearly, calmly. "You called it a dream. It would seem you were plunged into the middle of a vision."

Rosalind laughed, a shaky laugh, and said, her voice a bit stronger now, "I don't know where the knife came from. I've never seen it before in my life."

"It's kept in a glass case down in the library."

"Nicholas?"

He laid the knife back on the night table, gathered her against him again. He kissed her ear. She was at last warming. He began stroking her again through the soft muslin nightgown.

"The man who was stirring the pot," she said against his shoulder, "I told you I'd never seen him before."

He kissed her temple. And waited. And his heart pounded slow deep strokes.

"He smiled at me. He knew me. He said, 'You are mine.'"

He waited.

She pulled back in his arms and looked into his face. "It's all so clear to me now. I know who the man was in my dream. It was Sarimund."

There was more confusion in her voice than fear now. He tried to keep his voice light. "Since I met you, Rosalind, I must say my life has been anything but boring. So Sarimund is in the middle of this rich mix of chaos, no surprise there."

"First I dreamed of Rennat the Titled Wizard of the East and now Sarimund. What does it mean, dammit?"

He smiled at her curse, touched his fingertip to her chin. "We'll figure it all out."

"All of the whiteness, the dagger with the white blood, Sarimund speaking to me—you're right, it wasn't a dream, Nicholas, it was a vision."

"Yes," he said, "I think it was." Having a vision sounded all well and good, but he had no answers that he could get his brain around, and it nearly killed him.

"And that knife. Is it someone's message that there will be violence? Was that an additional warning for me to be careful?"

"I plan to keep you safe, sweetheart, I swear that to you. As for the rest of it—" He paused, stared down at her. "But not now, not now." He leaned down and kissed her mouth. He felt her jerk of surprise, felt her initial resistance, then she sank into him.

She whispered against his mouth, "Sarimund was a vision, but you're not. You're my husband, Nicholas, and you're naked."

He'd forgotten, truth be told. Her hands stroked up and down his back now, and she moved even closer, if that were possible. Her palms stroked down his flanks, his legs, then smoothed forward toward his belly. He wanted to laugh. Here he was ready to take his wife down on the bed and there was a knife not a foot away from them that had, five minutes before, been dripping white blood. Whose? Sarimund's?

He pulled back and closed his eyes when her hands pressed against him between their bodies, and her fingers touched him. He jerked away.

"Did I hurt you?"

He laughed. "Oh, no, my brain is dead, but nothing else. I beg you, Rosalind, don't move your hands, well, I take that back, yes, move your hands but not away from me. Touch me, Rosalind. This is about us now, only us, and I want you very badly."

When Nicholas lay on his back a short while later, a sleeping Rosalind tucked against his side, he stared up at the shadowed ceiling, listening to the light rainfall against the windows.

He suddenly realized he didn't like the way the room smelled. It wasn't musty, no, it smelled coppery. Then he realized what it was. The scent he smelled was blood.

He lifted his wife in his arms and carried her back to the earl's bedchamber, kicked the door to the countess's room closed with his foot.

She jerked awake when he laid her onto the cold sheets.

"Shush," he whispered between kisses, "it's all right now. Come close and I'll warm you."

She murmured against his neck as she settled once again against him, "Sarimund said I'd be with him soon, soon I'd be coming to him."

He kissed her eyebrow, then her eyelids. "Rosalind, did you see any resemblance between you and him?"

He felt her start. "Did I look like him? Oh, no, Nicholas, I told you, he was beautiful, like an angel, all golden, his eyes light, light blue."

"What do you think he meant when he said to you, '*You are mine*'?"

"Could it mean I'm a descendant of his? Sarimund lived in the sixteenth century, at the same time as Captain Jared. And he's here, at least his voice."

A descendant of Sarimund—he supposed it explained a lot, but what exactly he couldn't say. He kissed her again, pulled her close. She whispered against his chest, "I let you make love to me. I shouldn't have done that."

Laughter came up in his throat, but he managed to hold it in. "Do you feel better now?"

"Yes, you know I do, but that is not the point."

"The point, whatever that is, can go to the Devil." He kissed her forehead, and settled in.

He was nearly asleep when he felt her lips move against his shoulder, and somehow, even though she only murmured the words against his flesh, he knew what she said. *"The Pale—that's where all this is leading us."*

He fell asleep to the sound of the rain against the windowpanes and an image of a red Lasis in his mind.

It was the bright sunlight shining onto his face the following morning that brought him instantly awake, but it was the sound of Mrs. McGiver's loud shout that made him leap out of his bed, nearly dumping Rosalind onto the floor.

41

Rosalind yelled, "Nicholas, you're naked!"

He stopped at the door, whirled back around, and caught the dressing gown she threw to him. She pulled a sheet from the bed and wrapped it around herself.

The two of them raced down the long corridor.

There was another loud shriek.

They ran down the main staircase and pulled up short. Mrs. McGiver stood over Peter Pritchard's body.

Nicholas was at Peter's side in an instant, his fingers against the pulse in his neck. He breathed a sigh of relief—his pulse was steady and slow. Peter was wearing trousers and a shirt, and only his socks. His boots lay beside him. He'd probably come into the house and taken off his boots because he didn't want to disturb anyone. "He's not dead, thank God." But he was unconscious. Nicholas felt for injuries, but nothing seemed broken. He heaved him to his shoulder and carried him into the drawing room and laid him on a sofa. He said over his shoulder, "Mrs. McGiver, what happened?"

"Oh, dear, my lord, I was coming down to see Cook about the oatmeal—there were lumps yesterday, and that's just wrong—well, yes, I saw Mr. Pritchard lying here. I immediately went to him, my lord, and I thought he was dead because he didn't respond even when I pinched his arm on the inside just above the elbow like I do to my grandchildren when they're naughty."

"Then what happened?"

She sucked in her breath and blurted it out, "I thought that miserable ghost had murdered him. I was afraid, my lord."

"Who is the physician in these parts?"

"Andrew Knotts, my lord, skinny as a windowpane but he doesn't go out of his way to kill his patients. Oh, here's Mr. Block."

Nicholas saw Block pulling on his black coat over a white linen shirt not tucked into his trousers. He did, however, have his boots on. "Block, get the physician immediately. Go, man."

Peter stirred some five minutes later. Both Nicholas and Rosalind, now in a dressing down brought to her by Mrs. McGiver, hovered close, her feet, like his, unfortunately still bare. Rosalind dabbed a handkerchief dipped in rose water to his forehead.

"Peter?"

His eyes slowly opened. "My lord?"

"Yes. How do you feel?"

"There were three of you, but now there are only two, so I must be better."

"Yes, you are better. Peter, what happened? Mrs. McGiver found you unconscious on the floor."

"My lord!"

It was Marigold, breathing fast, racing to a stop inside the drawing room door. "There are visitors. They're coming fast, impudent as you please, and here it is barely dawn."

Nicholas said, "Keep yourself still, Peter. Rosalind is going to give you some nice strong tea. I'll be back."

He walked into the entrance hall to see

his stepmother standing squarely in front of him, dressed entirely in lavender all the way to the straw bonnet atop her head with two very purple curling feathers that quivered, chin up, looking like a banty rooster ready to take all comers. Arranged behind her were all three of her sons—Richard, Lancelot, and Aubrey.

Nicholas crossed his arms over his chest. "Well, now, it's true I've been gone from England for a long time, but isn't this a bit early to pay a morning visit?"

Miranda said, "You aren't dressed. There is a bruise on your foot. Your bare foot."

He shrugged. "Why are you four here in my house?"

Richard stepped forward. "We had meant to arrive last evening, but our carriage broke down and we were forced to spend the night in Meckly-Hinton."

His mother whisked around him to stand in front of him. As if she were somehow protecting him from Nicholas? "We were forced to stay the night at this miserable little inn called the Raving Rooster, set in the middle of a village that shouldn't exist since it has nothing to recommend it."

"And you got up before dawn to pay me a visit. May I ask why?"

Richard Vail, dressed in black, dark beard stubble on his face, gently eased in front of his mother again. He said without preamble, "We are here to warn you."

Miranda stuck her head around his shoulder. "I told him, why bother? You hate the lot of us, who cares if you croak it? Or if someone croaks you?"

"Mother," Richard said.

"Warn me?" Nicholas's voice was all languid and arrogant, and he knew it drove Richard mad. But Richard didn't look as if he wanted to kill him; he looked pale, he looked—frightened. Nicholas frowned at him. "I know the four of you would not shed a tear were I belowground, yet you all troop into my house at near dawn to warn me?"

"Yes," Lancelot said, his poet's face flushed with anger, his voice nearly breaking with it, "but I didn't want to come. Don't tell you a bloody thing, that's what I wanted, but Richard insisted, blast him. I don't know about Aubrey."

"Shut up, Lance," Richard said, not looking at him. His brother sucked in a curse.

Aubrey, with his red hair and bright intelligent eyes, nearly bounced forward. "I wanted to come, Nicholas. I don't even know you, so why would I hate you? You and your bride were quite nice to me at your wedding. Listen, Nicholas, the fact is, we are here. Mother is fatigued, though she has the energy of three Druid priests. Won't you invite us in? We really are here to warn you, that's no lie."

"My lord!"

Trying to edge past his half brothers was Block, towing a very tall, very gaunt man in his wake. The man's hair was nearly as white as his own hair had been in the vision.

"You are the physician, sir?"

The man gave him a short bow. "I am Dr. Knotts. Where is my patient? I hope it is serious enough to justify bringing me out at this unleavened hour of the morning. I say, there are quite a few people standing here in the entrance hall. Madam, I must say you look on the bilious side. Perhaps it is because of the vast quantities of lavender you're wearing. My lord, would you care to direct me?"

Nicholas eyed his stepmother. "Ma'am, you and your whelps will accompany Block to the library and he will give you tea. I shall be along shortly."

"But—"

Nicholas didn't look back at her. He directed Dr. Knotts to the drawing room. He heard grumbling behind him but didn't turn.

As he stood by the door watching Dr. Knotts gently shove Rosalind out of his way, he called out, "Come with me, Rosalind. You and I must dress now. We have unexpected guests."

Not twelve minutes later the two of them returned to the drawing room to see Dr. Knotts standing beside Peter, the doctor's arms folded over his chest.

He turned at Nicholas's entrance. "My lord, there is nothing to warrant leeches." He sounded disappointed.

"Do you know what caused Mr. Pritchard to collapse?"

"He carries the curse of youth, which is idiocy, but he assures me he was not drunk. I have no idea what made him faint, for that is what he did, pure and simple. He had no seizure, no sudden pain in his head or limbs. So I must conclude that he collapsed for the simple fact that he is young and untried and—"

Nicholas said, "He is older than I am, Dr. Knotts."

"Then it must be a stricture in his bowels. This is not uncommon, particularly in young men with excesses of male vigor."

Peter sat up suddenly, thoroughly alarmed now. "A stricture in my bowels?"

"Aye, lad, but it will work itself out. Now, I must be off." And Dr. Knotts, after bowing to both Nicholas and Rosalind, was gone within the next second, Block at his side.

Nicholas said, "Don't worry, Peter. I fancy the good doctor has no idea why you passed out. Odd things sometimes happen when you least expect them, but then they pass. How do you feel?"

"I am fine now, my lord. I honestly don't know what happened. I was feeling quite fine, and suddenly, I saw this bright flash of white and then you were leaning over me, speaking to me."

It was the light that had laid him flat, Nicholas thought. But why? He said to Peter, "I wish you to confine yourself to very light duty today, Peter. Let's not take any chances. Now, my stepmother and my three half brothers just arrived. Her ladyship and I must attend them. Rosalind, come with me."

She asked him again as they walked to

the library, "Richard wanted all of them to come here to warn you? That is nonsense, Nicholas, and you know it. I do not trust any of them, except perhaps for Aubrey. He seems harmless enough."

"Richard looks scared. No, he is scared. He's not a good enough actor to fool me and that alone gives me great pause."

In the library, they found the three brothers seated, drinking tea and eating Cook's gooseberry muffins. The Dowager Lady Mountjoy stood next to the fireplace, a teacup in her gloved hand.

"I never liked this room," Miranda said when they walked into the library. "It's dark and cold, and so I told that mad old man."

"I agree," Nicholas said. "Now, Richard, you will tell me exactly why you have descended on Wyverly Chase."

But Richard was staring at Rosalind.

"You're here," he said.

"Well, yes, I live here."

Miranda said, "Richard has had a dream, Nicholas, a dream that—"

"Why don't you let Richard tell us about the dream, ma'am," Nicholas said pleasantly, his eyes never leaving his half brother's face.

"Terrified about a silly dream, just like a girl," Lancelot said, and gave his brother a fat sneer.

"If you don't have anything useful to say, then shut up, Lancelot," Nicholas said. "Now, Richard, what is this all about?"

Richard rose. He looked straight at Rosalind and pointed his finger at her. "She killed you, Nicholas. I watched her kill you."

Rosalind didn't protest. She smiled at him and marveled aloud, "What a lovely thought that is—killing my husband and here we are newly wedded. Hmmm. Have you looked at your brother, Richard?"

"Of course I have! What of it? I'm very nearly as big as he is and probably more dangerous!"

That earned him an ironic look from Nicholas and another big smile from Rosalind. "Please, do tell me exactly how I managed to kill my husband."

"You think this is amusing, do you? You stabbed him, damn you. I watched you stab him."

Nicholas said slowly, "Did you happen to see the knife, Richard?"

"Why do you care what the bloody knife looks like? That is the least of your worries.

This woman—your precious new bride—who has no family, no known background—she killed you."

"Then what did she do?" Nicholas asked him.

Richard's face flushed, his eyes darkened. "You think this is all a jest? You're mocking me?"

"Tell him what she did, Richard," Aubrey said. "Tell him."

42

Richard gave Rosalind such a venomous look she wanted to cross herself.

"She dug out your heart and held it up as if it were an offering to some heathen god, your blood streaking down her arms, dripping off her fingers. There was blood everywhere. She was covered with your blood, Nicholas, splattered upward even to her face."

"What did she do with my heart?"

Lancelot took a step toward Nicholas, fist up. "You bastard, you don't believe my brother. He doesn't lie, damn you. Listen to him if you wish to live."

"I'm listening, Lancelot, but so far it sounds like a tale Grayson Sherbrooke would write, perhaps set at Stonehenge. You said this was a dream, Richard?"

"I'm not sure, actually, I was in a sort of waking state, so not really a dream, no. More like a vision. A vision of something that will happen. I was alone, in my bedchamber at home, and time lost all meaning to me and then the vision came into my brain, clear and sharp. I could even smell the blood when she cut your heart out of your chest."

Nicholas looked at each of them in turn. He saw bone-deep resentment in Lancelot, a sort of academic interest on Aubrey's face, flat contempt on Miranda's face, and on Richard's face—cold fear. He said to his half brother, "You came to warn me because—?"

Miranda stepped forward, her expression now venomous. "She held up your heart, you moron, and she chanted foreign words Richard didn't understand. Your wife killed you! And you have the gall to question your brother's motives in coming to help you?"

Rosalind spoke. "Richard, what was I wearing in this vision?"

"A white robe belted at your waist with a thin rope of some kind. Its ends hung down nearly to your knees. Your hair was long down your back."

"You are certain it was me?"

"Yes, all that wild red hair, your blue eyes. It was you." He frowned. "But it was as if you were in a different time, in a different place. I don't know, that doesn't really make sense, but I know it was you."

Nicholas said, "So now she's a vestal virgin of some sort or a high priestess?"

"I don't know," Richard said finally. "I don't know. There were no priests hovering about, no one else, only the two of you, you bound on your back and her leaning over you."

"Do you know why I cut out my husband's heart?"

Richard, for the first time, looked uncertain. "I don't know that either," he said slowly. "All I know is that you did it." He looked at Nicholas. "You asked me what she did with your heart. She flung it away from her, as if it were refuse, then she rose and stood looking down at you sprawled at her feet, and she was rubbing her bloody hands together."

"Like Lady Macbeth?"

"No!" Richard shouted at her. "There was no real blood on Lady Macbeth's hands, only her guilt made her believe that, but your hands were covered with Nicholas's blood."

Rosalind said, "We did have an argument last night, and I admit I wanted to smack him with a book, but I didn't even do that. This ripping-out-his-heart business, that would require a dedication to something fanatical. Another time, another place, I think you said." And she thought of the bloody knife in her own vision, the white drops sliding to the floor off the tip. Where had the blood come from?

"Be it elsewhere and in another time, you still did it, I saw you do it!"

"My lord."

Nicholas turned to see Block in the doorway, looking stiff and proper, though his eyes were a bit on the wild side.

"What crisis is upon us now, Block?"

"The old earl's ghost will not stop singing lewd ditties. Mrs. McGiver requests that you order him to stop."

Nicholas turned to his half brother. "Would you care to attend the old earl's ghost, Richard?"

Richard gawked at him. "A ghost? You're saying the old earl's ghost is real? That is nonsense. There are no ghosts. My grandfather is in Hell where he belongs."

Rosalind, seeing that Nicholas was primed for violence, said, "Richard, why do you find a singing ghost more unbelievable than me dressed like an ancient priestess plucking out Nicholas's heart and offering it as a sacrifice?"

"Let us go to the drawing room," Nicholas said. "Block, tell Mrs. McGiver we will take care of the ghost."

The door to the drawing room was open. Outside in the entrance hall stood Mrs. McGiver and Marigold, both listening intently, neither of them looking particularly alarmed.

Nicholas motioned the group into the room, placing his finger over his lips to keep them quiet. Once inside, Nicholas said toward the wing chair, "I am here. Rosalind is here. Other relatives are here as well. What is it you have to sing to us this morning, sir?"

A minute passed. Two.

Richard said, "It is as I thought. Servants are fanciful, they make things up, they—"

A creaky old voice sang out,

I am tired of strife
I am tired of trouble.

**He stirs the pot
And it boils and bubbles.**

**Once he comes the danger's near.
Once he acts then death is here.
Go to the Pale and slay the source
Else the future may change its course.**

"Don't be afraid, it's merely the old earl," Mrs. McGiver said kindly to Miranda Vail and the three young gentlemen surrounding her, all of them looking sheet white and ready to bolt. "He loves to sing, you know," she added, all confiding now, "and usually he doesn't make much sense. What he just sang, now that wasn't lewd. A warning it sounded like to me. I wonder who this *he* is? I don't like the sound of this, my lord."

Rosalind didn't either. She wondered who this *he* was as well. How were they supposed to get to the Pale to find and slay this bloody source to keep the future from changing from what it should be?

Nicholas said into the dead silence, "Thank you, sir, for your fine song. Your rhyming was inspiring as well."

Miranda said in a choked whisper, "There is no one here. We are the only ones in this room. This—this ghost—he sings like this all the time?"

"This was a trick," Richard announced to the room at large, "some sort of absurd trickery done by a servant who is hiding behind the draperies. One of you doubtless made up those ridiculous words for him to sing." He strode across the drawing room as he spoke. "Where are you?" he yelled, shaking his fist. "Come out from your hidey-hole now, else I'll gullet you." He pulled a knife out of his coat pocket and brandished it at the draperies.

The draperies didn't move.

Richard flung them back. There was no cowering servant there. He looked behind each piece of furniture. He found nothing at all.

"Where are you, you bastard?"

An ancient moan came from the depth of the old wing chair before it toppled onto its side to the floor.

Miranda Vail screamed.

* * *

Rosalind, Nicholas, and his four relatives sat at the breakfast room table.

Rosalind said into the strained silence, a smile in her voice, "Let me assure you again that our ghost is harmless." None of them looked too certain about that; indeed, Rosalind wasn't all that certain either that Captain Jared was merely the singing messenger. She said, "Enough excitement for the moment. We'll have a lovely breakfast."

"I could not eat," Miranda said.

"I can," Lancelot said. "I'm hungry."

"You are so pretty sitting there daintily spreading butter on your muffin," Richard said to his brother. "Just look at you, the image of a romantic poet. As for your gluttony, you'd best take care else you will strain your trouser buttons."

"I am not pretty, damn you!"

Rosalind called out, "Block! We are ready for another breakfast course."

Aubrey said, "This is a lovely room. Are you certain the old boy isn't dangerous?"

"I don't think so," Nicholas said. "He makes no threats. He simply sings and occasionally sends his chair toppling to its side." He shrugged. "One becomes used to it."

"You do not believe me," Richard said, and he drummed his fingertips on the mahogany tabletop.

Nicholas said, "Richard, tell me about the knife Rosalind was using."

"The bloody knife?" Richard smashed his fist on the table. "You're concerned about the bloody knife when what you should be thinking about is how to rid yourself of this vicious bitch before she murders you!"

"Cook has made some lovely toast and scrambled eggs, not to mention kippers and—" Block froze in his tracks at the violence he saw on his master's face, indeed felt in the air itself.

Nicholas rose slowly from his chair. "You will apologize to my wife, Richard, and you will do it now and with grace and sincerity."

Richard shot Rosalind a look. His voice was halting as he managed to get out, "I am worried about my half brother. He does not seem concerned, and any intelligent man would be very concerned. We all came here to warn him, but—"

"You are mucking it up, Richard."

Richard cleared his throat. "I apologize, Rosalind. I do not know you so I cannot judge your character, but I had the vision and that is a fact."

"Do you know, Richard," she said, her voice emotionless, "I have never even been called a bitch, much less a vicious bitch. This vision of yours—"

"It is a portent," Miranda announced as she forked down scrambled eggs. "Visions don't lie."

A portent, Rosalind thought, and set to her own breakfast, surprised she was ravenous. She looked up to see Nicholas watching her. Surely he wasn't thinking she'd cut out his heart. But that vision of Richard's—

Nicholas said, "Richard, the knife. I ask you again, what did it look like?"

"It had a curved blade, and there were diamonds, rubies, and even sapphires embedded in the hilt."

Nicholas nodded. "I wish to show you something after breakfast."

"After breakfast," Miranda said, voice hard as the brass candlesticks in the middle of the table, "we are leaving. Richard has delivered his warning. We have done our duty. What happens to you now is on your own head, Nicholas."

Nicholas carefully laid down his knife. "I would like all of you to remain here for several days."

"So you believe me then?" As Richard spoke, he shot Rosalind a cold smile.

"Believe that Rosalind stabs me and cuts out my heart? No, but there are unanswered questions roiling about. Perhaps amongst all of us, we can figure out what is going on here."

"There is something else going on?" Aubrey asked, sitting forward, his eyes glittering. "Something better than Richard's bloody vision?"

"Oh, yes," Nicholas said, "much better."

43

Richard's voice was barely above a whisper. "Yes, yes, that is the knife I saw her plunge into your heart."

Rosalind saw herself holding that knife as it dripped blood—white blood. What if it was indeed a portent? What if something happened, something utterly catastrophic, and she did kill Nicholas? No, it wasn't possible, it simply wasn't. But what was possible, what was fact and she and Nicholas had to embrace it, was that there was magic at work here, ancient magic. She thought of all the Celtic names of the wizards and witches in the Pale. She thought of Taranis, the

Dragon of the Sallas Pond, who'd been Sarimund's confidant of sorts. His was a Celtic god's name as well, and he'd claimed to be immortal. What if they were the same beings, but they'd somehow ended up in a different time, a different place? And somehow they'd spilled over into this world? Were they trying to come back, only something terrible had happened and they were stuck in the Blood Rock fortress? What if they wanted her to kill Nicholas because he'd descended from Captain Jared, who hadn't paid his debt to her?

How could such a thing be of help to them?

It didn't make sense. She'd been born almost three hundred years later, well beyond Captain Jared's time, surely a god would know that. But then again, maybe there were boundaries on ancient wizards and gods, restricting them to certain skills in a certain time, a certain place. Maybe they weren't all-powerful or omniscient.

It was time to act, she thought, time to discover what this debt was all about, time to learn who she really was, maybe *what* she really was. The possible *what* scared her to her toes.

She heard Richard Vail ask Nicholas, "What is the knife doing here?"

"This knife appears to have many incarnations," Nicholas said, and she admired his ambiguity.

"Lawks," Aubrey said, rubbing his hands together, "wait until I tell my friends at Oxford what is happening in my family—ghosts and knives in a vision that really exist. But wait, Richard, are you certain you never saw this knife before? It did belong to Grandfather; it was in this room when you were a boy, wasn't it?"

Richard still stared at the knife, as if mesmerized. "I don't think so, but that was a long time ago and I was young—" He shrugged and tried not to look frightened.

"Nicholas is not our family," Lancelot said to Aubrey, "not really. Our father detested him, claimed he was a bastard, but since he was the image of himself, he couldn't very well prove it, now could he?"

Richard said, almost as an afterthought, "Shut up, Lance."

Lancelot puffed up and looked ready to yell, when his mother said, "It's all terribly unfair, but, at this moment in time, Nicholas is the head of the Vail family."

"Unfair to whom?" Rosalind asked. "Richard is the one who has been disloyal to his brother. I mean, trying to kidnap me, surely not a very praiseworthy thing to do."

Miranda said, "And why should he be loyal to this unwanted stranger? Gone when he was but a boy and he only returns to collect his dead father's title. What sort of son does that?"

Nicholas said, eyebrow arched, "One that is disowned, perhaps, madam?"

Miranda shouted, "It's still not fair, do you hear me?"

"I don't think it was particularly fair for someone to try to kill me when I was a little girl," Rosalind said. "What do you have to say to that?"

"I have to say you are probably a harlot's brat and her drunken lover took a cane to you, deservedly so, that's what I say."

In a flash Nicholas was not an inch from his stepmother's nose. He looked intimidating, dangerous, and ruthless. In a voice so soft no one could hear what he said except Miranda and Rosalind, he said, "Listen to me, you vicious old bat, you will never insult Rosalind again or I will ruin you. Do you understand me, madam? No more new gowns since there will be no more money, no more entrée into society. In short you will be ignored and ostracized."

"Ruin me? Ha!"

Nicholas smiled down at her, and that smile surely had to freeze Miranda to the bone. Was the woman mad? Had she lost all sense, to bait a man like Nicholas?

"Heed me, madam, for I am quite serious. Not only will I ruin you, I will ruin your three sons."

Miranda opened her mouth to blast him when Aubrey said in a loud voice, "I say, Mother, I don't wish to be ruined. I don't wish to be booted out of Oxford. As for Lance, he loves his new waistcoats and his horses. Hmm, and our butler Davy as well, I think. Please rein in your tongue."

"I pray this bastard meets a foul end," Lancelot said, his hands clenched, his pretty face flushed.

Rosalind clapped her hands. "All of you will listen to me now. We have an unusual situation here and it behooves us to figure it out, not fight and insult each other. Nicholas is the Earl of Mountjoy. Get yourselves over your disappointment for it grows very tedious to hear the lot of you whine and complain and curse Fate. Now, Nicholas and I need to attend to some matters that don't involve any of you."

To her relief, Mrs. McGiver arrived in the next moment to show the Vails to their bed-chambers. Rosalind assigned Marigold to attend the Dowager Lady Mountjoy. "Stick close to her, Marigold," Rosalind said close to her ear. "She will complain endlessly, but you keep smiling and tell her you will see to everything, all right?" She dropped her voice another ten degrees. "She isn't to be trusted."

When Nicholas closed the library door a few minutes later, he turned the big brass key in the lock, then called out, "Sir, are you in here?"

No answer.

"Captain Jared, we need you," Rosalind said.

No answer.

She turned to Nicholas. "Why did you invite them to remain?"

"This vision of Richard's and his identification of the knife made me want to keep them close. I have this inescapable feeling they're all a part of this, whatever this is. I've learned over the years that having your enemy within your reach gives you a better chance to survive than having one lurking unseen in the shadows."

She stepped up to him, went onto her tiptoes, and whispered against his ear, "Nicholas, I know how to get us to the Pale."

He stared at her, nonplussed.

"Why are you whispering?"

"I don't know, it simply seemed the thing to do. My own vision of Sarimund last night before the whiteness awoke me—remember I told you he was chanting something? I didn't hear the distinct words, but they somehow remained in my mind. The words he was chanting, they're crystal clear now."

Nicholas wasn't surprised, not after she'd read the *Rules of the Pale* when no one else could. "Why now, I wonder?"

"Because time grows short," Rosalind said. "Everything is happening very quickly now. Listen."

Look in my book
The pages are free
Follow my directions
And come to me.

"Free pages?"

"Yes. Don't you see? I couldn't read the

final pages of Sarimund's book that Grayson found in Hyde Park and then I was unable to read the final pages of the shortened book here in your grandfather's library because the pages simply wouldn't separate. Sarimund is telling me I can now open them, so that makes them free."

She laid her hand on his forearm. "Nicholas, you and I are evidently the two main performers in a strange play. I do not want to cut out your heart. I really don't. I am very fond of you."

He kissed her. "We are performers, you're right about that."

"To work. Let's begin with freeing the pages in your grandfather's book," Rosalind said.

Rosalind's fingers hovered over the pages, then, easily, she turned the page. Both of them froze for an instant, aware of an unknown that was close—or was it somehow Sarimund whose spirit floated above them? Perhaps Sarimund was slapping her in the face, but she couldn't feel it because those slaps were behind veils of time, too thick for anything to come through. She was afraid to read the page, afraid of what it would do. She looked over at her husband. "What if—"

"Read the pages aloud, Rosalind."

"Yes, you're right. I cannot lose my nerve now." She read:

I wanted desperately to know if Epona had birthed my son, but Taranis would not tell me. He began singing a love song to his mate, which I found quite sweet actually, but I nonetheless wanted to kick him. Now was not the time to praise eternal commitment.

Taranis said to me before he left me at my cave entrance, "Go home, Sarimund. Your time here is at an end, but do not forget what happened here because what you saw must be told to the girl. You must see that she knows this specifically"— and Taranis said, "Repeat the words in your mind. Now," and so I did:

Turn the last page
And think of my might
Read the words slowly
And wait for the night.

Did the words come from me or from the Dragon of the Sallas Pond? I do not know. I am home again—so many humans, jostling each other, all of them talking at once—how did I get here? I do not know that any more than I know how I arrived in the Pale. I seem to remember being in the Bulgar, but then it is gone and nothing is there in my memory. I wrote down the rules for you, just as my purpose for being in the Pale was you.

You are the crown in my kingdom, the bringer of peace and destruction, the one who must right the grievous sin. It is a very strange thing, but as I write this, I know I am one with Taranis.

Turn the page now and think of my might. Aye, it is my might Taranis recognized, and mighty I am, the mightiest wizard who has ever lived in the here and now, and in the future and past, and all other places not seen by mortals.

You are a woman now, not the little girl who sang so beautifully. Good-bye. My heart is with you.

Sarimund.

Rosalind very slowly turned to the last page and stared down at a perfectly blank page. But she knew to her bones that beneath it was the stark white that had struck them last night, and within that stark whiteness was—what? She wanted to scream, but knew it wouldn't help. She had to find out. She closed her eyes and thought of Sarimund's might. *What might? That he was strong? That he could mold and form events to suit himself? That perhaps he was an extension of Taranis? What did he mean that she was the bringer of peace and destruction? Now that sounded important indeed, terrifying too, since it sounded like she was vital, but to what—*

"Rosalind! Come, wake up. Do you hear me, you twit, wake up!" A hand slapped her face, not hard. That same hand slapped her face again, and this time it hurt because she was back to herself enough to feel it.

"No, don't hit me again, that's quite enough. I'm back now, all right?"

"Excellent, that's more like it. Open your eyes." He gave her another light tap on her cheek. "Open your eyes."

She did and looked up into her husband's face. She blinked. "What happened?"

"You stared down at that damned blank page and just—went away, as if you'd fallen asleep. You must tell me what happened."

"Nothing," she said. "Nothing at all," but she knew that wasn't true. But what had happened was beyond her reach. "How long was I—away?"

"Twenty minutes. How do you feel?"

"Quite marvelous, really." She gave him a very big smile. "Now, Nicholas, we have to wait for the night. Look at the last page—it's perfectly blank, yet Sarimund's chant tells me to think of his might and wait for the night."

"Not very humble, is he?" Both of them studied the blank last page. No magic occurred, no words appeared, but Rosalind wasn't worried, odd, but she simply wasn't. "We'll wait, just as Sarimund said to."

Nicholas wished he'd sent his relatives on their way. Surely there was no need to have them here now. But Richard's vision—why the devil had his half brother had a vision that was appallingly violent and clearly showed Rosalind with that knife, cutting out his heart? He wasn't frightened simply because he knew that she would never do such a thing, even to an enemy. But what if she were under some spell? No, that was absurd. Who had sent such a vision to Richard? And why? What did it mean?

He said to Rosalind, "I wonder if I will be allowed to come with you tonight, if that is indeed what is to happen."

44

"Oh, yes, I know you will be with me. While I was away, Nicholas, that is, I was right here, but my mind was elsewhere—I saw you, and you looked fierce and cunning, and because I suppose I was elsewhere, looking at you through different eyes, I saw the rich red aura of magic surrounding you, and I knew, Nicholas, I knew. You are powerful."

"How do you know red is the aura of magic?"

She cocked her head to the side. "I don't believe I knew, but it is. Yours is a very potent magic, I know that it is."

"We spoke of this before, Rosalind. Why do you think me some sort of wizard?"

"Do you doubt for a moment that Captain Jared was a wizard?"

He plowed his fingers through his hair, and cursed.

"You are in his direct line. Your grandfather was magic, probably other past Vails as well, perhaps all the way back to the beginning when wizards first sprang from the earth. But I simply know there is more magic in you than in any of your predecessors. I know it."

"So you believe the being who plucked Captain Jared off his sinking ship did it for a specific reason—because Captain Jared was a wizard and that's what the being had to have. You believe that is why all the first sons of each generation dreamed of you?"

She laid her hand on his forearm. "Haven't things happened in your life you can't explain? You may begin with your dreams of me."

He didn't like this and she saw that he didn't, but she remained quiet, watching him. He was fighting this with all his will, and his will was formidable.

"The dream of you," he said finally, his black eyes hooded. "I was only a boy. One night you were simply there, and as you continued to come every night and sing that song to me, you—the dream—simply became a part of me, seeped into my bones, settled in my brain.

"The little girl that you were was a part of me for so long I ceased to question it. I was used to you, you comforted me when I believed I wouldn't survive.

"But understand, the dream was nothing special, not really, even after I told my grandfather about it and he told me about the legend."

"It is not a legend, Nicholas. I'm quite real. I was out of time for Captain Jared, but not for you."

He looked into her face. "Out of time—how very odd that sounds, yet—you are here now with me and you are my debt, mine alone. I would gladly pay that debt if only I knew what it was."

"You can't think of any more strange things that have happened to you? Do you so easily forget that you knew I would be at that ball the first time you saw me, Nicholas, and that is why you came, to find me, to meet me, to assure yourself that I was real?

Remember, you told me you knew me when you saw me?"

"Yes, I knew you. Yes, I knew you would be there. I don't know how I knew, the knowledge was simply there, dormant I suppose you could say, until I journeyed back to England after I heard about my father's death. And then, the moment I stepped foot here at Wyverly Chase, everything changed. But magic? As in I'm a bloody wizard, if there is such a thing?" He cursed again. "All right, all right. Here's the rest of it. One of the last dreams I had of you, you were no longer the little girl. You were a woman as you are now. I remember leaping out of bed, sweating, hating that the little girl was gone because she was mine, both she and her song, her skinny braids, her freckles, the strength that even I could see in her, and I saw her vibrant red hair and knew it was you grown up.

"I remember I lay back down on my bed and fell asleep again, immediately, and there you were, you the woman, and you sang that song to me. Dammit, that's how I knew you when I saw you. I didn't tell you before—it simply seemed too unbelievable."

You didn't think that was magic? She said,

"It seems it was time for you to come back to England. I'm thinking you were meant to come to me when I was eighteen, you were meant to marry me, and the two of us were meant to end it—whatever it is—and that's why you dreamed of me as I am now.

"When I was away from you in those moments after I read from the *Rules of the Pale*, Sarimund said I was the crown of his kingdom, the bringer of peace and destruction, the one who had to right the grievous sin."

She jerked away from him and pulled her hair, actually jerked it with her hands. "What is this wretched grievous sin?" She jerked at her hair again. "To understand magic, I suppose you must simply accept all the twists and turns, the questions that can drive a mortal mad."

Nicholas said, "Almost three hundred years is a very long time for this being who saved Captain Jared to wait. Wait for what? Like you said, Sarimund called it a grievous sin and those are the same words in your song. *I know of his death and her grievous sin.* Perhaps it is a sin committed long ago by a god or a wizard or a witch, something strong enough, something bad enough, to continue existing all these years—until the two of us came together."

"Yes," she said, "yes, we are one." Her heart was tripping. "You believe that our coming together brings us more knowledge, more power?"

He strode away from her, walking the length of the library, staring out the windows for a long moment before saying over his shoulder, "I am a simple man, dammit, a man of business. I own ships, I own property in Macau and in Portugal and here in England. Despite my wealth, I am still simple. Dammit, I want to be simple, I don't wish to be cut adrift from what is normal, what is expected, what I am used to." He turned around and smacked one fist against the wall. A portrait of a racing horse shuddered, the frame tilted to the left. "Here I am carrying on, and you don't even know who you are. I am a fool—but a simple fool. Forgive me, Rosalind."

"What happened to me when I was a child was not your fault."

He walked back to her, grabbed her hands, and held them against his chest. "If it means being magic to resolve all this, then I will give up my simpleness. We will wait for the night and see what happens."

"Open the door this minute, do you hear me? I want to speak to that wretched ghost! He is not in the drawing room so he must be hiding from me here in the library. Open the door now."

He kissed her quickly, set her away from him. "Shall we let my dear stepmother come in and try to find Captain Jared?"

"Will you tell her it's the very first Vail and not her father-in-law?"

"No, let Captain Jared amuse himself at her expense if he wishes to."

Nicholas opened the door, gave Miranda a slight bow. "My wife and I have to visit a sick tenant. Have yourself a fine time with our ghost."

Miranda gave both of them a malevolent look, turned her back on them, and said loudly, "Well, you dead old monster, are you in here? I don't see you. Are you hiding from me?"

There was only the sound of the ormolu clock on the mantel, its steady ticking like falling rain in the silence.

"So you're afraid of facing me, are you? Well, you always were a coward when you were alive and—"

A creaky old voice sang out,

A crooked root is what I see.
Not the rose you pretend to be.
A black-hearted witch with an ugly nose
Set big and lumpy on a rotten rose.

"I am not a crooked root or a rotten rose, you cursed dead moron! I *am* a rose! Lumpy? I have a beautiful nose! What do you know, you're only a bloody ghost with a big mouth. You're not even here, just your voice, and let me tell you, your rhymes aren't at all clever. Ugly nose indeed! Show yourself, I'll show you a lumpy nose!"

Captain Jared, smart ghost that he was, kept quiet.

"You never liked me, never accepted me. It wasn't my fault that mewling bitch died. She was a weakling, a drain on your son, an encumbrance. I didn't kill her, your son didn't kill her. She simply died from all the meanness inside of her.

"Your son loved me, he married me, and I gave him an heir—I gave him three heirs—yet my heirs still wait in the wings for that miserable Nicholas to drop dead. You always turned your nose up when I came here and for no reason. I hate you, do you hear?"

A soft rhythmic sound came from the corner, like a boot lightly tapping its toe against the floor.

Nicholas took Rosalind's hand and they left the library to a silent ghost and his furious stepmother.

They heard her shout through the closed door, "I am not crooked! It is you who were crooked your entire blighted life, pretending to be a wizard. Tell me what is going on here, you old sinner, tell me now, else I'll never leave! Why did my precious Richard have that wretched vision?"

Silence, then a deep pitiful sigh, and a depressed singsong voice:

She'll leave if I talk
She'll stay if I don't
She'll haunt me forever
Unless I'm more clever.
Prithee, just look at me now
Shrieked at endlessly by a lumpy-nosed
  cow.

"More clever than I? You're a dolt, to have you as a father-in-law fair to burned me to the core, but I survived. A cow? I'm a cow?

You should thank me, for I was the one who
sent you that little brat who cursed me with
those black eyes of his as he slunk behind
furniture so I couldn't see him, but I heard
him chanting curses, death curses. I told his
father how he spewed hatred at me and at
him, that I feared for my newly born son's
life, how he bragged that he would kill you,
kill all of us. Nicholas was always a spawn of
the Devil, I told his father, had thick bad
blood in his veins, and he believed me. A
man should believe his wife, curse you.

"At least now you're dead, save for something malignant that has managed to stick its
snout out of the ether. And just what is this
prithee business? Another of your affecta-
tions, no doubt. No one has spoken that
word for hundreds of years. Ah, but you must
always be the poseur, even dead. I believe
I'll have you dug up out of your grave and
burn your wretched skeleton. That'll see you
gone, now won't it?"

Nicholas and Rosalind had to lean close
to the library door when Captain Jared sang
softly, that ancient voice echoing eerily,

**The knife rises high
And brings the end near.
The knife starts to fall
And you choke on the fear.
The prince must win
Evil must die
Pay attention, madam, for the end draws
nigh.**

The prince will win? What prince? The end was nigh? Captain Jared sounded very serious about that. Rosalind supposed nigh meant tonight. They heard Miranda shriek and throw a hassock toward the fireplace.

Nicholas whispered against her temple, "Do you think he's hiding up the chimney?"

Rosalind shuddered. "If she was thinking aright, she would realize it isn't the old earl, that it is someone else. And all those things she told your father . . . It's evil what she did, Nicholas—claiming a little boy chanted curses, making threats."

Nicholas shrugged. "Whatever she said or did, when I think about the past, I am vastly relieved I was forced to leave England, forced to face what I was at my core, forced to make my own way. Had I remained, raised as a pampered earl's son, would I have become like Richard perhaps? Or like Lancelot?"

"You would have become exactly what you are only you would not speak Chinese and have Lee Po about to correct Marigold's English. I begin to believe she makes mistakes on purpose to gain his attention."

He couldn't help himself, he laughed, kissed her, said against her temple, "Captain Jared certainly has the old girl going, doesn't he?"

* * *

The day seemed interminable, so many hours to be got through until the sun set and it could be considered night. Nicholas and Rosalind did indeed visit tenants, happy to welcome the new countess, happy to see Nicholas now their roofs didn't leak, there was hay in the sheds for their animals, and grain grew in the fields.

They spoke to three more women who were willing to sing with a ghost and work at Wyverly Chase, and they managed to get through a tense dinner with Nicholas's three half brothers and his battleaxe stepmother.

Nicholas asked Richard as he sipped on a lovely Bordeaux, "You had this vision only once?"

"That's right. It was real. It was the truth. But I see you still have her with you. You are a fool, Nicholas, a right fool." Richard shrugged. "Why should I care? After she flings your heart into the bushes, I will be the Earl of Mountjoy."

Miranda hissed.

Richard turned to her. "What makes you dislike that image, Mother?"

Miranda waved her fork at her son. "A vision simply shouldn't happen to a fine, normal, wickedly handsome young man like yourself. It happens only to crazy old men like your grandfather, whose blasted ghost sang out a 'prithee' to me."

"I rather like his songs," Aubrey said as he chewed on Cook's ham. "I wonder if he will allow me to sing with him."

Miranda hissed again.

"All of you are bloody mad," Lancelot said and threw a slice of bread across the dining room. "I want to leave. There is no reason to stay in the same house with a murderess. And Nicholas amuses himself at our expense. He will doubtless try to kill us, or set his wife to do it."

Rosalind was beginning to think that dispatching the lot of them wasn't a bad idea.

"Not if his precious wife stabs him first," Aubrey said, and Rosalind saw him grinning behind a spoonful of vegetable marrow soup. "What with all that violent red hair, I imagine she has a formidable temper, is that true, Nicholas?"

"He wouldn't have the nerve to strike her," Lancelot said, his mouth full, "now that he knows she'll cut his heart out. As for that heathen servant of his, I swear the fellow is cursing me whenever I chance to see him. He looks foreign. I don't like him."

Nicholas said, "It's true, Lancelot, that Lee Po knows many meaty curses, some of them designed to tangle up your innards so you choke on your own guts. I'd keep my distance from him." Nicholas paused a moment, looked around the table. "You know, perhaps Lancelot is right, all of you should return to London. Perhaps after dinner. Or after an early breakfast in the morning. Thank you, Richard, for delivering your vision message."

Richard came right out of his chair. "No!"

Nicholas lounged back in his earl's chair, arched an eyebrow. "No? Why ever not?"

"I cannot," Richard said, his voice, his very

posture intense. His hands were splayed on the table, his knuckles white. There was something desperate about him, Nicholas realized, but what was it?

45

Dinner dragged on with no explanation from Richard. Nicholas and Rosalind finally left his family to tea and whist. Lancelot was in a vile mood, throwing down his cards as if each one were a weapon. Aubrey baited him, said he was pretty as any girl he'd ever seen, which Nicholas thought wasn't far from the truth. Aubrey's smile never faded, his good humor seemed inexhaustible. On the other hand, Aubrey spent most of his time at Oxford. He didn't have to live with this bunch.

As for Richard, he brooded, one booted leg swinging over the arm of his chair.

Nicholas didn't think he was brooding over his luck at cards. Why, he wondered yet again, was Richard so anxious? If Rosalind did stab him, as Richard claimed he'd seen in the vision, then why wasn't he raising a brandy glass?

It was a relief to leave the four of them behind the closed drawing room door.

"I wonder where Captain Jared is this fine night?" Rosalind said as they walked into the earl's bedchamber.

"He kept quiet and I can't say I blame him," Nicholas said.

They drew on cloaks over their clothes. "It might be quite cold in the Pale," Rosalind said as she tied the black velvet ties together.

Rosalind made certain there was always a good three feet between them even though they held hands. She didn't want to fall into the Pale with the both of them naked.

Nicholas said, "I feel bloody ridiculous, lying in bed, waiting. Waiting for what? How the devil will we get to the Pale? I have no flying carpet."

She shook her head. "We must be patient, and wait, no choice. Would you like me to sing to you?"

He sat up. "No, what I want is to see if you can now read the final pages of the *Rules of the Pale*."

She sat up beside him. "I can't believe I forgot about it. You believe Sarimund has removed the veil from them as well as freed the pages from the shorter book?"

"We will shortly see, won't we?" He fetched the book from the top drawer in his dresser.

She sat in the large comfortable chair in front of the fireplace, and Nicholas stood beside her, his hands outstretched to the sluggish flame.

Her fingers trembled as she thumbed to the end of the book. She looked down at the writing, then up at Nicholas.

He said, "You can read it now. It would make no sense if you still couldn't."

She looked down again, cleared her throat, and read:

This is the end, I can offer no more help since I promised not to meddle.

You are a gift, Isabella, never doubt that, you are brave and true, your honor bone deep. Many times, I have found, a gift is a debt to another.

I have but to warn you not to trust anyone or anything, be it a god or a goddess, a wizard or a witch. Do not accept what you see for it may not be real at all. Those in the Pale fashion lavish illusions and violent phantasms to drive the unwary mad. Be disbelieving. Be cautious.

But know that evil cannot touch you.

Good-bye, my sweet girl. You must sing, never forget to sing.

Sarimund

Rosalind stared down at the last page for a good long time before she raised her face to her husband's. "My name is Isabella."

He looked at her thoughtfully, stroking his long fingers over his chin. "It is a beautiful name. I wonder how Sarimund knew your name was Isabella some three hundred years before you were born."

"If that is indeed my name in the present day. Why didn't he tell me my last name as well?"

"Since we are speaking of magic, then we are naturally speaking of obfuscation. I now believe that to make a proper magical pronouncement, you must be infuriatingly murky; you must litter ambiguous metaphors over the landscape; and you must spice your pro-nouncements with otherworldly words that don't fit into any comprehensible framework. You must unveil only half clues, a lame bit of garbled nonsense here and bit of misdirection there. And withal, we simply must accept it.

"And as for Captain Jared's dreadful rhymes—if his ghost would show himself but once, I would wring his bloody neck. Hmm, I wonder if my hands would go right through his neck. I wonder if there are more rules—vital rules—that Sarimund is still hiding from us."

Rosalind cocked her head to one side. "Being a wizard, you would know, now wouldn't you?"

"If I am a wizard, then you, madam, are a witch." And he began pacing the bedcham-ber, his cloak billowing about his ankles. He said, "I am a simple man. I am, I really am. And I like the name Isabella."

"That must mean I am Italian. Oh, curse Sarimund, why didn't the moron write down my full name? Ah, yes, that would mean breaking a magic rule. You know, Nicholas, I'm thinking one must study obscure texts to think magically."

"Leave me out of it. All I want to do is to stride over my acres, watch my lands flourish, give Clyde free rein to jump over that fence at the back of my northern border, watch the barley and rye grow tall, and make love to my wife until I am unable to move. Ah, if we are blessed, to fill the Wyverly Chase nursery." He heaved a sigh. "Don't look alarmed and tense upon me. I have no intention of attacking your fair person." He brushed his fingers through his hair, making it stand straight up. "Well, I most certainly will think about how you feel when I'm deep inside you, but not now. Now I want this over with. Behold, madam, a patient man. Come lie with me."

And so they lay next to each other, again holding hands, a blanket pulled over their cloaks and their booted feet. Their talk dwindled. Rosalind was on the edge of sleep when she heard Nicholas say, his voice low and deep, "If we do not survive this, Rosalind, know that I love you. Like the Dragon of the Sallas Pond, you are my mate for life. I pray we will survive this journey, that we will enjoy a nice long life."

"I love you too, Nicholas. It would seem I've loved you all my life—no matter which life. It is amazing how you make me feel, how you make me want to skip and jump and sing and perhaps play a rousing waltz on the pianoforte."

He basked. This incredible woman he'd dreamed of for so many years actually loved him, despite—despite what? He wondered, and frowned. But he didn't ask because suddenly, all words, all thoughts faded from his brain and he fell asleep instead.

Suddenly both of them jerked straight up in bed.

"What the devil?"

"I don't know," Rosalind said, and clutched his hand.

They watched as the smoldering ashes in the fireplace suddenly ignited, as if fanned by an invisible hand. The flames roared upward, making a loud whooshing sound, as if all the air in the room were being sucked into it. The flames whipped up and out, and the sound of a high wind filled the room.

Nicholas cursed and grabbed her against him. He yelled, "Don't let go of me, whatever you do, don't let go of me. Do you hear me?"

She nodded, unable to speak, only stare at the roaring flames. The sucking sound became even louder. The flames turned bright blue, then the blue deepened into a rich royal blue. They watched the big chair whip round and round until it disappeared into the whirling vortex. The gigantic flame seemed to swallow the chair. But how could that be? They'd watched the vortex actually suck the chair into the fireplace, but it was too large to fit, surely it was. Yet it didn't matter, the chair was gone. The blue flames roared, leapt upward as if trying to reach the sky, and the sound of it was like the cackle of a hundred mad witches.

Then the huge funnel turned itself on them. They felt the incredible pull, and despite themselves, it jerked them to their feet and pulled them toward the roaring flames that now had leapt out of the fireplace and formed a huge funnel that was twisting wildly, reaching to the ceiling, filling the bedchamber, twisting and circling fast, the noise unbelievable. But there was no smoke, no particular heat.

It was madness.

Nicholas instinctively grabbed the bedpost against the incredible pull of the vortex.

Rosalind said in a calm voice, "No, Nicholas, it is all right. Let go."

He released the bedpost and the vortex

swooped them up, slapped them together, whirled them about so fast they couldn't see or hear anything except the deafening roar. She felt his hand squeeze hers as they were both spun into the huge column of blue flame that roared and shrieked around them. Her hair whipped into their faces, blinding them. And Rosalind thought to herself, *It is the Cretan light.* There was a tremendous crashing sound.

Then they heard nothing at all.

46

Rosalind slowly raised her head. Her brain was clear, her mouth dry, her hair tangled in her face, and she wasn't afraid. She was lying on top of Nicholas, who was now blinking his eyes, and he felt very good indeed.

His hand was on her cheek. "What happened?"

"I think that vortex of flame somehow deposited us in the Pale. It was the Cretan light written of by Captain Jared. Remember?"

He said nothing, merely lifted her off him and set her next to him. "It appears we're in some sort of cave. Look at the sandy floor, and the opening, just over there. I can't see the back of the cave—it's black as a pit back there. I wonder how big it is."

Rosalind didn't care how big the cave was; she'd have to be forced at knifepoint to go exploring.

They rose slowly and walked to the opening and looked out. Three bloodred moons shone bright overhead.

"Oh, my, it is beautiful."

Alien and unnatural was what it was, Nicholas thought, but the utter strangeness of it didn't concern him at the moment. He cursed, smacked his palm against his forehead. "Blast me, I'm a fool. Here we are in cloaks and boots, ready for cold weather and a hike into the mountains, yet I forgot to bring a weapon."

"Sarimund didn't say anything about needing one," she said, and moved closer to his side, and wondered if somehow Nicholas had been blocked from thinking of a weapon.

"He didn't say anything about wearing cloaks either," he said, and cursed again. "Well, no hope for it. All right, I know we aren't to build a fire because that will bring the fire creatures in to devour it. Is that right?"

"Yes."

"Then I'm wondering how anyone ever cooked anything if these fire creatures always flew by to kill the flame."

"We will ask the red Lasis when we find it. We've got to make friends with it, so it will protect us from the Tiber. I hope Sarimund comes to us soon. Remember, he said he was waiting for me."

He said, "I cannot imagine meeting someone three hundred years dead. Well, yes, I can—Captain Jared. Do you think Sarimund will be only spirit and song?"

"I saw him across from the huge kettle he was stirring. He looked very real."

Nicholas said, as he looked out over the land, "Hopefully we are in the Vale of Augur and that is Mount Olyvan at the end of the plain beyond that skinny snake of river. If Sarimund doesn't come, if we can't find a Dragon of the Sallas Pond to fly us over it, then we will have to cross it. If I remember aright, we can't cross the river until the three bloodred moons are full, and rise together over Mount Olyvan. I wonder why that restriction? The river doesn't look deep at all, its surface appears calm, and over there, it doesn't appear to be more than fifteen feet wide."

Rosalind said, "If you stick even your toe

in that river before the three bloodred moons are full, I shall kick you."

He didn't know where it came from, but he grinned down at her. "The moons aren't quite full, are they?"

"No. Tomorrow night."

A black eyebrow shot up. "You seem very sure about that."

She looked momentarily surprised. "Yes, I do, don't I?"

He eyed her a moment, then said, "Perhaps there is another way to get to Blood Rock, besides crossing the river or finding a Dragon of the Sallas Pond to fly us there."

She turned away from him suddenly and began to walk toward a single tree that stood on a small mound some twenty feet away. Nicholas called out, "Rosalind, no, we must remain together. Come back here."

She kept walking straight toward that tree, at least he thought it was a tree. Of all things, it was a bright yellow and had very long bare branches sticking out from the trunk, moving lazily about like thin waving arms. The only thing was, there wasn't any wind, not even a slight breeze to make those branches move and sway the way they did.

He yelled her name again, but still she

didn't turn. Then he called out, "Isabella! Come back here."

She turned then and smiled at him, a mysterious smile.

He said, "I want you to sing to me."

He saw that her hair shined as violent a red as the three bloodred moons above her head, and her face was washed of color, not as white as the whiteness that had shrouded them and their bedchambers the previous night, but her pallor was marked. Had it only been last night? It seemed like eons ago. He stared at her as she walked toward him. The thing was, she was Rosalind, yet, somehow, she wasn't. He would swear red sparks flew outward from her head, forming a crimson halo—or a blood halo. Her cloak and gown were gone and in their place, a long white robe, a narrow golden rope at her waist. He felt a spurt of fear and quashed it. "Please, Isabella, sing to me."

She took another couple of steps toward him, the hem of her gown brushing against some spindly bushes that didn't appear to have any color to them at all. She sang:

I dream of beauty and sightless night
I dream of strength and fevered might

**I dream I'm not alone again
But I know of his death and her grievous
    sin.**

She lowered her head and he heard her sigh, deep and broken, as if wrenched from her very soul. "She wants to kill him, badly. He's only a little boy, no bad in him, none at all, yet she is afraid of him, afraid that when he reaches manhood he will smite her down and exile all the other wizards and witches to a place beyond death."

He walked slowly to her. She didn't move. He reached her, but didn't touch her. "What little boy?" His heart began to pound in hard, slow strokes.

"His name is Prince Egan. He is Epona's son, hers and Sarimund's. I must protect him. I must save him."

"How do you know his name?"

In the turn of a second she looked at him out of Rosalind's clear blue eyes, not Isabella's. "The final page of Sarimund's book—neither you nor I saw anything save a stark white page, but you see, there was something written there. I can see his name very clearly now. I must hurry. Epona will know I'm here, and she will kill him."

"What do you mean?"

"Sarimund's spell, it's stayed her hand. She cannot kill him until I am here."

"But how?"

"I don't know. He must come soon to tell me what I must do to save Egan."

It had to be asked. "If you do not save Prince Egan, will I die as well? Or will I never exist?"

There, it was said.

Suddenly her red hair bristled as if lightning had whipped through it. "If I don't stop her then she will kill Egan. Then it won't matter, will it?"

A terrifying roar rent the silence from directly behind Nicholas. He whirled about to face a monster that looked a cross between a lion and one of those strange beasts that roamed the western plains in America. The beast roared again, its huge mouth open wide, showing knife-sharp fangs. This creature had to be the Tiber. He barely had time to thrust up his arm before the Tiber leapt on him, going for his throat, its fangs glistening beneath the red moonlight.

He yelled, "Run, Isabella, run!"

She picked up her skirts and ran to the lone yellow tree. She jerked off one of the long naked yellow branches, and ran toward the man and the beast atop him, raising the branch high over her head. Suddenly, Nicholas was on top of the beast, his hands around its throat. She would hit Nicholas if she struck the branch down now. The Tiber grunted with rage, globs of white liquid flew out of its great mouth, its hooves and legs flailed wildly. The Tiber shrieked and Rosalind saw its fangs were as yellow as the tree, and those sharp fangs strained upward, toward Nicholas's throat.

"Nicholas, pull him over on top of you!"

He arched his back, gained leverage with his legs, and kicked his feet with all his strength into the Tiber's belly. It howled and he rolled over and whipped his legs up and closed them around the beast's neck and hauled it down over him. She swung with all her might at the Tiber's head, a blow so powerful the branch shuddered in her hands and her arms trembled with the force of it. The Tiber twisted its head about to look up at her and she hit its head again, even harder this time. The branch split apart in her hands and yellow sand gushed out.

The Tiber said, "Nay, mistress, do not kill me. I saw the man reach out to you and believed he would hurt you. Do not kill me, mistress. A branch from the yellow Sillow tree is a mighty weapon, no human before has known to use it."

Now this was a shock, Nicholas thought, and released his legs from about the Tiber's neck. The Tiber slowly rolled off him and came to its four feet, shaking its shaggy brown coat. No, not entirely brown, there were dark blue stripes across his back. Then it stood there, head down, panting.

Rosalind dropped the stick, watched more yellow sand spill out of it. "I'm sorry," she said to the branch. "I'm sorry."

Nicholas came up to his feet. He stared from her to the Tiber, now rubbing its head against some outcropping rocks. "Look at me, Tiber. Sarimund did not write that you could speak. He wrote only that you were our enemy. How can you speak? How can we understand you?"

The beast raised its ugly head. "The Tiber is the enemy to everything, man included, but not your enemy, my lord."

My lord?

"I do not understand this," Nicholas said. "Sarimund wrote we were to make friends with the red Lasis so we would be protected

from you. Why do you call her mistress? Why
do you call me lord? Why aren't you our
enemy? We are human. I am a man."

"You will find that all things are possible
here in the Pale, my lord," said the Tiber, and
Nicholas was certain he heard a snicker in
the beast's voice. Before their eyes, the Tiber
began to shimmer. Slowly, it turned into a
dragon, and they both knew to their boots
that this was a Dragon of the Sallas Pond
that Sarimund had described. His snout was
gold, his eyes bright emeralds, and on his
back were huge triangular scales, studded
with diamonds. The dragon rolled its emerald eyes at them. "Behold, I am not a Tiber.
This is the first time I have taken its shape. A
nasty creature, the Tiber, all rage inside,
only eating and killing on its tiny mind. I had
no idea. I won't do that again, no matter the
possible sport of it."

The dragon slewed its mighty head
toward Rosalind and its tail thumped, making the earth shudder. "You have great
strength in your arm, mistress. Forgive me,
my lord, I honestly thought you were an
attacker. Now I see clearly that you are not.
And the mistress, she knew to strike me with
a branch from the yellow Sillow tree. It is an

amazing thing." The dragon bowed to her, folding its huge wings briefly over its head. Then it looked up and stared upward at the three bloodred moons.

"You are no god," Nicholas said, and stared at the dragon in its whirling emerald eyes.

The dragon slewed its head back toward Nicholas. "Of course I am."

"No, you cannot be, otherwise you would have realized exactly who I was immediately. You would have known I wasn't going to hurt her. You would not have attacked me." He shrugged, "Or, if you are a god, then you must be very new at it."

Rosalind said, "Taranis only sings, at least that is what I have read. You are speaking to us."

"No, I am thinking to you. I don't sing well."

The dragon stretched out his formidable wings and rose straight up, a dozen feet into the air, and hovered there, wings barely moving, dramatically silhouetted against the three bloodred moons, a fearsome sight, but Nicholas wasn't impressed; he was angry. He waved his fist upward. "Stop your games, dragon, I am not afraid of you. Is your name Taranis? Stop your posing and your pathetic efforts at intimidation. If you wish lessons in that fine art, ask me to teach you. Now, I command you to come here and tell us what is going on."

"I know who you are," the dragon said as his mighty wings flapped and he rose higher, whipping up the yellow sand that had fallen from the Sillow branch. A lick of flame snaked out of his mouth, and he quickly swallowed it, his massive neck rippling with the effort. "Yes, I know well who you are, my lord. I had flecks of desert sand in my eyes and did not see you properly." Then he winged higher and higher, until he was as large as the middle bloodred moon. He paused a moment, on purpose, of course, posing again, and they saw his black silhouette against the bloodred moon and he looked like a mad painting in a storybook. They heard a voice so close it sounded right behind them, "Beware the Tiber. He is more vicious than one of those Blood Rock wizards. Seek out the red Lasis. As for Sarimund, who knows what that human wizard will do?"

Both Nicholas and Rosalind whirled about but there was nothing there.

Nicholas shook his head. "Imagine, that

damnable dragon only thought that advice to us, curse him." He paused, lightly touched his fingers to Rosalind's hair.

Rosalind said, "The dragon, he called you lord and me mistress. I wonder why. If he is a Dragon of the Sallas Pond, then why all the games? Oh, yes, I forgot—a rule of magic."

"The next time he flies near us, I wish to know if being 'my lord' grants me special favors in the Pale."

He brought her close against him, felt the pounding of her heart against his. He said against her cheek, "How did you know to break off a branch from the yellow Sillow tree and strike the Tiber's head with it?"

She said. "I didn't think, I simply did it. Oh, dear, I believe the tree groaned."

Nicholas began to rub his hands up and down her back. She hadn't seemed to notice she was wearing a gown that a medieval lady might wear, or a lady from further back than that, a lady who tended altars at Stonehenge. "It's all right. You saved me and I thank you. I hope you gave that bloody dragon a powerful headache, it would serve him right." He stared down at her a moment, streaked his hand through her hair, twisted a red curl around his finger. "Rosalind, before the Tiber attacked, you became someone else, or rather, perhaps you shifted toward someone else. You realize that, don't you?"

Slowly, she nodded against his shoulder. "I know only that I am different here in the Pale, both how I look and my clothes. Where is Sarimund?"

She drew back in his arms. She looked away from him, out over the vast barren plain between the Vale of Augur and Mount Olyvan.

"Rosalind?" He tightened his hold on her and whispered against her ear, "Isabella?"

"I must stop her, Nicholas. I told you, now that I'm here, her hand is no longer stayed. She is evil, she will kill him."

He asked, "Is Epona also a seer? Did she look into the future and foresee her own death if she allowed her son, this Prince Egan, to grow to manhood?"

Rosalind spoke, but her voice was deeper, with an odd lilt to it. "I believe it was Latobius, the god of the mountains and the sky, who saw the devastation of Blood Rock come to pass. He is both a god and a magician, you know. He feels so very much. He is oftentimes in pain because of others' actions. Were Egan to die, it would distress him unutterably." She looked down. "My belt is gold, all thin threads twisted together. And my hair is longer."

"You look like a princess, or perhaps a priestess."

He sounded calm and accepting, but he didn't know what was happening to Rosalind, he knew only that he couldn't let it matter now. He heard a soft blowing noise and looked down. He took her hand and together, they watched the yellow sand blow over the two halves of the Sillow branch, though there was not the slightest wind to whip the sand up. He watched as the two branch halves came back together, their fit perfect. They watched the blowing yellow sand move over the branch, slowly disappear into it. Sealing it?

Without thinking, Nicholas picked up the branch. He walked back to the yellow Sillow tree and set the branch carefully against the jagged hole in the tree. It settled in instantly. He stepped back, heard a sigh of pleasure, and knew he should be surprised, but he wasn't. "I am a powerful mender of trees," he called back to Rosalind. "I did not even require a needle or thread."

"It is because you are a wizard," she said

matter-of-factly, and came up beside him. She touched the branch, bent it a bit, and nodded. It was again firmly attached.

Nicholas heard a loud popping sound off to his left, like a gun's report, and pulled her behind him as he whirled about.

47

There was another popping sound, and another, louder and louder.

Nicholas threw back his head and yelled, "Stop that infernal noise, do you hear me? It is not frightening, merely annoying. Stop it, I command you!"

The wild cannon shots stopped.

Silence fell around them.

"That was the dragon," Nicholas said. "I won't put up with such nonsense." His voice sounded cold and impatient. And now, like her, he looked different—his hair longer, framing his face in a wild black tangle, making him look barbaric, an ancient warrior primed for violence. He was no longer wearing his black cloak. He was now dressed in black breeches, a billowing white shirt, and black boots to his knees. He looked both dangerous and violent. She reached out her hand to touch his forearm. "Are you all right?"

He shook his head impatiently. "Of course. I am simply as I should be here in the Pale. Just as are you."

His Pale counterpart, just as Isabella was hers, well, it made sense. Or an illusion, just as Sarimund had warned them about. She said, "You look like a warrior."

"The differences in us, we will ask Sarimund, if that no-account writer shows himself." He felt only mildly curious at the changes in himself, and not at all alarmed. "Don't worry. We will deal with it. We must find a red Lasis."

When they turned back, they saw a beautiful creature as red as the bloodred moons in the heavens standing in the cave entrance. It looked sleek, as if its coat were brushed every day, the muscles in its legs thick, its back wide, its neck long and graceful. It looked like a cross between a Shetland pony and an Arabian. Its eyes were huge in its long narrow face, a dark vivid gray, and filled with a sort of glowing light.

The red Lasis said nothing, merely gazed at them. It had absurdly long eyelashes. Nicholas knew in that instant that the red Lasis was very vain about its long eyelashes, and he thought, *Yet another small curiosity.*

He said, holding perfectly still, keeping Rosalind plastered against his side, "Are you Bifrost?"

The red Lasis bowed his head.

"You are the oldest red Lasis in the Pale?"

Bifrost sang in a beautiful sweet voice,

Yes, I am he.
Yes, I am old.
I came before time.
So it is told.

Not more poetry and bad rhymes.

Bifrost said, "It is not such a bad rhyme. Yes, yes, I can hear your thoughts. You are harsh. Rhymes are difficult. Let us speak then in human talk."

Nicholas said, "Sarimund wrote you would protect us from the Tiber. But you were not here when we came into the Pale."

Bifrost slowly nodded. He chanted this time. "I am the only remaining red Lasis in the Pale. My mate was killed by a moon storm—" At Nicholas's raised eyebrow, Bifrost said, "The storm comes occasionally when the three bloodred moons are full. Perhaps every thousand years or so, there is a moon storm and the moons are shoved together. There is a horrible rending noise that brings all out to see what is happening. Huge flaming spears of sheered-off moon, glowing red, fall to the ground. That time, unfortunately, one of the flaming spears killed my mate, who was standing beside a sharp-toothed angle tree. I am alone. However, the Tiber don't know this."

Once in a thousand years? "When did this happen?" Rosalind asked.

"Perhaps at the last full moon, but I doubt that can be true whenever I think about it carefully. My cousins are black and brown, a dull bunch with no imagination, always complaining, the lot of them. Even the Tiber doesn't like to eat them, much too salty, so it is said. But the Dragons of the Sallas Pond say their meat is beyond sweet. However, the dragons do not eat meat so I wonder how they could know.

"The Tiber still do not realize I am the only red Lasis left in the Pale. They are that stupid.

"I came to see that you were all right, that you survived your tussle with Taranis's son, Clandus, a spoiled little buttel, that one. You both did very well."

"What is a buttel?" Rosalind asked.

The red Lasis batted his long eyelashes at her. "A buttel is a particularly noxious creature that is forever trying to make himself more important than he is. I would kill all the miserable buttel if I were not so depressed." Bifrost dipped his head down and sighed.

After a few moments of silence, which neither Nicholas nor Rosalind wished to break, he raised his head again and spoke with a bit more vigor. "Perhaps it was a foolish thing you did, my lord, telling Clandus he wasn't a god, though it is quite true. A Dragon of the Sallas Pond must do great deeds to gain the state of godness."

Nicholas said, "Who decides whether or not to make a Dragon of the Sallas Pond a god? What can possibly be higher than a god?"

Bifrost blinked his very long eyelashes,

his head down again so both of them could better see the amazing length and thickness. "On precious occasions, a golden shell cracks open and a dragon rolls out, all tiny and wet, its wings plastered against its body. It grows quickly, hopefully in both its brain and in its body, and is then offered tasks to perform."

"Rather like Hercules in earth mythology?" Rosalind asked.

Bifrost said, "I don't know of any Hercules, all I know is that if the Dragon of the Sallas Pond is successful, he changes—both his status in the Pale and his abilities. He is able to impress his will and wishes sufficiently upon all the wizards and witches who dwell in the fortress of Blood Rock to prevent them from butchering every creature here in the Pale. I will tell you, he once controlled them easily, but now their depravity makes them stronger, more conniving. Now they occasionally try to do him harm though they pretend to worship him, to admire him. They should be thrown into the river and sucked down by the demons who rule the underrealm. My mate once tangled with an underrealm demon and survived." Bifrost paused a moment, then looked at Nicholas. "You wonder what creature or being is above a god. There must be something, I suppose, else how do the Dragons of the Sallas Pond know what tasks to perform? Who judges them? I shall contemplate this mystery in those moments when I am not mourning the loss of my mate.

"Now Clandus is offended and has doubtless flown back to his cliff to huddle next to a fire in his mother's cave, his wings spread, naturally, to protect his fire from the flying creatures. It will be interesting to see what Taranis does after Clandus whines in his ear about how loathsome you and the mistress are. Taranis hates sulking, and that is what Clandus is doing right at this moment."

"I hope that a father dragon disciplines the son by smiting him hard with his tail," Nicholas said.

The red Lasis bowed his head in agreement, his thick lashes fluttering. They heard his deep voice, amused now. "It seems like only yesterday that Taranis and I wagered about your coming and what would happen. But again, my mate's death seems such a short time ago as well.

"I have waited for you, my lord, and you, mistress. It is a strange thing to see you, mistress, as a woman and not the small girl whose face Sarimund placed in my mind. As for you, my lord, you are yourself and yet also the boy.

"And there is Epona, a witch who is vicious to her soul, though I do not know if she has a soul; probably not. She kills cleanly, no madness for gore in her. There is not a wizard in Blood Rock who isn't afraid of her, or, at the same time, who doesn't admire her immensely. She is very dangerous, my lord. I pray you will not forget that."

Rosalind said, "But she wanted Sarimund."

"That is so."

"Because he is so beautiful?" Rosalind asked.

"That is so as well."

"What is your wager with Taranis?" Rosalind asked.

"Taranis wagered you wouldn't come, mistress, that the passage of time had distorted what should happen, but you are here. You are very powerful, both of you. I wagered you would come, that you would save Prince Egan, that my lord would indeed pay his debt to you, for both your lines are powerful."

Rosalind asked, "What was your prize if you won the wager with Taranis?"

"Taranis swore to intercede for me with the wizard Belenus. He is more powerful than he should be, Belenus is, with his big white teeth. The fiend cursed me to shepherd about the occasional magician who found his way to the Pale. He laughed, said since my mate was dead I had more than enough time to see that the few straggling humans who wander into the Pale do not end up Tiber victuals."

"What did you do to bring down Belenus's curse?" Nicholas asked.

"He did not come to my mate's interment. My grief was great, and so was my anger. I sent an army of black snails to invade his living quarters on Blood Rock. They naturally found their way into his bed to sleep with him at night. Belenus cursed me for it. And so I have protected the pathetic magicians who have come here for a very long time now, surely a millennium. Perhaps.

"At last you have come, both of you. Mistress, I watched you save his lordship by breaking off a yellow Sillow branch and striking Clandus with it. My lovely eyelashes thickened with the excitement of witnessing what you did so naturally, without a human's infernal questioning or doubts. I was convinced at that point that you were the two predicted to come to the Pale, even more so when his lordship reattached the branch to the yellow Sillow tree. I have seen that done only once in my life. By Epona. Ah, but withal, I must make certain you are indeed what you say you are." He stopped and suddenly opened his mouth and sang to the three blood moons in a beautiful baritone:

I dream of beauty and sightless night
I dream of strength and fevered might
I dream I'm not alone again
But I know of his death and her grievous
    sin.

Without hesitation, Rosalind sang back to him, joyously, her beautiful voice filling the silent Pale night:

I was small and I was weak
He left me broken, without a name
But I lived and now I seek
What to do to end the game.

"Ah," said Bifrost, "it is time for you to ride Taranis, the Dragon of the Sallas Pond, to the fortress on Blood Rock."

He fluttered his eyelashes at them again, then simply faded into the cave wall.

Rosalind called out, "No! Wait, come back here. Where is Sarimund?"

There was only silence. The red Lasis was gone.

They stood inside the cave opening, looking out beyond the river in the distance, at the far end of a vast flat plain to Mount Olyvan, and at its peak the dark brooding fortress of Blood Rock that speared up toward the moons.

They heard a scuffle, panting, grunts. Suddenly standing before them was Sarimund, and he seemed to shimmer, his golden hair brilliant beneath the bloodred moons. He muttered, "Ah, you are here," and he gave them a beautiful smile.

Rosalind stepped up to the beautiful man who looked like an angel. "I first saw you in a vision. You were stirring a pot. You told me I would be with you soon."

"And here you are, my beauty. Here you are. Ah, to see you as a woman grown."

"Are you my father?"

"I? Certainly not, but I will say that I have held you close for a very long time, the spirit of you, the promise of you. Now I am here and let me tell you it was difficult. Although Bifrost believed you would come, Taranis did not. He believed I had failed, that too much earth time had passed, but you are here and that proves that I did not." He cupped graceful hands beside his mouth and shouted, "Do you hear me, Taranis? I have succeeded. I am the bringer of peace—"

"—and destruction," Nicholas said. "That is what you told her."

"Yes, both she and I are the bringers of peace and destruction."

"Are you speaking to us, in English, or are you thinking all of this to us?"

"I speak beautiful English."

"But it is modern English you are speaking," Rosalind said.

"Even a dumb beast like the Tiber keeps abreast of things. His English is halting, but the grammar is well nigh perfect, which surprises me since he has the brain of a fig.

"You have met Bifrost, known as the Scholar. He was hollowed out when his mate was killed in a moon storm so long ago.

Everything lasts for a very long time in the Pale, affections included."

"Where is the Pale?" Nicholas asked.

Sarimund studied Nicholas's face. "The Pale is as close as those three bloodred moons above our heads, yet it is apart, a study in contrasts. But it is as real as an eternal dream. Am I not real? Am I not standing here before you? Do you not see me? Am I not speaking to you?"

"You could be another specter like Captain Jared," Nicholas said.

"His is not idle curiosity, Sarimund," Rosalind said, lightly touching his arm, a very real arm, the muscles rippling beneath her fingers. Whatever he was, he was no specter. "Listen, we are here because you brought us here. You set this all into motion almost three hundred years ago when you convinced Captain Jared that he owed the little girl the debt, didn't you?"

"Yes."

"Did you really bring a storm to destroy Captain Jared's ship, or was it all an elaborate illusion?"

He made a choked noise in his throat and his golden hair lifted, very nearly standing on end. "The little girl had no bite to her, no impertinent questions for a wizard, but you, the woman, do," he said, now visibly calming himself. "I am more powerful than you can begin to imagine, I can whip the skies into a froth of madness, I can—"

"Yes, yes," she said. "Then you wrote the *Rules of the Pale* and prayed I would find it, somehow, so everything would be in motion."

"No, I did not pray; a wizard casts his spells, and waits to see them unfold. And waits. And watches. And guides. Of course you found it."

"Well, yes, I suppose you did that right, though you were a bit on the late side. And you finally released the final pages for me to read, but still that last page was stark white and perfectly blank. I only realized a little while ago that you had written Prince Egan's name on that page."

Nicholas said, "You planned for the little girl to come to the Pale, but she didn't come because it wasn't yet her time. Nearly three hundred years passed before she came, not a little girl, but a woman."

Sarimund said, "I know. It has driven me quite mad to know I was so very wrong in my calculations."

Nicholas said, "How could this be? Why did you want her in the first place?"

"After I left the Pale, wondering if Epona had indeed birthed my son, Taranis visited me in my dreams one night. He dreamed to me that Epona would kill our son—Prince Egan—because she'd somehow divined what he, the man, would become. Taranis said I had to stop her or the Pale would be thrown into incredible chaos, and he didn't know if he would be able to fix it. He said there was no wizard, no witch, no creature here in the Pale to help me so I must rely on humans. What could a human do, I asked in my dream back to him. He puffed out a whiff of flame and I swear to you I felt a sting of heat. He told me I was a wizard and a human, wasn't I, and I awoke. He was right, and so I settled into my wizard's brain and cast about for other witches and wizards on earth as strong as I. I found two separate, very powerful wizard lines that stretched back into time, meeting at one point back in the times of the Crusades. One was the Vail line. In my time your powerful line was represented by Jared Vail, a ship captain then, but not simple. He was brave, many times too brave. Ah, he was filled with strength, but being human, living in your constricted civilized world, he did not realize what he really was. I knew then that Jared Vail was the one. And you were there in my mind, Isabella, in the same time, representing your powerful line, and you were so clear, so strong, so very magic. I knew that both of you would be successful."

She said, "You saw the little girl. Why would you believe a little girl would have a better chance of saving Prince Egan than a grown woman, namely me?"

"The little girl was a light so bright no evil could touch her. She saw everything clearly, she could not be deceived by either magic or evil. But now? Is your light still as bright, your eyes as clear? Is the little girl still burning bright inside you? We will see."

"What does that mean—*we will see*?" Nicholas asked. "You're telling us you do not know?"

"Now is now, even though in the Pale, the present can bleed into the future or shrink into the past, though time itself is not really a factor, and thus I cannot know what will happen."

Nicholas looked angry enough to strike Sarimund.

Rosalind said, "When the child didn't come, why didn't Epona kill your son?"

"The point of the spell was to stay her hand until you arrived, Isabella, until you could come to the Pale to save him."

Nicholas said slowly, "You froze time?"

"That is a crude way of saying it, but yes, Egan has remained a little boy. When you save him, Isabella, he will become the man, the great wizard ruler he was meant to be."

Rosalind said quickly, "There is a problem, however. I don't know who I am so I cannot know what the little girl was and how her strengths would aid—" She stopped dead in her tracks. She stared from Sarimund to Nicholas and back again. Sarimund smiled at her and slowly nodded. She swallowed. Then she gave them a brilliant smile. "My name is Isabella Contadini. I was born in San Savaro, Italy, in 1817."

"And your name is the same as it was then in Captain Jared Vail's time," Sarimund said, then leaned forward and kissed her forehead.

48

Sarimund gave her a graceful bow. "Yes, your birth was greeted with great celebration, Isabella. You already had an older brother, you see, so the heir to the duchy was secure."

"Duchy?" Nicholas asked, an eyebrow raised.

Rosalind grinned up at her husband. "Oh, dear, Nicholas, I fear you're not of high enough rank to have married me."

"Tell him who you are, my dear," Sarimund said.

"I was born to Duca Gabriele and Duchessa Elizabeth Contadini. My mother is

English, daughter of the Duke of Wroth-
bridge, and she married my father when she
was seventeen years old—my father was
visiting London as a young man, saw her riding in Hyde Park, and wanted to marry her,
and so they married two months later. I loved
hearing that story, nearly every night I asked
my mother to tell me of it after she had
shooed away my nanny to kiss me good
night." She paused a moment, and a spasm
of pain crossed her face. "My mother," she
said again, and pictured her glossy red hair,
the way she'd felt her heartbeat when she
held her close against her, how she smelled,
of violets, she remembered now. *My mother.*
Over the past ten years, she'd wondered,
usually in the deep of night, if she had a
mother, if she was alive and thinking of her,
wondering where she was, and Rosalind
would cry at the pain of both of them.

She whispered, terrified of the answer,
"Are my parents still alive?"

Sarimund nodded. "Yes, both of them are
in fine health."

"And my brother?"

"Raffaello as well."

She wanted to shout, to leap about. She
had a mother who had loved her, petted her,

who wasn't afraid of her because she was magic. Magic? But it was true, she remembered it well. And her father, standing beside her mother, tall, his thick black hair brushed back from his face, a perfect man who'd once let her sit beneath his chair while he conferred with an ambassador from Austria. She'd been so excited she'd vomited on the ambassador's boots. Her father, she remembered now, had laughed—once the ambassador had left. She frowned. Her father's eyes, had she seen them somewhere? She said slowly, "My grandfather died while my father was visiting England and so he became the Duke of San Savaro after his return to Italy."

She grabbed Nicholas's arms, shook him. "I have parents, Nicholas, and I remember them! They loved me, very much. I have a family!" She began to dance around in her excitement. Nicholas grabbed her and held her tight. He kissed her lightly on her mouth, kissed the tip of her nose, smoothed his fingertips over her eyebrows. He said, "Where is San Savaro?"

Rosalind grinned up at him, so excited her feet still danced. "It is on the spur of Italy's boot. San Savaro is also the capital city of the duchy. It is near Nardò, only five or so miles from the Ionian Sea. We had a summer palace overlooking the sea. I swam there with my brother. I remember one night I went down to the beach to swim under a full moon, not something I should have done, naturally. I heard my parents laughing. They were swimming in the sea, just like my brother and I did." She paused a moment, tapped her foot. "Do you know, I'm wondering now if they were simply swimming."

Nicholas laughed. "A woman is married for less than a week and she knows everything."

Sarimund ahemmed. "Isabella, it's time to tell my lord what happened."

Nicholas frowned at him. "How do you know she can remember what happened to her?"

Sarimund shrugged. "She could not be allowed to remember before, it would have been too dangerous. Mr. Sherbrooke would have felt compelled to contact her family in San Savaro, despite his own misgivings. But now the time is right. Tell him, Isabella, what happened to you."

Suddenly the knowledge was there, alive and terrifying in her mind, and she trembled.

"He was my father's cousin—his name was Vittorio. He knew I'd seen what he'd done because he was magic, you see, and he knew I was magic as well. He sensed me, he knew I saw him smother the small babe then lay it back in its dead mother's arms."

Nicholas said, "There was no one else there to see this?"

Rosalind didn't want to but she pictured that horrible scene in her mind. The dead babe and its dead mother and Vittorio standing there, staring down at them, a bitter smile on his mouth. She would never forget that, never. "No, only I saw him kill them."

Nicholas was frowning. "You were a child. Few people believe a child. Why would Vittorio take action against you?"

"If I'd told my father, he would have had the bodies of Ilaria and the babe examined. They would have seen the marks of Vittorio's fingers on her neck. Perhaps the physician would know the babe had been smothered."

Sarimund said, "Isabella, do you know why Vittorio murdered his wife and babe?"

She shook her head.

Sarimund said, "Theirs was an arranged marriage, naturally, but Vittorio was vicious and unnatural in his sexual demands. Mixed with the magic was madness, only his father Ignazio did not want to face it, he never had.

"There came a time, however, when Ilaria hated her husband more than she feared him. She took a lover, a young man who sang beautifully, a wandering young man who left soon after he'd made love to her. He never knew she bore him a son and Vittorio killed them both."

Nicholas asked her, "What did Vittorio do to you?"

"Tell him, Isabella. You remember."

"Vittorio caught me before I could get to my father." She fell silent a moment, looked over the barren plain, then shrugged. "I'm sorry, but I don't remember anything else."

Sarimund continued. "Vittorio didn't want to kill you. Even in his madness, in his fear that he would be found out, he still loved you, and he loved your father like a brother. But he knew you could not remain in Italy or you would tell your parents, and he knew your father would believe you. Vittorio knew your father was a very powerful wizard from a long line of powerful wizards. As far back as any could remember, there was magic in the Contadini line. In both your lines, there has always been powerful magic.

"Vittorio knew if he didn't do something quickly he would be executed for his crime, that or thrown into a madhouse. So he immediately caught you and gave you over to one of his trusted men to take you to England. I found this destination rather curious since your mother's family is English, but no matter, he must have had a plan, though I never learned what it was.

"It seems Erasmo—the man Vittorio put in charge of you—witnessed you go into a trance. He was very superstitious, and it scared him badly. He believed you a witch and evil." Sarimund shrugged. "So he tried to beat you to death. Indeed, he left you for dead in that alley.

"Ryder Sherbrooke found you and nursed you back to health. Ah, dearest Isabella, I am sorry your memory was closed behind the stoutest of doors, but it was for the best, for everyone. Erasmo told Vittorio you had died of a sweating sickness on the journey. He said there was nothing to be done to save you, and Vittorio believed him.

"Ryder Sherbrooke decided, rightfully so, that no search should be made for your family. He wasn't willing to take the chance that someone would try to kidnap you again."

Sarimund lightly touched his fingertips to her brow, touched his thumbs to her temples. "Do you remember now?"

She nodded slowly, never looking away from him.

She said in a child's voice, broken and sad, "I'm sitting cross-legged in a small cabin on one of Vittorio's trading ships, the *Zacarria*, and my hands are folded just so on my legs. I'm concentrating on my father. I know he and my mother are frantic because I was suddenly just gone, disappeared. Even though I know I'm at sea, far away from Italy, I still believe he can save me. My father is so strong, you see, so very good, and he knows me, knows what I think and how I think. He tells me I am his magic princess and he will make very certain my future husband is a powerful wizard so I will always be safe. He tells me that nearly every night before I sleep, right after Mother kisses me good night. He always smoothes my eyebrows with his finger, just like he does Mother's." Rosalind broke off, lowered her head, and the tears came, hot and thick. A child's tears, she realized, not really her tears, not a woman's tears, but remembered tears and perhaps they were the most painful.

Sarimund touched her cheek. "Tell him, Isabella."

After a moment, she said in that same sad child's voice, "I'm focusing with all my strength on my father, and I see him. He is striding back and forth in front of Mother, and he is very angry, and scared. She's trying not to cry. My brother, Raffaello, is there and he looks very angry as well. He is striking one fist against his open palm, cursing. I call to my father, once, twice, then I scream at him in my mind. I see him turn quickly to face me.

"But at that moment Erasmo came into the cabin to tell me we had finally reached England, that we'd docked at Eastbourne, and he was taking me ashore. I suppose when he saw me, he at first believed I was sleeping, but I wasn't. I stared up at him, through him really, and cursed him in another's voice, and in another language, yet he understood. It frightened him very badly. He screamed at me that he'd heard I was a witch and thus vile and evil, and so he dragged me off the brigantine and into an alley to beat me to death. A cabin boy tried to stop him. Erasmo clouted him and tossed him into the harbor. None of the other sailors tried to stop him.

"I awoke at Brandon House, and remembered nothing of what had happened. After six months, I sang my song and spoke. After I'd been at Brandon House for several years, Uncle Ryder told me why they hadn't tried to search for my family—he feared someone would try to kill me again. His son, Grayson, was my best friend. I think he feared for me and thus he stayed very close for many years, though he never said anything about it." She shrugged. "When Nicholas came back to England, I suppose he set everything into motion. And here we are now, in the Pale. Am I really magic, Sarimund?"

He smiled at her. "Oh, yes. Your line is long and powerful, as I told you, as is the Vail line. However, unlike the Vail line, who forgot their magic"—he smiled now at Nicholas— "that is not exactly true. Galardi Vail, your grandfather, liked to toy with wizardry, but he never imagined that it was actually inside him, waiting to be freed. Your line, Isabella, the Contadini line, never forgot, which is why you were so strong. It is only when you lost your memory that you lost your magic."

She nodded slowly. She said, "Erasmo was right. I was a witch, a powerful witch, and I knew it, but—"

"You still are. You are here and that makes you even stronger. Don't forget it."

She said in some wonder, "I remember now when I was a child in San Savaro, I knew my father was spoken of behind hands, and with awe and pride, mostly, when the rain fell and none had been expected, or when a woman birthed twins unexpectedly, or when disease struck the fields and yet the barley and wheat still grew tall. All believed it was my father's doing. He was magic and all knew it. He was also deeply good. He said I was just like him. I was his magic princess."

She turned to Sarimund. "My parents—do they still remember me?"

He nodded. "Oh, yes. Every day they think of you, mourn your loss. As for Vittorio, he is wedded to another lady and abuses her endlessly. She has borne him no children. His seed is lifeless, you see. When your father realized this, he knew Ilaria could not have borne Vittorio's child. And he wonders who the real father was, and wonders about those deaths and how you, Isabella, disappeared so quickly afterward. He remembers perhaps seeing you in that ship's cabin, but he can't be certain since he never saw you again through his magic, because the link was broken, you see. You no longer remembered him. Nor could your elder brother, Raffaello, ever find you and he carries his father's strong magic blood. Your mother grieves, Isabella, she still grieves. You have four brothers now, the youngest only four years old. It would seem that there will be yet a fifth brother born very soon."

"I have four brothers? Almost five?" She couldn't comprehend it, simply couldn't take it all in. But she did comprehend one thing very well: Vittorio had never been punished.

Nicholas said, "Sarimund, you said it was better she didn't remember because Ryder Sherbrooke would have contacted her family, she'd have gone home to San Savaro and still been in danger. My question is why in the name of Heaven didn't you simply strike down Vittorio? Then she could have gone home without risk."

Sarimund said slowly, "I know so many things, see so many things, but I am not of the physical world now, my lord. I could no more call down a plague on Vittorio's head than a Tiber could trap a red Lasis. Do you understand?"

"You mean you cannot cross from here to England?"

He smiled at that and shook his head. "No, I cannot even cross into England. Nowhere on earth, for that matter."

"But—"

Sarimund closed his hand around Nicholas's wrist. "If I'd been able, I would have blighted that evil monster to the pit of Hell. Ah, there is so much evil everywhere. Here in the Pale, evil flourishes madly."

Rosalind looked squarely at Sarimund. "After I have saved Prince Egan, after Nicholas has paid his debt to me, I will go home and see that Vittorio is punished. Now, Sarimund, what are Nicholas and I to do now that we are here in the Pale?"

49

Sarimund lightly touched white fingers to her cheek. "Once you have saved the little boy, the earthly wizard who stands beside us will pay his debt to you."

Nicholas said, "Very well. I will accept that here in this strange land, I am a small boy, who is also a prince. She will save the boy, and thus save me. So, tell me, Sarimund, does this mean that you are my father as well, back when all this began? Are you a Vail?"

Sarimund laughed. "My line is long and noble, perhaps more powerful than either of yours, but my line is not of your line, my lord.

Your father is your father, the Earl of Mount-joy, descendant of Captain Jared Vail. You are English through and through.

"You have come into the Pale as you were meant to do. You have become who you were meant to be. Time grows short now and it is time for you to act."

"Will Nicholas survive when he pays his debt to me?"

Sarimund was silent for a very long time. He turned to look up at the three bloodred moons. "When Taranis approved my spell, he dreamed to me that if I interfered in any way at all, then the spell would cease and all would be lost. I demanded then to know why he couldn't interfere; after all, he was a god, he lived in the Pale. He sang to me: *I do not meddle in the affairs of witches and wizards and they do not meddle in the affairs of dragons.*

"Therefore, since I promised not to meddle, I cannot cast my eyes to what came to pass, and thus I cannot know."

Rosalind grabbed Sarimund's beautifully stitched collar and shook him. "Damn you, wizard, that lame bit of reasoning is not good enough."

Sarimund eyed her, a gleam of pride in

his beautiful eyes. "It is the best I can do. If only you had come to the Pale when I first selected you, Isabella, the bright child so filled with magic light—then all would have come to pass as I foresaw it. Jared Vail would have been here to protect you.

"But the time was still far into the future. Actually, I have wondered if Taranis meddled and knocked time awry. He is occasionally bored, you know, and it would perk him up to create some mayhem."

Rosalind began shaking Sarimund, so frustrated she wanted to clout him. "You listen to me, Sarimund. I do not care if the magician Merlin himself knocked time awry, I don't want Nicholas in danger, do you understand me?"

"Since you are yelling," Nicholas said, grinning at her, taking her hand in his, "he certainly hears you."

He turned to Sarimund. His voice was emotionless when he said, "You believe I will die, don't you?"

Sarimund said, "I cannot know, I told you. But now that I have seen you, my lord, I realize you are formidable, that you will not be easily vanquished, but your powers are still crude because you do not want to accept your magic. You must forget your hidebound earth rules with all their constraints. You must allow yourself to believe and accept what you are and you will grow stronger here, stronger than the three bloodred moons. You will be invincible.

"Here in the Pale, magic is sharp and clear and embedded in the very air itself. Here, there is nothing to impede your ability—if only you will let your magic have its full rein. Here, you will find it obeys you, mayhap with some elegance. Elegance and grace of action is a very fine thing in a trained wizard."

Rosalind said, "The lines I sang when I first began to speak again—*I know of his death and her grievous sin.* Who are they? What does it mean?"

"The *he* is Prince Egan, you know that his death is very possible indeed. Naturally, Epona's is the grievous sin, which could come to pass if you fail. I planted the lines deep in your mind, so they would always be with you, a reminder, a trigger, I suppose you would say in your modern day, to make you see, to understand."

"But I did not understand."

"Perhaps my elegant lines were a bit too

subtle, but no matter, you are here. Ah, look yon, there is Taranis. He is the leader of the Dragons of the Sallas Pond.

"Listen to me, both of you. The balance in the Pale is always precarious. Taranis knows this very well. He made certain I knew it when he dreamed the danger to me so long ago."

Taranis, Rosalind thought as she and Nicholas turned to look at the magnificent dragon who was soaring through the night sky, silhouetted against the bloodred moons, coming closer and closer. The very air around him seemed to part with his passage. He flapped his huge wings lazily, remaining perhaps a dozen feet above them. His emerald eyes whirled in his great head as he studied them. He was much larger than his son, and he was elegant, all his movements lithe and supple, as if practiced for a very long time.

Taranis smiled, pleasure flowed through him, although no one could tell that. He opened his great mouth and sang, "I am Taranis, Dragon of the Sallas Pond. I am glad you are here. Time grows short. Come, my lord, Isabella, it is time to end this. Blood Rock awaits." He turned his great head toward

Sarimund and sang, "You have kept faith with me. A wizard with a dragon's honesty."

Rosalind said, "Do none of you speak simply here in the Pale?"

Taranis sang, "The cadence of simple words is boring. The air lies flat when simple words spill out of a mouth. Singing the words gives them life and interest, and relieves tedium. I have waited for you for a very long time, as has Sarimund. We will see how well he casts his wizard's spells, though this one is beyond old and perhaps unravels. Welcome, Isabella." Then there was laughter, deep rolling laughter that seemed to come from the belly of that huge creature.

"Go with him," Sarimund said. "Taranis is pleased, he knows it is all about to come to an end. The Pale has been teetering as would a man on a stretched rope. What would have happened had you not come now? I do not know, but the possibilities curdle my innards." He smiled at them. "Yes, I have innards." He shrugged and patted his belly. "Go with him," he said again, "be cautious, trust no one, and never forget, Isabella, *no evil can touch you.*" And then he simply wasn't there anymore. Nicholas found he was only mildly curious. He knew

Sarimund had simply vanished, impossible, yet it was so. *I can do the same thing,* he thought. *Here in the Pale I can do the same thing. Here in the Pale I can do anything.*

He said to the spot where Sarimund had stood but a moment before, "Captain Jared is at Wyverly Chase."

They heard Sarimund's voice as a sigh in the still air. "What a grand man he was. He was so very sorry he could not pay the debt, but it was not to be; time had shifted on itself. And so the dreams came to many firstborn sons, and generations passed, all waited for the right time. When the two of you were finally united, Captain Jared wanted to see both of you, learn what you were about. He tells me you will succeed. But his magic is now as weak as a flicking flame in a high wind. Alas, he cannot even sing as he used to."

The great dragon bowed his head to them and sang in a sweet high voice, "My son would like to burn you to your toes, my lord, but he swallowed his flame since it is forbidden that he expel fire until he has reached his maturity. The penalty is grave enough to make even an immature dragon consider carefully. I was pleased he was able to show some restraint. Unfortunately, his mother also believed it would be great sport. It is difficult to chastise her, for she is very quick to violence. I, however, am a god. I have knowledge none other have, dragon or man; I have visions that would blind others. I know what is and what could be. I am an extension of the Great Wizard. I am here and I am now, and will always be here. Let us go."

Sarcasm rolled out of Nicholas's mouth as he rolled his eyes. "You know 'what is and what could be.' Ah, I wish to take lessons in magic speak."

Taranis's eyes whirled madly. The ground shook. "Perhaps first, you should learn to sing properly."

Rosalind said, "He is right, Taranis. Perhaps when this is over you can give us instruction. But now, what are we to do?"

Taranis landed beside them and the earth shook beneath his weight. He lowered his great head and sang, "Settle yourself between my magnificent scales and hold on tightly."

After Nicholas and Rosalind managed to climb upon his back, he sang, "That's right, hold yourselves steady." He lifted himself effortlessly into the night sky.

I am riding on a dragon's back, Rosalind thought. *I am terrified and I wish to sing with the joy of it.* Her soft white woolen skirts billowed, longer it seemed now, billowing behind her. She and Nicholas clung tightly to Taranis's shining scales. His wings moved rhythmically, and her hair tangled about her head in the wind.

Rosalind tightened her hands together around Nicholas's waist. "Look at all the snaking rivers and lakes. They appear, at least from up here, to bulge inside their boundaries, like a man's veins rising on his hands. Isn't that strange?"

The barren land below them was a vast plain that led to Mount Olyvan, its peaks jagged-toothed, bleak, and desolate. On its highest summit stood the huge fortress of Blood Rock. It was like a Hieronymus Bosch painting—Nicholas could easily picture abundant sin and moral turmoil residing within that fortress, and endless suffering, and endless pain and wailing.

Taranis rose higher and they felt moisture on their faces as they passed through clouds the color of eggplant and as wispy as dreams before dawn.

Nicholas said, "Sarimund wrote that you,

Taranis, were the Celtic thunder god. The Romans wrote that Taranis was the god to whom human sacrifices were made. Your name is Taranis. Are you indeed he?"

"It is all of a piece," Taranis sang. "All knits together in this realm and in most other realms as well. There is sin, there is worship, there is some good and more evil, and there is unity and devastation. The ancient Celts knew both, as do you in your modern day. As do we in the Pale. Ah, but the Romans, they were something else entirely."

Rosalind rolled her eyes at this and said to Nicholas, pointing, "There are so many animals running on the plain. Ah, there are Tiber below running in a herd, at least two dozen of them."

Taranis sang, "The Tiber believe the meat of the red Lasis will somehow elevate it above other creatures." There was a snort, then, his voice singing higher, sharper, "But the red Lasis is much too smart. You should see Bifrost throw the fire spears in the pits he builds. It is one of the few things that give him pleasure since the death of his mate."

But Bifrost has hooves, not hands, Rosalind thought, *how could he ever build a pit or hurl a fire spear?*

"Existing in your tedious, mind-numbing world has given you such limited imaginations," Taranis sang into the high wind that had just sprung up near Mount Olyvan. He glided straight up, right at the fortress of Blood Rock. "There, I have distracted you, made you forget what is to come. Endless worry can limit a wizard's powers, make his magic freeze. Now, however, it is time for you to focus and think and remember. As Sarimund said, be cautious, believe nothing you see.

"Ah, I quite despair of all this, but Sarimund is so very confident. Even though I am a god, all is hidden behind a thick veil. Events are trapped in the folds of time, and since time is bounded by place, my vision is obscured."

In the next moment, Taranis came to a smooth landing on a wide flat expanse at the top of the black stone fortress that had frozen Sarimund's blood when he'd first seen it, and now froze theirs as well. They saw the streaks of blood snaking down the black rock, thin as the rivers cut in the land below. It looked fresh, a vivid red. It looked thick and heavy, the droplets rolled slowly, inexorably. Nicholas remembered Sarimund had written that the sight kept all creatures in the Pale away from the fortress because it terrified them. Nicholas suspected all were right to be terrified of this hideous pile of blooded black rock. The fortress rose high above them, impossibly high arches with sharp spikes coming downward a good six feet, towers that speared into the eggplant-colored clouds or passed through them, wide entrances with huge iron portcullises poised halfway down, and so much ugly black stone covering everything. *A marvelous illusion,* Nicholas thought, and fancied he would alter this damned illusion once he had the time to do it. He smiled. He turned when Taranis sang, his voice deep and smooth, "Go, my children. I shall return when the time is right. Don't forget that here, in the Pale, you are very powerful, you are ancient magic." Then he raised his mighty head and trumpeted. It seemed the very fortress trembled and the streaks of blood on the black rocks spiderwebbed, creating new rivulets, a terrifying sight.

Nicholas and Rosalind carefully climbed off Taranis's back. Suddenly Rosalind cried out, "Oh, dear, I cut my finger on one of the scales."

"Let me see," Nicholas said and took her finger. He didn't think, simply squeezed and more blood shot to the surface. Then he took her finger in his mouth and sucked the wound. He studied the prick for a moment, then looked closely at the drop of blood on the tip of Taranis's scales.

Taranis rose straight into the air. He hovered there, his great eyes on Rosalind. He sang so loudly Nicholas would swear all the beasts on the far plain could hear him, "I have mixed with your blood. A Dragon of the Sallas Pond mixed with a witch. Now, what will come of that? I wonder." And he glided upward, wheeled to the right, and was away. They watched him fly back across the barren plain, where from their vantage point atop Mount Olyvan, the herds of creatures below looked very tiny indeed.

"What did he mean mixing his blood with—"

Rosalind got no further.

50

A young man stood directly in front of them, paying them no attention, as he shaded his eyes with his hand, watching Taranis fly away.

"He did not speak to me," the young man said as he turned to Nicholas and Rosalind. "Surely he did not see me, else he would have spoken to me. My lord, mistress, my name is Belenus. I am vastly important in your history, a god—of agriculture, the giver of the life force."

Rosalind eyed the brightest red hair she'd ever seen. Only his incredible blue eyes were brighter. She felt like a faded copy standing next to him. He had big, very white square teeth. She said, "The Romans called you Apollo Belenus and named the great May first festival after you, Beltane. In this modern age, we still celebrate Beltane. Did you know that?"

"Modern age? An age is an age, nothing more."

Belenus bowed to Nicholas, deep and graceful. "I am relieved you are finally here. There is only a sliver of time. I feel it; all do. We must open the door and step into the seam that divides what Epona wished to happen from what actually will come to pass. You wonder how I know this. Taranis had no choice but to think it to me so I would not stand here like a dolt, questioning you but not understanding. I have no time to give you a nice cup of witmas tea." He grinned, showing every one of those big square teeth. "It is Epona's favorite drink. She tries to hide it from the other witches. Witmas changes its taste, you know. I prefer it when it tastes of the juice of the newly killed Tiber. Now, follow me."

Nicholas and Rosalind fell in behind the young man with his pale white skin, and his burning blue eyes, and that violent red hair. It seemed even redder now. Nicholas felt the power in him, felt it drawing him, though he walked in front of them, saying nothing, simply walking.

They passed through impossibly wide corridors, like rooms really, some lined with Roman swords and helmets, others with skeletons, all standing erect against the corridor walls, like soldiers standing at attention. They walked through chambers, all painted in vivid colors, from the deepest purple to a pale, pale yellow, filled with precious Greek statues standing immediately next to crude wooden statuary, carved by ancient hands.

"All of this is much too large, too vast," Nicholas whispered to her. "It is an illusion meant to impress us."

"Of course it is an illusion," she said matter-of-factly, "and it is well done." Rosalind called out, "Belenus, perhaps you have created too many rooms and corridors to impress us with your power. However, you said we must hurry. Why are you delaying us?"

Belenus stopped at the next chamber, one whose walls were painted vivid bright blue, the color of his eyes, Rosalind saw.

There were velvet-covered benches against all the walls, a sultan's large jeweled pillows stacked everywhere, and on the walls were niches where statues of the Celtic gods stood. How he knew this, Nicholas didn't know, but he was sure.

Rosalind looked toward Nicholas, at his long thick black hair, clubbed now at the nape of his neck, and that hardness about his mouth, the promise of infinite violence and cruelty. She felt also the promise of wholeness, perhaps of a long-missing justice. He was now of the Pale, he was now of Blood Rock. This wizard was unfettered; he was at home.

She said to Belenus, her voice imperious, the air shimmering around her, hot and alive, her red hair a fiery nimbus around her head, "You will lead me to Epona right now. I know that I must proceed alone and that my lord must remain here. There is not much time left. What must be done must happen now or else times can overlap and there would be confusion even I cannot fix."

Rosalind felt incredible power flow through her. She embraced it, felt it grow stronger, felt herself one with it. She said to Nicholas, her voice calm, remote, "I am more powerful than the three blood moons. I could lift them out of the black sky and juggle them. Perhaps I could even sing to you as I juggled the moons."

In the next moment, Rosalind stood in the center of a vast stark white chamber. It was as blinding a white as she and Nicholas had experienced at Wyverly Chase—had that happened only the night before? Or a hundred eons ago? There were many windows with white gauzy curtains blowing into the chamber. The windows were not open.

On the far side of the room stood a narrow bed draped in white gauze hangings. The hangings, like the draperies, billowed over it.

She called out, her voice sharp, impatient, "Epona! Come here immediately. I want Prince Egan!"

Time passed.

"Epona!"

There was only the dead white and silence.

Rosalind wasn't alone. She was standing tall, smiling, atop a large flat platform. Beside her was a smooth flat stone, an altar. On top of it lay a man, his arms and legs chained down. He was naked, unconscious, and it was Nicholas.

His eyes flew open, dark, nearly black. He smiled. "I will kill you," he said. "I will kill you."

"No, you will not." She raised the knife in her hand and brought it down in a firm clean line, and stabbed it deep into his heart. She jerked out the knife, then cut away the flesh. She reached into his chest and cut out his still-beating heart. She raised her head to the heavens and chanted words that had no meaning to her, and then she flung the heart away from her. A great wind came up and blew her hair away from her face, plastered her flowing white gown against her.

She looked down at the man, dead by her hand. And she saw that it was indeed Nicholas. She had killed him just as Richard had seen her do in his dream. She sank to her knees, blind with hollowed pain. She felt her own life seeping out of her, and welcomed it.

Silence fell around her, into her, pain roared through her head. Then she felt something move inside her, and it was awareness, and it was knowledge.

And she knew.

She stood and yelled, "A lie, it was all a

lie! You will not fool me again, Epona! Show yourself, you bloody witch!"

Epona seemed to fly in through one of the large windows, though it appeared to remain closed, and the white draperies flowed about her until she was standing directly in front of Rosalind. She was gowned all in white. The material welled up, then settled around her, leaving one very white shoulder bare. Her hair was black as a moonless sky. She looked very young and very beautiful, her mouth as red as the blood tracking down the fortress stones.

Epona looked her up and down, sneered. "You are too late, witch. I had told Belenus to delay you and so he did, because he, like all the others, fears me. Yes, it is too late and you have failed. Sarimund has failed."

"Of course I am not too late, you witless creature," Rosalind said. "That illusion—you plucked it right out of my head, didn't you? You also gave it to Richard Vail in a dream to terrify him."

Epona laughed.

Rosalind said, "Well, no matter now. At last I realized the truth and you will not fool me again. I heard you represented beauty, speed, and sexual vigor."

"And bravery!"

"As you wish. Perhaps some of that could be true. However, you strongly resemble your mother. You look like a horse, albeit a beautiful horse, perhaps an Arabian."

Epona flew at her, her nails sharp as daggers. "You bitch! I am a beautiful woman, all say so."

Rosalind laughed as she held up her hand. Epona's nose smashed against her palm. Epona tried to draw back, but Rosalind's palm remained stuck to her nose. She laughed again. "Not only do you look like a horse, your power is pitiful. Where is Prince Egan?"

"Let me go or I will say nothing!"

"Ah, is that a neigh I heard? By all the gods, I pray Egan does not look like you, Epona." Rosalind drew back her hand from Epona's nose and wiped her palm on her cloak.

"Bring him to me now."

Epona cursed under her breath, a strange mixture of ancient Celtic and Latin words, all of them crude and graphic. Rosalind gave her a very cold smile. She felt viciousness sing through her blood. "I will not ask you again, Epona. I will reverse the spell of the witmas tea if you do not obey me. Ah, I wonder what you really look like?"

Epona vanished. Rosalind remained standing in the middle of the room. The air was silent and still. The curtains were no longer blowing inward from those closed windows. She heard a child's voice, coming closer. A boy child, and he was speaking. "Who am I to meet? There isn't anyone left that I have not met."

51

Rosalind listened, and waited. Suddenly he was in front of her, arms crossed over his chest, and he looked her up and down. He was perhaps eight, a finely knit boy, dark eyes, handsome. "Who are you, woman? What do you want with me? She said only that you were another stupid witch, not even from the Pale, and she would dig out your ugly eyes with her nails. She said she would drown you into eternity. She is very powerful. I would believe her."

"I am Isabella. You are Prince Egan, Sarimund's son?"

"Yes, who else would I be?"

She smiled down at the handsome little
boy. "No, you are yourself, of course." Rosalind studied the boy. Did Nicholas look like
him when he'd been a boy? They didn't look
alike, precisely, but there were similarities,
the olive tone of their skin, the dark, dark
hair and eyes.

"I do not recognize you. Why do you wish
to see me?"

I am in time to save him, to save Nicholas,
and she wanted to shout with the relief of it.
She whispered, "Nicholas."

"No, I am not this Nicholas. I am Egan.
Why are you here, Isabella?"

"I am here to save you from Epona."

"How can you possibly save me when I can
outrun you, I can blight you into a white bug?"

Ah, the arrogance in his young voice. But
it was Nicholas, she knew to her soul that it
was, at least here in the Pale it was. She
smiled. "Did Epona not tell you?" She could
not bring herself to call the witch his mother,
not when Epona wanted to murder him.

Egan said, "No, she never tells me anything of use. I wish to become a man. Sometimes I think that I have been this small size
for far too long a time. But who can be certain of anything?"

"You will become a man, I swear it." *And soon,* she thought, *soon now.*

Suddenly, Epona was standing beside him, shaking her fist at him. "I am Epona. I am your mother."

"More's the pity," said the little boy.

"You will never be a man, you will never displace me!" In the next instant, Epona drew a knife and lunged toward the boy.

"No!" *No time, no time.* Rosalind hurled herself in front of the child, and felt the knife sink swift and smooth into her chest. She felt it sink into her heart, rend it clear in two, and settle deep inside her. She felt a great lassitude, a sense that time had somehow stopped, and she was trapped within it. She dropped slowly to the floor. She looked up at Prince Egan, who had fallen to his knees beside her, his small fingers hovering over the knife, but he did not touch it. A smile came out from deep inside her. "I have succeeded. You will be a man."

He said over and over, his hands fluttering over the knife, afraid to touch it, "No, you cannot die." His voice broke into a sob. He looked up at his mother. "You wanted to kill me, but she saved me. She gave her life to save me. You are more evil than even I believed."

"Now it is your turn, whelp," Epona said, and suddenly another knife appeared in her hand. "Your turn and then I shall rule and all will be as it was supposed to be. I always told Sarimund his spells were worth spit."

She raised the knife, but Egan didn't run. He jumped to his feet and faced her. He said, "You cannot kill me, you cannot. I am a wizard. I will not let you," and he pointed his finger at her and began to chant.

"You are a little nothing!" She raised the knife to plunge it into his heart, but the sound of running feet made her jerk up.

Nicholas ran into the white room, an ancient sword in his hand. He saw Rosalind lying on her back, so still, lifeless, a knife sticking from her heart. A small boy was leaning over her, his hand pressed against her shoulder.

"No!" He threw back his head and howled.

"Get out of here! She failed, you have no business here. He dies now, and there is nothing you can do about it, nothing!"

Nicholas felt pain so great fill him, choke him, he thought he would die with it. But he forced himself to look away from Rosalind, to look at the mad witch, at Epona, holding her knife poised and ready, knowing she'd killed Rosalind, knowing she would kill Egan as well if he did not stop her. It made the pain freeze. Now all he knew was wild rage. He wanted her blood on his hands, the smell of it in his nostrils.

Nicholas saw the witch rise off the floor, her white gown billowing around her, and fly directly at him, snarling, white teeth glistening. But now there wasn't a knife in her hand. Instead she held, in one thin white hand, a short ink-black spear, its tip so sharp it seemed to split the air.

Nicholas shouted, "Black witch, your demon lover gave you the sword, didn't he? Sent it up to you from Hell. What did he expect you to do with it—eat it with your hay?"

Epona hesitated a moment, screamed curses, and aimed the demon sword at him. Bright orange light shot from the end of it, lighting the still air, forming terrifying shapes.

He looked at his own sword, a very old sword, perhaps older than Captain Jared Vail, its handle bejeweled.

He then stared up at the creature who had killed his wife, his wife who'd willingly given her life for the boy. "You are a monstrous evil," he said, voice as soft as the night air. "It ends here, and I am the one to end it." And he leapt upward, slashing with his sword.

But Epona leapt up another five feet into the air, out of reach.

He was in the Pale. He could do anything at all. He rose straight up, his sword aimed at her. "Come fight me, witch, or perhaps you wish to gallop away from me?"

She hurled curses at his head and Nicholas flew nearer to her, only about six feet away from her, and he taunted her, laughed at her—"Your face is the color of fresh dead snow, and all those billowing white skirts—you are ridiculous, witch."

Epona howled at him. "You are nothing more than a mortal loosed upon us who believes himself powerful, but you are so new I can see the wet on your flanks!" She froze, moved farther away from him, hovered, then landed gracefully on the white floor.

He looked down at her, bored as a man six feet in the air could look. She yelled, "I did not mean to say flanks! A new colt has wet flanks, not a human."

Nicholas neighed down at her.

Epona suddenly wore bright red, the skirts still billowing out in an unfelt wind. She rose straight up again, pointed the demon spear at him, mumbled something very, very old, and hurled it at him.

His hurled his own sword. It clashed hard against the demon spear in midair, both hitting their tips together; then as one, they exploded, filling the room with a rainbow of lights. Then Nicholas dove for her, his hands outstretched.

She screamed, "No!" and in her hand was a knife. "You damnable wizard! You're dead!"

Nicholas simply thought it and the ancient sword was once again in his hand. He knocked her knife aside and plunged the sword through her, its point sticking out of her back a good foot.

She hung there in the air, staring down at the sword thrust through her chest. Her surprise was plain on her face. She looked up at him. "This cannot happen, it cannot. My demon chant, none can overcome it, but you have killed me."

"Yes," he said. "It is a very old, very powerful sword."

"But my demon spear—"

"Naught but weak and pitiful evil," Nicholas said, and reached out. He pulled the sword out of her body. She hung, as if suspended by unseen strings, until finally she fell onto the floor, on her back. He hovered over her and watched her eyes slowly go blank into death. He watched white drops of blood pool out around her body, seep into her gown, not red now, but white again. And the white mixed together. Her face began to lose its beauty, its youth. She began to change, her flesh growing slack, wrinkles digging into her cheeks, her forehead. She continued to wither until nothing but a skeleton lay on the floor, swathed in white. Then there was nothing save a small pool of white blood where her back had once lain.

Nicholas dropped to the floor and raced to Rosalind. The boy was gone. The knife was still in her chest. "No," he whispered and pressed his face against hers. "No, this was not to happen. You cannot die. You give your own life for the boy's? No, surely that was not to happen!"

"Nicholas, could you please pull out the knife? It is very cold inside me."

He jerked back, stared down at her. He was shaking his head, then suddenly—

"Yes, you remember what Sarimund told me. No evil can touch me. And so it didn't, just blotted out the world for a moment and sent me into darkness. But I am here again and I am all right. Please, pull out the knife. I tried to order it out of me, but I couldn't, and my hands don't want to move. I don't think I yet have the strength."

He couldn't, couldn't—he grasped the hilt and jerked it out of her. He stared down. There was no blood, only the rent in her white wool gown.

"Ah," she said, still not moving, "that feels much better."

He went back onto his knees. "I believed that monster had killed you."

"No, no. You killed her, just as you were supposed to, just as I knew you would. I was conscious, I simply couldn't move, couldn't speak. Where is Egan?"

"I saw the boy leaning over you when I came in, but then he was gone."

"Well, now, that makes sense, doesn't it?"

"Nothing makes sense in this accursed place."

Rosalind lightly touched her fingers to her chest. The gown was whole once again. "Ah, I am coming back to myself." Slowly, she sat upright, smiled at his hand cupping her elbow.

"You swear to me you are all right?"

"Oh, yes. Egan is gone, Nicholas, because

you cannot meet yourself, even here in the Pale. You know that."

Suddenly they heard Taranis trumpet.

Nicholas and Rosalind walked out of the strange stark white room. But there was no endless corridor with statues of warriors and rooms filled with colorful cushions. No, they were once again standing on the ramparts of Blood Rock.

They raised their faces to see Taranis hovering above them, his wings whipping the rivulets of blood outward on the black rocks, making them splatter to the rampart stones.

Taranis raised his huge head and trumpeted again, the sound echoing off the rocks, making the sky lighten to a pale gray color. The wind died. All was silent, save for the echo of Taranis's shattering bellow. She knew all could hear it—every Tiber, every Lasis, even the yellow Sillow tree. And the wizards and witches.

He sang to them, "All is well. All is well. You saved Prince Egan, mistress, as you were supposed to. Ah, Sarimund, finally, his spell succeeded.

"To know a modern man can kill a monster, it is gratifying. It is over. The mistress saved the prince, and you, the man, paid your debt to her. It is over and Prince Egan will rule as he was meant to rule."

Nicholas smiled at her. "I wonder how high I can jump here in the Pale?"

"As high as the eggplant clouds. After all, you can fly." She couldn't help herself, she threw back her head and laughed. "Ah, Nicholas," she shouted, and threw herself against him, her arms locked around his back.

He kissed her once, twice, unable to stop until Taranis cleared his mighty throat in what sounded like a muted roar. Nicholas released her, stepped back, and raised his head to the heavens. He spoke in a voice that shook the very rocks of the fortress. "Sarimund! She saved the boy who is your son. I paid my debt. Epona is dead. You heard Taranis, now Egan will rule over the Pale as it was meant to happen.

"All will be different now, all will proceed now in the Pale on a very fine path indeed."

He nodded, as if hearing a reply. He looked back at his wife and smiled at her. "Do you hear the rumbling? It is time for us to leave. The boy is now a man. It is time for the change to come." He gave her a crooked grin. "As much as I would like to, I cannot meet him. What would happen were the two of us to come face-to-face? I do not know and I don't want to know."

Nicholas lifted her onto Taranis's back. The dragon lifted into the sky above Blood Rock and hovered. He sang to them.

A new season for the Pale,
A new life force to leaven the plains,
A calm darkness to bless the nights,
And wisdom to light the spirit.

As they rose higher, they watched as the fortress began to tumble in on itself. Black rocks began to crash down the side of Mount Olyvan, the sound like mad thunder, deafening them. The turrets tumbled, the arches split asunder, the air was thick with rubble and dirt.

They watched until Blood Rock was no more, until the top of Mount Olyvan stood quite bare. Slowly, they saw Mount Olyvan begin to green, wildflowers spring up, bushes with incredible color begin to cover the mountain. There were yellow Sillow trees spouting from the very rock itself, glowing bright.

"Ah, the new kingdom," Taranis sang, "and a new leader for our land." And they watched a white fortress build itself, the stones fitting themselves together, rising into the air to great heights, brilliant white turrets springing upward, gleaming beneath a new sun that glistened over all the land.

Banners flew from the ramparts. They were white with three pale yellow moons covering them. They fluttered in a soft wind.

The air smelled different. It smelled whole.

They saw Belenus and Sarimund walk out of the vast white palace, onto the ramparts. They were speaking to each other. Another man appeared, a beautiful man, a young man, and he stood there, until Sarimund held out his arms to him. Prince Egan walked quickly to him and they embraced. Sarimund raised his head to look up at them. He smiled.

Rosalind heard him say clearly in her mind, "I thank you for saving my son, Isabella. Egan rules now. He is good. If ever you need me, you have but to call. My lord, your debt is paid. All thank you. Captain Jared Vail thanks you. Go home, Isabella, go home."

Taranis bellowed once more and raised

himself straight up. "Hold tightly," he sang to them, and flew straight up directly toward a sun the color of a ripe lemon. They looked down to see the land below become smaller and smaller, then disappear. The air was warm, like swirling silk sliding off their flesh.

All was brilliant and calm, the air so clear they could see through the gems that studded Taranis's back.

Rosalind heard singing—soft, compelling, a woman's voice, and it sounded familiar. It was her mother's voice. She saw a man's face, her father, and he was nodding at her, smiling, his arms open.

She felt Nicholas's arms tighten around her waist, felt his warm breath on her neck. She leaned back against his chest. She felt calm, at peace.

Was that Taranis singing to them?

Then neither Nicholas nor Rosalind knew anything more.

Epilogue

San Savaro, Italy

They heard cheering.

Their carriage rolled over the cobblestone streets into the sun-baked capital city of San Savaro. Crowds lined the streets, yelling and clapping, waving at them. Behind the crowds were shops and cafes, small parks, horses tethered to posts, carriages next to drays. And flowers everywhere, trellised, in huge pots, in small window boxes, growing out of every spot of green. The colors and the scents were overwhelming.

"What is this?" Nicholas said, staring at all

the people obviously welcoming them. "Surely they must believe we are someone else."

They'd left England a month after they'd awakened in their bed at Wyverly Chase to find Richard pacing the drawing room, his mother on his heels, yelling she wished to leave this house because that wretched ghost ignored her—*her!*—wouldn't even sing insults to her, wouldn't even tilt his chair to acknowledge her presence, and she was tired of her cursed stepson and that hussy of a wife of his lording it over them.

"But he is the earl," Richard said, "it is his right to lord it over us. He is Lord Mountjoy. The hussy is his wife. Accept it, Mother."

Rosalind had said from the doorway, "Madam, I imagine that our ghost has finally continued upon his chartered course. You see, there is no longer a reason for him to remain. Richard, everything will be all right now. All of us will be all right now. You may believe that."

Richard Vail stared at her, then smiled, actually smiled at her, then he smiled at his half brother, a smile so much like Nicholas's that it nearly made her weep, and he said, "Good. That's good."

A sea change? she wondered. She heard Lancelot's sneering voice from the corridor.

Perhaps it would be too much to expect a sea change in Lancelot.

"I cannot get over this," Nicholas said now, staring at the crowds of people. "They must believe we are visiting dignitaries."

"Or perhaps they are expecting the Pope," Rosalind said, and grinned at him. She hadn't told Nicholas she'd seen her father in the Pale, that her father had turned to look at her, and she'd known he'd seen her and known she was alive, and coming to him.

She looked up at the brilliant sun overhead and thought of the bright yellow sun in the Pale, and how Taranis had flown toward it, and then—simply nothing. How had they returned to Wyverly Chase to wake up in their own bed, still wearing their cloaks, still holding hands?

But they had. They'd also had some bumps and bruises and sore muscles. Rosalind's chest was a bit tender to the touch. Where Epona's knife had plunged into her.

The crowds thinned as their carriage, pulled by Grace and Leopold, nearly prancing what with all the attention they were getting, rolled out of the center of San Savaro. The cobblestone road widened and began to wind upward toward a crest upon which stood an immense yellow brick palazzo, the yellow as pale as a watery sun. As they drew closer, they saw that the entire length of the palazzo was showcased by a long row of magnificent Doric columns, surrounded by fountains spraying water high into the air from the mouths of nymphs and grinning satyrs. Ancient statuary stood in groups or alone on the grounds, and more huge pots of tumbling flowers than Nicholas had seen since they'd left their own gardens at Wyverly Chase dotted the green scythed lawn. It was elegant and graceful. Nicholas said, "Do you remember?"

"Yes. It doesn't seem quite so big now, if you know what I mean."

"No, not big at all," he said, and kissed her ear.

Their carriage pulled up with a flourish, executed with great panache by their driver, Lee Po, who could do anything, he'd assured Rosalind. He allowed both Grace and Leopold to stamp their feet and snort.

To Nicholas's astonishment, standing at the top of the endlessly wide two dozen marble steps stood a line of people—two men, a woman, and three boys, young, all of them,

Nicholas suspected, dressed in their finest. They were all waving madly.

He recognized Rosalind's mother immediately, and knew this was what Rosalind would look like in her older years. A beautiful woman, rounded and soft, with glowing skin, and that glorious red hair glistening beneath the hot Italian sun. She was wearing a green gown of the same style and color Rosalind had worn the previous day. She was holding a babe in her arms.

There was Rosalind's older brother, Raffaello, a tall, handsome young man who looked very familiar to Nicholas, and surely that was odd. Then he looked at his wife's father and stilled. No, he thought, it couldn't be possible.

"No," he said aloud. "No."

* * *

"They did not want to let you out of their sight. I wondered if they will let me snag you away when it is time to return home to attend Grayson's wedding in September." He paused and looked around. "Was this your bedchamber?" He pulled off his boots and began unbuttoning his shirt. He was hot.

"Yes. They didn't change anything in it."

Nicholas opened all the windows and leaned out to breathe in the unique scent of Italy. Her bedchamber faced the east gardens and the air was warm and smelled of jasmine. And what? Excitement, he thought. There was so much excitement in the air itself since they'd arrived this afternoon.

Nicholas said, "I like your brothers. And Raffaello is a good man," he said, turning to look at his wife as she pulled on a lovely peach silk dressing gown. How lovely that the gown beneath it was as sheer.

"Yes, I like them too. The young ones don't know what to make of us—of me—but they will come to accept me as their sister and you as another brother. I brought a dozen boxes of English sweetmeats. Those candied almonds, in particular, should help them accept us all the more quickly." She paused a moment, frowned. "How odd that Raffaello is a man grown now. I can see him so clearly as a boy."

"Your father, Rosalind, he—"

"Yes, I know. I wouldn't have realized it, though, if I hadn't seen the portrait."

"Your father is the bloody image of Captain Jared Vail." There, it was said aloud.

"Sarimund said our lines crossed somewhere back in medieval times, a very long time ago. Still—Nicholas, it's not as if my father is the exact likeness of Captain Jared. There are differences, just as there are differences between you and Richard."

"Yes, but Richard is my half brother, we live now, at the same time, only five years between us, not some three hundred years."

Wizardry, he thought, he hated how it twisted and turned in on itself and made no sense to a human brain. He said, "Let me see your finger, the one you pricked on Taranis's scale."

He took her hand in his and examined her finger. He stilled. "You've looked, haven't you?"

"Oh, yes. It becomes more clear every day. Do you think it is Taranis's mark?"

He said, "It must be, but why a bolt of lightning, I wonder?"

"I don't know."

Nicholas kissed the finger. "I wonder. I wonder," he repeated, and knew, simply knew, that in the future, in some way, that pale red mark would mean something in their lives.

She said, "Vittorio escaped."

"Yes, I know. Your father is powerful enough to find him."

"Yes, he is. He blames himself for telling

Vittorio he knew I was alive and that I was coming home. It is a pity his man, Erasmo, died. I would have liked to take him to the Pale and toss him in a fire pit."

"I'm thinking Vittorio killed him."

"You are probably right. I daresay my father will kill Vittorio for what he did. He will find him, Nicholas." And they both knew she was speaking of her father's magic.

"At least Vittorio's second wife is free of him." He walked to her and scooped her up in his arms. "Imagine. My wife, my simple red-haired wife, is a damned princess."

"Well, I'm only called a damned signora, no fairy tale in that title."

"You're still royal, thus a princess. My poor stepmother actually sputtered when I told her—I don't think I've ever really heard a person sputter before. I thought for a moment, once she believed me, she would curtsy to you before she caught herself."

Rosalind giggled. "Well, you did announce me as an Italian princess. Just before they left, she hissed at me that I was still a strumpet, a *foreign* strumpet, and we would learn that my father had disowned me. A princess, ha!"

He kissed her ear. "I appreciate that she has remained her malignant self, no change in her at all. Otherwise I might have to like her. Richard now, I begin to believe he and I will rub together very well. That makes me wonder if he will influence Aubrey in my favor."

"So long as Lancelot and Miranda remain nasty, I'll be content." She laughed and held him tight. "All right, I am a princess, a *foreign* princess. What do you think of that?"

He held her away from him a bit and looked into her eyes. "I'm thinking my foreign princess would enjoy visiting Macau. Actually, Lee Po suggested it. He allowed that you would take the population by storm."

She fell silent. "Do you think you could teach me Portuguese by the time we arrive?"

"Oh, yes, and Lee Po has already offered to teach you Mandarin Chinese." He began kissing her, then stopped suddenly, stepped back. "You should have told me your father knew you were alive and coming back."

"Would you have believed me?"

"No. Yes." He cursed, plowed his fingers through his hair. "Probably, dammit."

"Kiss me, Nicholas. We are magic, accept it."

He muttered under his breath, but not under enough. "A witch, my foreign wife is a damned witch."

She laughed, stood on her tiptoes, and whispered against his neck, "And you, my lord, are a damned wizard."

As he nuzzled her neck, Nicholas thought of one of the statues he'd seen, nearly covered with a wildly blooming red bougainvillea. It wasn't very large, but it was extraordinarily lifelike—a shining marble statue of a dragon with glittering eyes and scales that looked sharp enough to prick a finger.

The dragon's snout reminded him of Clandus.